d'Arc Conspiracy

Yann Baillieu

Published by Dolman Scott Ltd

Copyright **Yann Baillieu** ©2014

ISBN 978-1-909204-56-0

Dolman Scott Ltd
www.dolmanscott.co.uk

Dedicated to Jehanne des Armoises
my soul twin and the love of many lives
throughout time and space.

Contents

d'Arc Conspiracy

Chapter 1

The Discovery

My name is Yann Baillieu; I am just your average middle aged reporter working for *La Voix du Nord*, a provincial newspaper serving the *Nord-Pas de Calais* region of France. In my youth I played rugby and had copper chestnut coloured hair. It has now turned grey with many winters, oh and I love horses. I live at 7 Place Alexandre Dumas, Lille next to one of my intellectual teacher friends called Bruno Marinello. He shares my passion for science and delving into the mysteries of the universe, so for me he provides a welcome relief from the day to day tedium of my routine work. I love the connection with the musketeers that Dumas wrote of, maybe I was there at that period of time in the 1620s? Who knows? You see all my life I have been plagued with vivid memories and flash backs of my own past lives. They were and are always in the first person, so I knew from an early age that I was not remote viewing other peoples' memories but mainlining into my own subconscious. The mind is a strange and wonderful creation, we only use 10%, the RAM memory, in our daily conscious activities but it is the 90% subconscious ROM memory that holds the key to our past and what we are. It was and is interesting, sometimes annoying, but never ever scary; they are only memories after all. It was just a fact with me. I was born with the ability of recall, some would call it a gift, yet others a curse. As a child I was surprised to find that others couldn't remember events, people and places from other times. The subconscious therefore fascinated me; it called to me all of the time whether awake or asleep, such vivid memories.

Just recently I had suffered what I thought was a stroke and the doctors, after much deliberation and an MRI scan, diagnosed that I had dissected my left vertebral artery. It turned out to be neither a stroke nor a dissection but something more strange and interesting; I was built different to other humans. The physicians were excited and announced that they wished to write a scientific paper on me which was unusual. Personally, I was just relieved that it wasn't a stroke, especially with all the trauma that would entail. Sure, I had somewhat high blood pressure; who hasn't these days! My age now put me in the bracket where I had to be careful, not much chance of that with the pace of life as it is in a modern day metropolis such as Lille, France. Perhaps the unusual ganglion structure supplying extra blood and energy to my brain accounted for my ability to recall previous memories of other lives? Who knows? I was just glad that I was alive. It's such an exciting time to live, the internet had revolutionized my life, it had accelerated my studies into all the knowledge that had been kept secret from the masses for centuries, for it was way beyond the controlling forces that hold us all captive in darkness and ignorance.

Ironic for a journalist! That I should be part of that very control system of information and disinformation. Truth should be our business but the world doesn't require that on a day to day basis, just more of the same bland diet of mediocrity for the masses. Never mind the truth print the legend - had been a famous 19th century American journalism quote. My perspective wasn't the same as others. I didn't buy into corporate political lies and spin. I had suffered cancer in my mid 20s and had been given 3 months to live at one point. After chemotherapy and radiation I found that I had been given a second chance, so had embarked on a quest for information into the nature of our existence and this physical reality in which we find ourselves. I loved the works of the philosophers such as Descartes and Voltaire; the enlightenment had propelled us out of the medieval darkness and repression of religion. I was proud of the French achievement to rationalize our world view, despite its imperfections and the infamous *reign of terror*.

My own family came from Norwegian Vikings that had settled in northern France on the border with Belgium. I therefore speak French, Flemish, German and English due to my multicultural perspective and the excellent education system of such a multicultural border community. Bailleul, a small village just outside of Lille, had been our family home for 1200 years. Transgressed by the horrors of the Great War our warrior family had played their part in that infernal industrialized butchery machine. My ancestors had also been in the Marie of Lille and had played their civic part in the past. I had not. Being content with just surviving life and sharing the excellent company of my fellow intellectual friends Monsieur Vincent Callens and Monsieur Bruno Marinello, we would often share an aperitif and the local gastronomic delights of such a fine city. Le Lion Bossu was our favourite restaurant situated in the historic old quarter of the city. I loved their *l'amour de vie* philosophy and *haute cuisine*. We dined there often and it gave us an appetite for intellectual discussion, for me it was the oxygen of life, French society and civilization. Vincent even reminded me of a fine revolutionary from that defining period of modern France. When he wore his dark rimmed 18th century round glasses, it gave him the quintessential look of a natural Robespierre. His father had been an eminent surgeon in Lille and Vincent was now the Directeur of a local school. My good neighbour and fellow science enthusiast had worked with Vincent hence the connection between our lives.

My life had been pretty mundane for a number of years until one summer's day when a beautiful young girl with auburn hair and blue eyes walked into my life.

"Bonjour my name is Lily Chevalier!" she announced with a cheeky grin and a flick of her immaculate mid length hair. I looked up from my computer screen to observe a tall leggy young lady of obvious refined quality, aristocratic breeding and education. She stood there looking slightly nervous and blushed.

"I'm sorry. I don't believe I know you; are you lost?" I said.

"No, I'm your new assistant and partner!"

I coughed theatrically and reached for my coffee. Taking a sip to stall for time and take in the situation. I replied, *"Pardon Mademoiselle? Il doit y avoir une erreur?* I was unaware that I needed a partner or an assistant even."

"Monsieur Latteur the copy Editor thought you could make use of me after your recent illness."

"Mmmm, well I must say, I am honest enough to admit that he is probably right and he is a good friend of mine so I do trust his judgement."

"I think he intends that I take over when you retire," she said with a giggle and continued in a matter of fact way. She enjoyed observing my reactions.

I spluttered into my coffee. "I see Mademoiselle Chevalier, that's news to me!"

She blushed again and looked somewhat uncomfortable as she had perhaps overstepped the mark with her youthful confidence. My chivalrous qualities rose to the fore as I responded more in control of myself and I attempted to put her at ease in an attempt to halt the point scoring.

"May I call you Lily? Much less formal don't you think?"

"Yes certainly." She politely replied. "How shall I address you Monsieur Baillieu?"

"The name's Yann and I would be honoured if you would call me such, all my friends do." I smiled and extended my hand to shake hers. That simple moment of physical contact broke the ice and we became two ordinary people getting to know one another. With that she too visibly relaxed and the atmosphere eased as we both smiled at each other. "Would you like a coffee Lily or perhaps a glass of Perrier?" I remembered that young people tended not to drink coffee in the manner of us old journalistic hacks.

"Water would be nice, thank you Yann." She tried out my name and found that it came naturally to her tongue; age seemed no boundary it was a meeting of minds.

There was something familiar about this confident young lady that sat in front of me. She looked like somebody I had known from the past, yet how could she be? She was so young, not 23 years old at a guess.

In conversation it transpired that she had been studying for a degree at l'Université Catholique de Lille, gaining a distinction there she had applied for numerous jobs to begin her career ambition to become a journalist. Very quickly I discovered that she was also an aspiring novelist favouring genre akin to my tastes.

She continued. "I'm beginning to write a novel too. I don't know if you know this author but my novel is a bit in the style of Bernard Werber: somewhere between science-fiction, philosophy, and the fantastic, well at least that's one of my ambitions!"

I was entranced. She appeared to be a fellow spirit with the same interests and intellectual curiosity. As she kept talking the coincidences were remarkable and quite beyond chance.

"We seem to be on the same wavelength Lily, is there the remotest possibility that we have met before?" I blurted out my thoughts without inhibition. I felt naturally comfortable in her presence and I could see that she was the same with me. We talked at length about art and philosophy and I completely forgot about the exact reason of why she had walked into my office at *La Voix du Nord*.

Just then the phone rang and interrupted our in depth conversation. I relayed the message to Lily, "It's Jean Latteur, he wants us to go to Metz tomorrow to cover a cultural exhibition at one of the *Musées de Metz Métropole, La Cour d'Or*. It's our first assignment together!"

"How do we get there?" Lily interjected with an excited schoolgirl grin.

"We are taking the TGV! Leaving Lille Flandres at 7:00Hrs we will be in Paris by 8:00Hrs change and then in Metz Ville by 10:00Hrs. We are booked in at the Hotel Moderne for 3 nights!"

Lily had made a routine assignment suddenly more exciting. She simply continued grinning with a charming expression of youthful innocence.

"Welcome to the exciting world of journalism." I exclaimed. "Well almost time to clock off, best get home and start packing. Jean will e-mail details of the assignment to each of us. You can check the details online at home." With that I started to clear my desk picking up my laptop and smiled. Lily stood and beamed an angelic smile back.

"Our first case!" she said excitedly. "It somehow feels like we have done this before." She said as she nonchalantly shrugged off the *Déjà vu* sensation.

"You get that feeling too?" I said quizzically. "That's weird? Oh well more to the universe than we can imagine." I confided. "See you at the Gare Lille Flandres 06:30Hrs in the morning. Don't be late! *A bientôt mon ami.*"

With that Lily grinned again, turned smartly and left the room. Her leaving left a tangible void in the office atmosphere. How could someone so new be so familiar? That feeling wouldn't leave me and persisted all evening.

My concentration and train of thought were interrupted by a text beep from my phone which shattered the silence. It was Jean Latteur - would I like to have dinner with him this evening? We could discuss the assignment too, his wife Mimi was going to cook *moule vin blanc,* one of my favourites; I text back in the affirmative and continued clearing my desk.

I left the office and walked casually along enjoying the warm early evening air and the scents of the old market mixed with the delicious aroma of side walk cafés. The tourist season was in full flight and the city was busy. Finally I stopped at a florist and purchased some beautiful flowers for Mimi. Taking the metro tram from Gare Lille Flandres, I stood the short distance to Clemenceau Hippodrome, the stop that I wanted. Rush hour was always busy in Lille but it saved me driving and parking in the city centre. I walked from the tram stop the short distance to Jean and Mimi's house in the well to do suburbs of Marcq-en-

Baroeul. By coincidence their children Jacque and Nico attended the **École Charles** Péguy of which my good friend Vincent was Directeur. Both had a gift for music as Jean had and I hoped that after dinner he might play something for Mimi and me.

I reached the impressive dark green door of his substantial house and rang the bell. Mimi gracefully opened it dressed in her *little black* Coco Chanel dress. She looked stunningly elegant, she had lost none of her Parisian catwalk looks or figure. Her dark chestnut hair contrasted magnificently with her pale skin and whistful blue grey eyes. The waft of her perfectly matched Chanel perfume, *Allure Sensuelle*, caught my nostrils and transported me effortlessly back to a long lost girlfriend I once knew. Such was the power of smell to trigger an emotional memory deep in one's psyche.

"Bonjour Yann, nice to see you, *bienvenue* come in." With that we kissed on both cheeks three times and I presented her with the flowers. "They're lovely, thank you so much, you are very naughty!" She grinned and led me into the lounge.

By complete contrast Jean was exhausted after a hard day in the office and was having an illicit cigarette in the garden. "Drink, Yann?" Mimi's dulcet tones broke my observation.

"Un verre de vin blanc s'il vous plaît." I replied automatically whist still holding the thought of the perfume memory and the observation of Jean.

In an instant Mimi glided to my side and handed me the drink. "Santé!" She said enthusiastically. With that we chinked glasses.

Jean entered from the garden. "*Bon soir mon ami.* How goes it? Don't know about you but I'm shattered!" He sat heavily in his favourite chair and reached for his drink on the adjacent coffee table.

Jean relaxed visibly and smiled his usual naughty adolescent smile and made a joke. He was always telling jokes and in no time he had me laughing and telling my own. If only all bosses were like him, the world would be a better place. He was the main reason I liked my job so much.

"I'm sending you and that glamorous new assistant of yours off to Metz. We are doing a cultural spread over the next several weeks on medieval France. It's sort of a mini-series. We are contrasting many different regions with our own medieval experience in the *Pas de Calais* and I think it will be of interest to the readers. Treat it as a sort of historical summer holiday!"

"Sounds interesting," I thought out aloud. I could see several possibilities and articles lining up in my mind. It played to my sense of history and as yet unexplained fascination with that period.

"Jehanne d'Arc country!" I suddenly burst out with a spontaneous exclamation which exploded from my subconscious; wow, where did that come from?

Jean smiled, "I thought you would like the assignment. That's why I gave you the job instead of Michael."

I smiled back and thanked him it was soon time to eat and we made polite conversation around the dinner table. The boys joined us and I enjoyed talking to them about their experience of the day. After the extremely tasty meal of several small courses in the French tradition we settled back in the lounge. The packing would have to wait and I could sleep on the train. I would not be brilliant company for Lily but I was very much into enjoying the now moment in the universe. When I looked back all of my best memories were made up of such spontaneous now moments. What is important in life? When I contemplated this question it was happy times with good company and conversation that I remembered. My childhood holidays came suddenly into view, those long hot timeless days of youth that were spent with my father and sister; always an extraordinary adventure and inevitably they involved traveling to other countries so as to broaden our education. At the time I thought them expensive and frivolous but now I could see that in terms of memory they were rich beyond compare when matched against the normal mundane day to day life we shared.

My thoughts mingled with the lilting melody of medieval lute music. Jean had started to play and the heady mixture of alcohol and a delicious meal had relaxed me to the point of euphoria. The haunting sounds of a world gone by came alive as Jean magically plucked the strings. Suddenly I was there, for an instant my memory sparked and flashed as it reconnected with the past. It was like a vivid dream of images, colours and smells all triggered by the haunting strains of a medieval melody. So familiar, so familiar, yet I knew not why. A beautiful woman's face shone incandescently in my mind's eye. Her magical azure eyes pierced my soul as she smiled lovingly at me, a beautiful intimate mellow smile. Then in an instant she was gone! I tried to get her back but the moment had past and the iron door of reality had slammed shut.

Chapter 2

Metz

orning came far too quick. No sooner had my head hit the pillow after wandering back from Jean's at 2am in the morning than it was time to rise and shine. Instantly packing; I grabbed the necessary and placed it in my short stay suitcase. Shower, shave and ablutions over and I was off on my travels again. Mustn't be late for the 6:30am rendezvous with Lily at Gare Lille Europe. I rushed down the steps to the TGV Eurostar platform. Paris 07:00am flashed up on the board. Excellent, 06:32hrs - I was only two minutes late and no sign of Lily. I text her on my mobile with a cheeky wakeup message. After 15 minutes a pair of long legs clad in tight jeans hurriedly scurried down the steps and Lily came into full view.

"Nice shoes!" I said in greeting, for Lily was wearing a very chic pair of Jimmy Choo's.

"Thank you." Lily replied. "How did you notice?"

"It's a gift!" I laughed at her surprised expression, "One of my mottoes is - *shoes are art and life is theatre.* I should have been a girl really!"

Lily grinned and gave a sigh of relief. "I'm not used to getting up this early but at least I've made it." She grimaced.

"Never mind you'll soon get used to it. Once on board you can relax and I'll get you a coffee, *jus d'orange* or such."

With that the gleaming silver and blue TGV engine glided into view followed by its long train of snake like silver carriages. It came to an effortless stop, the doors opened and we boarded the carriage in front of us, just opposite to where moments ago we had been stood chatting. Lily stowed her bag and took her seat. I followed suite sitting opposite her. Not 2 minutes had elapsed and the train started its journey slowly gaining momentum as it left the platform.

Within minutes it had cleared the points and began accelerating to its normal cruising speed of some 250 plus kilometres per hour. I settled back in my seat and made conversation.

"Einstein is reported to have once said – What time does Oxford reach this train?! I suppose we could ask the same question of Metz" I smiled and waited to see if Lily knew what I was on about?

"Yes, it's all relative you know!" She grinned at her own reply and fumbled in her purse for some money. "I'm getting you a coffee and a croissant and a *chocolat chaud* for me; no arguing."

"*Merci beaucoup mademoiselle.*" I was impressed, very modern. Lily was good news, I liked her direct no nonsense approach. We made interesting conversation and the time flew past much as the flat scenery of *Picardie* flew past the window. Exactly on the hour we glided into Gare du Nord, Paris. A quick 20 minute taxi ride and we were in Gare du Est. Lily spotted the train waiting at its allotted platform and we jumped on board.

"Now we can relax!" I said with a sigh of relief. "Just one and a half hours to Metz and no more changes."

"Yes, it's a bit tight that one, only 40 minutes to catch the scheduled train." Lily obviously was totally aware of the need for efficient timekeeping when travelling TGV style, definitely no time to stop and stare. I could see that we already had the makings of a good team.

We settled down and reviewed the task ahead. I spread my notes and internet research documents on the orange brown table top that separated us. I was pleased to learn that she was excited about the trip and enjoyed history, for there is nothing worse than not enjoying your work. The 1 hour 20 minutes direct to Metz flew past as we effortlessly glided through the champagne countryside of northern eastern France. At 10:02 am precisely on schedule we pulled into Metz and alighted onto the platform.

"Well that was pretty painless," I smiled at Lily, "Now to find the Hotel Moderne, it should be just across the road." A 2 minute walk across Rue La Fayette took us to the door of the large impressive sand coloured building opposite the station and we entered the lobby and checked in at the desk.

"OK Lily 30 minutes to make yourself comfortable and then we'll go explore!"

"Sure no problem, I'll just freshen up." With that Lily shut her door and disappeared from view.

I went into the adjacent room and put my suitcase next to the bed. Going to the window I pulled wide the curtains and enjoyed looking at the view of the impressive station building opposite. Its stone *façade* had a sense of medieval solidity for it was built from the same local sandstone as used in many of the Metz city buildings. A single large impressive clock tower rose to the right of the main entrance. It all looked too grand for a simple railway station. Metz had been an important riverside city since Roman times as it was situated on the Moselle. The river and several water features dominated the geography of the city to the north and west of the old town. The old German quarter was situated near the station to the left of my view and was famous for its *Porte des allemands* which faced the German border not far away to the east. The sense of history was all around me despite the modern look of the large public buildings in this area. Metz is a very French city with deep German roots as it had been fought over and besieged for millennia by its belligerent neighbours. It was now the capital of the province of Lorraine which in earlier times was known as Lotharingia. After Charlemagne's death his empire was split into 3 parts at the treaty of Verdun 843, Emperor Lothair took control of the middle portion which stretched down into Italy and hence he gave his name to the province. Charles the Bald took what would become modern France and his brother Louis took what would later become Germany. The Germans had renamed the province Lothringen after the Franco-Prussian war of 1870 – 71 and it had remained German for 5 decades thereafter. In fact the epic battlefield of Gravelotte St. Privat was not a stone's throw away to the north east.

I was suddenly aware that even though I had never physically been to Metz I had for some unknown reason a lifelong fascination with this part of France. Well I was here now and perhaps some answers would leap out at me over the next two days as we explored? I certainly had found it very easy to learn German as a boy, perhaps there was a tangible connection? My thoughts were interrupted by a gentle but firm knock at my door. I opened it and Lily stood there dressed more like Lara Croft than the chic young lady with whom I had had the pleasure of travelling with.

"I think you look very business-like!" I nodded my approval.

"Well you said we would be exploring so I wanted to be more comfortable." Lily looked the part dressed in her chomped khaki trousers, trainers and an olive green tee shirt, all topped off with a feminine straw hat and a small army style olive green backpack.

"Right off to the *Porte des allemands,*" I grabbed my note pad and camera, "we just follow the Rue La Fayette back past the station and carry on around the outside of the old German quarter."

We then left the hotel in the summer sunshine and walked briskly along the route I had previously outlined. Following the railway line we came to Avenue Jean XXIII and continued the curving path towards our goal. The impressive large scale public buildings of the station area gave way to more suburban human sized housing as we strolled down the Boulevard André Maginot. I crossed confidently over the road with Lily and walked along the bank of the small river that runs to that side of the city.

"How do you know the way?" Lily enquired inquisitively, "it's like you know where you are going, are you sure you have never been here before?"

"It just seems familiar," I said with a shrug of the shoulders, "It's all changed but the water course is still the same as it was." That's spooky how did I know that? Why indeed should I say such a thing having not been here before? It seemed to unexplainably come from within. "You've got to go with the flow Lily! It's my journalistic sixth sense." I tried to laugh it off but I definitely somehow knew my way. I tucked that strange feeling away for later analysis.

Just 20 minutes later we approached the medieval structure of the barbican entrance to the city known as the *German gate* which was just beyond the modern road bridge. We continued over the pedestrian crossing and got to the twin towers on the city side of the famous gate. They loomed above us with their black pointed witches hats.

"This is it. A living history link that's still here after 600 years," I paused to take a picture, "Yes it's still……"

With that I step across an invisible threshold and through the arch that joined the twin sand coloured towers; the world went silent! Everything became instantly brighter in colour, the sound of the automotive traffic suddenly disappeared and was replaced by human voices speaking a strange part French part German dialect, carts moved drawn by oxen and the road bed was densely mud covered with interspersed patches of rotting straw and dung. I was surrounded by many people all were dressed in strange cut old woollen clothes of muted colours, the men with tight leggings and pointed shoes. I looked down at myself and found I was dressed all in black with the same sort of garments and hose. They felt tight, itched terribly and smelt! Oh my God, the smell was awful, everything smelt of dung, including me. I touched my clothes, they seemed real enough but very dusty. I brushed the dry dirt and could taste it in my mouth as the cloud of particles rose in the air surrounding me. I continued walking and approached the main barbican gate on far side of the short curving bridge with its arched structures and pillars on the north side. Deformed people sat begging with their backs against the wall and dogs roamed freely. Two soldiers armed with halberds stood by the outer portcullis and chatted casually. As I approached they stood to attention, smiled and greeted me. I somehow understood their strange dialect and answered them back in their own Lorraine Franconian tongue. I passed uninhibited and ………..

As I stepped through the arch of the outer barbican the noise, pollution and mechanical smell of the modern world hit my nostrils again. The bright colours were instantly replaced by the everyday world of colour that was so familiar and real. I blinked and stumbled. A hand grasped my arm as if to steady me. It was Lily; she looked into my eyes with a gaze of astonishment. "Yann, Yann are you OK?" she continued to support me as a friend supports a drunken man, "sit on the wall over there. You scared me. You seemed to blank off and then started talking is a strange German like language!"

"I'm fine honest, not sure what happened. I'll sit on the bridge wall and tell you what occurred," I sat down, now fully recovered and started to consciously marshal the events in my head, "This is very interesting, it all happened when I stepped through the arch at the other end of the bridge and it stopped just as abruptly when I stepped through the barbican arch this end." I went on to relate in as much detail what I had experienced whilst it was still vivid in my memory. Lily listened entranced and took in all of the detail.

"Hmmm…the language you spoke was a bit like the modern Alsatian dialect, but it sounded much more archaic. The dress of the people and soldiers you talk of definitely make it the medieval period, I would swear on that just from the description."

Lily went on to describe what she had noticed about my behaviour so as to corroborate the events that had taken place. "Your whole gait and stance changed as you strode towards the barbican. You were definitely not with me at all!"

"It's a flashback, no doubt about it, positive. I have had them all my life but never one as vivid as this!" I laughed nervously, "It's this place Lily, something triggered a massive displacement in my consciousness. It was so real. I was there. It was pure time travel Lily, pure time travel. Now what is going to happen when we walk back through the gate? Let's do the experiment!"

With that I stood up straight, stretched my legs and made my way back to the barbican gate. Gingerly I paused and stepped over the threshold like Alice entering the looking glass. To my utter disappointment nothing happened. I deliberately paced my steps as I walked past the arches and columns again. Still nothing, again through the other gate past the twin towers, still nothing;

I was disappointed. With Lily's encouragement I repeated the experiment several times, still nothing.

At this point Lily produced a pair of right angled copper metal rods from her rucksack and gleefully chirped, "Time for me to do an experiment of my own!" With that she held the rods one in each hand parallel to the ground and began to retrace our steps. I looked on in amazement as I had no idea of what on earth she was doing? She moved smoothly back and forth in straight lines between the gates. I watched as she homed in on some invisible force that she was testing for. The rods seemed to move by their own freewill as if by magic or witchcraft. At the threshold of the gates they crossed violently with several similar strong results between the two invisible portals.

"It's as I thought, this is an extremely energetic place! The ley lines are very powerful. Here you try." With that Lily handed the shiny copper rods to me. I grasped them at first too tightly and nothing happened. "You have to hold them loosely like this." She adjusted my grip and I retraced my steps exactly. To my utter amazement it worked! The rods seemed to have a mind of their own, they moved of their own freewill. The reaction was strongest at the thresholds.

"The flowing water concentrates the energy," Lily added enthusiastically, "It's particularly strong in the middle."

"Right, time for a café cognac and I'm buying! In fact the paper is buying," I said clapping my hands together, "Let's find a nice bar and relax, that's enough fun and games for one day."

"We had better take some photographs first. I think we got a little side-tracked. Now the sun is low in the sky I can get some good shots for the article." Lily ever practical and on the job whipped out her digital SLR camera and busied herself taking several pictures from various points and angles. "Nice buttress work!" She said pulling my leg and winked.

"Hey great joke and I thought you were such a nice girl!"
"Looks can be deceptive Yann Baillieu; I'm a tough cookie underneath this sweet exterior."

"I don't doubt it for one minute," and I laughed, "we make quite a team, don't you think?"

Crossing the busy road we entered the German quarter looking for a convivial bar restaurant. One thing was certain we would be discussing the day's events for most of the evening.

Chapter 3

The White Lady

he previous evening had been delightful and Lily proved to be excellent company. She was becoming almost like a daughter to me yet with overtones of a comrade in arms perhaps there was a past life connection? We had sampled the local cuisine and had wandered around the old town after dinner. I was beginning to get a feel for the place, it had changed, yet parts seemed somehow familiar. Now it was the morning of the second day and I was ready to explore again. I knocked on Lily's door, it was 08:00hrs.

"*Bonjour* Lily, time for breakfast!" I heard movement within and the door opened. Lily was dressed in a bath robe with her hair piled up under a towel on her head. Her face looked fresh and pink.

"*Bonjour* Yann, great evening, I'll be another 10 minutes or so."

"No rush, plenty of time, I'll go on down and wait for you. Enjoy! This assignment is turning out to be fun with you on the case. Normally I'm on my own trying to make conversation with total strangers."

Lily curtsied, "Yes my Lord!" and gave me a cheeky grin.

Her actions and unusual comment sent a strange tingle down my spine. I smiled, paused, and left. "À *bientôt mon ami*," I said cheerfully and with a degree of automation. What was that all about? I shrugged my shoulders and made my way down to the dining room. Fifteen minutes later a glamorous warrior looking Lily arrived dressed in a pink tee shirt, combat boots, urban disruptive grey, white and black combat trousers and a black military webbing belt with several pouches.

"Wow, you look ready for action! Just like an action movie star," I quipped.

Lily laughed and sat down," well you know us French girls' know how to dress to impress – with a chic feminine twist of course!"

"You certainly do! The buffet is over there, help yourself." Lily rose and made her way to the long table to one side of the dining room. Returning a couple of minutes later we started planning our day whilst nibbling croissants and sipping first orange juice and then some coffee.

"I thought we would head for Temple Neuf down on the river and then visit St. Etienne Cathedral after which we can have lunch at La Place Jehanne d'Arc behind the museums. How does that sound?"

"Absolutely fine, lots of photo opportunities and glorious weather too," came the spontaneous reply.

After breakfast we started walking towards the Moselle River on the other side of the city. Some 30 minutes later we approached the slope down to the famous river. The Temple Neuf church on its small island gave a good focus to the pictures with St Etienne rising in the background above the more modern city housing along the river bank. Lily clicked away and shot lots of pictures.

Thoughts of the oppressive dominance of religion in the middle ages flooded into my mind. The church had been all powerful and was the ultimate business machine then. Now banks and finance had taken over the world. You can always tell the priorities of a civilization by their tallest buildings. The Church did not only own the physical in the Middle Ages but they also owned the spiritual; they owned and controlled your very soul! There was no escaping the tentacles of the Church you had to work with them or face annihilation and eternal damnation if you were against them. This was usually preceded by a very public, very messy and painful death. Pain was their misguided way of driving out the Devil – my God they had a lot to answer for!

I knew that a branch of my own Baillieu family had been Cathars and as a rival business system to the official Roman Catholic Church they had been exterminated ruthlessly much in the way that the Nazis had eradicated the Jews in the holocaust. Whole provinces of southern France had been laid waste in the 13th century by Pope Innocent III. In 1208 the Cathars were condemned to death by that very man, and in 1209 Simon de Montfort led a papal army of more than 30,000 soldiers against the region. The killing went on for 35 years, claiming thousands of lives of men, women and children.

Massed burnings had taken place but diaries and other evidence had been found documenting the excesses of the Dominican inquisition. Perhaps I would write about this in my article? Time for a shakeup, the readership needed a shock to jolt them out of 2000 years of religious abuse and complacency. What is more the paper couldn't fire me; I was retiring, so I could say what I liked! Yes, that would give my article some decent teeth and a good deal of bite. I voiced my thoughts to Lily who nodded her approval. She hadn't looked at it that way before, but she immediately understood my line of attack. "Controversy is good for circulation," she added gleefully.

We mingled with the tourists, many of whom were doing exactly what we were doing. Walking into Temple Neuf Protestant church, I half expected a flashback or something of that nature, but nothing. Somewhat disappointed I contented myself by thinking and watching Lily making notes and taking pictures. The date of the church was post medieval period, so that may have accounted for the absence of a flashback in my personal memory. Oh well, upwards and onwards. We walked back across the bridge with its modern day traffic and then along the river bank quayside, finally turning right and walking the short distance to the entrance of St Etienne Cathedral. Now this was of Gothic medieval magnificence, an oppressive statement of Church power on Earth and dedicated to the glory of a vengeful God. The sheer scale of the monumental structure was so impressive; overwhelming it would have dominated the mind and soul of the medieval onlooker.

We entered and I left Lily to walk up a side aisle. I went into a side chapel for a few minutes of silence alone. There I lit a couple of candles and thought of my now departed family and those friends, those dear ones that I had lost on my journey through life. The energy of the site resonated within me, the material structure, harmonics and the sacred geometry of the space worked its magic as it was intended to all those years ago. The builders had used all of their skill to impress and magnify the religious experience of the masses. Part victim, part supplicant, the average medieval peasant had no chance of resisting such cunning intelligence. The Church had been the spiritual theme park of its day, complete with souvenirs and fast food. Pilgrimage had been the trend then and any church would be lucky to have some saintly relics or a piece of the original cross of Christ with which to entice the customers through the doors. It was a business. With those thoughts I continued my tour and caught up with Lily, we finally left after an hour and made for the old town and the museum area of the city.

The Musées de Metz - La Cour d'Or was and is situated in the north east quadrant of the city and housed in the old Austrasia palace complex which is part fortress part former Royal residence. I had planned to save the museums for last day and so we continued on towards Sainte-Ségolène et la Place Jehanne-d'Arc. The very name sounded promising for our research for how could any article on medieval French culture not contain a mention of her name. She was after all a national heroine and a Saint. We had grown up with the story book legend of the peasant girl made good, it was an important part of the core identity of France, especially in the post war years after World War I. Was it all true though? Most people failed to question the story any further than the political spin version much as the medieval peasants had failed to question the might and power of the state and aristocracy in the *Moyen Age*. It's all seems to be an exercise in power and the control of the masses. I thought for some minutes, it's always been that way, nothing changes, the faceless people of politics and power seek to dominate the citizens' mind in such a way that they become puppets of the state.

Many thoughts crowded through my busy mind as I walked the quiet streets of the old quarter of the city. Then I suddenly turned a corner into Rue Taison and became transfixed by the sight of a large red dragon suspended over the street by cables. It was totally unexpected and triggered a very deep memory. All sorts of images flashed in my mind: symbols of power, a woman's face, a crown, a white equal armed cross, a shield and a badge. They were all very personal. They were something to do with my core being, something very important to me, but what? My logical conscious mind reeled from the information overload that my subconscious had spewed forth in glorious Technicolor. The shield and the badge in particular stood out; a red dragon rampant with only two legs on a sky blue field. Very distinctive, it obviously meant something, but what?

Lily was totally unaware of my inner turmoil and continued walking at a pace uninterrupted. Interesting reaction my conscious mind said quietly and I made a mental note to analyse the images later. In fact I must make a sketch of them at the first opportunity, yes that would be a good idea. My conscious mind was happy with that decision and lost its sense of urgency to commit to immediate memory.

It was fast approaching lunch time as we reached the museum area. We continued past La Cour d'Or entrance and down a side street until we reached the Place Jehanne d'Arc. The little square was an oasis of quiet with its trees and neat hexagonal fountain. The water bubbled refreshingly in the midday heat and cascaded down its two ornate tiers of iron work. The whole scene presented an idyllic view. People sat chatting in the pavement café underneath the looming vista of Sainte-Ségolène church opposite which dominated the scene. Its impressive ornate twin towers seem to pierce the sky and attract the tourist cameras.

"Perfect Lily, shall we lunch here?"

"Yes, why not, how about the café Jehanne d'Arc just over there?"

"Sounds just the place considering our quest. I wonder why it's called that. Perhaps its proximity to the church is a clue?" I said quizzically.

"Who knows it's certainly intriguing," Lily puzzled, "I can understand Reims, Orleans or even Rouen having a café Jehanne d'Arc, but why here? I don't remember any connection with Metz being mentioned in my school history lessons?"

"I sense a story here Lily, we will have to dig a bit to find some answers but it could make for a point of interest in the article. I haven't seen much else to make exciting headlines yet."

I was finding Metz a bit too modern for my liking. It had been besieged, raised and rebuilt too many times to leave much of its medieval past. Its geographical location made it a major bastion against German invasion, for not much else stood between here and Paris. Perhaps Jean our editor would send us to other more overtly medieval cities in due course to make our job easier? I suppose in fairness though the idea was to contrast the different regions and their local histories against the overall historical backdrop. Intuitive thoughts danced and played in my mind, there was something compelling about this place, something undiscovered. You must look beyond the everyday modern reality to get to the heart of what lies buried beneath hidden in the layers of time. My conscious mind kept reiterating that point for some reason? Like a dog with a bone, it just wouldn't let it go.

We sat at a café table in the little square and within minutes a waiter appeared dressed in black and white with a pristine starched apron and black leather money belt. His black bow tie added a sense of formality to the proceedings and courtesies over he readied himself to take our order. The menu was comprehensive with several interesting gourmet options available on the lunchtime menu.

"A most impressive menu for a small café. I'll have an Absinthe and water as an *apéritif* please and Lily what would you like?"

"Mmmm, I'll just have a *verre de vin blanc s'il vous plaît*. I see you have a taste for *la fée verte* – the Green Fairy! You are an unusual man, Yann Baillieu." Lily sounded knowledgeable, "I thought the authorities had banned that in 1915?"

"True, but it's been reintroduced since 2000 and is now quite *de rigueur*! It has a delicious sense of being slightly anti-authority, which is why I occasionally drink it." A little of the rebel rose to the surface of my psyche as I answered Lily's question with a cheeky smile.

The waiter reappeared with our drinks and I went on to order the main course. Lily was fascinated by the sugar cube on a silver spoon that hovered over the green absinthe in its specialised glass. A small carafe of iced water stood next to the glass. The whole table started to take on the appearance of a chemical experiment.

"La truite avec les haricots et avec nicoaise de pommes de terre de crème s'il vous plaît" I said reading from the menu. The official looking waiter wrote silently on his note pad and then looked at Lily.

"Sounds nice make that two!" Lily obviously shared the same taste for fish as me.

The waiter repeated the action, smiled and returned to the café building.

While we waited for lunch to appear, I grabbed some white paper napkins and drew what I had seen in my mind's eye. My focus was particularly drawn to the rampant winged red dragon with only two legs. It seemed very familiar indeed. I was obsessed with its lack of four feet as it looked wrong, but it was aesthetically pleasing in composition; almost like a red sea horse in shape. I knew it was very important so I scribbled away furiously until I had captured its likeness exactly and my subconscious was satisfied. Lily watched with fascination, "I didn't know you were an artist Yann?" She picked up two of the sketches and gave an admiring glance to the tonal quality and rendering. "You are very talented!"

"It's nothing Lily; I have always drawn painted and constructed *objet d'art* ever since I was a small boy. Our family over the centuries has had quite a number of artists so I suppose it is in my DNA. I'm a very visual person"

We discussed the Impressionists and how they contrasted with the pre-Raphaelites before them. Our conversation moved to the 19th century obsession with all things Gothic and medieval including the legends of King Arthur and the Knights of the round table. Lily proved again extremely knowledgeable which made our discussion all the more interesting. After dessert, which was a light lemon sorbet to refresh the palette, we gathered up our belongings and headed towards Sainte-Ségolène church opposite. The middle open door, between the lofty twin towers with their impressive Gothic spires, had been beckoning us to enter throughout lunch. Now it was time and within a couple of short minutes we had walked up the stone steps and disappeared inside, the gaping void of the Nave swallowed us whole.

I immediately started to get *déjà vu* sensations. The most noticeable feeling was the sudden drop in temperature and the sense of being in familiar surroundings but in another time and space. Unknowingly I was in the exact same spot as I had been 600 years ago? My conscious mind had no knowledge but my subconscious was obviously heading for overdrive and jumping up and down to get attention. I could feel it stirring. My pulse quickened, I became clammy and a tingling sensation went up and down my spine giving me goose bumps.

Then it happened! I walked into a particular hot spot in front of the altar rail and POW! It was instant time travel. The modern internal vista of the church disappeared from view and I was instantaneously surrounded by much brighter colours and light. Medieval heraldic banners hung from the pillars of the Nave and the church was suddenly full of people dressed in muted medieval coloured clothing: dull greens, browns, blues, together with mulberry and straw yellow pervaded the scene. Then the smell hit me! It was so different to the world I knew, it was that distinctive farmyard odour mixed with incense, not quite as strong as the previous incident at the *Porte des allemands* but just as distinctive and pungent.

Interestingly, I wasn't caught off guard or traumatised this time; in fact I was quite relaxed. I seemed to be the focus of attention as I stood waiting by the altar rail. I looked down at my apparel; I was dressed in finely polished black armour with a hand and a half sword by my side. I recoiled at the thought of wearing a weapon in church but then noticed that several noble looking gentlemen in the congregation were wearing theirs. I reasoned that it was a status symbol as were the knightly spurs that chinked when I shifted stance. What was I waiting for? I looked for clues, the church was festooned with flowers and I suddenly guessed why! Oh my God it's a wedding and I'm the groom! An electric shock jolted through my body as I realised the enormity of the event. I looked at my squire a young boy of 11 or so dressed in black with a sky blue surcoat emblazoned with a two legged Red Dragon. It was the same heraldic device that I had been drawing in the café not a half hour previous. In truth I had lost track of all time, it could have been several hours ago for all I knew? The boy held my shield with the same device proudly displayed for all to see. It matched the sky blue cloak that draped over the *pauldrons* of the plate armour that covered my shoulders.

The great and the good were gathered in the front pews and my gaze was drawn to a regal looking lady dressed in a fine fur trimmed gown with the most elaborate hair beautifully pinned and mounted up underneath her medieval horn shaped headdress. She wore the arms of the Duke of Luxembourg conjoined with her own family. She smiled, I somehow knew her, her husband was absent which puzzled me but I felt she was very close to me. The thought came into my head; she is my *Liege Lady* I am sworn to defend and protect her unto death. Now she was sat here in Metz to see me married, but to whom?

A beautiful young maid sat to her immediate left, she turned and revealed her face - oh my God it was Lily! As large as life she sat there in the position of the eldest child of the House of Luxembourg, to her immediate left sat two angelic children, a younger sister with curly long pre-Raphaelite blonde hair and a slightly younger brother with the same hair but shorter. The whole family were dressed in their utmost finery.

I glanced back at the priest, a jolly bald man of large girth and the altar seemed to aid my focus as I tried to make sense of everything that I was experiencing. I can't be marrying Lily she is far too young!

Just then a trumpet fanfare resounded from outside the church at the entrance to the main square. The congregation stood and all eyes turned to the great door.

Then she entered, the lady in white, she stood, strong, proud and noble in the doorway. Her radiant persona pulsed visibly and the crowed congregation let out a muffled gasp of awe in wonder. About her luxurious dark brown hair was a simple garland of wild flowers, her samite white dress clung exquisitely to her athletic figure and glinted with the interwoven fine silver thread that caught the available light. About her waist she wore a narrow gold belt in the feminine tradition that highlighted the shape of her inner thighs and boyish hips. She was broad of shoulder yet narrow of waist but the most distinctive feature was her sky blue sword belt, scabbard and the long sword with cross hilt that it contained. Beneath her samite dress could be discerned shiny silver greaves and sabatons with spurs such as a knight would wear; she was every inch a warrior! Enigmatic, beautiful, strong, noble and proud, but who was she? This was no ordinary lady; she was a magnificent magical being.

Next to her was a finely dressed powerful man in black with many gold chains and an elaborate medieval hat like head dress. He supported her arm and wore the heraldic arms of Luxembourg enamelled on his gold collar plate; it was the Duke himself! It was the husband of the grand lady in the front pew whom I had sworn to serve until death. He was going to give the white lady away. Was she his daughter?

Just then the lady in white drew her sword and the congregation gasped with an audible sharp intake of breath. She held it aloft and then reversed the hilt so that it took the form of the holy cross of our Lord. She knelt and kissed the hilt then fell into prayer. The congregation hushed. Rising after some minutes in which the audience held its collective breath, she handed her precious sword to a page and adjusted her clothing. The man in black nodded to the trumpeters. Another fanfare shattered the silence of the congregation and catching my eye she smiled at me. With the reverberating echo of the fanfare still audible within the church the choir and organ took over with a medieval *Ars Nova chanson* by Philippe de Vitry. I recognised the music as one of my favourite pieces from the 1340s, as I gazed lost in awe, the lady in white began to walk in a stately manner towards the altar with her train following.

I swallowed despite my mouth being dry, this was a big occasion, a very big occasion. Emotion welled up inside of me, I felt love this woman, she was equal in spirit and determination, yet the marriage was arranged for some other purpose. I realised what was about to happen, I was about to wed the white lady…

The seconds seemed like hours as she made her way regally to my side in front of the altar. I could see every detail of her natural beauty. Her aristocratic high cheek bones, her flawless complexion with deep blue eyes and her immaculate swan like neck. She smiled with that knowing smile of recognition between two souls that have danced together through eternity. It was the most beautiful timeless moment ……

ZAP! The lights went out! The whole scene folded and collapsed in an instant and all I could feel was my body being shaken physically. Slowly as my senses came back into play I could hear Lily's distant voice getting louder and nearer, "Yann, Yann are you alright? Speak to me, speak to me."

My conscious mind engaged and I began to recognise the now familiar face of Lily Chevalier in front of me. She had hold of both of my shoulders and was gently but firmly shaking me back into the here and now. As she came into focus, I smiled and simply uttered a monosyllabic, "WOW!"

"You were really out of it! You started to worry me; it was like you were transfixed. The lights were on but nobody was home. That was really spooky!"

"I'm fine, I'm fine, it was nothing dangerous. I was time travelling. It was amazing, truly amazing." I swayed as I continued to adjust to my here and now surroundings.

"Well never mind that, I think you should sit down for a while and get your bearings. We sat in the front pews with Lily in the exact same position I had seen her in the time slip. Her visage and demeanour caused me to double take a breath which she noticed.

"Tell me what happened?" What did you see?" Lily was excited to find out what had happened.

"So much to take in Lily it will take some time," I started to relate my experience to her. She sat spell bound as I poured out the details to her why they were still vivid. "You were there Lily, you were there, plain as day!" I reiterated the point several times during the course of the story.

Lily smiled, "I knew we had been together before! I just had that feeling from the first time I stepped into your office and we met. Call it feminine intuition!" and she laughed.

"But who was the Lady in White? That is the million Euro question Lily! I wonder if we will ever find out?" On that note we gathered up our belongings and made our way back to the café Jehanne d'Arc.

Chapter 4

The Door

Half blinded by the afternoon sunlight we stumbled back into the street. I paused unsure of where I was but the café looked an inviting oasis below our elevated position on the steps of the church. Lily noticed the street name and gave an ironic chuckle, "all this talk of dragons in there, guess what the name of the road is?"

"I have no idea Lily, what is it?"

"Rue Boucherie Saint Georges – The Road of the Butchers' of Saint George. I wonder if they made dragon sausages?" Pleased with her own joke she gave a laugh.

I couldn't help finding it funny too and chuckled, "very appropriate my dear girl, that is a weird coincidence?" The connection was definitely there I felt it deep down. Perhaps the church had deliberately influenced the naming of the road in the past to expunge the name and power of the dragon cult. The word *Fairy Folk* came into my mind for some strange reason – what was that all about? Strange thoughts circulated in my head, they floated to the surface along with images and feelings of *déjà vu*.

"I need a café cognac Lily! Plus a good grounding dose of reality this is all getting very esoteric. I have never had such a barrage of non-stop past life images and experiences. This must be a special place for some reason?"

We sat back down in the café Jehanne d'Arc and the same corporeal waiter appeared as if by magic, *"Ah Garçon un café cognac s'il vous plaît* and what would you care for Lily?"

"Un café au lait s'il vous plaît."

"Qui Mademoiselle certainement." The waiter replaced his note pad in his apron pocket and disappeared smartly into the café.

When he returned with our drinks Lily engaged him in conversation as to why the café was named as such? The waiters eyes lit up and he became extremely animated as he told a strange tale of the false Jehanne d'Arc – Jehanne des Armoises who lived on this very spot over Sainte-Barbe gate now long gone. She married in the church of Sainte-Ségolène opposite in 1436 to a local knight Robert des Armoises, Seigneur de Tichemont. She even displayed the *blason la Pucelle* - coat of arms of Jehanne Du Lys, Maid of France on the board outside their dwelling. Lily made copious notes and paused several times to check with the waiter the spelling of the names.

She turned towards me and said, "Ah yes, I remember from my history lessons that individual knights from surrounding estates were responsible for the defence of gates and towers in cities and castles. It makes sense that he was charged with defending the Sainte-Barbe gate and therefore lived over it!"

I smiled to acknowledge her flash of inspiration, then sat silently so as not to disturb the flow of information, sniffed my cognac in its classic bulbous full bodied glass and listened intensely to the conversation. At one point I noticed my arm bursting out into goose bumps at the mention of the name of Robert des Armoises. I made a conscious mental note of the curious reaction that meant my subconscious was taking note of a specific piece of information. I also found myself strangely emotional as I listened to the story.

As the waiter came to his conclusion, Lily thanked him and sat back in her chair. "Well what do you make of that Yann?"

"Extremely interesting, it's one of those gems of knowledge that only the local inhabitants would know; perfect for the article. I knew there had to be a story here!" My cognac suddenly tasted better and its heady scent smelt even more delicious as I realised we had a story on our hands.

Then Lily made a curious statement, "Did you notice the hairs standing up on my arm when he told the story?" She paused to show me her arm as if to confirm that it was no illusion. She paused and then continued talking in self contemplation to herself, "Yes, amazing I have never experienced anything like that before!"

"I have," I said butting in, I gazed over the top of my cognac glass, "it happened just then, with me, it's usually a sign that my subconscious has recognised something familiar."

"Interesting, I never thought of it that way before." Lily sat backed in thought and sipped her café au lait.

I could see the cogs whirling in her mind as she started to see a story emerging from all of this. She was just like me! No wonder we got on, we were like two peas in a pod. I moved onto my coffee and sat sipping symmetrically and thinking in silence.

Finally Lily interrupted my train of thought, "I'll hit the internet on my laptop after dinner tonight and see what I can dig up on Jehanne des Armoises, she sounds quite a character."

With that thought we paid the bill and meandered back to the hotel Moderne. It was a pleasant summer evening and the air cleared away the dust and medieval cobwebs that were beginning to cloud our 21st century minds.

The evening passed quickly, we ate in the hotel and settled down to do some research on the internet. Very quickly with just a few keywords in various search engines, we started to piece together the story of Robert and Jehanne des Armoises.

"Hey look at this," Lily shouted, "there is a wooden door with their faces carved on the panels, in such fine detail too. The article says the door was originally found in Paris around 1850 when a hotel was being demolished, but judging by its style it obviously dates from the 1440s. Also we quickly found related twin portraits which were discovered above the fireplace of nearby Chateau Jaulny. They were almost identical to the door, in fact they looked copied; the door was therefore brought home to Metz and placed in the museum."

We were both starting to get excited at the discovery of the information. Now we could put faces to these enigmatic characters, two local historical figures who had left physical footprints in the sands of time. It was agreed this would make a good introductory article to our summer series.

"Time for bed Lily," I began to yawn and stretch in my chair, it was approaching midnight, "we have a good reason to visit the museum now."

"Qui, bonne nuit Yann. A demain matin."

"Bonne nuit mon Fleur d'Lily!" The nickname just leapt into my mouth.

"J'aime qu'il est minon." Lily grinned.

"Sorry it just slipped out," I smiled to cover my embarrassment, "it does suit you though, glad you don't mind, don't want to upset you on our first assignment."

With that we shut our individual doors and were soon asleep.

Next morning we stuck to our routine. I knocked on Lily's door at 08:00hrs then went down to breakfast. By 09:00hrs we had left the hotel and were walking the now familiar streets to the Musées d'Métropole La Cour d'Or. It seemed we had a date with destiny. Entering the museum we started to look at the collection of medieval artefacts in the Art and History section. The multi-arched vaulted ceiling gave an authentic crypt like feel to the exhibits and sent a chill down my spine. The whole place had been built as a combined palace-fortress which suited its present purpose perfectly.

Lily was on the hunt scouring the museum for the one artefact she really wanted to see. We both had a sense of expectation? Turning a corner, we simultaneously spied the door. It was resting in a semi reclined position so as to highlight the beautiful detailed carving of the faces. We stood awe struck as it was much more detailed than we could see from the pictures of the internet. The 3 dimensional photographic quality portraits of Jehanne and Robert were exceptional. The artist had obviously been highly skilled, making it a perfect treasure of the medieval wood carvers' art.

Then came the eureka moment, Lily let out a series of profane expletives, "*C'est quoi ce bordel! Mon Dieu! Mon Dieu! C'est vous! C'est incroyable!* It is YOU!" Stand sideways again like you were just a moment ago. The mouth, eyes and nose are all the same! The only difference is the beard. "Don't move, don't move!"

In seconds Lily had her camera out and was clicking away excitedly, she had forgotten entirely about the museum's no photography policy. Luckily nobody came and the room remained empty at such an early hour of the morning; it was 10:13hrs precisely. I could see a resemblance in the carving, but I could not compare it visually with my own face. Instead I had to rely on Lily's judgement until I could see the photographs and compare my visage with the carving.

I was duly a little dumb struck and watched bemused as an animated Lily danced around excitedly. If she was right and it was a big if, then it made sense of my experience at the *port des allemands* and the church. Could I really be remembering episodes from a life as Robert des Armoises? I could feel my subconscious nodding in approval with a self-satisfied grin of affirmation. We continued our journey of discovery in the museum which took us up until lunchtime. "Time to go eat," I whispered to Lily we've been here 5 hours already!"

"Yes let's go back to the café Jehanne d'Arc where we ate yesterday. It's just around the corner."

No sooner had Lily uttered those words than we found ourselves back at the same table with the same waiter again.

"Perfect *déjà vu*!" I gleefully said half in jest.

"Yes, absolutely Yann," Lily smiled and relaxed with her now familiar *verre de vin blanc.* In between sips she flicked through the pictures on her digital SLR, murmurs of revelation broke the silence as she alternated between pictures of my face and the face of Robert des Armoises on the door.

"Here Yann look at these two," she handed the camera to me," I'm not a policeman, but if this was an id photo fit for murder, I think the jury would hang you!" She grinned, it was a large grin of satisfaction and ultimate triumph at the definitive proof she now possessed on her camera.

"Yes, I can see what you mean especially the distinctive shape of the mouth; absolutely identical. Quiet amazing, "I'm not sure we should write about this in the article though, best stick to the historical detail."

"Yes, agreed, the world might not be ready for such a discovery."
"Certainly the church would get upset at the very concept of a *do it yourself* universe with no need for priests or a religious control structure and the loss of such power."

"We wouldn't be terribly popular at all would we?" I flicked on the camera display of pictures and instantly sat bolt upright, "It's her, it's her, it's the lady in white! There on the photo of the door was the exact same profile image of the woman I was getting married to in my flash back. It is definitely the same face."

"Well that clinches it, we know that the lady on the door is Jehanne des Armoises, so the lady in your flash back must be her, in which case you were Robert des Armoises, seigneur de Tichemont!"

"She is beautiful, so beautiful," I kept flicking the images backwards and forwards studying every contour of her face. Each different light angle gave a new insight into this beautiful enigmatic woman that carried a sword and wore spurs to her own wedding. My heart yearned to meet her again, such fire, such passion, I had been touched once by her magic and nothing would ever be the same again. My mind had encoded and remembered every detail and locked it away in my subconscious.

The waiter came over with the bill and we engaged him in conversation again. Our questions were much more precise and targeted. He answered them to the best of his knowledge and the picture clarified somewhat. Lily made yet more notes and again made sure of the accuracy of the names and places for further research back at the hotel.

Chapter 5

Dragon Lord

s we left the café Lily took the initiative, turned to me and said, "Do you fancy trying out an experiment?"

"What do you mean?" I replied half guessing what she was about to say as our minds were beginning to work in unison.

"Let's go back into the church and deliberately try to access the subconscious memories you have. Now that you know the connection it should be easier to get back there and retrieve the stored data." Lily began to get excited as she could see something interesting might happen. "After all the universe is just a giant information machine. It'll be like trying to access a website that you stumbled across previously!"

"OK Lily let's give it a go. I need to find the lady in white again just to know what happened?"

With that we crossed over the road and climbed the several stone steps into the now familiar Sainte Ségolène church. It was quiet with no visitors and the ancient sacred atmosphere was visibly tangible. The musty smell of the pews and dusty prayer kneelers rose to greet us as we moved. I walked towards the hot spot in front of the altar and stepped into the magic square. Nothing! No change, no colours, nothing. Disappointed I tried to reproduce the conditions of the previous day by jostling backwards and forwards several times.

Lily watched quietly, "you are trying too hard," she said having intuitively grasped the mechanics of the situation, "relax your conscious mind and allow your subconscious to access the memories held inside and communicate with them. Haven't you ever studied meditation?"

I could tell that she was getting impatient for a result, "only once when I was learning Goju Ryu Karate many years ago. I'm familiar with the concept of Zen and Zanshin - a meditative state of relaxed awareness yet one of being totally alert. In order to function efficiently on the battlefield in extreme situations Japanese Samurai would empty their mind of all distractions and function on subconscious instinct. That way they could allow their reactions to be driven directly by their subconscious which is able to operate ahead of normal space time and so gain an advantage by being already in the space ahead of the opponent. They could then strike the winning blow first with their razor sharp katana which was usually enough and not be harmed in the process!"

Lily stood with her head quizzically on one side with the eternal *trust a man to think of that expression*. "Yes, well it's like that except much more peaceful. Let's try together."

She took my hand and led me to the front pews where we had sat previously. "Right Yann now sit quietly, take deep breaths, breathe rhythmically, focus on the Rose window above the altar and let you mind go blank. That shouldn't be too hard for a guy should it!" She smiled impishly at her own joke.

I was already starting to understand the concept and beginning to visibly relax. The sacred atmosphere and the quiet started to settle my noisy mind. The multiple colours of the stained glass window became more vivid as I contemplated the dancing patterns of the sunlight driven mandala. Seconds seem to slow down and stretch into hours as time decelerated and then stopped. The Rose window began to blur. Holding Lily's slender fingers, I could feel the pulse of her heart beat in tandem with my own starting to slow down in synchronization and then begin to fade away. I slackened my grip on her delicate feminine hand in empathy as my conscious mind relinquished control. Then as I relaxed I stepped through the looking glass of my mind into another world.

The church was suddenly full of the same medieval people I had seen previously. I recognised the faces of several members of the congregation especially my Lady the Duchess of Luxembourg who I now knew to be my patron. She smiled at me and there was obviously a definite bond between us. Next to her was her eldest daughter as I had seen previously, I knew not her name, she suddenly turned and caught my eye then beamed a beautiful smile of recognition; it was definitely Lily! I hadn't realised how pretty she was in her own right until that moment. I looked back towards the altar and felt an electrifying jolt as my eyes met the eyes of my Lady in White. She now stood with me in front of the priest and I gazed into the blue liquid pools of her eyes that revealed the unfathomable depths of her very soul. The hypnotic effect of the Lady's sea grey eyes were enhanced by distinctive black edges to her irises which made her gaze totally irresistible, the spell was complete, my heart was hers forever. Lost for several seconds I swam in her soul and connected with her innermost being. She was exceptionally beautiful, strong, complicated and tricky but oh what a bright spirit burnt within her breast. She was a truly magnificent, wild and exciting creature; a royal warrior princess of ancient Scythian lineage.

I felt suddenly humbled in her presence and wanted to bend my knee to her. She was undoubtedly of high noble birth, a shadow fairy Elven princess from the darkest forests of my imagination. She smiled, her moist lips parted to reveal perfect white teeth framed by pale translucent skin that flawlessly covered her exquisitely structured high cheek bones. Mesmerised I followed every contour towards her delicate ears that were partially exposed under luxurious auburn chestnut hair. Every part of her anatomy was feminine perfection in divine classical proportion, with the notable exception that she had broad strong shoulders and narrow boyish hips.

My soul felt like weeping at such royal born magnificence. The wild flowers arranged in a neat circlet about her brow complimented her soft visage. We came to the vows and she spoke in deft eloquent tones, her courtly speech shone through with each syllable ringing clear. Words seemed to escape me as I attempted to repeat the words of the priest and I twice had to clear my throat. My lady looked askance at me, nudged my armoured cuirass with her elbow and spoke under her breath directly to me, "come on Robert, don't you want to marry me? You are much more decisive when in battle! Has a mere slip of a girl taken your voice away?" It was a direct challenge and she was enjoying every second of it.

I still stood there in disbelief that we were to be married. Then came the rings; symbols of eternity and infinity. Rings of power from the mists of time and legend, they glinted in the candle light. Made from pure white gold with a raised pattern of standing stones exactly mirroring an ancient stone ring from Hibernia, it was a pagan reminder of the fairy lineage of the dragon princesses; a direct connection across thousands of years to pre-Christian times. They were rings of power and memory; dragon rings imbued with sacred power. For dragon princesses contained the *living waters of knowledge* rich with alchemical hormones such as serotonin and melatonin, their body fluids gifted to their chosen dragon lord with clear sight and precognition. It was pure undiluted magic and the church was in fear of the power of these Elven fairy goddesses. Hence throughout time they had sought to burn, violate and destroy these witch princesses and erase their sacred royal bloodline.

It was a power struggle to the death and the church was ruthless in their prosecution of this dynastic genocide. That was what they were frightened of, that is what fuelled their bloodlust and mania for the destruction of all witches. In a blinding flash of Biblical revelation I suddenly understood everything. I was a humble knight yet I now realised that I possessed Dragon DNA. I was a match for my lady in white because I was genetically similar. I was sworn to protect her as I was my Dragon Liege Lady the Duchess of Luxembourg, she too contained the same sacred DNA that gave access to the Fairy realms of knowledge and clear sight. It all started to make sense as I remembered…

I looked back into those mysterious blue pools that my Lady Jehanne possessed. I stood erect and held my shoulders back suddenly alive and engaged in the process of sacred union with my dragon princess. My hand tightened on the hilt of my sword as I mentally swore to protect her from all adversaries. The overt Catholic Church ceremony was ending yet I understood the secret occult ceremony that had been taking place below the level of the public driven display. In full knowledge I turned to Jehanne and pressed her supple athletic feminine body to my hard body armour and gazed back into her eyes. Our lips met and electricity exploded within me, such power she contained, I reeled from the mind shock. Heaven and Earth seemed to stand still and everything faded from view.

I came to and sat shaking slightly, my heart pounding, I was back in the everyday Metz present day reality with a jolt.

"I understand, yes I understand, she was a dragon princess!"

Lily looked amazed, "a what?"

"A dragon princess, Jehanne des Armoises was a dragon princess; she was a source of pure clairvoyance and power. She wasn't a peasant girl at all she was a royal princess; very very royal indeed. This is incredible Lily, incredible!" I was so excited I grabbed her and hugged her tight. "And you were there Lily! You were beautiful and your mother was a dragon princess, so that means you are! You must share the same special DNA."

"What are you on about? I'm just Lily Chevalier an ordinary student graduate starting her first job."

"Yes, but think of it Lily you may in all probability be a dragon princess? Yet the knowledge within you has been suppressed by your modern materialistic upbringing!"

"Oh I see what you mean it's a case of reactivating my DNA which contains the inherent abilities you have just witnessed in your time slips!"

"Yes that's it Lily, the present population like those before them have been controlled and kept deliberately dumb by those in power such as the church and state, those that wish to control the world in order to support their own greed and thirst for power."

In a blinding flash of revelatory realisation Lily jumped up and shouted, "That's it, that's it, why you can remember you must be a dragon lord, you must have the same DNA. Yet you have lived all your life without knowing just as you outlined to me just then. You forgot the obvious - it applies to you!" Lily sat back down with a satisfied grin on her youthful face. She continued, "We are both dragons that's why we clicked from the first instant, we just fitted together like we have always known each other! If your time slip is anything to go by then we have definitely known each other in different periods of space time - we are Time lords, masters of time and space! No wonder the forces in control of this planet don't want us to realise our own power - we are unstoppable."

We both sat in total silence for several minutes contemplating the gravity of our discovery. The altar and fabric of church was still there, the sun shone through the Rose windows the same, everything was as it was but we were different, we were aware of the dormant power that lay within us; nothing in this world would ever hold us back again.

d'Arc Conspiracy

Chapter 6

A Rite of Passage

After an hour of debrief we left the church, my head was still reeling from the aftershocks of what I had experienced. It was a pity that there was not more original fabric from the medieval period to explore in Metz; I would have to be content with what I had already discovered.

Soon we were back at the hotel and it was time for a shower to freshen up. "I'll see you for dinner at eight, Lily." It had been a paradigm fuse blowing day and I wanted now to do some further research in order to plan tomorrow's agenda.

"Yes, no problem I'm going to have a lie down and then a shower. That's enough excitement for one day! I also want to have a little think about what exactly happened." Lily looked tired so I smiled gently and watched her safely enter her room.

"Thanks for being there today," I said warmly, "this experience would be nothing without you. It seems I am the lock and you are the key. We make quite a team together."

Lily smiled and shut her door bringing with it a deep sense of finality that meant I was on my own once again. The shower was hot and refreshing. I enjoyed the tingle of its energy on my skin which was a reality check of sorts. I thought of Descartes and the nature of our everyday existence; just how do we know what is real and what is illusory? Is the universe just one giant illusion, yet we think it is physical and solid? Timeless questions percolated through my head. This is why science invented experiments I thought. If the same outcome is achieved each time then we can formulate a law, which is usually backed up by mathematics of some sort, be it an equation or calculus; cause and effect appeared to drive the universe simple as that. Yet, how could I quantify my experience today, it was totally subjective but so real; was it just fantasy?

I sat in my bathrobe and tapped the keys of my laptop idly reviewing the information on Jehanne and Robert des Armoises. I kept pausing on the image of Jehanne taken by Lily and each time I felt a warm sensation of love welling up in me.

What about the other portrait, the one at Chateau Jaulny? I looked at it online; not the same feeling there was no connection. Yet, I was intrigued by Robert's distinctive red hat which was obviously symbolic and deeply significant to those that knew its meaning. I loved the twin dolphins of the pedestal that supported the circular wreathed head of his portrait. They were my favourite creatures, that couldn't be a coincidence; it was a definite cause and effect connection. Jehanne had a sun or green man carved on the door yet it was not painted on the portrait above the chimney, she had been given the same ubiquitous dolphins as Robert. The later copy made by an unknown artist had obviously omitted this important feature. For me the green man represented the wildwood and her love for nature and in particular trees, for she was an Elven fairy princess; it was therefore totally appropriate. The carvings secretly encoded such information; I just had to remember what it all meant?

I finally made my mind up; it was a lightning trip to Chateau Jaulny in the morning before taking the TGV back to Lille via Paris at 17:00hrs. I would stretch the rules of the assignment a little! Jean wouldn't mind if it meant an interesting story and we had now had loads and loads of detailed information on which to base the article. I searched online for a hire car company in Metz and found one, as the hour was late I decided to phone instead of book using the internet. I was lucky the office was just closing and I managed to secure a small Renault Scénic for an early start in the morning. By now it was 18:00hrs, time to chill out so I set my alarm for 19:30hrs; time for a rest. Lying back on my bed I closed my eyes, relaxed and prepared to doze off.

Instead of blackness I started to see bright colours it was the looking glass calling to me again, the question was should I resist it or should I take the plunge and step in? I made the conscious decision to enter the circular lake of colours not knowing if I would ever find my way back again without the aid of Lily. I paused for a moment then leapt in....................

I was totally shocked; for there next to me on a large four poster bed lay my dragon princess totally naked. A large fire blazed away in a huge grate and the light danced off of her ivory white skin. As it flickered it threw into sharp relief every contour of her perfect feminine form.

"I've been waiting for you Robert where have you been?"

I found myself replying automatically, "I had to say goodbye to the last of the wedding guests and make sure everything was bolted and secure for the night," my voice was slightly deeper and I spoke with an archaic accent using dialect Franconian, yet I understood perfectly.

I found myself naked too, I distinctly felt the fur of the bed cover as it played with my skin, I looked longingly and then slid effortlessly alongside my lady, "You are incredibly beautiful Jehanne. I do love you so much." I traced my fingers over her body and paused just short of the livid scar above her left breast. It had healed now but it was a constant reminder of her pain and suffering at the hands of the English. I kissed it gently, "You have healed well my warrior princess."

"Yes it's been seven years since the crossbow bolt found its mark as I scaled the walls of Les Tourelles at Orleans. Jehanne seemed unperturbed by the wounding and trauma suffered that day, "the armour took away most of the sting. Luckily it was high enough to miss my heart." She placed my hand on her warm beating breast and spoke softly as she reminisced. "St. Catherine was at my side that day!"

"Yes, I remember, the army thought you were dead, the English thought you were dead, and even I thought you were dead, but you miraculously survived! I remember them helping you mount your horse once the wound had been bandaged. They handed you your banner and you winced as you held it aloft to inspire the troops; then we cheered, oh how we cheered. The English couldn't believe it – witch magic they called it, scared them to hell and back!" I chuckled softly at the memory, "No wonder they wanted to burn you so badly!"

I kissed her neck and then gently her lips, her back arched as she warmed to my embrace. "You saved me Robert, my handsome black knight, not once but twice, stole your dragon princess away from under their very noses."

"Not before you suffered their insane tortures my love. God I hate them, their accursed church and all their deceptive workings. They masquerade as saints, but behave like devils. They are pure evil incarnate!"

"Hush my chevalier noir, they are winning at the moment, but their God is false and in the end they and their workings will fall and the people will be free, but the people have to free themselves. We can't do it for them. We are an old race midwifing the birth of a new type of human."

"You are right my darling. They slaughter us when we show them the truth and they still can't grasp how this magnificent universe works. Our Lord spoke those very words at his moment of suffering – forgive them for they know not what they do."

My gentle caresses were beginning to arouse the warrior angel I now held in my arms. As the soft sensual touches increased in intensity and urgency Jehanne started to writhe. She kissed me in return with amazing intensity and power responding to the rhythm of our dance.

Then she whispered softly in my ear, "You may drink from my living fountain if you wish Robert." She indicated by pressing on my shoulders that I should slide down her body so as to stimulate her further. Within minutes she gushed forth her divine waters and I drank a deep and heady draught.

The effect was instantaneous, the serotonin and melatonin within the clear sweet smelling liquid stimulated my psychic receptors and jolted my consciousness into hyperspace. I could see the world at my feet. All the silly games humans play, the misery and the suffering caused by them. I could see the English being thrown out of our country in the not too distant future. The rise of empires and the demise of France in the New World and the ultimate triumph of the English language, yet they too would fall, but not before they had defeated the Germanic threat of the black soldiers with their lightning strike insignia on their collars and red arm bands with black spiders. Then I saw beyond that to the fall of religion and the new age of enlightenment with its golden age of truth, science and logic.

I accelerated my travel, it went way beyond this tiny planet and time seemed to stand still. I saw millions of populated worlds similar to our own and basked in the radiant light of the universe. I was enfolded in a blanket of pure love and I understood the hidden mystery of everything. There was only bliss and oneness with the source, it was as if I had died; no pain, no suffering, just pure universal love. As the glow subsided I returned to the arms of my warrior angel, warm and soft she embraced me; so tender, so perfect, so wonderful.

Her soft voice whispered gently in my ear, "Now you understand my chevalier noir. This is the wondrous gift of true sight that is mine to bestow on the man I choose. You are now my dragon lord and I am your dragon princess. I contain the key within me that unlocks the door to the Fairy realm. I give it to you freely and as a token of my true love, for no man can take it by force."

I wept at the beauty of the moment, her words of affirmation and the revelation of true knowledge I had received. "It was incredible Jehanne; I saw the truth of your words. I understand everything you say now. It is a wonderful gift and I am my lady's humble servant forever." I stood naked in the firelight and then knelt before her royal presence and bowed my head.

"Hush, hush Robert, arise, you are a dragon lord, you are my equal and you have taken your first flight into the Elven fairy realm. Hush, lie with me and sleep, sleep my love."

Then the alarm on my mobile phone went off and I was jolted back to reality as if attached to a bungee rope. Oh my God, what was that all about? I lay naked on the bed, it was 19:30hrs and I could hear Lily showering next door.

Chapter 7

Chateau Jaulny

he day was overcast with the threat of thunder. The dramatic sky made the journey to Chateau Jaulny some 40 kilometres from Metz all the more memorable. We picked the car up around 08:00hrs having skipped breakfast due to time constraints as our TGV ticket was booked for 17:00hrs that evening. We were on a mission to investigate the mysterious twin portraits of Jehanne and Robert des Armoises that had been discovered recently after some plaster work above the main fireplace was removed by a workman during renovation works. Apparently the portraits had been covered up deliberately by the resident des Armoises incumbent at the start of the revolution to protect them. The internet pictures were not good quality and I wanted to see how I felt about being there. With our new found abilities we were both excited as to the possibilities of what we may discover if our memories were triggered. The assignment had become personal and liberating old memories told us much more than any history book ever could. It had become a spiritual quest into the understanding of our collective psyche; a pilgrimage of the soul.

The clouds rolled in and the wind increased as I drove the blue Renault Scénic southwest through the rolling flat agricultural landscape to the little village of Jaulny. As Sieur d'Tichemont Robert would have had other properties surrounding Metz of which he was protector in addition to holding the Sainte Barbe gate should the Republic of Metz be attacked and besieged he would also derive income from his feudal tenants. Tichemont was just a short distance northwest from the city and could be clearly seen on the internet map, but there were only a few houses there now and open fields so Jaulny was a much better bet to investigate, especially as time was so short.

Lily and I were beginning to understand the duties and way of life in medieval times under the feudal system. Lily had once been the eldest daughter of the Duchess of Luxembourg. I knew we had a deep connection and that Robert had worked for the Duchess; I also had an intuitive insight into her name then it began with a letter Y. I was sure of that. I just somehow knew it. I also knew that we were a team and that we had probably worked together in back then. Lily confirmed my feelings by spontaneously commenting without prompt, "I feel we have taken this journey before, it all seems so familiar. I feel very safe in your company!" She then went back to observing the scenery as we entered Jaulny.

Lily's behaviour reminded me of my father's tendency to suddenly make a seemingly random comment and then carry on with the task in hand. His behaviour seemed curious as he would lecture me in such away about how useful the monarchy were at maintaining stability within the country, when he knew that at an early age I favoured a republic. The discovery that Metz had always been a republic began to answer some of the questions about myself as to why I had such a strong preference at such an early age. I knew that previous memory might account for that. I also had a deep love for my father that was far beyond anything I had since known; the same was not true of my mother, which also puzzled me as a child and beyond. He died when I was 21 and I still missed him terribly. Lily had the same effect on me, even though we had known each other for less than a week. It was a feeling of unconditional loyalty; that I would happily die protecting her to my last breath. It was the same with my father and he with me.

We drove up the small inclined road that ran the length of the outcrop of rock that the small chateau was built on. It was a good defensive position and I noticed that the approach to the entrance was anticlockwise in true castle fashion so as to hinder the right handed sword arm of the attacker. We drove into the entrance courtyard between the outer towers, a single one to the right and a composite one to the left. I parked the car just to the left of the large rusty iron gates that hung from the tall stone pillars of the entrance to the chateau. The building was constructed in a squared off U with extremely thick external walls containing a minimum number of small shuttered windows on the landward side. Larger picture windows had been added at a later date on the open side to enjoy the panoramic views afforded from on top of the rocky outcrop. The two main blocks towered over the central courtyard in the heart of the U shape which made it the perfect killing field for any attack on the main chateau entrance.

It was not a substantial large chateau in the grand sense but it was easily defensible with good solid walls and a built up parapet running length ways on either side of the rocky outcrop. It felt Scottish in layout and architecture which I had observed on my holidays to the highlands and lowlands of Scotland. I knew from my family history that the Flemish Baillieu family had gone on to become the lowland Scottish Baillie's of Lamington, Lanarkshire. Lorraine and Alsace had a very mixed architectural heritage with many influences as it was perfectly positioned in the buffer zone between the Latin world of France and the Teutonic world of Germany.

"Well Yann, we are here but how are we going to get inside to have a look at the portraits?"

"A good point Lily, we could pose as tourists and enquire as to accommodation; we know it's a hotel? The problem with admitting we are journalists is that people usually want paying! I think we have blown our budget on this trip with the car hire so we will have to be resourceful."

Lily sat thinking for a moment then sat bolt upright, "I've got it I will say we are getting married and would like to consider Fort Chateau Jaulny for our honeymoon, due to the connection with Robert and Jehanne des Armoises!"

"Mon Dieu, Lily! That will never work we look more like father and daughter." I was shocked in a pleasant way.

"Not a problem – you're quite a catch! I'll let my hair down which makes me look older and wear sunglasses. Leave it to me; I'll do the talking, you just play along. I'll boss you around a bit and they will be convinced we've been married forever never mind engaged!"

I laughed out loud, "You're one hell of a girl Lily!" And with that Lily unpinned her radiant shoulder length hair and donned her dark Von Zipper sunglasses. "You just need a raincoat and a beret and you could be a World War II spy!" I joked, but was secretly amazed as it did make her look older. It was as though she had done this before. She was amazingly confident and well-rehearsed.

"Right now let's spike your hair up a bit, raise your collar on your jacket and put your sunglasses on – perfect!"

We both check our new look in the vanity mirrors built into the sun visors of the car and to my surprise it seemed to work.

"I'm impressed Lily. I think this might just work!"

"The secret is you have to believe in yourself 100% Yann, it's all just acting and theatre; smoke and mirrors."

Lily seemed totally confident so I was happy to let her lead the way. She exited the car and instantly changed her character, she then pushed open the giant iron gates which they groaned and creaked eerily for won't of oil. Either side they were hinged on tall 5 metre pillars of local stone topped with carved vases of flowers and joined by a row of formidable iron spikes. The small courtyard yawned before us like the giant mouth of a stone monster. The chateau was designed to intimidate and entrap the attacker, be they modern day visitor, local medieval peasant or a foreign enemy. On either side of the flagstones leading to the main door loomed the large fortress like wings of Chateau Jaulny. Many small windows and shot holes peppered the solid thick walls making the courtyard the perfect killing ground. I felt the hackles rise on my neck as it brought back familiar memories. Then I stepped on the first stone of the main entrance and instantly a flash of lightning arced overhead followed by a tremendous reverberating boom.

In the flash I saw Lily spontaneously change. She was now dressed in a black cloak with a hood, as she turned I saw that her left breast was covered with a radiating white equal armed cross, it looked like the Babylonian black sun symbol as used by the German Teutonic knights of old. Its shape sent a shock wave through my mind, it was so familiar. From within the hooded cloak I saw her teeth flash a familiar grin. She reached for her sword and grasping the pommel drew the shiny silver blade. Looking down I saw that I was carrying a heavy crossbow which was loaded with a vicious armour busting quarrel, its heavily waxed point protruding over the loading stirrup. Suddenly aware I was careful not to point it towards Yvette, the name just sprung into my mind, for one slip of the trigger and the deadly bolt would go straight through both her body and armour. I knew that the sinister purpose of the wax was to deliberately adhere to any glancing surface it met and punch a deadly hole through the shiny exoskeleton of the target and then pierce the fragile flesh and bones beneath. Yvette of Luxembourg turned back in the dark and reversing her sword banged loudly three times on the door.

The bell rang and I was immediately jerked back to the 21st century by the electronic high pitched sound of modern technology. The sky lightened and the large oak door creaked opened. A neat well-dressed lady with a soft spoken aristocratic voice bid us welcome and asked us to enter.

Lily replied in an equally refined accent that I hadn't heard her use before. I was impressed. I followed in the manner of an automaton my conscious mind was hurriedly analysing the stream of data it had just received. I was certain that it was a real memory. Specific details of the entrance were different but it was definitely the same place; I was certain of that. I knew we were on a mission, I could feel the tension and the adrenaline running through my veins. I had been excited, totally alive and was acting with a definite purpose, but what was that purpose?

We were ushered into the main entrance hall with a large stone staircase opposite which went up and off to the right, two large oak panelled doors loomed impressively to the left and right of the hall. But which room contained the famous chimney with the portraits above the fireplace? Would we find out or would our cover be exposed? I could hear Lily engaging in conversation with the lady concerned who was obviously the present owner but my conscious mind was elsewhere acting like a voracious sponge absorbing every minute detail on view.

My attention was drawn to a fake replica suit of armour that stood on the mezzanine landing of the staircase. Above it on the wall to the right a large brass dish hung just below a tapestry wall hanging to give a medieval ambience. To the left of the staircase hung a stags head trophy. Nothing rang true, it was as though I had entered a theatre with a fully dressed medieval set; it was good but not genuine. I knew from past experience that I only had to touch a genuine artefact and I was catapulted into the depths of my subconscious; scientists called the process psychometrics.

I reasoned that the flagstones which were genuine had triggered off the incident as we entered and Lily was a living conduit to the medieval world of my past life as Robert des Armoises. She was the key!

Excited with my discovery I switched back into here and now mode and started to pay conscious attention.

"Is your fiancé OK my dear?" I heard the aristocratic lady enquire.

Lily replied immediately without batting an eyelid, "Oh yes he's a little deaf from when he was in the Foreign Legion. Operating machine guns without hearing protection, not a good idea don't you know, but what can one do in a combat situation? He's my universal soldier!" With that she turned towards me and kissed my cheek endearingly, gave me a big squeeze and winked.

Mon Dieu! She was good; so natural and convincing, the aristocratic lady's eyes became quite emotional as she swallowed Lily's story hook, line and sinker. "You'll be wanting our best bedroom for the honeymoon then?"

I coughed loudly and nearly choked at the implication! "Honeymoon?" I blurted out the word uncontrollably.

"Yes my darling I thought this splendid little chateau of your ancestors would be so perfect. Don't you agree?" Lily slapped me heartily on my backside and winked again.

I regained my composure and using a sensible upper class voice responded, "why of course my darling, anything for you my

Princess; no expense spared. I love my Yvette she used to be a Paris catwalk model you know!" I smiled, kissed her on the cheek and patted her on the backside. Lily blushed and turned back to the Lady, who was now totally convinced we were so hopelessly in love and absolutely genuine.

"May we look around the chateau Madame?" Lily broached the vital question.

"Why of course my dear; It's so refreshing to see two young people so in love!" The aristocratic lady beamed and I coughed again.

"He was gassed in the Gulf War, poor chap." Lily said without batting an eyelid.

"Please feel free to wander around my dear I have several jobs that need attending to so take your time. This is the only way out so I will see you as you leave to complete the booking details." The aristocratic lay started to move off.

Lily caught her eye and made one parting shot, "Certainly Madam you are very kind, we may consider having our reception here too instead of in Metz after the church ceremony at Sainte Ségolène and the civil registration." Lily was now firing on all cylinders and really getting into character, so much so that she even had me convinced about the whole affair!

I smiled and held out my hand which she gently squeezed and then looking deep into my eyes she winked and whispered, "Job done." With that the aristocratic lady departed and we were suddenly left standing alone hand in hand.

Letting go I immediately congratulated her, "Wow that was a seriously impressive performance Lily, where did you learn to act like that?"

"I was leading lady in several small school productions back in Besançon before attending Lille University."

"You certainly know how to act!" I laughed and beamed a smile, "lead on my beautiful fiancée!"

Lily pushed her shoulders back straightened up and without hesitation went through the oak doors to her right with determination. "I think it must be this way?" Lily entered the room and took an immediate deep breath. I knew she instantly what she had seen. I rushed to her side; there above the large fire place were the twin portraits of Jehanne and Robert des Armoises forever gazing into each other's eyes. The gold leaf looked as fresh as the day it was applied as did the delicate light blue grey paint of the panels. Jehanne was wearing a flower bud fairy cap and Robert the distinctive bright red Phrygian cap with the point falling backwards. I was struck by the symbolic significance of the portraits. They were obviously encoded with many underlying meanings which only those privy to the dragon secrets would know. As Lily clicked furiously away with her camera, I attempted to absorb the feel and detail of the remarkable portraits.

I was struck by the twin supporting downturned dolphins on each pedestal that supported the circular laurel wreaths that contained the head portraits. The Dauphin was the obvious intention but I was also aware of my keen love of dolphins with their imagery of freedom and spirit of playfulness. My conscious mind then noticed that Jehanne's pedestal was painted differently to the wooden door carving. I was certain that on the original door she had her own cryptic symbology which meant to me that the portraits were idealised copies of the door from a later date, possibly one hundred years or so after the carving. The door had been carved and sculptured as exact portraits from real life and contained a near photographic image, whereas these were much more bland and two dimensional. I was convinced that I was now looking at a tribute painting to their life executed by the family at a later date. It was a lasting memorial to record the image of two illustrious members of the Armoises family for posterity.

The link with cave painting was inescapable. They were quite beautiful and emotional to gaze upon, the children or grandchildren had immortalised the loving couple of whom they were so proud. A sense of wonder filled my heart as I stood quietly gazing at the miracle and power of art to convey information across the ages.

The alarm on my mobile phoned sounded. "It's time to get back Lily if we are to make the TGV for Lille!"

"OK Yann, two more minutes." Lily continued to click away frantically as though her life depended on it.

Then as if on cue the aristocratic lady returned to see how we were getting on. Lily immediately reverted into her role of fiancée and confirmed that we would be booking the chateau as part of our nuptial celebrations, but that we still had another venue to look at. With that we bade farewell and left the chateau without fuss.

"My turn to drive darling now that we are almost married!" Lily held out her hand for the keys.

"You were magnificent in there, but remember you shouldn't boss your dear fiancé around so much when you find one!" I surrendered the keys without further protest.

We jumped in the car which started faultlessly and we were off. For some strange reason Lily decided to take an intuitive route that was different to our original. As we left Jaulny and entered the adjacent commune of Landremont I suddenly banged on the dashboard to gain attention and shouted, "Stop the car - Stop the car!" Lily checked her mirrors and jammed on the brakes bringing us to an immediate halt. To compound her amazement, without hesitation I flew out of the car door and started running back to the sign. Lily parked the car safely and then moments later came to join me by the side of the road.

"Look Lily, look!" I exclaimed pointing at the commune sign.

"What is it Yann? Mon Dieu!" Lily swore under her breath. "It's the Dragon from your shield!" She stood dumbstruck.

I was transfixed. Just as with the image of the carvings with their ability to convey information across space time, there in front of me was the very image I had seen on my shield in Sainte Ségolène church. It wasn't just my fanciful imagination conjuring illusions, here was the same device used as a heraldic blazon just metres from Chateau Jaulny, the home of Jehanne and Robert des Armoises. Lily regained her composure, went to the car and retrieved her beloved camera.

"How's that for feminine intuition?" She beamed as she clicked away, "had we gone your route we would have missed this priceless gem! Oh yes, Lily Chevalier is on the case!" She laughed and carried on clicking.

Chapter 8

Champagne

he journey back to Metz went swiftly. There was so much left to explore now that we had opened Pandora's Box. Domrémy the alleged birthplace of La Pucelle - The Maid was just down the road and the whole border area following the source of the Meuse and Moselle seemed to have its own magical character. To the west lay Verdun scene of one of the bloodiest sieges and battles of World War I showing that geography is the mother of battle. The ever expanding Germans would always try to penetrate the plains of France through the same geographical gaps. To the northwest lay Luxembourg the intriguing principality that was pivotal to the Jehanne des Armoises story, for the Duchess had been a great patron of her around the year 1436. The rough hilly terrain of the Belgian Ardennes rose to the north, scene of the last ditch Battle of the Bulge in the winter of 1944 again involving the Germans, who made an unexpected offensive thrust through that sector on the border between the Gallic Latin tribes and the Teutons. Metz was strategically at the centre of events in this part of Europe, no accident then that Robert des Armoises, Flemish soldier of fortune should be stationed at this crossroads of history.

One thing puzzled me though about the Landremont heraldic blazon, the red dragon was surmounted on a saltier cross argent, field azure, it was the Scottish flag; what was the connection? I was sure that in the church I had seen just the distinctive red dragon on a field of light blue. I knew that it was heraldically incorrect to place a colour on a colour; a badge on a national flag however was acceptable. Could my memory be mistaken? It was a conundrum that would play on my mind for the whole journey home to Lille.

The journey by TGV to Paris was quickly over and soon we were enjoying a 3 hour stop over. I decided to treat my Fleur d'Lily to dinner so we took a table at a restaurant near Gare du Nord. "Champagne and oysters, it's on me!" I triumphantly announced much to Lily's surprise as she imagined it would be a quick cup of coffee and a pastry on the expense account that had now run all but dry.

"Well it's not every day you make a ground breaking discovery about yourself and gain a glimpse on how the universe works, is it?"

"I'm still blown away by the whole experience!" Lily confided in agreement.

We chinked glasses in the sure knowledge that the short journey from Paris to Lille would be even quicker after a bottle of my favourite beverage!

"It will take several days for all of this to sink in, Yann." Lily said reflectively as the bubbles tickled her nose. The meal was superb and of Parisian standard. I ordered a Tornados Rossini bleu and Lily surprisingly ordered the same!

"We really are in tune with our character and behaviour!" I confided my observation as I sipped my Champagne.

"Yes, it's remarkable; I feel we have known each other all our lives!" Lily grinned and relaxed back in her chair, "that was delicious thank you so much, Yann."

"My pleasure, my wonderful Fleur d'Lily, it's not every day one can dine in such surroundings with a beautiful young lady; Santé!"

I raised my third glass of Champagne and toasted our friendship, "Un pour tous et tous pour un!" I used the famous Musketeers' toast from Alexandre Dumas' epic story of friendship and adventure to seal the bond between us. It seemed wholly appropriate given the flash back memories I had experienced.

Lily decided to add another toast, "to the fellowship of the Black Brethren!" It came from her deep subconscious and sent a peculiar tingle of familiarity down my spine.

I decided to order another bottle of Champagne which we duly started to drink. I suddenly looked at my watch and realised we had but ten minutes to board the TGV for Lille. "Drink up Lily we must fly!" Without further ado Lily grabbed the half full Champagne bottle as I paid the bill and leaving a generous tip, we ran out of the restaurant in a none too dignified exit!

Finding the platform fairly easily we jumped aboard the waiting TGV and sat back in our seats giggling like school children. "That was close!" Lily said as she drew a much needed breath, "you're quite something, Yann Baillieu. I salute you!" With that she took two restaurant Champagne glasses out of her handbag and to my utter astonishment, poured me another glass of Champagne. She then delicately passed it to me with a very unladylike cheeky grin, "and I'm sure that your more than generous tip will cover the price of two glasses!"

"Excellent! A lovely souvenir from my comrade in arms; I shall keep the glass on the mantelpiece over my fireplace in lasting memory of our trip and this moment. You are quite a character yourself Mademoiselle Chevalier; Santé!"

I raised my glass to my stunningly beautiful confederate much to the amusement of the other passengers in the carriage. The champagne having kicked in Lily put her iPod ear pieces in and started to close her eyes. "Wake me up in Lille – Robert..." Her last words echoed in my mind as I stood guard over my sleeping comrade in arms. Images flooded my mind as I sat looking at her angelic face framed by her lustrous auburn hair. I saw castles, and sieges, battles raging and men dying. It was brutal warfare at its worst; bloody and extremely violent. Arrows rained down as men hacked each other to pieces with sword and pole axe. The noise and clanging din of weapon on armour sounded in my head in a cacophony of sound. I saw the fluttering banners of France and England above a seething mass of shiny armoured knights thrashing like a shoal of fish. The studded and leather clad men-at-arms fought hand to hand with the quilt clad common soldiers in furious melee. Both sides taking casualties from arrow and crossbow quarrel, their armour to no avail. Everywhere was awash with blood, hot red gushing blood, spurting like geysers from men's' arteries as they were severed by vicious blows from the butchers' weaponry.

Yet, amidst the carnage I saw a young girl in shining armour mounted on a magnificent white steed of sturdy proportion. She held aloft a virgin white banner bearing a flurry of golden fleur d'lys that sparkled in the sun, they surrounded a picture of a man on a cross with an angel on either side; the words Jhesus Maria embroidered in gold proclaimed her holy mission. Her right hand held aloft a long shining sword as she urged the men on to victory. Her bronzed cropped chestnut hair flowed freely exposed in the breeze so that all may recognise her. She was the very vision of an apocalyptic angel of doom and hope. Such beauty surrounded by such carnage; she gave hope, inspiration and encouragement to the soldiers of France in their darkest hour.

Suddenly the electric glare of Gare Flandres, Lille flashed in my eyes and I snapped out of my waking dream. I shook Lily from her slumber and we made our way from the train to the solid ground of the platform. The cold night air hit my face and the change was complete. I was finally home and the dream of the last three days was broken...

We had another three days to write our article for La Voix du Nord. Lily and I shared a taxi and I bade her bon nuit at her apartment address. The door of the taxi slammed shut with a finality of permanent separation but I knew I could see my Fleur d'Lily bright eyed and bushy tailed at 09:00hrs in Editor Jean's office. Jean wanted us to report on our mission and outline the details of our article to him personally. The content of the story we could write together was already crystallising in my mind as I inserted the key to my front door. A quick shower and I was glad to fall into bed as it was now well past midnight.

At 09:00hrs sharp Lily and I entered Jean's office, for the next 45 minutes we off loaded our joint experiences with the aid of Lily's PowerPoint presentation of images. All the while Jean sat there listening with only the odd quip thrown in. He was naturally sceptical but fascinated with the wealth of intuitive detail we had collected.

"Well that's certainly an interesting tale," he said. Then getting straight back to the nitty-gritty, "Right, a double page centre spread to kick off the series with, lots of patriotic imagery and a touch of the occult a la Da Vinci code should hit the mark. Conspiracy and the paranormal are quite fashionable now and it should sell well. I like it! It will add a splash of historical colour to the usual summer events and lack of news during la grand vacance."

Lily and I looked at each other and smiled. "Excellent!" I said to break the silence and clapped my hands together as I stood up. "We'll get onto it right away."

With that we left Jean to get on with the business of the day and we returned to my office. Upon entering I was amazed at the amount of paper work that had piled up on my desk, plus the hundred or so e-mails whilst I was away.

"Don't worry Yann; I'll write the article, you just get on with clearing your desk of all that paper!"

"Are you sure Lily? That's very kind of you, normally I have to juggle and do everything at once."

"Yes, sure, it will be great fun and I can write it from my perspective observing you." Lily had already seen how this was going to work and the fact that Jean liked the memory flashbacks meant she could write the article and include what happened to me in these episodes. Jean had indicated that the article needed to have a new fresh perspective and that people do like a genuine mystery story, so the way was unexpectedly opened to write up our tale in full and not to make it just another sanitised politically correct historical tourist guide.

I was pleased at the outcome as it meant that our experiences would reach a wider audience and stimulate debate and discussion as to the whole issue of our existence on this tiny blue planet.

Twenty four hours later Lily presented me with her article.

Chapter 9

The Book

A week later just before our next assignment in Orleans, I made two astonishing discoveries. The first occurred as I was getting my car out of the garage. Instead of just shutting the up and over door I decided to go back in and look at the open wall cabinet containing some 200 miniature fantasy figures that I had painted in the early 1980s They were placed there because I had nowhere else to put them and at least in the garage they were accessible and on view.

To my utter amazement there on the top shelf in the townsfolk section was a knight on horseback with a banner and a squad of 7 men-at-arms. I remembered that I had painted them at random without reference to any books. At the time I was puzzled by the fact that I had painted the heraldic blazons in a stylised way that I hadn't used before. Now I knew why; for there was the Landremont red dragon on a sky blue field proudly displayed over and over on shield, surcoat, jupon, trapper and banner. My jaw dropped in disbelief as I held the precious tangible icons in my hand. I now knew absolutely for certain that they had been a product of my fertile subconscious mind.

This led directly to the second bombshell discovery. I had always been an artist and had painted in water colours since being a small boy. Often I would paint for relaxation and some five years previous I had engaged myself in an unusual project. I had decided in a completely arbitrary moment of inspiration to construct a 3D pop up picture book on heraldry and the medieval history of France instead of my normal 2D flat illustrated paintings. The project was largely an experiment with the aim of publishing a small book for marketing to young people via *La Voix du Nord*. The whole work had blossomed into a complete work of art containing several pages of heraldry painstakingly rendered in fine watercolour.

I now sat down in total disbelief at what I was seeing. The book lay open on the coffee table in my lounge and I sat in silence for several minutes before breaking out into a huge smile. Wow! It was an excellent example of my subconscious in action as at the time I had no conscious idea of what I was constructing. The whole project had been hijacked by my own hidden memory for its own purposes of expressing itself into being.

I decided to invite Lily to dinner on the night before we would leave for Orleans in order to show her my discoveries. I desperately wanted to see her reaction to make sure I was not deluding myself in wild fantasy and hallucination. I duly invited her to dinner on the following Sunday night.

Originally I had intended to cook at home but decided at the last minute against the idea as it would make far too much mess and work; the assignment and deadlines came first. This would be an emotional trip as we were heading for the epicentre of Jehanne d'Arc's finest hour which would lead to her major influence on French culture and history for posterity; for it was the miraculous lifting of the English siege of Orleans in 1429 that raised her to the status of national superstar. The legend of la Pucelle – the Maid started in Orleans.

I had an intuitive premonition that this for me would be an emotional journey, for my senses were beginning to home in on this past life with stunning clarity.

Lily turned up on time at 19:30hrs sharp which surprised me as I had been used to her using her lady's prerogative of being fashionably late. I invited her in for an aperitif which would be a civilised way to start the evening. "I have something to show you, Lily!" I announced with dramatic flair as I popped the champagne cork and made her jump unexpectedly. The perfectly chilled champagne poured smoothly into the tall fluted glasses and turned a reddish purple colour as it mingled with the blackcurrant Cassis liqueur already in the bottom quarter of the elegant crystal vessel.

"Magnifique, Kir Royale! My favourite," Lily exclaimed with the adolescent excitement of a teenage school girl, "you spoil me."

"Only the best for my comrade-in-arms," I responded in debonair fashion, "I have to look after my precious Fleur d'Lily!"

I raised my glass in salute as did Lily and we both stood eye to eye, *"Un pour tous et tous pour un!"* "One for all and all for one," Lily repeated the toast joining in enthusiastically as we chinked glasses.

With that she sat back down on the settee and relaxed visibly. "What has Monsieur Baillieu to show me then?" She said with a giggle as the bubbles tickled her nose again and she fondly remembered the train journey.

"Well I was going to keep it until the end of the evening but seeing that you are interested and we have an early train to catch tomorrow I shall show you now!"

With that I walked over to my lounge book case and drew out the slim hand illustrated volume rendered in fine watercolour and gold leaf, applied to a brown leather binding. "See what you make of this my petite Fleur d'Lily!" I handed her the A4 sized antique looking tome with a flourish and sat back with my drink to observe her reactions. Lily studied the cover intently. "It's beautiful Yann, quite exquisite; where did you buy this?"

"I didn't. It's all my own work," I said modestly.

"You made this!" Lily's face lit up and her mouth opened wide in animated caricature fashion. "It's amazing, really, really beautiful; you are so talented."

"I don't think so but it did become literally a labour of love as you will see."

Lily examined the covers and studied the rich water coloured pictures of the principle characters interspersed with scenes from the medieval story told within its rich leather covers. The corners were bound in riveted brass so as to give it that medieval feel of authenticity. The Gothic script of the title was rendered in meticulous calligraphy and read, *In the Shadow of the Dauphin*; its hand embossed gold leaf shone in the flickering candle light of the room which gave the whole volume luxurious warmth.

"It reminds me of Froissart in style," Lily said knowledgeably.

"Precisely that was my intention but Froissart with a twist darling and it did get a little out of hand with my original simple concept as you will see!" I smiled gently and waited for Lily's reaction.

I was not disappointed for as she opened the book Lily let out a squeal of delight. "Wow! It's 3 dimensional; how totally amazing!"

She then proceeded to lay the book out flat on the coffee table underneath the pendulum light in order to bring the pages into full illumination. As she did so up popped a scene of a medieval chateau set in rolling country side with a small boy playing with his falcon in the foreground.

"It's truly breath taking, Yann," Lily held the book level with her eye and rotated it a whole 360 degrees to observe the fine detail. "Astonishing, the quality of the water colour illustration is worthy of an art gallery!"

"Glad you like it, I have never shown anybody this; you are the first to see it. I painted it in 2004 for my amusement and relaxation."

Lily read the story neatly written in medieval Gothic script while I continued to explain. "I made myself a quill pen, well several actually. Then I taught myself to write using them. Strangely I found it easy to do."

It had been a mystery to me as to how I could do that without training for I just seemed to know what to do. Now with my experiences in Metz I had a good idea as to why this was.

After Lily had fully savoured the first two pages she turned slowly over to pages three and four. Her eyes grew wider as she absorbed the sheer detail of the armoured knights on horseback engaged in combat, banners flying, heraldic emblazoned shields and jupons colourfully arrayed which all combined to produce a rich feast for the eyes.

"I'm speechless Yann, truly speechless!"

"You ain't seen nothing yet, try the animating levers then rotate it and open the door!"

Lily found that by pulling tabs the knights moved in combat and the horses reared up, then she rotated it 180 degrees and found that the scene had switched to a peaceful castle with a wooden door in an arched stone wall surrounded with flowers set in a garden enclosed by medieval crenulated walls. In the near distance towers and turrets shone in the painted sunlight.

Lily's deft slender fingers opened the door and she immediately drew a breath and yelled. "*Mon Dieu!* It's the two figures on the door, even the pose is the same; it's the door from the museum in Metz! I don't believe it!"

I laughed at her reaction, "that's exactly how I felt." I said with satisfaction and a certain feeling of vindication.

"But, I don't understand, you said you made this five years ago?"

"Precisely it was literally a labour of love and just evolved from my subconscious. I had no idea why I was so obsessed with finishing it and then the unexpected twist of the love story. Turn to the last two pages, go on, go on!"

Lily turned to pages 5 and 6 and her eyes started to mist up with emotion, "it's beautiful, so sad."

She had been instantly moved by the content of the story that told of how the knight had lost his love to the Black Death and was left alone and desolate despite being successful in battle and life. He stood tearfully alone on the ramparts of his fort chateau.

Lily sat staring at his face and reflected. "It's amazing, truly amazing. It is as if you have just made this after our trip to Metz, but you can't possibly have put this together in the short space of time since we have been back."

"Exactly, you are a witness to that very fact Lily, a very important witness. Did you notice the name of the battle depicted in the middle pages?"

"No, I was too absorbed in the detail of the heraldry to look at the writing on the page."

"Have a look again," I said quietly.

Lily turned the page and read, "Patay 1429, it's the battle that sealed the success of Jehanne d'Arc's campaign and lifted the siege of Orleans!"

"Yes, precisely and where are we going in the morning?" I said with a smile.

"Orleans! Ah now I see your reason for showing me this tonight."

I poured Lily another Kir Royale and she placed the open book reverently on the coffee table.

"Now I will show you the second part of the show!"

"What there's more!?" Lily sipped her aperitif and sat back up straight on the edge of the chair.

"Yes, behold!" With the dramatic flourish of a stage magician pulling a rabbit out of a top hat, I reached under the table and produced a tray bearing a squad of miniature painted soldiers surrounding a knight on horseback bearing a red dragon banner.

Lily looked intrigued and mystified. I waited for the penny to drop. I carefully stationed the caparisoned dragon knight with his faithful squad of men-at-arms one by one next to the book. The pendulum light illuminated the heraldry perfectly! Every man bore a shield or badge of the red dragon exactly the same as their liege Lord who displayed multiple copies on his jupon and horses trapper. He held aloft a banner with the same device on a field of pure sky blue.

Lily still looked quizzically then suddenly spotted the connection as she consciously took in the heraldic significance of the assembled scene. Her eyes opened in disbelief!

"*Sacre bleu, non,* it's the exact same red dragon motif! How, when, why?"

"A long story *mon petit* Fleur d'Lily, but with a paint brush, 1982 and they are just eight figures from a collection of over 200 fantasy role playing miniatures from my gaming days."

I tried to be precise because I sensed that it was as if Lily was scribbling the details down in her mental note book. As we sat finishing our drinks the church bell struck 20:00hrs.

"Time to eat! What perfect timing." I announced as I stood up.

"Yes, I'm hungry now after all that food for thought." Lily stood and placed her champagne glass on the table. "Notice I'm leaving the glass behind!" Lily laughed again at the memory of our TGV trip.

"I know a nice little restaurant in La Madeleine not far from here. We can walk there no problem and the rest of the evening is yours to command my lady!" I bowed theatrically then helped Lily on with her black cut jacket. "Nice tailoring, very sci-fi!"

"Thank you. Yes, you're not the only alien in town!" Lily laughed again but I detected a note of truth underneath her riposte.

"Well, you are a Dragon Princess those genes have to come from somewhere?" I grabbed my own black leather jacket and left everything exactly as it was.

94

Chapter 10

Timelines

The evening air was deliciously warm and we chatted freely as we strolled casually along past the Hippodrome in the direction of La Madeleine and towards the centre of Lille. We walked along the Rue du Général de Gaulle until we came to the T junction with Rue Pasteur.

"This is one of my favourite local restaurants Lily, it is very very good." I said as I pointed to the Restaurant de L'Orangerie. We entered and I was greeted by Lucie who I knew well.

"Your usual table Monsieur Baillieu, right this way." She deftly showed us to my table in the corner. The ambience was perfect, subdued lighting, warm dark red table clothes and candle light.

We ordered an aperitif and studied the menu. After some consideration we settled on *the L'ardoise de foie gras de canard maison et sa crème brûlée as a starter followed by Pavé de saumon rôti, millefeuille de poireaux et pommes vapeur* for our main course. As we waited Lily started the discussion in earnest.

"When was Robert des Armoises born, Yann?

"I think it was 1403 according to the internet information why?"

"Well, if Jehanne des Armoises died in 1453 as recorded then he would have been 50; how old were you when you made the book 5 years ago?" I knew that Lily had hit on something big and my mind started racing for the answer.

"Of course I was precisely 50 years of age! Wow! I must have produced the book in response to the death of Jehanne whom I dearly loved. You're a genius to see the connection, Lily. You're right; I suddenly wanted to make a book on heraldry and the history of France which focused my creative skills on that period. Then I guess my subconscious continued to hijack the project with escalating force once it had been given an effective platform on which to communicate!"

I could see in an instant how it all worked; my subconscious was responding in chronological synchronicity with that of Robert des Armoises. In fact, if there was only the eternal now, then we must both be physical projections or aspects of one spirit linked by a single mind which operated in a higher timeless dimension.

Quick as a flash Lily immediately launched in with another profound insight. "Yes, that makes some sense if we imagine our separate physical past lives as chronologically synchronous with what we perceive to be our present. It would be very similar to a number of trains setting out on parallel railway tracks. If one train were to be emotionally derailed the shock waves would be felt on board all the other trains!"

In a single moment of inspiration we had grasped the true nature of time and space.

"Yes, that's it!" I shouted! "Our consciousness must reside in a higher dimension with no time only the eternal now, so our subconscious mind is present simultaneously in all of our physical incarnations."

Lily became highly animated and took out her limited edition Greta Garbo Mont Blanc pen and started drawing on the table cloth.

"Imagine our many lives on this spherical 3D planet as having 2 dimensions rather than the 3 that we perceive; each separate life would therefore be stacked like a pancake one on top of the other. As we wander about the surface of this planet, we would be at certain geographical points, at certain times of our lives. Imagine that these coincide and collide when we visit places in synchronicity. The emotional event effect would be doubled or trebled and therefore magnified to create the dejà vu time slip experience exactly as in Metz; also when you produced the book and the soldiers!"

I leant forward to look at her geometric doodling. "Interesting, this looks like mathematical topology? Gaston Julia would be proud of you!" Lily laughed at my fractal mathematical observation.

"I'm honoured that you compare my insight to one of France's most famous mathematicians."

"It would account for dejà vu; the coming together of time and place with the subconscious orchestrating the proceedings on two levels of pancake without the conscious mind being aware on either." I realised that we had grasped a primary truth that was testable in scientific terms by examining the timeline for Robert des Armoises life with my own. "We have a testable theory, Lily. The coincidences of time and place should be self-evident when we lay our two lives side by side."

"Place is of course space, so we could mathematically substitute one for the other; so it is technically a theory of time and space. Lily had realised the profound nature of our discovery and enquired further to clarify the detail, "When precisely did you paint the red dragon figures?"

"It was 1982; I remember it well as I was not enjoying my job at the time so I threw myself into a parallel world of fantasy or more accurately drew on my subconscious memory as we now know." We both raced to do the math but Lily beat me to the draw!

"You were 28! That means it was 1431 in Robert des Armoises' life and Jehanne was about to get burnt at the stake on May 30, hence the urgency."

"Mon Dieu, Lily! You're absolutely correct! I wrote several games with the same reoccurring theme. If I still have those scripts in the attic we can examine them as primary evidence for parallel details. This is so exciting!"

I stood up, circled the table and knelt beside her. Taking her hand I kissed it passionately. The restaurant immediately broke into a spontaneous round of applause as they thought I had proposed!

I ignored them and only had eyes for my genius comrade-in-arms. "Time for home, Lily; I will escort you to your door."

"Merci beaucoup mon chevalier! Vous êtes très courageux et beau!" Lily curtsied theatrically and smiled as I helped her put her jacket on.

"Ssssh not so loud Lily, anyone knowing you will think we are already married!" Lily realised her *faux pas,* laughed and blushed a bright scarlet.

I announced our spoof engagement to the restaurant with an exaggerated sweep of the hand. *"Madame et Monsieur Chevalier noir; Quelle équipe!* What a team!"

I paid the bill much to the amusement of the waiter who winked at me, gave my "fiancée" a red rose and was then totally bemused by Lily's doodling on the table cloth which he puzzled at for quite some time whilst scratching his head.

With that we left the merry restaurant scene, I walked Lily to her door as promised. I then headed for home and a good night's sleep before our rendezvous set for 06:00hrs on the morrow.

Chapter 11

Orleans

Monday morning dawned and I met Lily at Gare Lille Flandres. It was no effort as the bright July sunshine had painted the sky early. We had established the routing now so we settled back in our seats and relaxed for we knew that we would be in Paris in precisely one hour. Lily opened the conversation, "thanks for a great evening last night, Yann. I'm starting to wonder when you are going to stop blowing my mind with all of these revelatory bombshells!"

"You and me both; I have the feeling that we are looking at an iceberg of information and as such we have only scratched the surface."

I sipped my coffee reflectively and then dipped my croissant in its hot black liquid body.

"Well it's certainly exciting. I feel that we are performing a ground breaking experiment which has all sorts of ramifications for humanity. The nice thing is that we have an outlet to the public for the information and Jean seems to be backing us to print the truth." Lily beamed and looked excited.

"How can you be so enthusiastic and positive at this time of the morning my beautiful Fleur d'Lily?"

"Youth!" She replied and laughed, "It's as simple as that."

"Absolutely, you are inspirational! I have the feeling that you play a bigger part in all of this than you know; the best is yet to come."

Paris Gare du Nord came and went in a blur of commuter flurry and we headed over to Gare d' Austerlitz by taxi to catch our SNCF normal service train to Orleans.

The short hop to the Loire valley was over in the blinking of an eye. We read rapidly through our internet notes and familiarised ourselves with the ground plan of the city. "I hope we are not too disappointed?" I confided to Lily, "It looks pretty modern to me, rebuilt in the grand style of the late 19th century after the Parisian model."

"Well good or bad we will uncover something and it may not be what we expect. It's an emotional place set at the centre of things, so it must hold a lot of memory energy?"

"Yes, quite right, I must remember that we are also dealing with the 96% invisible universe and not just the 4% visible!" Lily had given me quite a thought. Her young mind was much more open to the new ideas and concepts science was discovering; the great unseen quantum universe beneath the atomic level seething with energy held within it the fine matter realm in which our immortal spirit and subconscious memory dwelt.

She was both beautiful and intelligent; a wonderful combination.

We pulled into Gare d'Orleans which shone under its sparkling new stainless steel and glass undulating double waveform canopy in the morning sunlight. Alighting from the train I noticed straight away that it had a lovely harmonic feel to the open space beneath its roof due to the lack of sharp angular projections; it was an architectural triumph. We had booked in at the Best Western Hotel d'Arc which lay just a short walk away at 37 Rue République. As we strolled casually we passed the Centre Jehanne d'Arc to our left, crossing the busy inner city ring road we checked in. We took the small elevator to our rooms on the second floor. As we reached our adjacent rooms I turned and said, "Same routine see you in 20 minutes. We'll use the statue of Jehanne d'Arc in the Martroi as our inspirational and spiritual base. What do you think, Lily?"

"Yes fine, that's a good idea." With that Lily went into her room to unpack and change, "See you in a moment then!" She shouted as the door shut.

I entered my room next door and laid out my notes on the table by the window. As a General plans a battle I studied the ground for advantage and clues to our point of attack. The cathedral of Sainte Croix would provide a solid medieval foundation to the whole expedition and fine tune our minds for whatever we would experience and discover in the few short days ahead.

La maison Jehanne d'Arc looked promising and if original would trigger a memory response I felt sure. Apart from that the city was now large and modern, sprawling out beyond its ancient medieval walls. I had in my possession several old maps of the city taken from the internet and enlarged so that I could clearly see the detail. One of them gave the positions of the English bastions during the siege and yet another details of the major campaign victories including the all-important Battle of Patay 1429.

The Pont Georges V would also be a key feature as it ran south out of the city across the Loire River to Les Tourelles the site of the famous assault that marked the turning point of the siege and the wounding of Jehanne d'Arc by arrow. As expected the Loire would be at a low due to the dry summer weather so there would be some lovely photo opportunities for Lily. Unfortunately the modern road system and tramway had swept Les Tourelles and any other medieval structure away, so I naturally expected very little to be seen or occur there; busy in the day time with traffic it didn't look that promising.

The English had an army of only 3000 men and had laid siege to three quarters of the city wall with various bastions. The defenders had a massive advantage in numbers plus internal lines of communication. Supplies had been brought in regularly at night by barge under the very noses of the English so the citizens had not starved. The cannon had caused intermittent damage to buildings but were few in number and silenced by skirmishing parties when they became too much of a nuisance.

Professional soldiers conducted the siege, pay and plunder were their meat and drink, getting killed for no reason was not in their game plan; it was in essence a giant game of chess.

Likewise on the defenders side the citizens left the risk and business of war to the professional soldiers and the trained militia, neither of whom again were keen to get slaughtered. The very idea of hoards of lower classed armed masses was considered abhorrent to the aristocracy and the knightly class, much in the way that the Romans had continually feared a slave revolt. It was these masses that Jehanne d'Arc planned to activate and turn into an unstoppable wave that would sweep the English out of France. The Dauphin would ride that wave somewhat nervously to his advantage and to the advantage of the Armagnac party that supported him. He would go along with the plan until it got too dangerous for his own comfort and risk the destruction of the rigid class structure.

Then they would discard their self-made saintly puppet, disown and betray her to a fate worse than death at English hands. Once she was dead they would go back to the status quo and carry on business as usual. We were here to experience the high tide of her achievement; the miraculous deliverance of Orleans from the hands of the enemy. It would make her into a superstar in the eyes of the populous and secure the throne for the Dauphin.

The game was afoot, the stakes were high and I was ready to experience anything my subconscious could throw at me. I knew the memories might be painful. I had tasted their gall on the TGV at the end of the Metz affair. I reasoned that it would be good for my soul and good to reveal the truth of L'affaire Jehanne d'Arc. I owed it to her, the people proclaimed her an angel as they rushed to touch her, she was my angel and I loved her deeply.

There was a loud coded triple knock on the door and I knew that Lily had beaten me this time. I opened the door and there stood my glamorous associate hair flowing with sunglasses perched on the top, backpack in place, camera ready to go, shorts and army boots and the most amazing Andy Warhol style T shirt emblazoned with the saintly image of Jehanne d'Arc across her chest.

"Nice shirt! How on earth did you manage to buy that since we arrived here?"

"I didn't. It's just something appropriate that I ran up to wear on our quest. I'm really getting into this whole affair. I have a surprise one for you later!" Lily did a twirl and curtsied elegantly.

"Wow, I'm impressed. I love your creative colour skills; very funky!"

The T shirt was electric pink with blues and purples and highlighted in yellow and green!

"I took a jpeg image from the internet, tweaked the colours and screen printed it; it's a little hobby of mine." Lily was quite the artist; it was gorgeous and certainly would get her noticed.

"Can't wait to see the one you made for me?" My curiosity was aroused.

"Yes, it's very special, plus I have another surprise for you. I shall reveal it at dinner tonight! It's my turn to be the magician and conjure up something for you. I have been thinking ahead and I have a little plan!"

We set off north back along Rue République to the centre Jehanne d'Arc to gain an overview of the siege and Jehanne's life. As expected no memory time slips occurred due to the modern fabric of the building and position, now well outside the medieval boundaries of the old city. The centre did have an original coloured illustration in the style of Froissart which dazzled the observer with colour and detail. Made in the 1480s it was not contemporary with her life but it was still a good find.

Returning an hour later we past our hotel going south towards the main square or rather hexagon as place du Martroi is built on a geometric basis. As we neared the open space we could see the central statue on its plinth; Jehanne d'Arc mounted and armoured on her horse with her sword arm extended horizontally with the tip dipped in salute. I found the bronze sensitively composed as it did not celebrate her victory with brazen bravado. Jehanne was always proud that she had never raised her sword in anger, she preferred to carry it more as a status symbol; she was ever far more fond of her sacred banner which was worth ten hundred swords in battle.

To the left the delightful Jules Verne themed carousel played a merry tune and entertained the children. To the right the tram tracks carried their sleek silver carriages to and throe around the periphery of the hexagonal public open space. I was reminded of the Flemish word for witch – Hex! Perhaps it was a subconscious reference or decision that had deliberately made the geometric shape so visible in acknowledgement of her occult status?

Leaving the statue we walked east along Rue Jehanne d'Arc towards the Cathédrale Sainte Croix. Its impressive facade with twin towers loomed over us as we approached much as it did in medieval days. A wave of emotion came over me as we approached but it did not develop further. We passed l'Orangerie a small cafe and decided to break for mid-morning refreshment. As we sat in the pleasant warm sun the siege seemed a million light years away in time and space. Lily enjoyed the sun's warmth and sat with her face upturned to catch the rays of light. As we observed the cathédrale its visage started to tune us into the medieval mind-set.

Entering the structure we found it lofty and detached; its Spartan decoration being a complete contrast to the more ornate Catholic churches and cathedrals that we had been used to. We lit candles and said prayers for our departed loved ones. Then we returned to place du Martroi. Orleans had suffered extensive Allied bombing during World War II which had destroyed much of its medieval fabric and in some way sanitised its etheric memory.

Following the main street with its tram tracks we continued south into Rue Royale and then branched off to visit *La maison Jehanne d'Arc* at 3 place du Général de Gaulle. Its period facade looked promising but again held no memory as it was a modern reconstruction but it did house an interesting collection of artefacts, costumes, weapons and dioramas; including a large model of the attack on Les Tourelles. It was a beautifully constructed model and had been painstakingly researched to give an accurate picture of the structure of 1429. When viewing the *bastille des Augustins barbican, boulevard des Tourelles* and Main gate with its distinctive four towers, the atmosphere immediately changed and we both became much more aware of her presence. The accuracy of the model was the key as it triggered the subconscious. The delayed reaction it stimulated would only become apparent in hindsight later on that day.

It was then that we had a great stroke of luck. Whilst continuing our walk down Rue Royale after leaving the exhibition we noticed several book shops to our left. With further investigation we came across an antique and second hand bookshop of note called *Libs'Old* on the Rue Bourgogne. There in the window were two large volumes for sale entitled; *The Life of Jehanne d'Arc* by Anatole France dated 1908. The weighty tomes looked comprehensive and detailed so we decided to look closer. Entering the shop we asked the young studious assistant if we could peruse the said volumes from the window. Turning the pages we both agreed that we had stumbled upon a treasure trove of detailed information which would be invaluable to our investigations and save many hours of internet searching.

"I have an idea, Yann. We could perform an experiment, a sort of blind test. Yes, we would only consult the books after our time slip experiences in order to check them for accuracy and detail."

"Great idea, Lily!" I said enthusiastically, "that would make our investigation much more scientific and we could see for certain if our subconscious memories are accurate."

With that in mind Lily called the young male assistant over and began to negotiate a price for the books. She told a tale of how she was a poor student from Lille studying history and that I was her blind father to whom she would read passages to on long winter evenings! The books were far too expensive for her pocket so she wondered if there was any chance of discount on the price.

The assistant went to ask his manager and came back saying that she could have the two volumes for €300 instead of €400!

"Well that's dinner paid for!" Lily said quietly to me under her breath as we left the shop clutching our purchase.

Playing my part I held her hand tightly and followed cautiously. Once around the corner I couldn't resist a comment, "Lily Chevalier, you'll never go to Heaven!"

"Been there, done that and got the T shirt; they threw me out! Seem to remember it was something to do with knowing you and the Black Brethren."

"That may be truer than you know young lady? This planet needs a lot of help."

Reaching the Rue Royale again we turned south and continued to follow the tram tracks. Within 5 minutes the vista opened out and the mighty Loire River spread majestically before us. The multi-arched Pont Georges V beckoned us across to the site of Les Tourelles on the far bank. A shiver went up my spine at the emotive view and tears welled up in my eyes at the thought of the memory.

It was too late in the day for further investigation so we took the tram back to our hotel and well-earned rest.

Chapter 12

A Secret Revealed

ily came down to dinner clutching two neatly wrapped parcels, one slightly thicker than the other; my curiosity was immediately engaged.

"Bon soir, Yann!" Now it is my turn to blow your mind." She said with a grin and flicked back her beautiful auburn hair. Lily ordered an aperitif for us both, it was Kir Royale again, which she knew I associated with a celebration.

"Wow! This is becoming a quite a habit, what's the occasion, Lily?"

I'm going to keep you in suspense a moment longer! Let's order first. I'm hungry."

My mind started to race; what could it be? She was obviously savouring the moment supreme! I scanned the menu and went for the seafood starter, followed by the local fish a form of carp. Not too surprisingly Lily ordered the same plus a bottle of the dry white Loire valley vin blanc to complement our choice.

"Garçon a bottle of the Pouilly-Fumé if you please," then she turned to me and continued, "the smoky minerality of the Sauvignon Blanc grape will bring out the delicate flavour of the fish exquisitely! What think you?"

"*Absolument mon chéri!*" I was lost for words but managed to recover the situation with a burst of confidence to cover my ignorance.

The waiter was impressed with Lily's choice and mentioned his approval to her. She smiled graciously and then returned to business.

"Now, monsieur Yann Baillieu, it's my turn to amaze and astound you!" With a beautiful smile she touched my hand, which sent an electric shiver through my whole body and handed me my present. It was exquisitely wrapped in royal blue paper with a flurry of gold fleur d'lys, gold ribbon and a flourish finished it off perfectly.

"I can tell you are a Dragon Princess, the merest touch of you hand is enough to send my nervous system into ecstasy!" Lily blush but she knew it was true. "Your taste in gift wrapping is as impeccable as your manners; I'm so impressed and it's not even my birthday."

"Go ahead you may open it. I want to take a picture of your face!" With that she reached for her camera and sat back waiting to catch a pure Facebook moment.

I started to unwrap the soft package and my mind began to intuit the nature of its contents through touch. I guessed it was clothing and could see it was black; the plot thickened. A hood appeared shrouding a grey T shirt bearing a Jehanne d'Arc image but it was a black hoodie that gripped my attention. Obviously, Lily was trying to make me trendy! Then I opened it up fully and suddenly leapt up from the table. For there emblazoned on the front was the white cross of the Black Brethren in perfect mathematical proportion exactly as I had seen it on Lily in my flash back time slip. My mouth gaped open in astonishment, Lily clicked continuously away on her camera and giggled.

"Now I know for sure that I have got it right! Your reaction confirms it."

I was rendered speechless as tears of emotion and remembrance welled up in my eyes. I traced the outline with my finger and the touch confirmed that it was real and not illusory. Regaining control of myself, I could see that it had been beautifully hand stitched in appliqué onto the chest of the midnight black hoodie.

Breaking my silence I stammered, "How did you know? It's, its perfect!"

"First a toast!" said Lily as she put her camera down and raised her glass. "To Yvette of Luxembourg, high priestess of the Black Brethren."

"To Yvette!" I raised my glass and chinked it against hers. The very name echoing from her lips reverberated in my soul. She knew, somehow she knew much more than I had revealed; my prediction had been correct, Yvette/Lily had played a very important part in l'affaire Jehanne d'Arc and beyond.

As I watched she opened up her own identical but thinner parcel to reveal a twin matching hoodie emblazoned with the distinctive white cross. "Tomorrow it is full Moon and we shall make good use of them!"

I started to see that this was all part of "the little plan" that she had mentioned earlier.

"A-hah! Now you have blown my mind you can tell me more over dinner." As if on cue the seafood starter arrived and as I listened Lily unfolded her tale:-

"It was the night of the Chateau Jaulny trip when I arrived home. I expected to just fall asleep after my shower, but like you in the hotel room the coloured lights of the looking glass well beckoned me; so I jumped in and this is exactly what I experienced.

I was Yvette of Luxembourg, my mother told me right from being very young that I was special. I knew this because I could see events before they happened and I could see and converse with dead people. As I became a teenager my mother talked to me again and told me that I was a Dragon Princess and that I would have a special mission of great importance to perform in my 23rd Year.

In that year there came into my life a freelance knight called Robert des Armoises who had fallen out of favour with the Duc du Bar for surrendering a castle of his without permission to my mother's allies. My mother recognised instinctively that he was a dragon knight and had turned up exactly on cue as she had foreseen to help in a mission of incredible importance to the fate of France.

A royal princess of the Dragon line would play the part of a peasant girl in order to fulfil the prophecy made that a young girl would raise the populous of France in revolution against the English Goddons. The name Les goddons intrigued me and my mother explained that the English were called that by the French because of their continual blaspheming using the phrase; *God damnation*. The Dauphin would become king and be crowned in Reims by her actions. History would, thus be corrected and all powers held in balance again to preserve the future. This would keep humanity on track in its spiritual and political evolution.

I, Yvette of Luxembourg, would act as high priestess and fairy Elven navigator to a group of seven souls that would form a secret Brotherhood called the Black Brethren. Robert des Armoises would lead the seven to support and protect *la Pucelle* – the Maid in her mission.

As my mother was Duchess of Luxembourg and related by marriage to Philip, Duke of Burgundy she could not be seen to openly support the Armagnac cause against Burgundy's allies the English - Goddons. The plot had been conceived by Yolande of Anjou who had enlisted my mother's help as a fellow dragon queen.

Jehanne was the 12th daughter of Ysabeau of Bavaria and her father was the King of France; the *sang royale,* the royal dragon blood ran in her veins. She was taught to speak eloquently in a courtly manner, to converse in 4 languages, to joust and to commend armies. She was the living golden arrow that would be fired to trigger the ousting of the English and set France on course for nationhood again. Even her name would be a clue, d'Arc - the

Bow. The Dauphin gave a coat of arms to the d'Arc family of a bow and 3 arrows argent, the centre one golden tipped and fletched representing Jehanne supported by two arrows crossed argent to represent the two brothers of her adopted family, all set on a field of azure royal blue. Jehanne herself would be given the coat of arms of, a sword upturned argent, bearing the crown of France gold, supported on either side by the royal fleur d'lys of France gold; by her sword she would win back the crown of France!

You just have to know the code and I remembered. Then internet research confirmed what my subconscious knew to be true."

I was totally amazed and sat silently like a school boy listening to this incredible story from his learned teacher. All the meanwhile Lily nibbled at her starter and barely drew breath.

The main course arrived, Lily poured me another glass of Loire vin blanc and continued her story:-

"The white cross kept shining in my mind. It was beautiful, so pure and mathematical in construction; so precise. I stood in front of it and knew that I was the living book that had recorded its secrets for then and this present time. I could see that you and I had been together many times throughout history and that we had worked together in ancient Greece to defeat the Persians and allow western democracy to flourish in Athens.

The living cross was a symbol of reincarnation; it encoded this message in an acceptable form to avoid persecution from the Catholic church. They were the very same organisation that had perverted the message for their own greed, power and control; for they had no power on a do-it-yourself spiritual universe. They posed as holy and pious when the reverse was true. Stories of heaven and hell were invented to scare the ignorant masses into submission and slavery; whilst all the time they waged a genocide war of annihilation against the old fairy races and their clairvoyant powers.

In ancient Greece the Divine proportion or Golden Mean and its relationship with reincarnation was known and held in secret by the Pythagoreans, they in turn had gained the knowledge from the Egyptians. The Pentagram and the Dodecahedron were visible geometric manifestations of the Golden Mean ratio – Phi Φ and as such therefore symbols of reincarnation.

This was due to the reiterative properties of the ratio which enabled it to maintain its proportion at any scale; it could literally spin its way from the invisible fine matter sub-quantum universe into the coarse atomic matter universe yet maintain its structure. In that way spirit could interlock with matter!

It is the one constant that can endlessly repeat itself and contained miraculous mathematical properties, Phi squared is itself plus one and the reciprocal of Phi; one over Phi is itself minus one. It is totally unique. It can also be expressed as the irrational constant 1.6180339... which along with Pi 3.1415926... describes the invisible and the visible universe. Pi describes the material world with its 2D circles and 3D spheres that make up our atomic reality. So the ancients reasoned that Phi must be to do with the spiritual; the invisible part of the universe; hence its status."

Lily paused for breath and realised that she had been doodling on the table cloth again with her Mont Blanc pen. She had barely touched her fish, but I didn't want her to stop as he was about to divulge something of great importance. My subconscious knew what she was about to say and was hanging on the edge of its seat, it was screaming in my ear EXACTLY! My conscious mind was still playing catch up and was totally bemused by Lily's virtuoso performance.

Lily took several small mouthfuls and sipped her white wine. She took up her pen and started to draw the cross on the table cloth.

"I checked modern research and several sacred geometry websites and it confirmed that our DNA is a double helix spiral based on a ratcheted dodecahedron with pentagram side sugars. The whole amazing living molecule and the key to our physical existence is based on the Golden Mean! The ancients were right. Spirit can interlock with matter across the dimensions due to the unique mathematical properties of the Phi Φ ratio.

So Robert des Armoises constructed his blazon and heraldic arms to encode this ratio secretly for those of the Black Brethren who could read it and would know its secret meaning. The symbol, a white cross, would be eminently acceptable to the Catholic Church and its fanatical priesthood who were ignorant of its true meaning. It would also be a message to leave to his future self that he had walked this way before.

This is what he did; he knew that Phi Φ can be calculated by using the square root of 5 plus 1 divided by 2, so he took 5 squares arranged in an equal armed cross after the fashion of the Swiss national emblem. He extended the outer line of each arm to 1.6180339 units of its original length. Then he added one square more in the middle but half the size. Then by drawing the diagonal cross lines and erasing the original square construction boxes a beautifully proportioned cross is seen and the underlying construction hidden!

The rooted 5 squares, plus 1 divided by 2!"

Lily grinned triumphantly and sat back in her chair as she watched the light of revelation flicker in my eyes.

"Yes, of course, I remember now. You have it exactly; absolutely correct! Wow!"

Lily picked at her fish in satisfaction and I sat back sipping my wine in total admiration of my dragon princess.

"Fleur d'Lily you are truly a marvel; how clever you are! Your mother chose well in selecting you for the mission all those years ago."

Lily grinned, raised her glass in silent salute and drank freely. Then pausing and replacing the glass firmly on the table. "Oh one last thing, what did it all symbolise and mean. That came to me last night after you showed me the dragon shielded figures and pop-up book.

The blazon is a variation of the Babylonian black sun symbol as used by the Teutonic knights and German forces ever since. Ours however is the white sun of spiritual illumination and as such represents the inner spirit of the person wearing it, radiating outward into the material world, represented by its four symmetry square shape. As such it is a microcosmic reflection of the macrocosmic whole of creation as it extrudes itself into the physical world; unstoppable, infinite and irresistible! As above; so below!

Cheers..."

Lily raised her glass and drained it in one. "Now what shall we have for desert?"

I laughed out loud and started to applaud my confederate. "Wow! You have taken my mind and blown every fuse in it several times; you are truly amazing!"

Lily laughed too and simply said, "The lemon sorbet looks nice!"

Chapter 13

Les Tourelles

ily knocked on my hotel bedroom door at midnight, exactly as we had arranged at dinner earlier that evening. This was all part of her "little plan" that she had mentioned. She was excited and definitely up for an adventure of the consciousness kind. With that in mind I was happy to let her take the lead and we slipped out of the front door of the hotel unnoticed. Once on the pavement she instructed me to raise my hood and immediately I felt a change in my perception of the city.

I became much more focus and determined, it worked I felt a definite sense of déjà vu. We followed the tram tracks south towards the river. Passing through the deserted hexagon place Ste-Pierre du Martroi and continuing down the Rue Royale. Jehanne's statue cast interesting shadows and I could not resist touching it and absorbing its energy in the light of the full Moon. Lily snapped away using a variety of aperture light stops on her camera to add atmosphere to the pictures. She was also determined to record the whole episode for analysis. This included video clips which she proceeded to make by flicking the switch on her camera.

Lily chose to use the shadows for moving in which were strong due to the full Moon and clear sky. As wraiths in black we moved silently onward towards the Pont Georges V. The whole feel was extremely clandestine and I could sense the connection with the past; the only thing missing was my crossbow and sword. Pausing briefly we absorbed the vista as the panoramic view of the river opened up. Then it was time to push on across the bridge with just the noise of the river for company we glided silently on. The lights made patterns of reflection on the moving water as we crossed over the many arches. I thought of the wave nature of the universe and the creation of our reality. Were we real or were the reflections real? I felt that we were becoming living reflections of our past selves.

I stopped Lily and asked her to record that idea on video lest I forgot. The Moon shone full and was reflected by her white radiating cross which resonated in my mind; it was the perfect blazon for this kind of work and made identification easy. Stray quarrels from crossbows can be very messy if loosed at the wrong target. My mind was linking into Robert and the connection was getting stronger with every step across the bridge.

Once on the south bank we found ourselves at a traffic intersection. "Sit down over there Yann and face the city, close your eyes and see if you can time slip." Lily had foreseen this and knew that there would be too much traffic in the day time to focus. Now all was quiet and deserted; perfect!

Nothing happened; for fifteen minutes or so I tried to connect but there was not even a flicker of the coloured lights and well of memory. "Lily, have you any ideas why it is not working?"

Lily sat beside me and thought. She gazed in silence and I watch her face lose expression, the effect lasted only seconds and then she snapped back into the present. "Of course, we are in the wrong place! The cathédrale Ste-Croix is further right than it should be. My senses tell me it is a couple of hundred metres east to the correct place where Les Tourelles and the original bridge stood."

"Of course Lily; this must be a modern bridge in a different position! Well done, you are definitely the fairy sighted navigator as Yvette was."

"Follow me and I will match the position of Ste-Croix with what I saw then we will have the exact location in which to meditate."

We both stood up and dusted ourselves down then Lily silently moved eastward along Quai des Augustins and I followed in her footsteps.

"This is it!" Lily stood by a simple stone column with an iron crucifix. At its base was a simple inclined plaque set on stone and built into the quai Les Tourelles wall that lined the river bank. "Let's focus our minds and sit here. The epicentre of events must still resonate in this position."

Lily gazed momentarily at the city and then sat with her back to the stone plinth. I walked the little square and could feel the energy starting to trigger my memory. Then as I turned to face the city and Lily I started to see coloured lights and the well of memory opening like a gate between myself and the plinth with its simple iron cross. I walked forward and... ... ...

She gave the armed populous hope. For too long they had suffered at the hands of the nobility and knightly class. Just as they had lost patience with their own lords and masters of war so they despised and loathed even more the English Goddon scum besieging their noble city.

The time came when Jehanne was mystically inspired by her voices to lead an attack on Les Tourelles. All watched for a sign, whilst the army commanders deliberated on the best way to attack, but the populous and Jehanne were not listening. Suddenly she stood up, this small frail girl dressed in armour and clutching her precious sacred banner.

"Victory is ours if we attack now!" She declared with her delicate feminine voice as loud as she could above the clamour to arms.

The populous listened only to her; every ear was tuned to her voice, every eye strained to detect her slightest movement or intention. The white and gold *Jhesus Maria* banner was held aloft for all to see and everybody watched it wave in the wind , then they stood as one and started to move inexorably forward with the will and purpose of one body. For la Pucelle commanded more than just their flesh and blood, she commanded their souls. It was her spirit that moved them forward.

Divine will and the angels were with la Pucelle as she started her advance towards the outer breast works and bastille of Les Tourelles. The mass of the populous rose with her and broke into a trot behind her banner.

It looked for all quite impossible, a lone girl in armour with a white and gold banner charging an armed foe, entrenched behind solid defences.

Such a sight had never been seen before but in that lay the magic, for not one citizen wanted her to be harmed and all would sacrifice themselves before they would let their mystic angel fall. The armed wave enveloped the outer walls; scaling ladders rose and up climbed the first wave. The English were at first taunting and laughing but then as they saw the witch with her banner and the heaving unstoppable multitude pour across the ditch in front of their breastwork their laughter turned to terror and fear.

Upwards and onwards they poured trying to break the English spirit. Then it happened a lone English archer with a bees wax tipped armour piercing arrow took aim and fired his deadly shaft at la Pucelle. With deadly accuracy it found its mark just above her right breast between shoulder and neck. Her diamond hard cuirass was punctured with a deafening thwack and the force knocked her backwards from the scaling ladder. She fell onto the heaving masses that followed her. They caught their fallen angel as she plunged towards the ground and thereby prevented further injury to her person.

The English cheered. "The witch is dead!" They shouted loud and jeered. As others on the bastille battlement took up the call the populous started to lose heart. For they had seen their angel fall and doubt crept insidiously into their minds. Gradually they attacked with less urgency and vigour. Then as morale crumbled totally they fell back to their original positions. The English poured arrows onto them and many shields, like spiny hedgehogs, bore evidence of their onslaught and deadly penetrative power. So they bore their fallen angel back to her tent and gathered around her. The call for help rose in their voices as they prayed for a miracle and the life of their angel to be spared.

Then I stepped forward I was dressed in black and bore the white cross of the Knight Hospitalier at my side another dressed the same but of slighter build; it was you my trusty Fleur d'Lily. My presence was enough to still the crowd who parted so that we could approach. For all recognised the badge that we bore; the Knights of St. John were long famous for their healing and deeds of heroism in the crusades.

I threw back my cowl and people caught a glimpse of my face with dark goatee beard. You smiled at the fallen angel and knelt beside her litter. She winced in pain and shock from the effects of shock. Under her breath she mumbled prayers to her Saints and the Madonna.

I drew a flask from my belt and gave the angel a few drops of a pungent brownish liquid. She relaxed and tried to smile through the pain. Her eyes penetrated my soul as she gazed intently at me.

You then placed a wooden peg in her mouth so that she could bite on it should the pain prove too intense. Then I took the arrow and broke the shaft so that her cuirass could be unbuckled and removed.

That done, I saw you unbuckle her chain mail suit as she leaned forward; the pain made the angel cry out which elicited a gasp from the crowd.

I knew that the arrow had no barbs and could see that it had penetrated through the rings cleanly which was a good sign as it meant that it could be withdrawn smoothly. Now she was down only to her bloody under garments so I took my dagger and cut her chemise, then I pulled the cut material apart and ripped it away to expose the wound.

I could see that the shaft had penetrated a good three inches into her frail feminine chest, but high enough not to have pierced any major organ. Now came the moment of truth, I pressed on her pale white flesh and grasped the shaft stub; with one quick firm pull I plucked it from her body.

She arched and screamed in pain as the deadly iron tip was drawn. I passed it to you as you have the better eye sight and you held it up to the candle light to inspect it. You nodded and said that it was clean and whole, no foreign matter clung to the vicious sharp iron warhead which was a good sign for it had pierced her flesh cleanly.

Taking another small flask containing cognac from my belt pouch I poured a small quantity into the wound to cleanse it. The angel winced. Then I squeezed her flesh and noted the colour of the suppurating liquid as it came back out of the wound. I was satisfied that it was clean and free from excessive amounts of blood so I smiled to reassure the angel. Thrice more I repeated the procedure whilst murmuring prayers and incantations to calm the fallen angel. You bathed her brow with a cloth soaked in cold water. We worked well as a team, I was proud of you, Yvette of Luxembourg. You smiled at me as you could read my thoughts.

Then came the moment to seal and bind the wound. I drew a candle from my pouch and lit its wick from the nearby candle providing illumination inside the tent. I waited for the wax to melt and then plugged the wound with its clear warm liquid. I began solidifying quickly and its dissipating warmth gave comfort to la Pucelle who smiled for the first time.

You reached into your haversack and produced some clean linen. Then you made a pad and placed it on the now sealed wound. I took her left hand and placed it on the pad and bade her to press firmly to keep it in place.

"You will be fine my beautiful angel, fear not." I whispered gently into her ear. "You have many angels and Saints watching over you and you are much loved. We will not let harm befall you."

La Pucelle smiled and fire returned to her eyes. "I shall lead them back. My voices have promised victory this day and that I shall enter the city by the bridge tonight."

"You shall, but first we must bind your wound. Then protect you as best we can, lest the English finish their deadly task with another arrow!"

Yvette handed me clean linen strips and I began to bind the padded wound and shoulder so that it was comfortable and supported.

"You will have to use your left arm to raise the banner my resurrected angel, but you will succeed. I thought you dead, the whole of France assembled here before Orleans thought you dead and most of all the English Goddons on their ramparts thought you dead, but you will rise again as our Lord did and you will be victorious! My clairvoyant Lady, Yvette of Luxembourg, has foreseen your victory this day and I, Robert des Armoises with my Black Brethren, shall protect you from further harm."

Yvette dropped her cowl and the crowd gasped to see that she too was a girl of great beauty. For up to that moment she had been assisting anonymous. Several of the crowd crossed themselves and they whispered that it was a miracle for never had they seen women in arms before.

Jehanne laughed, "You will steal my thunder, sister. You are truly welcome though in my hour of need. Together we will rid Orleans of the English Goddons that infest its walls. Then we shall crown the Dauphin at Reims!"

Robert laughed too as he knew that la Pucelle had regained her fire. Jehanne had been wounded at two past the clock but by four she was harnessed anew and emerged from the tent. A tremendous cheer arose in the crowd and spread like wildfire throughout the camp. In the distance the mystified English Goddons became concerned for they could sense that the French were far from beaten.

Then came the supreme moment; Jehanne spied her sacred banner being taken forward without her permission by a lone soldier. She was furious and so incensed that she broke into an immediate trot towards the bastille of the English Goddons. Reaching the bottom of the scaling ladder she scurried up it and grabbed the leg of the wayward soldier and started to tug hard at his boot in order to retrieve her banner. The soldier now somewhat unbalanced shook the banner from side to side as Jehanne attempted to pull him down. Cheering broke out in the army as they read this for a sign to attack! They cheered and offered prayers as they en masse ran at the walls of the bastille and started up the scaling ladders again. Everywhere they cheered and shouted for their angel that had been delivered from the jaws of death. The noise was deafening and a religious hysteria gripped them; over the battlements the fanatical zealots poured.

The English became terrified as they spied the witch they thought dead resurrected. It was a bad omen; many crossed themselves for they knew their fate was sealed. Then they cracked, the moment came when they were mentally beaten and the men-at-arms started to flee their positions. Only the hardened professional knights refused to be intimidated but they were few, only some 50 in number and the armed populous were legion.

Then came the spark to ignite the bonfire; Jehanne turned at the top of her scaling ladder having retrieved her banner and shouted at the top of her voice, "CITIZENS OF OLEANS, ATTACK NOW AND VICTORY SHALL BE YOURS - FOR GOD HAS SPARED ME AND OLEANS SHALL BE FREE!"

The cheering reached a crescendo as the impulse of energy transmitted outwards from the source that was la Pucelle. The roar was deafening and rose above the clash of arms. The English Goddons ran, only the hard core of professionals fought resolutely as they retreated towards Les Tourelles.

Coincidentally as the banner incident had spontaneously launched itself the professional commanders had pre-arranged that an incendiary barge should be floated in position under the draw bridge to the main gate of Les Tourelles. The haphazard timing was perfect! The barge with its lethal cocktail of tallow, oil, wood, tar and gunpowder ignited under the wooden bridge leading to the small chateau looking gate that guarded the entrance over the many arched bridge before Orleans. The fire raged and burnt the dry timbers so rapidly that the retreating men-at-arms were faced with a giant wall of flame as they fled.

The English Goddons were now trapped between the armed populous screaming blue murder and a curtain of flame that was rapidly devouring their only escape route. Many braved the flames and some made it to sanctuary, but most faced with certain death by burning plunged into the chill waters of the mighty Loire.

The masses poured onto the rear guard of the English Goddon knights as they continued to fight, but many less brave citizens had already stopped to plunder what could be had. Enough, however, remained to complete the victory. The fight was hopeless for the English. By the time it came for the professional knights to cross the burnt bridge the timbers were so charred that they collapsed under the weight of the press and all were drowned in the Loire River.

Victory was total. Jehanne climbed the ramparts of the bastille and walked among the cheering masses as they raised their pole arms in salute. She watched as they hacked down the hated English flags and banners from their poles. Reaching the edge of the burnt bridge she knelt and gave prayer to her saints and Mother Mary.

By evening's fall she entered Les Tourelles with the other professional commanders across the hastily erected new bridge. As dusk approached she entered Orleans by the main gate across the many arched bridge that spanned the mighty Loire River exactly as she had predicted and had promised the citizens earlier in the day.

The legend was born and all of Orleans rejoiced that evening.

Watching from the shadows dressed all in black, with hooded cowls and displaying simple white radiating crosses, stood seven mysterious figures.

"Sehr gut, Robert. Alles in ordernung!" A thick German accent broke the stillness of the evening twilight as the citizens scavenged among the corpses for anything of value. "You have done well today; our little angel has performed well. Without your intervention it might have gone differently?"

The voice belonged to a strongly built German knight with an intelligent and aristocratic character. I answered in German and I knew in my mind that he was my friend of long standing; Ritter FreiHerr Johannes Jakob von Eltz, a Dragon knight of renown. He hailed from Burg Eltz am Mosel and had been my companion in arms these past three years. I looked at my fellow Black Brethren, gathered like ravens at the feast they stood watching the final act of the day's events. Their faces hidden by cowls but illuminated by the Moon and the flickering torches that dotted the scene of carnage; I knew them all very well, Ulrich Voss the healer, Ruprecht of Müden, Tomas, Guillaume and Thibault of Metz, the last 3 were my chosen men-at-arms. In their centre stood our priestess Yvette of Luxembourg weeping for the souls of the departed and praying; she turned to me, her lip quivered and she fell into my arms seeking comfort and reassurance. The site of war was too much for her innocent young heart.

The scene faded and I found myself at the foot of the cross on the quayside that marked the historical position of Les Tourelles. I held Lily in my arms and could feel that she was still not in her body so I placed her gently against the plinth with her back to the wall. Feeling a little shaken I stood up straight to relieve the cramp in my arms and breathed the early morning air deep into my lungs. I noticed that Lily was still sat in trance. As I watched, her face softened and her eyes flickered. Then she was suddenly back in the present with me.

"That was quite interesting!" Her voice seemed distant but gathered strength as she continued, "we shall have to compare notes back at the hotel and see if I experienced what you did?" With that she stretched and stood somewhat slowly so I helped support her and together we gazed at the view of Orleans in the early morning light.

Gradually the sky turned light blue on the horizon to the east and we could see the Cathédrale Ste-Croix catch the sun's early rays. With that as a sign we made our way back across the modern pont Georges V and followed the iron ribbon of the tram tracks all the way back to our hotel. Jehanne still sat majestically on her horse in the Martroi and we paused for a moment to reflect on our experience.

"She was quite a girl!" Lily broke the silence with a simple observation, "and now I have met her face to face. It was a very bloody and brutal time. I still have those images in my head. Hold me a minute, Yann"

I placed my arm around her and gave my brave confederate comfort. I could see tears in her eyes and one trickled down her cheek.

"All those dead people, such a waste of life, it was so terrible. How can human beings do that to each other?"

"It's because they can't see what we see and they don't know what we know; simple as that my beautiful Fleur d'Lily. They are evolving souls as we are but they haven't reached the stage that we are at yet; they will in time though."

After a few minutes Lily regained her composure and we continued our journey to our hotel.

We said our goodnights and hit the sack at 5am having agreed to meet for brunch at midday in order to compare our time slip experiences. Then the fatigue of oblivion over took me and I slept like the dead, my consciousness finally at rest.

Chapter 14

Les Enfants Perdus

I awoke to a sunny morning at 10:11hrs. The light streaming in my window was more than enough to wake me, plus I was on an adrenaline high after the incredible events of the night before. After a shower and a shave I sat down and wrote copious notes on my visions in the time slip. Lily had suggested we do this so that we could compare our individual memory experiences without prejudicing the evidence.

The recollections were so vivid that I had no problem remembering all of the detail. I even remembered the individual names of the Black Brethren, which meant we could research them on the internet later in an attempt to confirm them as historical fact if at all possible.

I could hear the shower running in Lily's room so I knew that she was up and about too. The plan was to meet in the hotel foyer at midday and then to wander down to the Martroi for brunch and swap stories. I was curious to hear of her experiences as this was the first time that we had jointly jumped into the looking glass of memory. Had we seen the same scenes, felt the same feelings, tasted the same air; I wondered?

The day was deliciously warm so I dressed comfortably in my new Jehanne d'Arc T shirt Lily had given me and chomped black trousers, then headed out of my room armed only with an A4 notepad and some pens. I didn't have long to wait as Lily descended the stairs within minutes of my arrival in the lobby.

"Morning Yann, trust you slept like the dead? I did! I'm beginning to feel like your ghoul fiend! I'll tell you why when we have brunch. I'm really hungry." Simultaneously she looked at her watch to confirm that it was indeed still morning.

"Hah ha, good one! Nice play on words - Yes perfect thanks, out like a light and up fresh and ready for the next adventure."

"Oh yes, have I got something to tell you, and I have already planned what we are going to do tonight." Lily grinned with that – I know something you don't - cheeky expression of hers that always had me intrigued and wanting more.

"You are incorrigible my petit Fleur d'Lily; *prendre l'avantage, on y va!*"

With that I opened the main door for her and bowed theatrically, "*après vous mademoiselle.*"

"*Merci, mon chevalier noir!*" Lily curtsied and smiled sweetly.

Once in the fresh air we turned south and headed down Rue République towards place Saint-Pierre du Martroi. The tram tracks bought back instant memories of the night before and the early morning walk back. I silently contemplated Einstein's analogy with time for it was the tram tracks and ornate public clock in Zurich that had first led him to theorise on the true nature of the space time continuum in 1905 whilst he worked at the Swiss patents office and gave private tuition. I found myself musing in a similar fashion over the nature of consciousness and memory. This was going to be an interesting working lunch and I looked forward to it with anticipation and a hunger for knowledge that I had not experienced before!

Once in the hexagon place du Martroi we paused to look at Jehanne's statue just as we had done earlier that day as dawn was breaking. Her immortal presence seemed to ground and centre our thoughts amongst the turmoil of tourists, trams and daily life. Soon it was time to head past the carousel and along the Rue Jehanne d'Arc towards the cathédrale Ste-Croix which stood beckoning in the Porte de Bourgogne area of the city.

I knew now that the original medieval cathédrale was far different from the present construction as I had seen it clearly in my time slip. This explained the sterile atmosphere we had experienced within its cavernous body which contained numerous more modern memories layered over the ones that directly connected and concerned us. Emotion was the key; any original fabric seemed to contain memory and engendered an immediate response when we either touched it or were in close proximity. It was as though matter stored memory, much as a tape recorder. Finally I voiced my ideas to Lily as we strolled along in the sun.

"If the universe is just a thought form that creates matter and space from energy then all matter contains memory!"

Lily continued strolling and then added, "Space too! Remember as Einstein said; Matter is thick space and space is thin matter – Space tells matter how to move and Matter tells Space how to bend! You are exactly right; now my stomach is grumbling and telling me it needs some solid memory to quieten it!"

"How did you know I was thinking of Einstein? That's amazing!"

"You're just so transparent; remember as you told me I am a dragon princess! I'm just exercising my powers."

I laughed at her directness which bought my high minded insight to ground instantly.

"I agree, l'Orangerie is not far now; my turn to get breakfast."

We settled ourselves at one of the pavement tables nearest to the cathédrale and ordered orange juice, fresh croissants, coffee and a yoghurt for Lily. The waiter was a little perturbed at our timing as they were about to start serving lunch but said he would see what he could do? Whilst Lily was being charming with him I opened up my A4 notepad and placed my Pentel black and gold Stylo liquid fountain pens on the table.

"Lady's first," I said politely, "I'm dying to hear your experiences from this morning!"

Lily smiled and began to tell of her impressions in the time slip. It was like playing poker. I sat straight faced trying not to give visual clues as to the accuracy and concurrence of her story with mine. As she hit each marker point exactly it grew more difficult not to shout enthusiastically in affirmation. It was obvious from her concise account that she had experienced the identical time slip I had, yet precisely from her perspective of events. She had seen what I had seen and heard what I had heard. There was no doubt about it her account was completely synchronous in every detail.

I found myself subconsciously ticking off the chain of events in my notes as she talked. Lily's notepad was as yet unopened but I knew she was reciting it word for word, just as one lays a winning hand down in poker card by card. She knew it was a winning hand and was enjoying every minute of it.

Then came a difference, the atmosphere changed instantly and I began to listen more intently to the subtle detail. I turned to the back of my notepad and started doodling visual notes as she poured out the story.

"All the time you were healing Jehanne, I kept feeling this evil black presence behind me. It came from a person yet it felt like a giant black cloud engulfing my soul and pulling at my back; literally clawing at my soul and sucking my energy. I didn't look directly at it but caught glimpses in my peripheral vision. It emanated from a large powerfully built knight that carried a yellow shield divided into four quarters with a black cross. I stayed focused in helping you but it kept distracting me; its negativity drew me like a magnet. I recognised it as dragon energy but from the dark side."

Then Lily leant forward and grabbed my arm for reassurance. "It was awful; pure evil. I have never felt its like before! Then

I woke up and you were standing by me." Lily's face blanched at the memory, her eyes misted and her whole body started to tremble with emotion.

"The knight disappeared to the east of Les Tourelles." She opened a tourist map of Orleans she was carrying in her back pack and spread it out on the table. "We must go back to Les Tourelles and investigate. It's still there, I know it is, I can feel its presence; right here!" With that dramatic statement she took one of my pens and drew a large black cross on the map at Rue du Coq Saint Marceau just near the cross marking Les Tourelles.

I was moved by the intensity of emotion Lily had displayed, looking down I found that I had drawn a large black cloud made up of many children's faces. What could it mean? My subconscious had obviously been listening to Lily's tale and had connected directly with the source of the evil; but how could children be evil?

The moment passed and Lily sat back and relaxed visibly. We both started to nibble at the croissants, orange juice and black coffee. The warmth of the sun dispelled Lily's dark mood and she put her Von Zipper sunglasses on. She looked extremely chic as she raised her face to absorb the rays of warmth. Her sun kissed auburn hair, fine delicate bone structure and smooth skin made her the epitome of a young intelligent French woman enjoying the time of her life.

An hour flew by and I reluctantly paid the bill. I didn't really want the moment to pass, but time had marched on despite my willing it to slow down. Lily disturbed the silence. "We have to investigate this, Yann. We are needed!"

"Absolutely, my petit Fleur d'Lily, the day is yours to do with as you will. We already have more than enough information for our article; anything else we discover is a bonus."

Lily stood, stretched and then gathered up her unopened notebook. Grabbing her camera and back pack she announced dramatically, "To Les Tourelles!"

I walked alongside her, but I could feel that there was purpose in her stride. Lily was totally resolute and focused in her mission. It was obvious that she was being guided by her inner most intuition.

We jumped a tram at place du Martroi and found ourselves very quickly at Les Tourelles by the cross and monument. "This way, Yann, it's drawing me like a magnet. The energy is so powerful it involves many, many souls."

I followed Lily's lead which took us eastward and then off to the right a little into the Rue du Coq Saint Marceau. I started to sense the negativity as we started to move into the road. "I can feel it now too, very powerful like a black cloud, very oppressive, very sad." Lily barely heard me she was still walking with a determined gait; totally focused on her mission.

Within minutes we found ourselves outside a cabaret club come restaurant called l'Insolite. The doors were shut firmly as it was early afternoon and the dinner revue show only opened in the evenings. A large menu with the tariff clearly marked invited bookings by telephone or internet. Next to that was a large poster of the acts currently performing on stage; it was clearly a dining restaurant of some excellent standing with live entertainment.

"This is the building. I can feel it!" Lily was pressed against the window with the palms of her hands touching its surface. "Whatever it is, it lives in here!"

"I feel it too. There is no way in, the only way we can gain access is by booking a reservation for tonight. It's Tuesday so I don't think it will be tremendously busy. What do you think?"

Lily punched the telephone numbers into her mobile and pressed connect. She had obviously already thought and was taking decisive action! The line was engaged so we knew that they were answering calls and probably taking bookings. "I'll keep trying!"

We walked back to the cross and sat on the wall overlooking the river. Finally she made a connection and I could hear from her conversation that they had some places free for this evening. We had agreed previously that we would go for the menu Polisson at €89 each. It included:

Kir Royal
et ses Petits Fours
Cassolette de Fondue de Poireaux
et ses Saint Jacques poêlées au Cidre sur Riz Coloré
Glacier du Soleil à la Vodka
Lapin Moutardé à l'Ancienne en Saveur d'Estragon
et son Assortiment du Jardinier
Gratiné de Fromage sur Briochette et Lit de Salade aux Noix
Douceur de Feuillantine au Chocolat
Café
Bouteille de Champagne par personne pendant le repas

It seemed rather delicious and was all inclusive so I voiced my approval as Lily finished the call and closed her phone.

"Well if we are going to face ultimate evil it might as well be on a full stomach and with a glass of champagne in one hand!"

My jollity met with a frosty reception! "This is serious, Yann, the negativity is sickening and incredibly concentrated. Perhaps you can't feel it like I can? But it has a holocaust feel to it, so many souls suffering, trapped and crying out for help."

My bubble burst and I bowed to her feminine sensitivity. A chill ran down my spine, despite the warm summer sunshine. The lady was in no mood for messing. Lily's mood had darkened to the extreme and I considered myself told well and truly.

As a result we walked back to the tram stop in silence pausing only occasionally for Lily to look back over her shoulder in the direction that we had come. Each time I noticed that the tears had increased in her eyes and flowed now down her cheeks. As we waited I put my arm around her and gave her a reassuring hug. "Whatever it is? We will face it and overcome it together my Fleur d'Lily. I will not let you down; promise!"

Lily smiled and kissed me on the cheek. "I always feel safe with you! You are my shining knight."

"Well whatever it is it can't harm us as we are at present in the physical universe, so we will face it and defeat it!"

The cloud lifted and we enjoyed the sun's radiant warmth as we waited several minutes for the tram to arrive. We decided to have another look at the maison Jehanne d'Arc as I wanted to study the dioramas and Lily like the costume display. After that it was time for a leisurely stroll back to the hotel and a rest before changing for dinner.

We arranged to meet in the hotel foyer at 19:30hrs and then to grab a tram from just outside the door back to Les Tourelles. Lily arrived on time and looked stunning in her little black dress and a matching pashmina with a faint silver stripe.

"Wow! How good do you look?" I complimented her and then took a long look at what I was wearing. My unpressed light grey travel trek jacket with matching Chinos and a simple tight black T shirt was no match for her suave appearance.

"Simple and elegant, no? Easy to pack and carry, plus I can deploy it at a moment's notice should the situation demand it! It is my secret weapon." Lily laughed at the expression on my face which was totally in awe of her. Then with a confident smile she gave me a twirl.

"Absolutely stunning my girl, whatever awaits us will be totally blown away by your good taste and style!"

With that she linked arms with me and we stepped out into the warm night air. The tram arrived and we duly found ourselves back at Les Tourelles some 15 minutes later. The city was bustling with summer night activity and the tourists were busy soaking up the atmosphere. The atmosphere for us however changed dramatically once we had crossed the river and alighted from the tram.

A sense of foreboding and negativity charged the air as we walked towards the cabaret restaurant l'Insolite. It felt like high noon in a western film with a gun battle about to break out. The tension rose as we walked side by side down the side walk. I had flash backs, we had done this many times before, sometimes with just the two of us, but sometimes with more of the Black Brethren following in our wake. It was dragon power; we resonated and magnified the individual energy we each possessed when in each other's company.

A few short minutes and we turned to enter the cabaret restaurant; it was show time. The maître d' asked for our reservation details and then escorted us to our seats. The tables were set in long lines coming away from the stage curtain between each seat in opposite pairs stood a single red rose in a simple but chic black glass vase. Lily remarked that it was blood red in colour and that she saw a child's face in each one. Her observation sent a chill down my spine as we sat opposite each other on the end of one of the table arms.

The restaurant was busy and many people had already taken their places. Unlike us they were oblivious to the atmosphere of evil that oozed from the fabric of the building.

"I can feel the horror, be strong; are you sure you want to go through with this?" I said under my breath.

"I am ready. I am stronger than you think!"

A look of determination spread over Lily's face; she looked every bit the psychic warrior she was; the subdued lighting chiselled her features perfectly and her hair sparkled with fire. The waitress introduced herself and bought us our Kir Royale aperitif and Lily surprised me by raising her glass and confidently uttering the toast, "Good hunting!"

That inspired me and I knew that she was not mentally intimidated by whatever lurked in the dark recesses of this place. Our battle preparations were interrupted by the compare as he took to the stage and introduced the opening musical number. Our mood lightened with the visual distraction as we watched and enjoyed the spectacle.

There then appeared a comedy act duo who presented some contemporary political satire as we ate our starter. It was at that moment I noticed a form materialising next to Lily. I caught it out of the side of my eye but when I looked directly it disappeared. I noticed that Lily's skin was showing goose bumps.
"Lily..." I went to say something but she immediately cut me short.

"I know. I can see it!" She whispered out of the corner of her mouth. "It's all under control. I'm going to lure it in." With that Lily became more flirtatious and started to use her powerful feminine energies. Although aimed at me I noticed the apparition gaining substance until I could see it clearly even when looking directly at it.

The whole experience was amazing we had been joined by a ghostly spirit made of ephemeral energy that was now obviously paying close attention to Lily whilst ignoring me completely. As

I watched spellbound the entity reached out to touch her hair, but its ghostly finger slipped right through the strands. It had taken up a position in between her body and the chair. Then it sniffed her perfume and began to touch her intimately. It was horrible to watch, I had the feeling that it was a predator sizing up it next prey and lusting for the taste of her young fresh flesh. It was becoming sickeningly aroused.

I was quite distracted from the cabaret and felt a wave of repulsion creep over my body as the apparition pawed and molested my beautiful innocent companion.

"Can't you feel what it is doing? It's so repulsive, evil and perverted." I said covertly controlling my anger.

"Yes, I know exactly what it is doing! I'm in total control, don't worry I'm luring it in by giving off victim energy signals. I can sense it's done this many times before with murderous intent but I am holding back my disgust and horror."

"You are braver than me; it's so creepy and disgusting to watch. The entity is richly dressed in medieval clothes and I don't like what it's doing to you one bit! I can feel the anger rising in me, it's my protective nature; I can't help it!"

"You go it will detect and then latch onto you. Now is your chance to investigate and find the source of its negative energy. I will distract and hold it here for as long as I can."

I intuitively understood what Lily was saying as it somehow was an echo of a familiar past. The entity was supporting itself by drawing off negative energy from other souls nearby, they were its victims and too weak to break free. I was an energy vampire enslaving and using other weaker spirits to feed its insatiable ego.

I left the table and proceeded to the gentleman's toilet. I was uneasy about leaving Lily entwined in the clutches of this obscene apparition but I trusted her judgement and knew that I would be of infinitely more help by finding the spirit source of negative energy that it was feeding off.

I located the door and descended down an old stair case into the cellar of the building. The musty smell attacked my nose and I felt a distinct temperature drop as I entered the space below the modern current street level. The fabric of the building here was considerably older and definitely felt medieval in construction and materials. The word Medieval took on a new meaning as I kept repeating the syllables to myself; medi-evil, medi-evil, medi-evil. The lights flickered and dimmed increasing my apprehension.

This was not a nice place. I quickly relieved myself and started to wash my hands in the basin. It was then that I could feel the hairs on my neck starting to rise and I had the distinct feeling that I was being watched by something in the shadows. The lights began to flicker and I heard the distinctive sound of a child sobbing, faintly at first but then it grew stronger and nearer. It was a lone child's voice but as I listened I heard many more in the distance. My heart began to race and I could feel it beating inside my chest as I drew ever shorter breaths.

Then I felt something tugging at the hem of my jacket. I somehow controlled the overwhelming reaction to jump with super human endeavour and looked into the mirror in front of me.

I was a young boy of no more than 12 years dressed as a page in rich medieval clothes but there was something very wrong, very wrong indeed; they were totally soaked in blood! His white face was stricken with terror; blood flowed from the corners of his mouth and mingled with the tears that flowed freely down his cheeks.

Transfixed I stared into the mirror not daring to move and held my breath as I allowed his spirit to make contact with me in its own time. I dropped my wet right hand to my side and extended it backwards in an open gesture. I felt the child grip it hesitantly and I felt the temperature drop simultaneously from my warm flesh.

"What is your name little one?" I said whilst still staring into the mirror.

The boy looked startled and instantly recoiled as though bitten by a rabid dog letting go of my hand.

"Don't be afraid I'm here to help you little one. Focus your mind and tell me your name. I can feel you when you touch me and I can see you in the mirror."

I saw his terrified white face begin to relax and his face quivered into a tearful smile. I extended my hand backwards again in a gesture of friendship and felt him touch my palm with his index finger.

"That's it, good boy, I felt that. Now focus your energy and tell me who you are and how I can help?"

The child tightened his grip on my hand and tried to mouth words. I noticed an obscene gash appear across his throat and knew instantly that this was the mortal wound that had killed him. The innocent child had died by having his throat cut and the blood drained slowly from him.

My stomach knotted in revulsion of those that could perform such an act. I began to guess that it was probably the depraved creature that was at this moment latched onto Lily above.

"My name is Jeudon; I was an apprentice to the furrier Guillaume Hilairet." The voice came into my head. I smiled and turned towards the boy then dropped down onto one knee so as to be less intimidating. The boy recoiled but maintained his grip.

"Well met Jeudon, you remind me of myself when I was a page to the Duc d'Orleans in 1415. I was 12 at the time, the same age as you at a guess? I mean you no harm. I am here with my friend Lily upstairs to help you." I forced myself to smile despite his terrible wounds. As I watched in amazement I could see him take on visible form in front of me. I could now see clearly what had befallen him before he died.

"Sire, how is it that you are made of flesh yet were once a page?" "It's a long story Jeudon but we all come back and have many lives. You seem to have become stuck in this awful place. My friend Lily was Yvette of Luxembourg, we knew Jehanne d'Arc at the time of the siege."

It was as if a candle was slowly flickering into life before my very eyes as the truth of my words began to penetrate his mind and free his soul. He started to cry but this time it was with tears of joy.

"You are the first to be able to see me. Normally I am invisible to everyone who comes here."

"Yes, Jeudon you live in spirit and most people can't see you but I have a special gift. Lily thinks you are being held captive is that true?"

"We are many, let me show you." With that Jeudon tugged on my hand and pulled me through the door and towards the stairs. I couldn't pass through the door as he could so I had to stop and open it first. Jeudon laughed for the first time in 600 years, "I forgot you are solid!"

The lights flickered and dimmed but I could still clearly see Jeudon holding my hand. Then I heard him cry out, "You can come out. He is my friend. He can see me!"

At that the sobbing stopped and a scene of indescribable sadness emerged from the physical stairway. Many, many young children of all ages came towards me all bearing horrific injuries. Many had wounds to their neck and limbs indicating the barbaric manner in which they had been dispatched. Many had been bled to death slowly and then been dismembered.

The look of fear in their eyes was heart breaking to behold and I felt as though I had been doused in ice cold water. The lights flickered flared and went out as their collective electromagnetic energy interfered with the flow of electrons in the copper wires above me. I was overcome by sadness and grief. Lily was right it was a holocaust, so many innocent lives cut short and their souls held captive by the monster that sat above.

Some 300 passed by me and I seem to absorb all of their pain and sorrow. As I did so it was replaced by anger and an avenging violent rage which started at the base of my spine and flowed upwards through my central nervous system to explode in my brain. I felt the energy within me glow and give me strength. Jeudon looked at me, "Now you know the truth, monsieur. The monster that did this sits with your friend and his name is Gilles de Rais!"

I exploded with rage, now I knew who we were dealing with. A battle hardened aristocratic Breton dragon knight and companion of Jehanne d'Arc at the siege of Orleans. He had gone over to the occultism, satanic worship and child sacrifice in 1433 to satisfy his sadistic excesses.

"Lily and I will avenge you Jeudon and you together with the other children can return to the light." I knelt and made the sign of the cross in the air with my right hand in the same manner as a priest.

He smiled and began to fade before my eyes as did the other children that surrounded me. I was now in full battle mode, my fury aroused. I strode up the stairs and back into the main darkened dining hall. Barely containing my rage I sat opposite back Lily. I could see that the monstrous energy vampire was still obscenely entertaining itself a Lily's expense. Sensing my anger it turned towards me, it could obviously feel my disgust and hatred for it.

"You look like you've seen a ghost, Yann!" Lily looked shocked at my appearance and could feel the violence that boiled beneath my flesh.

"I have seen too many, Lily. We must destroy this depraved thing that sits before us. He has no power now." I stood up and boomed out in a strong loud voice, "I name thee Gilles de Laval, Baron de Rais, child murderer and satanic egotist; be gone from this place!"

The apparition started to glow red and flew at me grabbing my throat. I felt the wind leaving my lungs as I was knocked into my chair. I struggled to breathe. My own energy rose but was no match for this demon spirit. Then the room exploded and lit up with an incandescent bright blue light. It emanated from Lily's head, body and finger tips. It engulfed the seething red spirit that clung to my throat and surrounded it.

As the blue energy intensified in brilliance so the red ball of energy diminished and contracted in size. Brighter and brighter Lily glowed, her face turning into that of a vengeful goddess venting her utmost fury and spite on the object of her annoyance.

I could feel my throat loosen and air return to my lungs. I coughed and spluttered. The red light reduced to a pinpoint and then exploded into a fading burst of light like a spent firework. With that the blue light emanating from Lily brightened in colour and then in an instant dissipated into the room. Lily sat once more calm and serene in front of me.

The audience in the dining hall applauded as they obviously thought it was all part of the cabaret act!

The waitress came over, "everything alright Madame?" She enquired with an air of concern.

"Yes, no problem, my partner obviously had something nasty stuck in his throat! He's fine now, no need to worry." With that Lily took a sip of her wine and continued with her main course. Then she dismissed the waitress with a wave of her hand and a smile.

I felt the rage inside me subside and my pulse returned to normal. "I seem to be late for my main course, mustn't let it get cold! It looks delicious. I will tell you the details later my darling when you are not eating." I smiled and Lily raised her glass.

"I think you will find it is job done when you return to the source of the negativity; one up to us then, Santé!" Lily could sense a change in the atmosphere.
I lifted my glass somewhat shakily and chinked glasses. "Yes, it feels that way. I am glad you are on my side my angel of light."

"I think I will take a walk and go see for myself." Lily smiled then excused herself and exited the room discretely. After several minutes she returned grinning from ear to ear, "No problem, it feels perfectly normal down there. You go have a look as a lady can't go where you go! See what you think?"

I sat for a moment then made my way to the foot of the stairs. It felt a lot different, very normal now, just warm and pleasant; I smiled to myself. Entering the *Hommes* I decided to wash my hands and to splash some water on my face in an attempt to freshen up. The room went suddenly cold around me and condensation formed on the mirror.

Then I watched writing appear on its smooth glass surface;

You have freed us, Merci

A warm orange light began to materialise in front of my face. It took the shape of a boy's face; it was Jeudon. He smiled a radiant smile and the light of his soul shone brightly in his eyes. I smiled back and with that he faded.

I was moved to tears by the experience which was so far removed from anything I have ever witnessed. I dried my face and looked at myself in the mirror. Regaining my composure I made my way upstairs and back to our table.

"Job done?" Lily enquired as I sat down.

"Absolutely, job done," I raised my glass, "Santé!"

Chapter 15

Patay

The imagery of the mutilated children played on my mind. I had been a soldier in many of my past lives, used to bloody battlefield carnage but even that was no preparation for the horror and sadness that I had witnessed.

After the show Lily and I walked back to our hotel linked arm in arm. The whole riverside was lit up electric blue punctuated periodically with white spotlights. The cathédrale Ste. Croix looked particularly dramatic as it was illuminated in such a way that it dominated the city skyscape.

As we crossed the many arched stone bridge from Les Tourelles to the old city I paused midway to share my experience with Lily. For upwards of an hour I poured out the details as I stared into the flowing waters of the Loire. Lily listened in silent horror as the terrible imagery unfolded. At some point she put her arm around me and held me tight with her head on my shoulder, her beautiful long auburn hair falling forward to hide her tear stained eyes. It felt like the loving action of a mother comforting a traumatised infant who had experienced a nightmare. I found her soft feminine touch reassuring and healing. Emotions welled up in me and I was able to let what I had seen pass in a single cathartic act of confession. My tears dropped into the Loire and mingled with the flowing clear waters that would eventually take them to the sea.

We moved onto the Martroi and ritualistically touched Jehanne's statue. Lily broke the silence and voiced my thoughts. "How could such a pure spirit have mixed with such violent people?"

I gazed into the face of the angel of Orleans and thought for several minutes. "That is the true miracle, my Fleur d'Lily. She was a beacon of hope shining brightly amidst a sea of violence and madness; in a brutal vicious world she stepped up to the mark and made a difference. I continuously marvel at her courage and strength but even more so now after what I have just witnessed!"

Lily paused and reflected, then spoke in a contemplative voice. "The English called it the Hundred Years War it was such a long, long time; the holocaust and World War 2 only lasted a relatively short six years by comparison. The dreadful imagery of the Nazi death camps forms the only point of reference that I can compare to what you have described."

Lily cast her head down in deep thought and it was my turn to put my arm around her shoulders. "It's not over yet." I said after a pause of several minutes.

"I know, Yann. I've been thinking of that ever since we left the cabaret." Lily pulled her pashmina tighter around her neck to gain some insulation against the early morning chill.

"We must go out to Patay before we leave. Good or bad we must feel and experience what happened there." I had now lost my initial enthusiasm of some days earlier but I was determined to see the experiment through to the end, despite my unexpected encounter with Gilles de Rais.

"Yes, I agree. We must see the mission through in order to collect all the data, otherwise we might miss something important and regret it later." Lily tried to smile but she was painfully aware that it might not be a pleasant experience.

We agreed to spend the afternoon on the battlefield before departing on the early evening train for Paris. The best solution we finally decided was to take a taxi out to the site some 26 kilometres north west of the old city and to arrange for the driver to pick us up an hour before the train was due to leave. Several trains were available at that time of day so we had some flexibility built into the plan. The only reserved seats were for the Gare du Nord, Paris to Lille TGV at 19:00hrs. Having made our final arrangements we walked the final leg along the Rue République to our hotel and bed.

Weary from mental, emotional and physical fatigue we said our goodnights and went into our individual rooms. Within minutes I was fast asleep in a dreamless world of oblivion.

I awoke mid-morning disturbed only by the sound of Lily's shower in the next room. The images of the night before haunted me and I had to make a conscious effort to exclude them from my thoughts. Action seemed the best remedy so I busied myself with shaving and then packed my bag. Reaching for my mobile,

I text Lily that I would see her in the foyer. Breakfast was no longer a hotel option so I sat waiting for Lily and thought where we might go. When she arrived some 15 minutes later I quickly settled the bill and collected the receipt for my records.

We headed for Gare du Orleans on the tram and checked the times of the train back to Paris.

"I'm getting hungry!" Lily exclaimed. "Fancy a croissant and a coffee?"

"Good idea, then we can dump our bags and grab a taxi."

Some inner voice was spurring me on. I knew that time was short and something important lay waiting for us to discover. It was that deep inner knowing that lent urgency to the proceedings. Within minutes Lily re-appeared clutching two large take away cups; a coffee for me and a hot chocolate for herself. From her back pack she took out two almond croissants that she had also purchased. We chose a seat and enjoyed our al fresco dining whilst admiring the elegance of the wavy roof structure.

"If you look at it in strips it looks like reels of film." I found myself fascinated by the clever play of light from the clear glass panels that interspersed the silver metal roof material.

"Yes, it is beautiful, just like me; elegant, chic yet highly functional!" Lily laughed and several crumbs spluttered from her mouth.

On the horizon I could see a small gathering of houses. "Is that Patay, Monsieur?" I enquired enthusiastically.

"No Monsieur, that is Lignerolles; Patay is just beyond it." The driver blankly replied.

Then in complete contrast from the back seat Lily suddenly shouted, "Stop the car, stop the car!"

The driver did not immediately understand the urgency of her instructions and therefore continued someway before he slowed and eventually stopped the car by the side of the desolate road.

"You OK, Lily?" I turned in my seat to see what had transpired.

"Yes, fine I just had a strange vision that's all." I could see from the expression on her face that Lily was desperately trying to make sense of what she had seen. "I saw a golden eagle standard and lots of soldiers carrying oblong shields crossing the road. They were definitely Romans and not Napoleonic troops or medieval knights. I know my history."

"OK, we'll go and investigate; it might lead to something?" I thanked the driver for stopping and asked if he could let us out here and then return to pick us up at 16:00hrs. I paid him up front with a €50 Euro note and the promise of more when he returned at which point he suddenly became most helpful!

He assured us that he would be back here at that precise time and that we could expect him to be punctual. With that he swung the car around and sped off into the distance back to Orleans and civilization.

The transition was abrupt and final, as we suddenly found ourselves in the middle of nowhere. We stood alone under the hot midday sun with only our intuition to guide us.

"I know the battlefield is here. I can sense it." Lily sounded positive. "Let's walk back to where I saw the Romans.

Within 5 minutes we had reached the spot where Lily had seen her vision. To the right of the road was a rough patch of ground containing many large stones and to the left in the distance was a lone small wood with a pylon that seemed to line up with the rough stony ground. In front of us stood some more pylons with power cables that crossed the road and connected with the wood to the east, in the distance we could just see 3 farms and the military airbase; we knew that Orleans lay over the horizon beyond that. Due to the flat nature of the terrain it was hard to make out any other distinctive features except for the fields of ripening wheat that swirled all around us.

We wandered off of the road onto the rough ground, Lily knelt down and touched one of the stones and shut her eyes. "It's a Roman road! That's why I saw Roman soldiers carrying an eagle; they were marching along it!"

"Well done, Lily. You are amazing! In 1429 the English army were retreating from Meung to Janville when the heavy cavalry of the vanguard under La Hire and Xaintrailles surprised them; they were probably following the old Roman road?"

"That makes sense." Lily nodded her agreement.

I was picturing events in my head and looking northeast towards the small wood. "The English archers were concealed just in front of a dip when our cavalry scouts flushed a stag out which bounded through their position. That caused them to raise a shout which gave away their position."

Lily continued the description as she started to see the events in her mind. "Yes, the vanguard then knew where they were and attacked before they had time to deploy their stakes and draw their longbows. They hit them front, centre and on both flanks; literally riding over them. The main battle under Alençon and Dunois followed up and engaged the men-at-arms on the ridge to complete the victory. By the time Jehanne and Richemont arrived with the rearguard it was all but over. Talbot and Scales were capture over there and Falstolf made off in disgrace. Then the pursuit hunted the remainder down."

"Result; the English lost 2000 men and we only lost 5! An amazing victory indeed, it was the first time the English had been defeated in an open battle for a long, long time. It sealed the relief of Orleans campaign and sent shock waves through medieval Europe."

We both stood gazing into the distance trying to piece together in our heads what had happened that 18th day of June, 1429. Eerily Lily suddenly broke the silence with an intuitive statement from her deep subconscious. "We were both there!"

Goose bumps immediately spread all over my arms as the truth of her insight hit home.

It was then that I noticed a strange shadow laying in the crop of green wheat just to the right of the small wood in the distance some 200 metres from the road. "Hey Lily what's that? Let's walk along the field boundary to those trees over there. I think I can see something in the crop!"

Lily looked towards where I was pointing. The sun was a brilliant yellow orb overhead surrounded by a deep blue sky so she shaded her eyes with her hand. "You are right I can see something too, let's investigate."

The scene looked very similar to the van Gogh painting *crows in a cornfield.* It immediately conjured up in my mind that powerful image of the black harbingers of death flying in that he depicted so graphically in the picture. I had visited the van Gogh museum in Amsterdam long ago when young, the picture had transfixed me for several minutes at the time and now my memory banks dredged it to the surface of my consciousness. I remembered it was his suicide note; life had closed in on his tortured soul. He could see no way out, so he shot himself in a field exactly like this. I then thought of the doomed English that died on this field ridden down by the heavy cavalry of France. The image of the crows turned into ravens that bore white crosses on their wings, then the vision subsided as Lily tugged at my sleeve.

I stepped onto the ploughed field and immediately felt like an extra-terrestrial as we left the safety of the tarmac. We started to walk along its rough edge towards the trees. It was a strange sensation as I had never done this as an adult before being only used to the familiar paved surfaces of cities. Deep within my childhood memory there lurked a certain familiarity with the feel of walking on rough earth. I felt instantly reconnected to my childhood, a sense of discovery and the land.

"What are all these lines in the field, Yann?" Lily was brushing the wheat with her hands as she walked in front of me. The tactile sensation seemed to reinforce the experience for her. It reminded me of the opening memory scene from the film *Gladiator* as Maximus is about to go into battle against the German tribes.

"I think they are where the tractor tyres leave an imprint in the soil when sowing the seed."

"They remind me of tramlines. It gives such a beautiful structure to the landscape, like staves on a page of music." Lily stopped and took several photographs. Nearing the small wood, we could see that some of the crop to our right had been flattened. It was a sense of curiosity that led me to deviate into the field to investigate further. I used the tractor tramlines so as not to destroy the delicate plants and cause unnecessary damage. Lily followed close behind on the line parallel to mine and continued to click away with her camera. Several times she paused and flipped it to video to record our journey and audible thoughts.

Suddenly I stood at the edge of the immaculately flattened crop that spread in an arc; both directions from my position. I was totally astounded. I had never seen anything like this before! The crop was undamaged, just lying there as though somebody had carefully thrown a bucket of water over it. I could see no mud or mechanical damage at all. It was a miracle.

"Wow! What on earth is it?" Lily had caught up with me and now stood at the edge of the circle too.

"I have no idea!" I gazed in awe at the perfection of the circular rim I was observing. Beyond I could see another smaller circle at the centre of the strange construction.

"It feels like a church!" Lily whispered in a reverent manner out of the side of her mouth.

"I know what you mean. It's that same feeling I get when I walk into a sacred building." I found myself talking in an equally quiet tone not wishing to disturb the magic.

"What do we do now? Shall we enter?" Lily was finding it hard to refrain from plunging into the heart of this new mystery. "I feel like Alice in Wonderland again!" She unconsciously extended her hand towards me and I felt it touch mine with a burst of electricity. I gently extended my fingers and gripped it. Then together we took a pace forward and stepped into the circle. It seemed a sacred act, there was no dramatic transition as we had experienced with our time slips but there was a sense of energy that seemed to be flowing and spinning in the direction of the lay of the crop.

Lily's knees buckled slightly as the energy impacted on her muscles and other physiological systems. "It feels like we are standing in running water!" Lily held my hand tighter as if to steady herself in a current.

"I know I feel it too! Let's split up and walk around the ring, it looks pretty big to me. Then we can go into the centre circle." I felt a sense of ritual was needed in order to respect the sacred feeling of the temporary structure.

We wandered in opposite directions. Lily went clockwise with the lay and followed the flow of the energy intuitively. I decided to go anticlockwise and found myself looking for mechanical damage to the stalks but I could find none. It became an obsession as I wanted an answer to this conundrum. Dropping to one knee I periodically checked the crop at its base, some of the nodes seemed to have grown longer on one side which accounted for the flattening effect of the wheat. Occasionally I found some that had exploded from within. In disbelief I collected some to show Lily. The most amazing thing was the total lack of mud, footprints and mechanical damage; even the white patina on the surface of the leaves was undisturbed, yet on touching it I could see my finger prints had left an impression.

Joining back up with Lily I recorded my observations on video as I related my findings to her. Lily interjected with her own observations as to the nature of the energy that she could feel and said that her camera had malfunctioned several times as she explored.

Then together we made our way into the smaller centre circle of the formation. There was something about the harmonic proportion of the pattern that resonated with my soul. It seemed more than just two simple circles, there seemed to be an underlying geometric structure that was distinctly present yet somehow invisible. I noted my feelings on camera to which Lily added that she could see stars in her head when she shut her eyes?

Reaching the centre point we found a delicately woven twirl of crop with a single stem of wheat protruding upright from its midst. I marvelled at the sensitive delicacy of its weave. I was sure that previous generations would have said it was the work of the elves and fairies had they witnessed this miracle.

"Wow! It looks just like a delicate birds nest." Lily was on her knees examining the fine structure through the lens of her digital camera.

I found myself lying flat on the ground beside the nest. I looked up at her; the sun tinted her hair with a fiery red as it shone through the individual strands of her auburn locks. "I've died and gone to heaven! You look just like a Goddess!" I sighed as Lily's beauty struck my soul.

She grinned and poked her tongue out mischievously and said in a coy fashion, "I'm only me!"

"Well you – is pretty good my dragon princess!" I deliberately skewed my grammar to emphasise the playful nature of my observation.

Lily laughed and lay down in the circle. We both looked up at the clear azure blue sky and discovered within ourselves a great sense of love, healing and peace. It seemed to emanate from the formation itself and the energy that had created it.

I drifted off to somewhere in time and returned minutes later only to find that two hours had past! "Hey look at the time!" I said as I sat bolt upright checking my watch. "It's nearly 3 o'clock. We've only got another hour."

Lily woke from her alternate state of deep meditation and shook the cobwebs from her mind. She slowly started to focus with one hand shielding her eyes from the bright sunlight. "I've just had the most wonderful healing dream." She spoke with a wistful fairy voice and stretched as she lay on the ground.

We both stood up. I could clearly see that the sun had moved substantially in the sky and I noticed that Lily had slightly red suntanned face as we had forgotten to use sun block.

"We should measure the diameters of the circles." Lily said returning to her logical conscious self. She looked into her back pack which lay to one side and pulled out a ball of string. "This will do, grab one end and walk across to the edge of the circle on that side." I did as she asked. Lily walked to the opposite side of the circle from me and touched the standing wheat with her end of the string. She bade me do the same and told me to pull the string tight. She then looked along the line of the string towards me and asked me to adjust my position until the white cotton cord touched the centre stalk. "Pull it tight!" She shouted and then taking out a knife she cut the string precisely. "Let go!" I did as she requested and she wound the piece of string up. "Right let's do the same with the big ring, inside diameter and outside diameter, same procedure." Within ten minutes Lily had collected 3 neatly wound balls of string which she tucked carefully into the backpack along with what was left of the original ball.

"Ah, I see, you are going to measure them later when we get back to Lille." The penny finally dropped as I understood what she was doing, "most ingenious!"

"Then we will know the exact dimensions of this miracle." Lily smiled, "I have a hunch that it's maybe important and when we analyse the data we might find something interesting?"

As I stepped out of the circle I had an intuitive urge to visit the small wood immediately to our front right before returning to the road. I felt that I couldn't leave this place without investigating the anomalous clump of trees; it too seemed sacred. Carefully we made our way along the tramlines without damaging the standing crop back to the edge of the field. Then we continued along the boundary towards the wooded area.

After several minutes we stood on the threshold of the trees and gathered our thoughts. The energy of the circle had completely blown away our previous medieval thought patterns and I was therefore caught totally unaware. For as we stepped into the wood the time slip vortex appeared. Multi-coloured lights danced in the air and we plunged into the din and clamour of a full on battle. The electrifying jolt had all the hallmarks of a car crash! I was mounted on a strong bay chestnut coloured horse with a black mane. My crossbow was held to my eye and I squeezed the trigger. I saw the English man-at-arms fall to the ground as the deadly bolt struck home with tremendous force in the middle of his chest. I was shocked as I realised that I had just killed him stone dead. He had had no chance.

My thoughts were rudely interrupted by a longbow arrow that thwacked against the visor of my sallet and luckily glanced off at an oblique angle. I spied the perpetrator, slung my crossbow, drew my sword and spurred my horse to the gallop. Within seconds I was on him, he ducked but my scything sword found its mark and blood spurted from his head as his helmet came off. The gaping wound in his neck continued to spray blood over my horse and black grieves as he went down under the trampling hooves.

All around the hue and cry to, "Hunt down the English Goddons," roared from French throats. Nine months of siege with its deprivations and terror had hardened the hearts of the French mounted men-at-arms. Many in their throng had lost blood relations at Crecy, Poitier and Agincourt, now it was payback time.

Finally the aristocratic mounted chivalry of France had caught the crooked stick wielding archers of England out in the open and totally unprepared; it was total carnage, with only the English men-at-arms putting up any sort of worthwhile resistance.

Everywhere I looked; I saw blood and body parts. Battle madness reigned supreme and I was part of it.
As the mounted knights charged on followed by their loyal men-at-arms, I reloaded my crossbow. The weapon was light in comparison to the heavy siege crossbows that employed complex mechanisms to span them. I could use either the hook on my belt in conjunction with my leg muscles and the crossbow's stirrup or a simple hinged lever designed for use on horseback; being mounted I decided to use the latter and reached for an armour piercing quarrel with leather flights from my quiver. Regaining the reins I swung my horse around using my knees and continued the chase. Firing from point blank range I despatched another archer with a bolt to the face; his paltry short sword being no match for my hunting crossbow.

An impressively caparisoned knight galloped up with a retinue of men-at-arms. I twisted in my saddle and raised my crossbow intuitively to defend my head.

"Relax!" A loud voice boomed out in French, "Good shooting, I'm glad you are on our side yet I see you do not wear the white cross of France but that of a Knight Hospitalier. Who are you, Sir?"

I looked at the 3 royal fleur d'Lys that his azure shield bore surrounded by a red border with eight white roundels, more properly described in heraldic terms, Azure three fleurs-de-lis Or, a bordure Gules bezanty Argent. I knew straight away that it was the gallant Jean de Valois, Duc d'Alençon, Commander in Chief of the Royal Army. Behind him to the left I saw a shield bearing, Azure three fleurs-de-lis Or a label Argent, a sinister bendlet Sable overall, I knew instantly that it was Jean Bastard of Orleans the commander of the siege these past 9 months. He looked anxious to continue the pursuit and engage the English men-at-arms on the ridge ahead so I decided to make it short and sweet.

"My name is Robert des Armoises, sieur d'Tichemont from the République of Metz my Lord." I did my best to bow my head whilst in the saddle and added a flourish with my free right arm.

"Ah yes, I know you and your black ravens, you are forever guarding the angel. Where are they?"

I scanned the horizon 360 degrees and located *la pucelle's* banner rearward some distance by the old Roman road. I could just make out four black figures that sat motionless on their horses behind her entourage.

"There my Lord are four of the Black Brethren watching over Jehanne and her banner." I pointed with my crossbow, "Others of our number are yet in the field despatching the English Goddons to Hell."

"France and my sovereign liege the Dauphin are most grateful Sir Robert. You have our thanks."

"Our pleasure my Lord we but do our duty and the bidding of our Lady Luxembourg."

"Interesting, that's more than her son does! You must explain something of these intricacies another time when we are not so busy. I have been waiting for this day for a long time!" With that he raised his sword hilt to his lips in salute, clapped his visor shut and then signalled his men forward at the charge.

As he disappeared into the fray, I headed my trusty steed rearward to rejoin my sacred band of Brethren. As my horse gained ground I saw Yvette remove her hood and wave. I glanced at *la Pucelle*; she met my gaze and smiled, then raised her banner high. Our eyes locked momentarily and our souls connected; I felt warmth spread through my body. I was truly alive at this very moment it time. She raised her sword and touched the hilt to the place near her neck where the arrow had pierced. I raised my crossbow to indicate that I understood her message of thanks. With that I spurred my horse onward. She did the same and her entourage and men-at-arms followed her. As she passed, her gaze was firmly fixed forward but I could see the fire of the Holy Spirit burning brightly in her eyes which were set intently once more on her sacred mission.

As I urged my horse forward with my knees to rejoin Yvette it somehow stumbled on a corpse and was thrown forward. Multi-coloured lights appeared in a circle and I found myself on the floor in the middle of the small wood. Lily stood over me and held out her hand to help me up.

"That was careless, you do all that fighting and then your horse trips as you trot over to see me!" She laughed to see my embarrassment as I brushed the leaf mould from my clothes.

"Hey, don't tell me you saw the whole thing?" I said suddenly realising that she must have witnessed what I had experienced.

"Yes, I saw the whole thing. I just sat here guarding our precious angel with Ulrich, Tomas and Thibault whilst Johannes, Ruprecht and Guillaume played hunt the English with you!"

I dusted myself off and stood up smiling like a small boy that had been caught out doing something naughty.

"You do realise what we are stood on don't you?" Lily looked me straight in the eye and was suddenly serious.

"Well, I can feel the negative energy but I guess you are going to tell me anyway."

Lily smiled and then looked serious again, "It's the grave pit! It contains the bones of some 2000 English soldiers that died here on the 18th day of June in the year of our Lord one thousand four hundred and twenty nine."

"Mmmm a sobering thought but it was their choice. We had best get back to the road. The taxi will be here in 15 minutes and we have a train to catch."

Quietly we made our way out of the wood and along the edge of the field back to the road. Lily paused to take a couple of last photographs, one of the wood and one of the mysterious circle with the airbase in the distance.

Within minutes of reaching the road the taxi arrived exactly on time and did a three point turn to face in the direction of Orleans. The driver smiled at me when he saw that I was covered in mud, twigs and leaf litter. By the expression on his face I could see that his mind was working overtime trying to guess what we had been up to!

Some thirty minutes later we found ourselves back at Gare du Orleans with our train for Paris due at 17:00hrs. We collected our luggage from the driver. I thanked him and then paid him in full with another €50 Euro note.

"Just time to grab a quick coffee and a bottle of water, my treat," Lily looked tired now and I could see it would be a quiet ride home back to Lille.

Chapter 16

The Crop circle Connection

After a good night's sleep we met with Jean in his office at La Voix du Nord just off the Grande Place in the centre of Lille. He was extremely interested in our account of what had transpired in Orleans. Understandably he censored the Gilles de Rais episode but was more than happy to have us write about the arrow time slip and the Battle of Patay. Pictures of the Maison Jehanne d'Arc and Les Tourelles monument were accepted for the article.

Lily and I spent the rest of the morning roughing out the copy and viewing the photographic footage. It seemed that we had been there forever as we reviewed the evidence. We then came to the circle pictures which we analysed and that was when we had a shock; on the last picture of the circle we spotted an Unidentified Flying Object! It was a metallic looking structured craft of saucer shape with a raised central section. In profile it looked as though someone had cemented two dinner plates together. Would anybody believe us? On that frame there was no point of reference so we looked at other frames for clear evidence that would deny the charge of hoax.

"I'm amazed I saw nothing through my view finder when taking the picture and we both saw absolutely nothing!" Lily spoke in hushed tones to avoid other workers in the over hearing our conversation. We had taken some stick over the paranormal flavour of our last article so she wanted to be doubly cautious not to become a laughing stock.

"Well, I have nothing to lose as it's the end of my career, but for you my Fleur d'Lily it is the beginning." I understood her caution and left the decision on how to play this one to her.

"Thanks, Yann. I will stick my neck out though if we find more hard evidence that provides undeniable proof that we didn't hoax the whole thing!" We continued to look at the photographs and finally found what we were looking for. There on one of the early shots from the Roman road was a frame showing the small wood in the distance and there at the back of the right corner was a partially exposed UFO identical to the full on image that first alerted us.

Lily smiled as she enhanced the frame and zoomed in on the anomaly. "We have it!" She exclaimed and sat back in her swivel chair; I went over to her screen to take a look.

I spent several minutes examining the image in depth and finally gave my decision. "You are right! It's a bit pixelated at that resolution but it will stand up in court. I'm quite happy to publish and be damned."

The whole experience had just taken on a much larger perspective. The craft was clearly behind the trees which eliminated a hoax as the size of the craft could be calculated which proved it was not a model. I estimated it to be some 26 metres in diameter with a height of approximately 10 metres in the central raised portion. Lily also noted that the shadows of the trees were distorted in the vicinity of the saucer.

"The space around the craft must be warped by its energy field and therefore the light from the sun bent as it passed through the UFO's space."

I was getting very interested in the photograph as it resonated with my teenage studies on Einstein and relativity. "Matter tells space how to bend and space tells matter how to move! The mass of the craft was refracting the light rays; perhaps that is why we couldn't see it with our own eyes? It literally cloaked itself from our normal vision."

Lily started to understand, "Yes, that's it! The craft was distorting the space around itself so that we just saw around it but it couldn't fool the camera. The energy field must pulse at a particular frequency and the camera caught it momentarily when it was uncloaked and therefore visible."

Lily sat back again with her hands clasped behind her head. "Wow! This is so cool!" She said with a satisfied tone of vindication.

"I wonder if the circle or military base has anything to do with the craft?" I threw the obvious conjectural point into the ring of discussion.

"Or the other way around; may be our own consciousness created the UFO and the circle?" Lily threw in her thoughts on the subject which completely caught me unawares as I was being very detached about the whole incident.

"It's a bit of a coincidence isn't it? You feel compelled to visit a spot in the middle of nowhere, then I see Roman soldiers, we find an anomalous circle in a field and a UFO appears!" Lily had the bit between her teeth and was not going to let go of this line of enquiry. "You're not an alien are you?"

I laughed, but she was being deadly serious, "Might account for your difference in vascular plumbing to the brain and memory ability?"

"Well, best not tell anyone otherwise they might put me in the zoo next to the Citadelle!"

Then it was Lily's turn to laugh out loud and make a joke of it, "I can just imagine you there; I would come a feed you every day!"

"So long as they don't autopsy me I don't mind!" All sorts of dark thoughts penetrated my head as I thought of the military base we had seen. "Time for a glass of wine and lunch, let's go to the Le Pot Beaujolais just on the corner near the Opera house?. I'm buying before they dissect me!"

Lily grabbed her bag and we left the office and stepped out into the bright midday sun shining on the Grande Place. As we a walked along Lily suddenly said, "Do you mind if we go to the book shop across the square I want to buy some things?"

"Sure no problem, lunch can wait a few minutes." I replied in a quizzical fashion assuming that she wished to purchase a book. After 5 minutes of rummaging in the stationery section Lily found what she was looking for, an extending tape measure and a pair of compasses. As she paid for the items at the cash register the penny dropped.

"This is about you balls of string and the circle isn't it?"

"Sure is; I've got an idea and I want to see if it works!"

"I know this is going to be one of those lunches where we end up nearly getting thrown out for drawing on the table cloth!"

"Sure is! If that happens I'll just use my feminine charm and you can look innocent."

Lily smiled and giggled as she grabbed my arm. It felt like Dad and daughter time again so I thought to myself, whatever, and joined in with the madness. We didn't have far to walk just a couple of hundred metres to the corner opposite the Opera.

Lily chose a table inside away from distractions and ordered from the menu. With a large glass of *vin rouge* I settled back ready to watch the floor show!

"I have a little idea based on something my mathematics teacher once showed me in high school. I want to see if it works and this is the first opportunity I have had to test the theory."

Lily carefully laid out her props on the clean white table cloth with the precision of a surgeon. I loaned her my Swiss army knife to open the packaging on her new acquisitions. She gave me the tape measure and asked me to extend it to a length of one metre. Then she proceeded to measure the 3 balls of string one at a time by passing the twine through her fingers over the metre measure and counting. After several minutes and a bit of rechecking she had 3 precise measurements written on the serviette:

9.28: 30: 41.68 metres.

"It's a good job I had a hundred metre ball of string; that last one nearly used up half of it!"

She continued with the conjuring trick.

"Right, now these are the 3 diameters of the circles we measured. I kept seeing stars as I mentioned and I think I know the connection? I got the idea from the roundel insignia on the military transport planes on the way to Patay. In the night I dreamt of the insignia but they mysteriously changed from French roundels to American stars within the circle. Then I remembered this morning what my maths teacher had shown me; watch!"

She took from her bag her A4 notepad and after a pause for calculation drew a small circle with a radius of 4.64 millimetres using her newly purchased compasses. Then she drew a bigger circle using a radius of 15 millimetres by extending her compasses after using a small ruler to adjust them to the new measurement. Finally she extended them even further and drew a larger circle with a radius of 20.84 millimetres.

"Now for the mathemagic!" My attention was 100% as with the deft mesmerising effect of a top conjurer she reeled me in for the finale of the trick. I sat silent on the edge of my chair in anticipation.

Then taking her ruler and a sharp pencil she began to draw straight lines tangent to and touching the centre circle; one after the other in sequence she laid them down with the precision of surgeon. To my astonishment a perfect 5 pointed start appeared!

"It works!" Lily exclaimed in triumph as the last line connected with the first point, *"C'est magnifique!"*

I was amazed and found myself applauding audibly. "That's why you could see stars, your subconscious could see what you conscious mind couldn't. You intuitively knew that we were standing in harmonically proportioned flattened circle of wheat."

"And it is the sacred pentagram, the geometric symbol for reincarnation. Let's see if I can repeat the trick."

Lily now flushed with success redrew the original 3 circles afresh and to the exact same dimensions. This time she drew straight lines tangent and touching the centre circle but touching the outer largest circle; one after the other she drew them with deadly accuracy, each one touching the last one until seven lines were constructed and the last one met the starting point.

"There you go; a perfect heptagram! Absolute magic, no?"

I sat and stared at the neat diagrams, the numbers 5 and 7 had been deliberately encoded in the circle of flattened wheat near Patay. I then remembered back to my classics days with lectures on Greek number theory; 5 represents LIFE and 7 the virginal number of MYSTERY and SPIRIT. The name Athena in Greek had the value 777 as she was thrice virginal, because 7 cannot divide exactly into 360 and Jesus in Greek had the value 888 which was thrice perfect.

"I've got it! Spirit inhabits matter and gives rise to life; life and spirit are inseparable."

"That makes sense, what a profound message. I wonder who or what sent it and why?" Lily was pleased with my insight which gave some meaning to the enigmatic rings in the crops.

After lunch we walked back to our office and Lily inked her drawings in. She then photocopied them for me and coloured some of them in for pinning on the wall display board by her desk. Using her inkjet printer she also ran off several copies of the photos containing the circle and the UFO. Within minutes several other journalists and co-workers had stopped to look at her handy work and to ask questions.

Passions ran high as the debate developed and Jean came to see what all the fuss was. "You'll have us all seeing crop circles!" He said jokingly, "Back to work we've got a paper to run."

Gradually our colleagues drifted off as the novelty wore off. "What did he say they were, Lily?"

"Crop circles, but I think he just made that up." Lily answered robotically as she was busy typing out a neat copy of the Orleans article that we had put together.

"Sounds kind of exactly what they are; that's a good name for it."
I found myself tapping it into a search engine, selecting images
and then pressing the enter key, suddenly up popped several
pictures of crop circles, each showing astounding precision and
remarkably complex geometry. Page after page I viewed like a
lost child in a candy store, there were hundreds. "Hey, Lily stop
what you're doing and come look at this!"

Lily came over to my desk and her jaw dropped in disbelief. "Oh
mon Dieu! What magic is this?"

"I had no idea such things existed. I hit upon the best website
first time. It's URL is www.crop circleconnector.com, try it on
your machine."

Lily went back to her computer and was soon looking at the
amazing images. We were both astonished at the precision of
the geometry which was extremely detailed and highly accurate.
Further research revealed that they occurred all over the world
but the epicentre was definitely in southern England around the
Avebury and Stonehenge area. At the click of a mouse a whole
new world opened up before my eyes. It seemed to be a very
ancient world of stone circles, monoliths and prehistoric pagan
religion based on the Sun, Moon and Venus. I knew instinctively
that I was connected with that world and so was Lily.

Further research that afternoon on our own photographs revealed
several other frames with anomalous shadows probably due to
an invisible object distorting the space around itself, plus one
other shot of a small object in the distance but too small to be
recognised except for its distinct lack of wings.

As I took the metro home that night thoughts kept circulating in my head. What had been a started as a historical quest had now developed into something far more profound and now with present day relevance. That night I fell asleep holding my pop-up book and dreamed of my Lady des Armoises.

Next morning it was the usual Friday end of the week workday. I texted Lily on the way into the office to see if she had experienced any dreams, time slips or revelations in the night? The mysterious reply came that she had experienced a sudden burst of energy which had disturbed her sleep around 04:00hrs but with no other phenomena associated with it, so she had just gone back to sleep.

I decided to have an early breakfast at Café Le Rihour just a stone's throw from my office at La Voix du Nord. I read the early addition of our paper to catch up on local events whilst eating. At 09:00 hrs. I walked into my office. A white piece of paper sat on my computer keyboard propped up against the screen. It read;

Yann

One of your circles has landed near Forest-sur-Marque! No joke!!! A Monsieur Larché was out walking his dog early this morning and reported seeing a large flattened area of crop. Might be worth investigating?

Etienne

I knew Etienne from the 24 hour news desk had seen Lily's pictures on the wall the day before and so he had probably given this story more priority than he would have normally. It was a good lead, so I rang him to check that he definitely wasn't joking? He confirmed that normally a citizen walking a dog with a mundane story would not have attracted his attention but having seen Lily's pictures yesterday he had told us as quick as possible.

Just then Lily entered the office. "Bonjour, Yann. How are you today?"

"I'm fine thanks, slept really well and didn't get woken up with a burst of energy either. Hey, take a look at this." I handed her the single sheet of white A4 and waited for a reaction.

"Mmmmm, interesting I think we should take a look don't you? It seems more than a coincidence."

"I'll ring the car pool and see if they have a vehicle available. It's the end of the week they should have something we can use?"

Ten minutes later, after a quick phone call and a bit of wheeler dealing, I reported to Lily that we were all set and had a car from 09:30hrs. We cleared our desks as quick as possible and then made our way to the car pool a couple of blocks from the city centre.

The city was busy as usual but we managed to clear the traffic near the centre fairly quickly and headed out northeast towards Lac du Héron a small nature reserve on the out skirts of Lille and the satellite communes of Hem and Forest-sur-Marque. Turning off the main road at the roundabout towards the village of Hem we started our search. The place was deserted as resident population were either at work or on holiday. I looked for the boulangerie as that would be the local centre of gossip and people would have been buying their fresh baked baguettes and croissants from the early morning.

Luck was with us as we quickly found the boulangerie pâtisserie Delhaye Guillaume at Place de la République. In his scribbled note Etienne had neglected to give an address for Monsieur Larché, again fortune was with us as the lady shop assistant knew him; for even though he lived in Forest-sur-Marque he walked his dog to Hem every morning to buy fresh bread. He had indeed mentioned seeing an unusual patch of flattened wheat to the side of the road that morning. We thanked the lady and jumped back into the car and headed south back out of the village to the turning from the main road. We continued over the junction in the direction of Forest-sur-Marque the next village. Lily kept looking westward out of the passenger side of the car and I kept glancing eastward. As the road hit a slight bend Lily shouted she could see the lake ahead, at that moment I glanced eastward momentarily and saw an enormous patch of flattened wheat many times bigger that the crop circle near Patay.

I pulled the car over and parked it as best I could off of the road so as not to interrupt the flow of traffic. The road was very quiet so I did not envisage a problem. Armed with her camera Lily was first out of the vehicle and started taking pictures immediately. The she switched to video mode to record her thoughts and the atmosphere of the place. The whole area was deserted with the exception of the bird life on the lake.

"Have you got your string?" I said as I changed my shoes in case of mud.

"Sure have, a whole new 500 metre ball and it looks like I'm going need it; the area looks pretty big to me!"

We entered the crop and carefully made our way along the tramlines to avoid causing unnecessary damage to the crop. A sense of excitement and expectation arose in both of us as we neared the flattened area. We paused at the perimeter of the formation and looked for signs of mechanical damage or human intervention. There appeared to be none; it was pristine.

"We'll phone Monsieur Larché later to check his story as he may have disturbed the site but it looks untouched to me." I scanned the formation from where we stood for foot prints but I could find none. "Well nobody has come down this tramline my prints are the only ones and they go only one way.

"It's the same on my tramline." Lily said as she caught up with me having taken several photographs along the way. She stood for several minutes taking close up photographs of the crop from our position on the edge of the formation. "Here goes, un, deux, très," and with that she walked into the circular rim of the crop circle. I followed her lead and could only feel the gentle swirl of energy that went in the direction of the lay of the wheat.

We followed the same procedure we had established in Patay; Lily went clockwise and I went anticlockwise. It was a big circle with a precise rim, inside lay 4 large flatten circles with standing centres at each point of the compass, the centre contained a fifth flattened circle but with a thin 1 metre ring of standing crop.

It was an amazing construction made with extreme precision. I could see that all 5 circles were of the exact same dimension and I marvelled at the sense of symmetry displayed. I could find no damage anywhere, only expanded nodes and bent wheat that was not broken. I tested my own footprints and could see that the crop was instantly damaged and showed forensically that I had been there. I even found several exploded nodes which I collected as samples. The crop had clearly been acted upon by a force that left no mechanical damage, it had to have been microwaves and electromagnetism that were responsible for the effects I observed. I wasn't sure but the more evidence I saw the more I became intrigued and wanted to know more. Dew drops still clung to the leaves as did the white dust like patina spore bloom that leaves have naturally.

It was time to measure the dimensions of the circles with Lily's string; firstly the dimensions of outer rim; next the diameter of each of the 5 large circles within the perimeter ring; then the diameter of the 4 standing crop circle centres; finally the dimensions of the centre standing ring that was only a meter wide.

"Hey, have you noticed that you would have to flatten the centres to create the circles manually using string and a board." I pointed out this sudden revelation that was of importance to Lily.

"Of course, you would have to stand in the centre to measure the radius as it was being made! That fact alone shows that it is not made by simple human mechanical means." Lily was impressed as it dawned on her exactly what I was saying. "The inner ring is unbroken too! It is a miracle. I have witnessed the impossible; mon Dieu!"

We then sat in the centre circle to meditate and feel the energy. I made several rough sketches of the details and pattern's design. Satisfied that we had recorded enough data we both lay back in the crop circle to look at the sky. It had the same feel of peace and healing that we had experienced at Patay near Orleans. This experience was something totally new for us and we both tried to record every detail in our memory banks.

After an hour or so it was approaching two o'clock and time to head back to the office in the centre of Lille. Reluctantly we had a last walk through and around the circle and then headed for the car.

Once back in the office Lily shared all of her collected data with me and I put duplicate copies on my laptop and desk PC so I could continue to analyse the data freely.

"What do you think about sending the data to the crop circle connector; do you think they would be interested? I'm sure Jean won't mind?" Lily said enthusiastically as the fires of youth burnt brightly within her; the spirit of the chase was upon her and she was in full flight. The circle had energised her soul!

"Well we had better check with him as he may want to run the story as an exclusive?" I always erred on the side of caution as the paper did pick up the cheque for all of this.

We ran the story by Jean and showed him the photographic evidence. He was sceptical about the phenomenon which was something totally new to France but he could see no reason why we shouldn't share the information on a larger scale and so gave us the go ahead provided we had an article written by Monday.

I made a few phone calls and managed to track Monsieur Larché down once he was home from work. Lily e-mailed the best of her photographs to Mark Fussell and Stuart Dike of the crop circle connector along with a short report on the two circles we had visited, including their dimensions.

It was now early evening and I suggested to Lily that we go eat at my favourite restaurant unless she had other plans, also that there was a Saturday night gathering of my teacher friends at Vincent Callens' house in La Madeleine. Both invites were taken up enthusiastically by Lily so we closed down our work stations and gathered up our belongings; then we left the office for the weekend.

The local crop circle report would fill in the regular article slot after the story of our Orleans trip so we had more than covered the next couple of issues of the paper. We strolled towards the Opera house and turned right into the Rue Faidherbe that led to the main station and the metro terminal. The restaurant Les Charlottes en Ville lay on the left and I explained to Lily that I was a regular there as the food was excellent and the atmosphere cosy, plus it was convenient for the metro.

I was in the mood for another celebration to mark the appearance of our own crop circle in Lille; I somehow felt it was a personal gift from beyond to mark our journey of discovery. Who or whatever had made it was in tune with our minds and seemed to appreciate our contribution to history via Jehanne d'Arc. Lily ordered our now Kir Royale aperitif and we sat discussing the week's events and then our personal lives and histories.

Both of us were more than content just to enjoy the moment and watch the world go by after such a hectic week of adventure. I learnt that Lily's father had lived in Lille and that her mother was a concert pianist of some note. When she was a young teenager Lily had moved away with them to live in the mountains close to the Swiss border. She was the oldest of three; had a younger sister Clara; a younger brother Darius and they all loved their beautiful Bouvier Bernois mountain dogs. I was surprised to find that she had spent a year attending a famous English preparatory school in Broadstairs on the southeast coast, when only 10 years of age and that she had returned there as a gap student for another year before attending Lille University.

I reciprocated with some of my life's adventures and managed to drag up several old funny stories to make her laugh. In the course of conversation I began to realise that what looked random in my life had a pattern and that it was no coincidence that she should walk into my office that fateful day just a few short weeks ago.

The meal was exquisite and after settling the bill, I escorted my Fleur d'Lily home safely.

"A bientôt, mon chevalier noir," Lily said as I left her at the door of her apartment. The simple phrase echoed in my head as I walked the streets towards Place Alexander Dumas and home.

Next morning, I started work at home on the Lille crop circle diagram following what I had learnt earlier from Lily. I made several accurate drawings and pinned them to my notice boards in both the study and in the kitchen. There was something compelling about the design and dimensions of the circle, it spoke to my subconscious direct and I could not help staring at them for long periods of time. I knew the design was familiar, so familiar yet I could not consciously recognise the encoded message.

In frustration I texted Lily, she responded in an upbeat manner and said that she had already decoded the design and that it would be good for my soul if I tried to puzzle it out myself! Then she texted me 5 minutes later with the message that she would reveal the answer at the party tonight. After another 5 minutes she texted me;

This is what you require (33.85:30):10:(5.64:5):3.09 metres
Go figure???! LOL =:^D XXX

Now I could analyse my sketches properly so I set about re-drawing them precisely using my old geometry equipment and lots of sharp pencils. Within an hour I had the answer; I scanned them into my home computer and printed off lots of copies. Then I set about my geometric dissection of the harmonic proportions in the same way Lily had demonstrated with her circle analysis. I could see immediately that the 4 satellite circles contained hidden pentagrams with respect to their radii ratios of 1:30917 and 5 connected straight lines drawn tangent to their centre circles. I then tried to find other patterns:

Outer rim (33.85:30) = 30/33.85 = 0.8862629 = Squaring the circle – solution; when a square is constructed tangent to the inner circle of the rim, it precisely squares the outer circle such that the square's perimeter is exactly the same distance as the circumference of the outer circle.

Using my calculator I realised that the exact diameter of the outer rim circle must have been 33.851372 metres which would give the precise ratio necessary to give an exact ratio of 0.886227 – The inaccuracy I felt sure lay with our measurement and not the circle makers. I sat and stared at my proof for an hour, continuously checking and re-checking my drawings and calculation; it was staggering!

Squaring the circle was the old Greek conundrum of reconciling Heaven and Earth; Heaven the circle with Earth the square, such that both had the exact same dimension of circumference and perimeter. It was the same message as Patay the reconciling of the invisible Spirit with the material plane of existence; invisible with the visible.

I then moved on to the centre standing ring:

Centre standing ring (5.64:5) = 0.8865248 = Squaring the circle – solution; when a square is constructed tangent to the inner circumference of the standing crop, it precisely squares the outer circumference of the standing crop such that the square's perimeter is exactly the same distance as the outer circumference of the standing crop. This would be precisely correct it the true measurement were 5.6418953

They were identical! The outer rim and the inner circle of standing crop where precisely the same geometry; both squaring the circle.

My mind was totally blown by the sheer devastatingly accurate geometry being displayed in of all things a wheat field just outside of Lille. I reviewed all of Lily's photographs as a slide show and just gazed in wonder at the mind that had created this elegant miracle.

I grounded myself by doing household chores and then taking a shower. I was still mesmerised by the precision and detail of what I had witnessed. I was sure that I had missed an obvious connection that my subconscious was screaming out but I couldn't see the wood for the trees. I would have to wait for Lily's solution that evening to fill the gaps; perhaps she had decoded the obvious? I found myself drawn again to the crop circle connector on the internet as I had a spare hour to kill before meeting Lily. The hypnotic effect of the myriad of designs that had occurred in June and July struck a chord with my inner self as I now understood the geometric perfection being displayed. I noticed that the very next weekend there was the Crop Circle Summer Lectures in Devizes, Wiltshire, England. I contacted the organisers Karen and Steve Alexander by e-mail to enquire if tickets were still available? I intuitively knew it was the right thing to do as we needed to plunge into the heart of the phenomenon in order to understand it more fully.

I texted Jean to tentatively suggest that this was a worthwhile line of enquiry and that we might need the end of the week off plus the Monday following. His answer came back pretty quick and emphatically stated that we could go but would have to fund the trip ourselves as it wasn't directly related to our series of articles or in France!

Happy with his answer I decided to wait for an e-mail reply from Karen Alexander before telling Lily. Evening was fast approaching and made ready to leave for the party. Lily was expecting to meet me at Vincent's house in La Madeleine as it was equidistant from our addresses.

It was a pleasant summer's evening as I walked over the bridge that spans the auto route from Lille centre to Marcq-en-Baroeul. I reached Vincent's house in Rue Jean Mermoz at 18:45hrs ahead of time. Richard and Bruno were already there along with Heidi and her best friend Déborah the new mathematics teacher from Vincent's school, École Charles Péguy. Bruno was interested to know what adventures I had been on that week. So I drew a quick verbal sketch of our trip to Orleans as I enjoyed an Absinthe and iced water aperitif. Déborah was particularly interested in the decoded geometric solution to the crop circle at Patay, but our conversation was cut short by the arrival of several other guests which broadened the conversation. We seemed to hit it off immediately and I felt strangely comfortable in her company. It was as if we had known each other forever. There was also something very familiar about Déborah's face and her empathy for the subject. I could feel my subconscious was tugging at its lead but my conscious mind had no idea what the connection was at this point in present time.

Then the bell rang and I answered it being the nearest to the front door. There stood Lily in her little black dress with a mulberry coloured tailored jacket and matching Dior handbag, she looked absolutely stunning. In her other hand she clutched a bottle of Pouilly Fumé.

"I thought they might like a taste of the Loire!"

"You are a treasure Lily come on in and meet the gang." She gave me the bottle to hold and then unbuttoned her jacket. I took it carefully and hung it up on the hooks by the front door, "You have exquisite taste my Fleur d'Lily such good tailoring and colour choice!"

She smiled, "*Merci, Monsieur.*" I then escorted her through the main living room and into the kitchen. There I introduced Lily to Vincent who was busy selecting some more cheese from the fridge for the guests in the garden. Vincent owned a 1900s Lille town house with a long narrow garden, he had sensitively restored it over the years and it retained many of the elegant original features. The guests sat and mingled outside as it was such a nice evening. I introduced Lily to them and she spent the first part of the evening mixing and making friends. Many asked about our latest articles as they had read them in the paper.

As the sun set Lily came over to me and with a cheeky grin she enquired, "Did you decoded the pattern hidden in the circle?" She was fishing for clues as to how far I had got with the problem.

"I could see clearly that it was 4 symmetry and that there were pentagrams in the 4 large satellite circles, then I discovered the squaring the circle twice which blew my fuses. That was as far as I could get before I had to get ready to come out. I know there is more my subconscious is screaming in my ear but I just can't see it! What did you find?"

"Well done you did well and you are going to like this a lot! It encodes the sacred cross of the Black Brethren!"

"No, are you sure? You must be joking, it can't possibly…"

"But is does, I am 100% sure and here is my proof." Lily reached into her Dior handbag and withdrew a crisply folded piece of white paper. "Go ahead and open it!"

I took the paper from Lily and slowly unfolded it. Even though I was prepared for the result it still gave me goose bumps when I looked at the design. Sure enough the cross was there!

"The trick is to draw diagonal lines at a tangent to the 4 satellite circles; they delineate the cross precisely and in the correct proportions. The clever bit is that the width of the outer rim encodes the value of Phi Φ 1.6180339 and the centre standing circle gives a square as you have found. It is without doubt a neat and geometrically eloquent solution to the illuminated cross of the Black Brethren." Lily looked very pleased with herself.

"It is as though the circle makers have read our minds. I could never have come up with such a wonderful solution!"

As if just on cue my phone vibrated indicating the arrival of an e-mail. It was Karen Alexander saying that they had 5 spare tickets left due to cancellations. "It's the number 5 again! Meant to be; say how would you like to spend next weekend in England?"

"When, where, what, why, how?" Was all Lily could splutter. "Leave Thursday, come back Monday, Devizes in Wiltshire, England, a crop circle conference, for our research, by car and tunnel sous la Manche!" I was pretty sure that I had answered all of her questions succinctly.

"Formidable, let's do it!" Lily was as ever decisive and positive.

"Right, that's settled, I'll book it in the morning..."

✠

Chapter 17

Adam's Grave

The last week of July started well. We were both able to catch up on our work in the office and to cover some local stories around Lille. Lily and I spent the evenings researching our next target Reims and also the mysterious world of crop circles.

The Crop Circle Connector proved a great source of knowledge in this area and I found myself subscribing for the season so that I could look at the past season archives. Lily spent a lot of her time looking at Karen and Steve Alexander's Temporary Temples website and again trawling through the archive photographs of years gone by.

I had decided to drive to Wiltshire in England as that would give us the flexibility to move around once we were on site. Devizes proved to be fully booked for accommodation during the conference but I was able to secure a reservation at the Castle and Ball hotel in Marlborough some 20 kilometres away. The upper class market town looked typically English and centred on the main high street with a famous public school at one end and the majority of town housing at the other. We chose to stay three nights; from Friday into Monday morning.

The journey would be fairly quick as I decided to take the Eurotunnel from Calais to Folkestone in order to minimize the Channel crossing time. Friday dawned early and I drove my black Renault Laguna around to Lily's apartment. Even though it was 04:30hrs Lily was up, dressed and ready; she had decided that she would be able to nap in the car on the way so was content just to fall out of bed with her small suitcase and into the nice warm car.

The sense of adventure and expectation hit us as we left Lille on the autoroute for Dunkirk. Within the hour we were in Calais on the final leg of the journey and gliding into the Eurotunnel terminal at Sangatte. The majestic swans and herons bought the landscape alive in the early morning mist as we drove over the raised viaduct to the ticket control area.

I presented my e-reservation print out at the check in desk and we found that we had enough time to stop off at the terminal for a quick coffee before our 06:45hrs Shuttle. I changed some Euros into Pounds Sterling whilst Lily looked in the perfumery. Then we purchased our coffee and croissants at the café near the entrance of the building on our way back to the car.

Within five minutes we had cleared UK border controls and were sat waiting to be loaded at the embarkation point. The light for our row turned green and I followed the car in front as it snaked its way along and down the ramp onto the platform beside the Shuttle. Dousing my headlights I followed the instructions of the loading operative and pulled left onto the waiting train. Then I drove silently along through the aluminium coaches to our space.

The lady in a Eurotunnel day glow safety jacket clutched her two way radio and waved us into place. "Handbrake on, open your windows and sun roof please; have a pleasant journey." She said in a perfunctory way as she smiled and then moved to the next vehicle in line.

I complied with her request whilst Lily read the overhead illuminated tickertape sign to me in English. Having finished our coffee as the Shuttle silently left the platform we both flipped our seat backs into a 30° position and lay back for a short doze.

Forty short minutes later we pulled out of the tunnel as Folkestone came into view through the small carriage side windows. The Shuttle glided to a halt and we finally drove onto English soil. Lily noticed the white horse on the hillside overlooking the town and pointed it out to me.

"I think you'll be seeing a lot more of those where we are going, they are very much a part of the landscape of southern England and Wiltshire."

"Didn't Jehanne ride a white horse?"

"Yes she did, that's because she heralded the downfall of the English and symbolically heralds in medieval days always rode white horses to gain attention; later on trumpeters would ride white horses for the same reason. These are much older Saxon and Celtic horses that are carved into the sides of hills. The turf is cut away and the white chalk exposed to complete the art form!"

I explained at length that the white horse was an ancient symbol of the Celtic Iceni tribe in Norfolk and also of the Anglo-Saxon people of Southern England.

"Ah yes, The Vale of Pewsey has a famous Alton Barnes white horse carved into the side of Milk Hill near Adam's Grave. I have seen it on the web and Google Earth." Lily spoke with interest and authority, I was impressed, she had obviously done her homework.

She continued, "The East field at Alton Barnes seems to be a major site for crop circles through the years. It sits just below Adam's grave on Walker's Hill.

The name Adam's grave rang a bell with me. "That is right the Anglo-Saxon chronicle mentions that there was a great battle there in 592AD. The local King Ceawlin had his royal hall there; Tolkien used the imagery for Théoden's hall and the Riders of Rôhan in his books."

"I love those Lord of the Rings films!" Lily exclaimed as she started to find some modern day relevance in my history lesson.

By 07:30hrs French time we were on the M20 and heading towards Maidstone the administration capital of Kent County, England. I asked Lily to turn the car clock back an hour to show UK time and we settled down for the 3 hour drive to Wiltshire.

The roads were busy with commuter traffic especially as we pulled onto the M25 from the M26 link. I decided not to take a coffee break at the services as I could see the traffic building up so we pushed on around the M25 to the M3. We stopped at the Welcome Break Fleet services once we had cleared the rush hour traffic. The English school holidays had just started a few days earlier so the major rush for the West Country had already started.

By 10:00hrs UK time we were driving down the long hill to the Amesbury roundabout on the A303.

"Can we go and look at Stonehenge?" Lily said excitedly.

"Yes, why not it is very much part of the ancient landscape and has been the site of several crop formations in the past; especially the Julia set mathematical fractal in 1996."

"Ah, I saw that it was amazing. I read the story on the crop circle connector!" I realised then that Lily had obviously succumbed to the magic of the circles and subscribed also. I was impressed again at her thorough research.

"The story goes that the formation appeared in daylight; a commercial pilot flew his small plane over the field at four thirty in the afternoon and saw nothing, then when he flew back at just after five it was there; a large precise mathematical fractal lay in the crop just south of Stonehenge the other side of the 303! I think it was just over there," Lily pointed just front and to the left of the Stonehenge turn off junction whilst I waited for a gap in the traffic.

As we chatted a break in the traffic occurred so I pulled off of the A303 towards the famous megalithic circle of stones that are some 3500 years old. We both experienced a strange sense of being *home* as we drove passed the monument and then pulled into the car park.

Leaving the car we walked to the ticket office and purchased two admission tickets then went through the turnstile, turned right at the gift shop and walked through the underground tunnel, then up the long ramp onto the other side of the road.

The sense of history hit us as we walked out into the sunlight and up to the ring. The black crows welcomed us with their throaty chatter as they fluttered and hopped from stone to stone.

"I've been here before!" Lily said breaking the silence.

"When; as a little girl?" I said as I gazed at the magnificent megaliths.

"No it was thousands of years ago and again in many lives since."

I remained silent as I too could identify with that feeling of returning. We walked anticlockwise around the outer ring in silence, passed the Heel stone and returned to the start position. After that we chose to sit and contemplate the stones in our own personal space for some 30 minutes. All sorts of memories crowded into my head as my mind spewed forth the triggered contents from its subconscious store. Rituals, robes and archaic people flooded my vision; I knew for sure then that I too had been here before; many times. I had come home.

The cloudy sky obscured the sun but I could tell that it was fast approaching midday so I decided to go and find Lily. She was sat on the grass at the apex of the inner horseshoe silently meditating.

"Without blinking or moving as I approached she said, "I was a priestess of the stones!"

I understood immediately, she had been a priestess many times in many lives and in many parts of the world; Neolithic England, Ancient Greece, Ancient Rome, Anglo-Saxon England, Viking Norway and Iceland; finally Luxembourg in medieval Europe. Her list was my list. I could see myself with her many times and in many rôles; always together, always on a mission, always part of the same team. The words - *soul clan* – bubbled to the surface of my consciousness and at last I understood intuitively the truth of its deep meaning.

"It's time to visit the Barge Inn for lunch my Fleur d'Lily!" I touched her on the shoulder and an incredible feeling of electricity flowed through me. It seemed to emanate from the living stones themselves, flow through Lily and enter my body where it connected with my soul; very powerful, very deep, very ancient.

We walked back to the car linked arm in arm and headed back the way we had come to the Amesbury roundabout.

Taking the first left we drove passed the army camp at Bulford and then the tank training grounds with their yellow warning signs marking the road crossing points. Twenty minutes later we were in Upavon and heading for the Vale of Pewsey. The sense of coming home was growing stronger every minute as the magical landscape wove its spell.

At the Woodbridge roundabout, I intuitively carried straight on ignoring the sign for Pewsey to the right. I knew that an inner auto pilot was navigating my way directly from my subconscious, so I just gave in to it.

The car snaked effortlessly through the twisty narrow lanes as it passed through several hamlets; it too seemed to have a mind of its own.

At last we drove over a humped back bridge that crossed a main railways line. Five minutes later we wound our way into the small village of Honey Street within sight of the Alton Barnes white horse. I turned left at the timber mill just before the canal bridge and glided silently along the single track road that led to the hidden Barge Inn. Several houses backed onto the narrow lane which gave it the feel of private property but I knew that the inn lay just around the corner.

I parked the car and we clambered out of the vehicle. The camp site was half full and our eyes were immediately caught by a magnificent Native American tepee that sported a multitude of rainbow coloured streamers from the tops of its poles.

As we walked up the gentle slope to the main door of the public house we saw several barges sat lazily on the canal; children, dogs and ducks all mingled effortlessly around them in idyllic harmony.

People sat at wooden trestle tables enjoying the weather, the English flat beer and lunch. The scene was very different from France but it did have a certain Anglo-Saxon charm about it.

We sat at one of the tables next to some croppies. Lily wanted *fish and chips* as it was Friday and we were in England; the land of clouds as she called it! I decided to have the same plus a pint of what the English call *real ale*. Lily wasn't sure about my drink choice but eventually I persuaded her to try a half of the quintessentially English drink.

"It's similar to Belgian beer; you'll like it!" I said enthusiastically. Lily made a face as she could see that I was joking, but she decided to give it a go. I then left her chatting to the croppies who all seemed very friendly whilst I went inside to order.

Whilst waiting for the drinks I chanced to wander around the bar and into the back room where I stood reading the notice board for several minutes. I knew from the internet that the famous East field had been visited with a deceptively simple looking formation on Bastille Day – July the 14th. I hadn't thought much of it but now I could see the map position and the amazing photographs of the complex woven floor pattern which drew me like a magnet. I decided to tell Lily that we should pay it a visit. Just then the barman called me as the fish and chips were ready so I paid and carried the tray back outside.

I found Lily deep in conversation with the croppies so I asked them what they thought of crop circles? The answers varied from the esoteric to the, *it's all pensioners and plankers!* One of the croppies explained the *double entende* associated with the word *plankers* which made me laugh and caused Lily to blush.

They explained enthusiastically that in the late 80s early 90s the government had used two old age pensioners called Doug and

Dave to quieten the hysteria associated with the massive crop formation that were appearing. They claimed in the newspapers to have made all the circles and patterns with nothing more than a wooden board and some string. Dave had worked for the Ministry of Defence and had since died and Doug was now very ancient; yet still the formations came and in ever increasing complexity.

I laughed and said, "His ghost must have been making circles in France recently then!"

The group became interested in our adventures and listened carefully as Lily unfolded the story of the crop circles at Orleans and Lille. I was amazed at the high level of emotion and passion displayed by the normally reserved English, plus several Dutch and a German couple when the subject of crop circles was raised. They said they were regarded as anything but normal and that the majority of the people wandered around close minded, like mental zombies; all you needed was a spark of intelligence and an open mind.

They also mentioned that the formations were increasing in complexity in tune with the Mayan 2012 end of time. I found myself thinking; perhaps that was something to do with our experiences which seemed to be accelerating and increasing in complexity too?

After lunch we said our goodbyes to the several people we had been talking to. I was gratified to learn that at least two of the couples were attending the conference in Devizes over the weekend.

Driving back out through the wood yard we turned left over the small brick bridge and carried on along the road past the Post Office. Then straight on, we continued over the junction that goes left to Stanton St. Bernard and right to Pewsey. The incline of the road increased considerably as we climbed and skirted right around the base of Walkers Hill. Then cresting the hill we followed the road until we reached the Knap Hill car park. I turned right onto the rough gravel surface and parked the car facing towards Adam's Grave.

We disembarked, stretched our legs and gathered our equipment together. A short walk over some rough grass with multiple tyre tracks took us to the base of Golden Ball hill with its spectacular view over the East field.

We stood at the gate with Woodborough hill in the far distance across the wide Vale of Pewsey. Away to our right Adam's Grave rose up majestically above us just the other side of the main road. I pointed it out to Lily and said that it was also known as Woden's barrow which betrayed its more recent Saxon origin. The whole place felt somehow magical and alive with ancient energies.

Just then a shock of blonde hair came into view below us, followed by a man wearing a beret. I thought that unusual as the English were not known for wearing that very distinctive piece of head gear. May be they are French or Scottish I thought to myself as they came ever closer? The lady owner of blonde hair was very striking. She wore dark sunglasses and led the way with a determined stride up the narrow track towards us. As she neared our position I could see her fine aristocratic high cheek bones and lithe athletic body more clearly. She looked almost Elven in her ethereal beauty yet she had a strong determined warrior countenance. In her hand she carried a camera and on her back a knap sack very much like Lily's.

We hadn't long to wait as they neared our observation position rapidly. The lady avoided my glance and busied herself with unlatching the gate whilst her companion turned to observe the formation in the East field below. My curiosity peaked when I saw that his beret sported a shiny silver sheriff's badge with a single 5 pointed star. I took it as mark of coincidence, the pentagram and the number 5 just hit me; so I spoke to him. "Afternoon, have you been to visit the crop circle?"

The lady looked directly at me and smiled, there was something very familiar about her. Then her companion answered my question. "Yes, it's very interesting, deceptively simple in its design just a single circle with a double *arc* but the floor pattern is absolutely incredible, such a complex weave, like woven fabric."

The word *arc* leapt out at me as yet another coincidence and as such it hit my subconscious with a resonant jolt.

"That sound astonishing, we shall go and have a look!" I then asked for directions and if there were any hazards to look out for apart for the cows. The aristocratic lady continued to gaze at me from behind her dark sunglasses; I could feel her high vibrationary frequency resonate with mine, it seemed to trigger my subconscious into action which was trying desperately to attract my conscious attention. I noticed then that her companion had bought his beret in Paris as it had the date 1998 and the French rugby logo at the back.

"Excuse me monsieur, are you French?" I asked politely, "you seem to be wearing a rugby supporter's beret!"

"No, I'm from Gloucester actually. I bought it on a trip over there at an international match in the Stade de France 11 years ago."

I had some difficulty understanding his accent but I was amazed at how friendly he was towards me. Again I had the distinct feeling that I knew him from somewhere.

He turned towards Lily and exclaimed, "Snap! You're dressed the same as Roselinde." The aristocratic lady went slightly pink and blushed behind her sunglasses but then managed to force a smile.

Lily looked surprised at the sudden attention paid to her, "Yes, I suppose I am!" she replied looking at the aristocratic lady.

"Well it's been very nice meeting you; enjoy the circle we must be going now!" Roselinde gave her companion an icy glance as she obviously felt that her name was not public property and with that started to walk towards the car park.

After some seconds the man said the same and disappeared into the distance to catch the lady up. I stood watching them for some time and at one point I felt sure that the lady turned her head towards me and smiled.

Lily and I then went through the gate and descended down the single track to the valley floor. We had to negotiate a few thistles but managed without too much problem to avoid painful injuries.

I had counted the number of tramlines over on the way down so I knew how to access the formation cleanly. It was just as well because once level with the crop of wheat I had no reference point to guide me.

Together we walked along the correct tramline which took us directly to the formation. We were both extremely careful not to damage the wheat but I found myself gently brushing the seed heads with my fingers as I walked which reinforced the moment for me with touch. After 10 minutes we stood on the edge of the formation, it was magnificent the whole circle was woven with sheaves of wheat plaited at right angles to one another.

"Incredible, it is so beautiful, what could have done this?" Lily was totally awe struck by the size and complexity of the formation.

"I have simply no idea my Fleur d'Lily, it is quite wonderful!"

Then we both stepped into the circle to join several others who were engaged in meditating, observing or just chatting within its circumference.

I understood now why Karen and Steve Alexander had called their website Temporary Temples, for we were definitely stood in a sacred space. Lily photographed the lay and chatted to the other people in the circle. I was content to investigate the stalks for elongated growth and exploded nodes. Finally I decided to chat to the same croppies as Lily.

After an hour we made our way back up the single track to the car park. We stopped to chat to a delightfully feisty Dutch lady called Janet Ossebaard and her friend Andreas Müller. It turned out coincidentally that she was not just a croppie but a famous crop circle author and had given many talks on the subject. I instinctively found myself using my Vlaams and again felt a deep past connection with her.

"So, that was the famous East field, well I'm not disappointed it was astonishing!" Lily sat back in her car seat and reviewed the photographs she had taken on her digital camera. "The Devil is in the detail; I wonder how many people actually take a really close look at this phenomenon before they dismiss it out of hand?"

"Not many, most just have such closed minds; by any stretch of the imagination we have just witnessed a miracle! I replied earnestly. "It's our job to rattle their paradigm cages!"

She smiled and then put her camera on the back seat. Starting the car I reversed and pulled onto the main road, heading towards Lockeridge and the A4. The short drive to Marlborough took no more than 20 minutes and we were soon outside the front door of the Castle and Ball Hotel in the middle of the high street.

It was now 17:00hrs as we checked in at the reception desk in the quaint hotel. By 18:00hrs we were ensconced in our rooms and ready to go out on the town. I said that I would meet Lily in the bar and that we would have an aperitif before finding a restaurant. The barman recommended eating at Godot's Bar Brasserie in Kingsbury Street which he said was also good for several other restaurants, so I asked him for directions.

Lily joined us and we chatted to the barman for some time as he was so convivial. We left the hotel at around 19:00hrs and strolled to Kingsbury Street. Reading the menus of the various restaurants we decided that the cuisine was good but that it wasn't really for us.

Suddenly Lily had a flash of inspiration, "Hey, Yann why don't we go back to the Barge Inn?"

In exact synchronicity I had had the same idea; it was if we had both received a subconscious text message at the exact same time! I intuitively felt that it was right so agreed with Lily immediately. We made our way back to the high street and jumped into my black Renault. Soon we were heading back out of Marlborough in the direction of Silbury Hill and Avebury.

After 5 minutes I found the turning off to the left for Lockeridge and we were soon driving through the small village towards Alton Barnes. The sky was clear and still light as the hour difference with France had kicked in. We soon passed the Knap Hill car park and skirted once again around the base of Adam's grave. The sight of the hill looming over us bought back déjà vu sensations as we wound down into the Vale of Pewsey.

I interrupted Lily's conversation by suddenly blurting out the thoughts that had flashed into my head, "They had a palisade across the road back there and a big gate. The Saxon Royal Hall was built on Adam's grave which was called Woden's barrow back then in 592AD. I remember the whole area was fortified and laid out to guard the fertile wooded valley below. There was a surprise attack and I lost my left eye to a spear thrust as I fought in the shield wall. It was a terrible defeat."

"I know I was there! I saw it happen! It was a bloody day." Lily interjected. "We lived here for some 20 years before that fateful day."

Her comment seemed perfectly normal to me now that my consciousness had expanded to accommodate the realisation that we had been together in many many lives.

We were soon driving through Honey Street and over the small brick bridge that spans the canal. I turned right into the timber yard and carried on past the houses to the Barge Inn.

The atmosphere was alive with people enjoying the summer evening underneath the gaze of the white horse in the distance. I parked the car and we walked to the main entrance of the pub. The bar was busy but they were still serving food so we squeezed in at one of the tables.

Without looking in my direction a distinctively feminine aristocratic voice said, "I know you?"

I suddenly realised that I was at the same table as the lady Roselinde whom I had met that very afternoon! The gentleman with the beret sat opposite her and was engaged in conversation with several female members of her entourage.

"This is a fine coincidence, how did you recognise me?" I said thinking of the unlikely probability of meeting the same two people twice in one day.

"Yes, a splendid coincidence but of course there is no such thing it is exactly how the universe works as everything is connected. Plus you have a very distinctive voice."

"That's right Dad!" The man with the beret joined in with the observation.

"Dad?" I repeated the strange phrase which I found both endearing and disturbing!

"I'm Billy the Kid and this is her Royal Roselindness, together with Helena, Patsi, Jane and Kristina. I call them the Witches of East field!" They obviously all knew each other very well as they were not at all perturbed by his quirky introduction!

I smiled and introduced our party. "This is Lily and I am Yann from Lille in France; pleased to meet you."

They seemed pleased to see us and we joined in effortlessly with the party as they were about to order their meals. Our food arrived after several minutes and we were able to join in with our new found croppie friends. It all seemed so natural and as though we had known each other before. Billy talked in depth on Indian philosophy and the nature of the holographic illusion that we call everyday reality. The "witches" joined in with very profound points of view and I was immediately struck by the richness of this new strange world that I found myself in.

Helena was extremely forthright and regaled the assembled group with tales of her trips to India. I soon found myself answering all sorts of enquiries about myself and my life in Lille. The main question seemed to be why there was a distinct lack of crop circles in France? Lily and I were delighted to advise them that the situation had now been remedied with the advent of crop circles appearing both at Orleans and Lille.

I learnt that Patsi was an art teacher when I complimented her on her colourful Native American inspired outfit. "Is the tepee yours?" I asked.

"No, mine is less grand, the group that owns the large tepee are all from North Wales. They are having a drumming ceremony tonight as it is a full Moon. You are very welcome to stay and join in, everybody is invited!"

I noticed that Roselinde was quietly taking in the whole scene, then she spoke softly, "Have we met before? I feel that I know you from somewhere? I thought that this morning."

"I don't think so, but you do look very familiar." I could feel my subconscious tugging at my conscious mind but I failed dismally to grasp the connection.

The moment passed and Lily engaged the group in conversation about crop circles asking each for their impressions and experiences. The stories were very illuminating and strayed into many areas of study from the nature of consciousness to UFOs.

I offered to stand a round of drinks and asked everybody for their preference. At the bar I suddenly changed my mind and ordered two bottles of chilled champagne and 8 glasses. It felt like a celebration so I thought I would act on my intuition and go with the cosmic flow of the universe.

I carefully carried the tray with the bottle and glasses back to the table in the corner.

"Ladies and gentleman, in order to celebrate our new friendship, I hope you will indulge with me in one of the finer inventions to come out of France!"

Everybody applauded and then Roselinde turned to me and said, "I adore champagne; how did you know it is my favourite drink?"

"I don't know? I just knew!" The stark simplicity of my answer shocked me. It was direct and honest with no attempt to gild the lily or qualify the statement. Looking at Lily I realised the pun and continued, "My answer is very short as I have made no attempt to, as you say, *gild the lily* and as you can see our Fleur d'Lily certainly needs no gilding, for she like you, is perfect the way she is, no!" Roselinde blushed as I continued, "Your royal spirit burns so brightly my lady that you cannot hide it from me behind those dark glasses; santé!"

The table went suddenly quiet as Billy, Helena, Patsi, Jane and Kristina felt the electricity that crackled between us. Roselinde looked down, then smiled, raised her head towards me and lifted her dark von Zipper sunglasses. It was the very same action that a medieval knight would have used to raise their visor in order to see clearly during a joust.

At last I saw directly into her soul through those beautiful clear sea grey eyes that finally held my gaze. I knew then in an instant exactly who this mysterious aristocratic lady was for my soul resonated in recognition of her *sang royale* blood; she was a Dragon princess of the highest echelon. I resisted the strange urge to bow and drop down onto one knee and busied myself with pouring the champagne. I popped the cork which broke the silence and then carefully poured the 8 large glasses which drained the bottles perfectly.

Sitting back down I passed the glasses around the table leaving Billy and myself to last. Helena called for a toast so thinking quickly on the spot I found myself looking at Roselinde and saying, "To this moment and the moment yet to come!" Everybody repeated the toast and took a sip of the clear effervescent nectar.

"Very good Dad, a declarative statement based on the eternal now!" Billy adjusted his beret and joined in with his own interpretation of my toast. "Enjoy the now, for there is only the NOW!"

Roselinde contemplated Billy's words looked at me and added, "This is just such a moment; you have captured its essence perfectly my chevalier noir!"

The words came so naturally from her lips that I failed to notice immediately what my lady Roselinde had said; then it hit me like a thunder clap! "Say that again..."

She repeated it with a quizzical expression and with some hesitation as she suddenly became extremely self-conscious. I smiled to reassure her. Then I asked, "Why did you say chevalier noir?

"I don't know? I just knew; it seemed to be the right thing to say!" Roselinde smiled, replaced her sunglasses and took a sip from her champagne glass.

Our *moment* over I was suddenly disturbed by the sound of Native American drumming coming from outside in the camping field; the drumming ceremony had started perfectly on cue. Helena and Patsi finished off their drinks and excused themselves as they were eager to leave the table to join in the ceremony. "Bearcloud is coming!" Helena said enthusiastically above the noise and the chatter in the bar. "We must go and greet him!"

I stood up with Billy and allowed the ladies to pass. Then Lily decided to go with Jane and Kristina just after the others as their curiosity was now getting the better of them.

"Time for another pint, Dad!" Billy raised his empty glass as a gesture and went to the bar. I was a little nonplussed but assumed that it was a compliment to be called, Dad; by Billy the Kid no less!

"Merci, mon ami but I have had sufficient English beer for one day!" I responded honestly as I patted my abdomen.

I was suddenly alone with Roselinde at the table. I decided to speak my mind, "I have never known you, yet I know you; does that make sense?" I spoke reflectively as I played with my empty glass somewhat nervously.

Roselinde touched my hand which sent an instant electric shock surging through my central nervous system. "I feel the same. I know there is a deep connection. I can feel it. I felt that bond between us when we met on Knap Hill briefly this afternoon but I wasn't sure. Could it be Anglo-Saxon?"

I listened to her soft words that were spoken with precise diction and sensitivity.

"What makes you say that?" I said in response to her candid disclosure.

"My name is Roselinde Saxmund which I have always felt is a little more than a passing coincidence."

"Well, Roselinde Saxmund, I am delighted to make your acquaintance. We shall have to delve a little further into this affair. My name is Yann Baillieu and I write for La Voix du Nord the local paper in Lille, France but for now I think we should go and enjoy the drumming."

Her radiant smile told me that I had said exactly the right thing so with that we left by the back door that led out onto the canal tow path.

The full Moon was rising over the beautiful Barge Inn to our left as I helped Roselinde down the bank and onto the level surface of the camping field. We joined the others sat cross legged on blankets around the fire in front of the tepee. The drums were beating and Bearcloud chanted a haunting Lakota refrain entitled *Return of the Eagles.*

I realised then that this was *the perfect moment to come* that I had toasted in the pub not an hour ago.

The drumming ceremony ended at 01:00hrs and I walked Roselinde back to her camper van in the corner of the field. We swapped mobile phone numbers and agreed to meet up at the conference in the morning.

I then returned to the fire and sat next to Lily who was busy talking to Billy as they fire gazed under the full Moon.

"I think it's time to go home my, Fleur d'Lily?" I whispered gently. Billy said his goodbyes and gave me a hug which came from the heart. Lily and I made our way to the car which started first time. I drove along the single track road and back through the timber yard. At the road I turned left over the bridge and continued through the village and up to Adam's grave. As we crested the hill I felt an urge to stop at Knap Hill car park for one last look.

We sat for a few minutes and watched the valley below as it slumbered quietly under the magical full Moon. The whole scene was amazingly beautiful bathed in soft moonlight and I thought of the Saxon connection with Ceawlin and the royal hall. Perhaps Roselinde was right; perhaps there was a deep connection with this mystic landscape and the Anglo-Saxon past of 592AD.

I certainly felt strangely very at home here, in the land of clouds and so did Lily. It was now nearly 02:00hrs so reluctantly I swung the car around in the car park and we headed down the road to Lockeridge and our hotel bed beyond.

Chapter 18

Devizes

aturday dawned together with the first day of the summer crop circle lectures in Devizes, Wiltshire, England. Lily and I left Marlborough at 09:30hrs for the short 30 minute drive. The clouds rolled over the open landscape with intermittent bright bursts of sunlight and artistically cast light and shade on the surrounding ancient landscape. After 10 minutes journeying we passed Silbury Hill to the right of the A4. It triggered many Earth mother goddess images in my head and the enigmatic question; why did they build it? I knew from my own internal subconscious knowledge that the answer was simply religion. Somewhere to the right beyond lay Avebury stone circle the giant Neolithic cathedral of Northern Europe; I made a mental note to visit it as a pilgrimage before we returned to Lille on Monday night.

Next we passed the Wagon and Horses pub which looked straight out of Tolkien's *Lord of the Rings* and could have doubled for the Prancing Pony at Bree, then came the Beckhampton roundabout where we took a left towards Devizes. The whole open landscape had a magnificent feeling of space, it was much more undulating than northern France but made of the same primeval ocean floor that created the dense layers of chalk that were common to both. I was conscious that many battles had been fought on this landscape from ancient times through to the English Civil War; perhaps emotional energy was somehow tied up with the crop circles and the chalk down landscape; emotional memory had soaked into the very land and been preserved. It lay dormant just waiting for the same souls to trigger and bring forth its potent message into the present conscious mind.

Oliver's Castle, Roundway Down, Bishops Cannings the names leapt out at me as I remembered the crop circle images associated with those evocative names. The crop circle connector archive had impressed itself deeply onto my subconscious and triggered many memories of many lives. I felt at home as though I was intimately connected to the very landscape itself. I knew that it was more a case of the land owned us rather than we owned the land. I could feel the truth of the statement in my bones made of the same chalk as the land.

All too soon we entered Devizes, with its castle like army barracks on the left and County Police Headquarters on the right it was a place of power in the landscape. In total amazement I spied that their badge carried the same white cross as the Black Brethren! The only difference being that the centre was a circle instead of a square; squaring the circle I thought silently to myself and smiled. I immediately felt the restriction of modern life close in on my esoteric thought. The magic fell away as I entered the town and was replaced with a friendly openness that welcomed the visitor with warmth. I looked at Lily and could see that she was still not quite awake and fully conscious. We travelled silently as she was just content to take the surrounding vista passively into her memory.

We then headed for the centre of town, passed a duck pond and came to a roundabout. Even the concentric rings painted on the road took on the feel of a crop circle. Turning right we skirted the main town centre with its confusing one way systems, people were going about their mundane lives oblivious to the miraculous happenings in the fields that surrounded them and then we drove by the Wadworth brewery. At the junction we turned left into the market place. The car park was filling up but I managed to secure a space opposite the Bear hotel. From there it was just a short walk along to the Town Hall and the conference venue.

The doors were already open so we collected our tickets from the front desk. An attractive young girl with long blonde hair offered me a programme. She looked very like Karen Alexander so I guessed that it must be her daughter Kayleigh. We turned left into the downstairs hall to be greeted by a busy scene of chatter and excitement. To the right Steve Alexander had a large stall and was busy selling his latest photographs of the current season's crop circles, together with his year books and DVD's from past seasons. The enigmatic images and the sublime geometric messages in the crop were everywhere to be seen. It was truly a feast for the soul.

Within 5 minutes an elven haired Karen ethereally entered the room and announced that delegates should take their seats in the Assembly Room above as the lecture programme would be starting shortly. I introduced Lily and myself to Steve and chatted briefly as people started to make their way out of the room. Lily said she would go on ahead and find a couple of seats for us whilst I finished talking.

After a few minutes I wished Steve *bon chance* and headed up the plush wide staircase to the Assembly Room above. A sense of history permeated the building much as it does in a palace. All around me were portraits of past Mayors, officials and civic dignitaries from Devizes. It was a deliberate display of tangible permanence yet here we were about to discuss a transient mystery of such a miraculous and ephemeral nature that seemed so diametrically opposed to the solid reality invoked by the building; the juxtaposition was quite exquisite!

I continued through the large stately doors where I was greeted by the elegant presence of Karen, her angelic long blonde hair perfectly framing her delicate porcelain features and smiling face.

"Welcome, you must be Yann Baillieu, I recognise you from your photo on the internet."

I was slightly shocked but also pleasantly surprised; Karen had obviously looked at the La Voix du Nord website.

"Enchanté Madame Alexander, it is a pleasure to meet one so dedicated to this incredible phenomenon!"

"We are all very interested in the two recent French crop circles that have appeared. I'll introduce you to Michael Glickman later; he is just dying to know all the intricate details. Maybe you can come along to his party tonight?"

"I would be honoured to attend." I said politely, "may I bring my colleague Lily?"

"Of course you may, we would be delighted to meet her. I'll give you the address late on." Karen said in a no nonsense down to earth north-country English accent.

"Merci et bon chance!" I smiled and left her to greet more delegates who were trying to get in at the last moment.

Entering the room I looked around for Lily, she was sat near the end of a row mid-way in the auditorium, to my right. The room was now crowded and had a wonderful cosmopolitan atmosphere; I could hear many different languages and accents of English being spoken. I entered the row silently and took my seat next to Lily. I had just started to make conversation when the lady in front of me turned around and said, "I do believe, I recognise that splendid accent!"

I immediately recognised her! It was Roselinde Saxmund, sat with Helena to her left and Billy to her right.

"What a perfect coincidence!" I exclaimed.

"There is no such thing as a coincidence in the universe, it was meant to be." She replied philosophically.

"Absolutely, I can't believe that out of all the seats here, Lily has placed me right behind you!"

Lily smiled and joined in the conversation, "I had absolutely no idea it was you at all. I think it is, how you say, karma?"

"Too right, Dad, Lily's spot on!" Billy couldn't resist commenting as it appealed to his esoteric nature and interest in Indian gurus and their insightful teachings. "It's an example of the interconnectedness of all things as we navigate this holographic illusion we call reality; souls seek each other out to resolve past issues."

Roselinde smiled and generously acknowledged that Billy's insight was probably correct. At that moment Karen started to talk into her microphone and the audience hushed its conversation. She welcomed everybody and introduced the programme for the day. I was impressed at the sleek efficiency of the organisation and the professionalism she exuded.

From her outline notes the speakers seemed to be presenting many thought provoking concepts based on first hand factual observation and detailed research. It was going to be a very interesting day! Yet, as I listened I found it very hard to concentrate for I was bathed in the vibrationary frequency of Lady Roselinde's aura. There was something very royal about her that connected us together from the past.

Michael Glickman was the first speaker after the opening introductory session and delivered a tour de force of dry wit and incisive factual geometric information. The subject of crop circles was dear to his heart and I felt that he more than any other living person in all humility projected a true vision on the depth and majesty of this miraculous phenomenon.

Next up was Daniel Rozman who appeared the very living embodiment of a young Rene Descartes, that immediately drew my attention and I switched full on. His lecture was entitled,

"Some Pow'rful Hand Unseen" an enigmatic title. He began by playing a haunting refrain on a Navajo flute thereby capturing the audience and holding them spellbound. His awakening from a City commodities trader to realising his full potential as a philosopher and novelist mirrored Descartes own journey from being a Lawyer to becoming a philosopher in very precise parallel detail. His entry into the world of crop circles was facilitated by the discovery of Euler's Identity a mathematical equation linking several constants which bizarrely was the subject of a famous crop circle I had seen on the Internet. He had seen the same photograph in a national newspaper and plunged headlong without reservation into a 3 year spiritual journey of immense personal triumph. Even his initials DR reflected my observation comparison with Rene Descartes; DR I RD. Listening intently I was stunned at the depth of his knowledge, clarity of intellect and perception. I remarked to Lily under my breath that she should meet him to intuitively see whether I was correct. She had already reached the same conclusion!

Midday came and we broke for lunch, Roselinde suggested that we head for the local tea rooms around the corner from the town hall. Lily, Helena and Billy came too which gave the breadth of conversation more scope than I would have wished. I was closing in on my intuitive emotional memory and was narrowing down the connection between Roselinde and myself to a limited number of possibilities.

The subject of Anglo-Saxon England arose and I had a very strong response to the Battle of Adam's grave when it was mentioned. I suggested to Roselinde that we undertake an experiment that night after Michael's party; fortunately she had been invited too so we made plans to visit Adam's grave underneath the waning Moon at midnight.

I knew that I was only grasping the tip of a very large iceberg of connection between us but I felt an overwhelming urge to get to the root cause of such a powerful emotion. Roselinde confided in me that she too felt the same and therefore was intrigued to discover more.

Having made our plans we settled the bill and returned to the conference. The other speakers were excellent and a whole new world opened up before us. The final talk of the day was by Jaime Maussan with details of the Mexican UFO presence. He was a hero of mine as I had been interested in the *OVNI's over Mexico* since viewing the *Messengers' of Destiny* video in 1991. I was thrilled to know that he was visiting Michael's party too so that I would have a chance to speak to him.

I wanted to know more about a possible connection between the UFO's and the crop circles, also as to whether he recognised the type of craft that we had captured on our photographs at Patay. I offered Roselinde, Helena and Billy a lift in our hire car to the party at Horton, a small village situated on the back road through Pewsey vale.

They graciously accepted and with that we all left together as Karen locked up for the night. Roselinde navigated without error and we soon found ourselves outside Michael's cottage in Horton. Walking around the back following the noise we found the door wide open. Many people we had seen at the conference were there and everybody was in a chatty mood discussing the season's events. Everybody seemed extremely friendly and many were obviously acquaintances having studied crop circles together for nearly two decades.

Jaime was most interested in our photographs of Patay and confirmed that indeed the craft appeared to be similar to those photographed over Mexico City. He also conferred upon me a sense of urgency; that these events seemed to herald enormous Earth changes. I could identify with that as I told him how I too could feel the acceleration in my own life with the time slips that were happening.

Michael was a marvellous host as he held court like a wonderfully generous medieval monarch. He too was interested in our story and I left Lily to fill him in on the details and seek out young Daniel whilst I sought out Roselinde. The time quickly passed and we said our farewells as the clock approached midnight. The whole landscape seemed alive under the newly waning Moon as it lit up the sky and land below with a wondrous silver white glow.

The five of us drove along Pewsey vale passed Stanton St Bernard a tiny hamlet near Honey street. At the junction we turned left and wove our way up the side of Milk Hill to the Knap hill car park beyond. There we locked, and left the car. Then the party headed across the road towards the peak of Adam's grave on Walkers hill. The terrain was rough and the incline steep. Roselinde seemed so familiar with the trail that she could have attempted it blindfold. It was all so familiar to me that I started to remember events and images from a past life and see the landscape as it once was long ago.

The earth works that supported the log palisade was still there to be seen even after 1400 years. As we crossed the outer ring ditch the well of lights appeared.

Transfixed I looked into Roselinde's pale face. I knew from her expression that she too could see them so together we turned towards the time slip vortex and stepped into the circling orbs. The transition was instant and shocking as it was suddenly early morning daylight! The area was filled with dwellings and the royal hall sat on top of Adam's grave. I could see exactly why its alternative name was Woden's barrow as all around were Saxons.

Looking to the rear I could see the large shut wooden gates that barred the Lockeridge road. Either side there were watch towers with slumbering guards. The concentric rings of log fortification provided stout defence against attack as we had to zigzag left and right to enter each layer by its main gate. The dwellings within the layers consisted of long thatched huts each with a double horse headed gable at either end. Smoke drifted lazily upwards from a central square hole in the middle of each roof. It was early morning and the whole royal encampment was barely awake. Only a few guards watched and chatted amongst themselves as they stood near the gateways. They were dressed in green tunics with copious amounts of brown leather and fur. Each had a green or brown shield with a white horse or some similar personalised emblem on its painted war board. Helmets were few in number with the Phrygian cap being the most common head gear. Each carried a belted sax and a long 2.5 metre ash spear.

Roselinde walked with ease even though she was finely dressed in a deep green long dress clasped at the shoulders with a matching pair of fine filigree gold enamel brooches, by contrast her long blonde hair was plaited and soldier like. Gold thread was woven into every inch of her garment and on her wrist she wore a solid gold torc.

Each guard stood to attention and bowed his head as she approached; she acknowledged their salute with a cheery greeting in a guttural Anglo-Saxon dialect. I heard myself answering also in the same dialect. I knew that my name was Cuthwulf and that I was King Ceawlin's youngest brother, as such I was the personal body guard and guardian to my niece Aelfwynn who was indeed Roselinde. She had grown into womanhood and was now some 20 summers old. I had taught her to ride and fight as a warrior. We had laughed together, cried together and I had watched her grow up into a fine princess. I felt a deep wave of familial love and protection sweep over me as I resurrected my subconscious memories; she was of the blood, a princess and I would gladly die for her my dear brother's only daughter.

Aelfwynn turned and smiled gently at me. The early morning sun suddenly crested the top of Golden Ball hill. The bright shards of its yellow light lit up her face and blonde hair with a lustrous glow. Just then all hell was let loose; several arrows zinged past us in the air and impaled themselves in the stockade wall with multiple thwacks. I instinctively threw her to the ground and covered her body with mine. An arrow hit my shield and penetrated its linden war board to protrude some 8 centimetres on the other side.

It was a major attack and we had been caught totally unawares. Several of the guards now ran to alert the slumbering warriors as others died where they stood. Within seconds we heard the sound of several war horns blowing. Warriors rushed in all directions as confusion reigned, then came the deep shock and sense of betrayal; we were being attacked by our own Saxon cousins!

Ceol, Cutha's son, our own King Ceawlin's nephew led the surprise attack; it was an inside job! Several heavily armed thanes came across the ditch and running up towards us. I stood to face them with Aelfwynn behind me. I drew my sword and braced myself for the onslaught. Aelfwynn pushed past me and drew her sax. As they thrust at her with their spears I parried the blows with my shield and prevented their sharp vicious iron points from injuring her sacred royal body.

Like lightning she darted inside the ash hafts and stabbed at the bodies that held them fast. Blood spurted as her sharp sax found its mark. Yells and screams erupted all around as battle madness took hold. I lunged using my shield to knock over another two warriors who suddenly felt the wrath of my blade as I hacked into their fallen bodies.

Then I felt a searing pain blind my left eye as a spear found its mark. Death was prevented by the thick ridge of my left eyebrow which deflected and took the full force of the sharp spear point; blood ran from my eye socket and dripped onto my tunic. Aelfwynn ducked under the spear and thrust her sax deep into the warrior's thorax. He screamed an involuntary howl of pain and fell to the ground where she administered the *coup de grace* with a swift thrust to the throat; blood spurted into the air and covered her green and gold dress.

There was nothing glorious in this deadly combat; it was a pure fight for survival. We retreated upwards towards the royal hall. With my good eye I could see that the shield wall had been formed and that it held for the moment. Above me I could see her father, my brother, Ceawlin descending to join the fray. "Protect my daughter at all costs!" He shouted, his face purple with rage, "Retreat as best you can, we'll rally on Woden's barrow hill yonder if we lose this one."

My only concern at that moment was for Aelfwynn's safety. Despite the pain we edged away from the fighting and around the base of the royal hall towards the back gate that over looked the East field.

Once through the gate we descended the steep escarpment to the enclosure below that held our horses. Aelfwynn saddled two sturdy ponies and led them to where I stood watching for the enemy to appear. Silently, she brought them to the gate and we mounted. Then once through the gate we headed down the track into the wooded valley below.

The lights of the time slip well appeared and we rode through them into darkness. I awoke led on the hillside with Roselinde some metres from my side. I could see the stars high above me and the nearly full Moon which was passing to the west of our position indicating that it was well past 01:00hrs. Roselinde awoke and stood shakily. Finding her feet she made her way to my position.

"Are you OK?" She shouted.

"I was going to ask you the same thing." I replied.

"What the hell happened?" She said breathlessly.

"Welcome to my world! I assume you saw what I saw and experienced what I experienced? My eye still feels sore."

Together we sat on the side of Adam's grave as she quickly recounted her experience whilst the memory was still fresh. Indeed, she had lived through the exact same event and had experienced what I had experienced in graphic detail.

"I have named it a *time slip*! We somehow find ourselves mentally back reliving a personal memory from the past. This time it was without a doubt the battle of Adam's grave in 592AD. The time and place triggered a common memory that we both share."

"It was so real! I hate violence. Yet, I found myself doing indescribable things to other human beings. I killed people!" Roselinde was shaking visibly and her milk white skin looked even more pale than normal as was illuminated by the ghostly white light reflected from the Moon.

"They were other times, you were different; you were a former physical version of your higher self. It was the inner warrior that lies beneath which surfaced and saved me on that fateful day. I owe you my life, thank you princess Aelfwynn!" I now realised the magnitude of the event and the supreme irony that the princess had saved her bodyguard from certain death. "My life is your life; I will have to repay that debt in some other time and some other place. We now know the connection between us; it is my weird. We have witnessed the soul clan bonds that bind us together."

Momentarily exhausted we lay back down on the hillside. She was suddenly a fragile woman again. A sense of warmth flowed through my body as her dragon energy fired up my system which then produced its own inner heat. Breathing deeply I began to recover my composure. Above the Moon looked down on us kindly, the same Moon that had done so 1400 years ago.

Several long minutes passed; then a disembodied voice shouted from above, "You alright, Dad? Have you seen the Ice Queen of Orleans?" It was Billy the Kid and he had a note of deep concern in his voice.

"We're fine!" Roselinde shouted back, "Just took a tumble in the dark."

His words echoed in my head as I realised what he had shouted; was it another of his amazingly intuitive observations? My mind was in turmoil as it tried to figure it out.

Billy continued, "Cool, you had us worried, one minute we could see you then you disappeared from view. It's a very steep hillside."

Roselinde and I picked ourselves up and dusted off the thistle down and bits of grass that adhered to our clothing. Luckily we had somehow missed the sheep excrement that littered the more gentle slopes of the hill. Roselinde laughed at my concern for such a very basic thing after the raw nerve jangling excitement of being catapulted into a pitch battle nearly 1500 years previous.

Together we climbed back up the steep escarpment to the crest of Adam's grave where we took shelter in a small hollow depression just short of the summit.

"What have you been up to Roselinde? Your hair looks a total mess!" Helena pitched in with anxious concern for her wayward charge.

"I'm fine we just took a tumble through time; I'll explain it all later, no harm done." Roselinde replied in her extremely articulate and aristocratic voice. I waited to see if she would mention any further details but she didn't so I remained silent.

Lily knew what had happened though, she smiled at me from close up as she picked off pieces of gorse and the thistle down that had been missed from my neck area. "You can't fool me, Yann Baillieu. One dragon princess always knows what another is thinking; it's a sort of psychic sisterhood!" Although Lily was speaking under her breath and in French I was aware that Roselinde knew exactly what Lily was saying even though she was several paces away and engaged in conversation with her own entourage.

We then all sat huddled together observing the stars above and the valley below with its mighty East field shimmering in the Moonlight whilst each engaged in quiet conversation with their immediate neighbour.

I checked my mobile phone for the time and made a general comment to the others. "It's quarter to two - we had better start getting back to the Barge in a moment." My words fell on deaf ears as people were enjoying the moment.

Suddenly, I saw an intense bright red light appear to my right at the far end of the valley near Bishops Cannings. As it came nearer I could see clearly that at its centre it had a bright white magnesium flare like core which twinkled. "Hey, look what's that?" I shouted to attract the others to the presence of the object.

"It's probably an Army helicopter, Dad." Billy said in an unconcerned voice. "They fly out of the Army Air Corps headquarters at Middle Wallop and buzz the crop circles all the time. It's probably on its way home after an exercise."

Then as I watched, it suddenly accelerated silently and travelled a good 2 or 3 kilometres to Stanton St Bernard. "That's no helicopter, did you see the way it moved?" I was extremely curious at the behaviour of the unknown object we were observing. Silently it continued and I could clearly see the whole valley floor lit up beneath it.

Then it came to the East field, "Shall I take a picture." Lily asked as she readied her camera for action. The incandescent unidentified flying object stopped and hovered.

"You might spook it, they can read our minds." Billy said, "And nobody will believe us anyway; best just to be cool, watch and enjoy!"

As if on cue and knowing that it had an audience the object split into two piercingly bright lights. The magnesium star like centre hovered motionless in the sky whilst the strontium red part started to dance erratically around it! The whole valley lit up in an amazingly silent pyrotechnic display. The show continued for at least 5 minutes and I could see that it had attracted an audience from the several tents on Knap hill below. Finally the two lights came together into one object again and then dipped down into the East field, where upon it extinguished itself in the crop.

"Oh my goodness," Helena exclaimed, "That was amazing! Bright blessings; it must be a sign from the circle makers."

"That was well cool, Dad!" Billy put his arm around me and gave me a hug.

"It definitely wasn't a helicopter!" I said in total amazement.

"I got a picture of it just as it dropped!" Lily exclaimed. "It's definitely a real object. I've captured it on my camera."

"The East field is a very special place. It was no accident my father built his royal hall overlooking it all those years ago." Roselinde said in an ethereal voice as she gazed wistfully into the distance. Only I knew what she meant.

"Time to go!" I said as tiredness started to overtake me. The air was turning damp and the night air chilly as the temperature dropped. The dew point had been reached and the land was becoming sodden.

Due to gravity we found it much easier to walk back down the hill to the Knap hill car park. I could see that the place was alive with activity and I also noticed that a large white Ford transit van had parked sideways on next to my black Renault Laguna. The occupant was sat observing the East field form the side sliding door.

"Hey, it's Cozmic Dave!" Billy shouted and waved from behind us. Hearing Billy's yell the person in the van stood up and waved back. Billy ran ahead to chat with his friend. Several short minutes later we crossed the Lockeridge road and caught up.

"This is Cozmic Dave, Dad or Louis XV as we call him; what a coincidence!" Billy introduced him with a certain pride. He did look very French though with a dreadlock ponytail and the profile of a lanky 18th century aristocrat. I mentioned it to Billy who confirmed that that was exactly why they called him Louis XV!" Billy wanted us to know all about his friend and the French connection which was obviously a fine coincidence. Also that Cozmic Dave spent the winters in northern France near the Carnac stones in Brittany where he had a cottage.

"Pleased to meet you, Sir!" I said as I shook hands with him.

"What's Billy Bob been telling you?" Cosmic Dave said with a laconic smile.

"Nothing; so far as we have just met you!" I replied Lily, Roselinde and Helena all shook hands with our new friend.

"I used to be a professional footballer, then a sound technician for the *Tourists* with Annie Lennox and Dave Stewart; that lasted 10 years. Then I worked for *Iron Maiden* but I fell off of a speaker stack in America and landed on my skull. Since then I have been, sort of retired; pleased to meet you all. Falling off the speaker stack is why everyone calls me Cozmic, it's my claim to fame!"

I was amazed at how genteel and refined Cozmic Dave was. He told us of his interest in Earth lights, energies and the stone circles. Pointing to Adam's grave he showed us the pale orange balls of light that came from within the hill and flew up into the sky.

"Ah, that's why they call this hill to the left Golden Ball hill! It's due to the earth energy lights." I said aloud as I made the connection.

Cozmic Dave went on to explain about Earth energies and the world grid, the sighting of Avebury, Silbury Hill and Stonehenge, and their connection with UFOs for over 5000 years. It turned out that Avebury was situated exactly on the Michael Mary line.

We dropped Roselinde, Helena and Billy back at the Barge Inn and said our goodnights. Lily and I went back to our hotel in Marlborough and finally got to sleep around 03:00hrs.

Day two off the conference was extremely interesting and all the speakers proved to be excellent. Steve's crop circle film of the season's formations so far was breath taking and put them firmly into perspective as awesome harbingers of change. Even though I was relatively new to this phenomenon I could see the continuous progression from the early days some twenty years or more ago. Afterwards both Lily and I attended the speakers' dinner together with Roselinde, Helena and Billy in the Italian Restaurant just over the road from the town hall which rounded of a most successful weekend.

On Monday Roselinde and I walked the Avebury Ring. We joined the others for lunch at the Red Lion in the circle and then went to visit some of the nearby crop formations that had just formed, one at Morgan's Hill, near Bishops Cannings from the day before which was an exquisite 4 symmetry pattern and a brand new one at Silbury Hill that sported a very unusual plaited centre.

At 18:00hrs we gathered together for a last meal at the Black Horse public house and coaching inn opposite the Cherhill white horse on the A4. Not wishing to let go of the moment I intuitively asked Roselinde if she would like to visit Reims with Lily and I the following week. I instinctively felt that there was as yet some unknown important reason for her to be there; time seemed to be closing in on our new found friendship and a sense of urgency overcame my normally reserved demeanour. It was quite unlike anything I had ever experienced before but I simply knew that Roselinde just had to be there.

We left the pub at 21:00hrs and stood together in a ring holding hands under the gaze of the white horse opposite. The orange sun was fast setting in the western sky and it seemed the natural time to depart. We hugged each other and kissed on both cheeks. I held Roselinde's gaze and made her promise to come to Reims. In my mind I had the twin images of two cathedrals, the Neolithic cathedral of Avebury from 4000 years ago and the mighty cathedral of Reims from 600 years ago; one sat inside the other conjoined by sacred energy, time and space.

As dusk fell we walked to the car, pulled out onto the A4 and headed back to Folkestone and the midnight Shuttle. An unexplained tear formed in my right eye, dropped onto my cheek and fell silently to be absorbed on my black Oakley hoodie.

Chapter 19

Chess

It was early on the following Friday that Roselinde Saxmund made her way to the railway station at Saxmundham in Suffolk, England the home of her ancestors. She was taking the early train to London in order to catch the Eurostar to Lille. It was a journey into the unknown; a journey unlike anything she had experienced before, for it was only the weekend before that she had met an intense French journalist by the name of Yann Baillieu and his attractive young assistant Lily Chevalier at the Devizes crop circle lectures in Wiltshire, England.

There was a mysterious connection that deep down linked them through several lifetimes. The Saxon connection had played itself out on Adam's grave but there was much more to come, she could feel it deep down in her bones. Her subconscious memory was screaming the answers but as yet her conscious mind was still playing catch up.

The connection was so compelling, so forceful and so intense, that she found herself inexplicably on an early morning commuter train bound for the city. Something deep within her soul was calling her to France. It lurked dark and foreboding in the recesses of her mind and needed urgently to be exposed to the light of day in order to make sense of her life. She had embarked on a soul journey of discovery from which there would be no turning back.

It was a normal Friday for the commuters that boarded the 08:21hrs from Saxmundham bound for London Liverpool Street. The city was exactly 2 hours and 3 minutes away a fact that the zombie like commuters were all too aware of in their clockwork existence. Roselinde knew that there would have to be a short 5 minute stop over at Ipswich in order to change trains and make the connection with the mainline service; she nervously bit her lip as she contemplated the tight schedule and crossed her fingers that the journey would go smoothly and allowing for the short taxi journey required, get her to the Eurostar terminal at St Pancras on time to catch her scheduled departure.

Just then a text message came in on her mobile. It was Yann in Lille; he had managed to change and secure a cheaper ticket for her. The Eurostar would now leave London St Pancras at 14:04hrs instead of earlier as initially planned. She became agitated immediately, for she disliked last minute changes and would now have nearly 4 hours to kill. It was all so contrary to her normally well-ordered yet Bohemian life. Roselinde text Yann to indicate her displeasure and the fact that she definitely, was not cheap!

Yann replied some 10 minutes later. He apologised profusely with the caveat that the paper was paying for it and that he was trying to keep within budget. It was also all such a rush. His reply did nothing to change her humour or indeed allay her annoyance.

After a subsequently seamless uneventful journey, the train pulled into Liverpool Street on time and Roselinde alighted with the grey faced commuters, who rapidly scurried to exit the station. She made her way to the taxi rank and hailed a cab. The connecting journey of some 3 miles was swiftly over in just 12 minutes. She exited the taxi, paid the driver and stood looking at the magnificent red brick gothic cathedral like architecture that was St Pancras Station. This was it; no turning back. Her stomach churned at the thought of returning to France. Her father had taken her there once as a small girl with her sister when he was an RAF pilot and they lived in Germany on the border with Luxembourg. She had never forgotten the dark misgivings she had experienced then and had quietly put them to the back of her mind but now they confronted her head on.

She entered the station through the new glass entrance and made her way to the Eurostar booking office with the intention of picking up her reserved tickets from the desk. Her attention, however, was captured for several minutes by a beautiful bronze statue of a man and a woman embracing under the clock. The evocative pose summed up something of how she felt for she was rushing off to meet a strange Frenchman that she had known for barely five minutes yet somehow she felt she knew him intimately. It didn't make a lot of sense, it wasn't *normal* but then again she didn't do *normal*. She was determined to follow up the coincidence, see the mission through to the bitter end and therefore steeled her resolve to face the challenge of returning to France.

With some 3 hours to wait Roselinde made her way to the Arcade shopping mall by the platform concourse. She had always loved books since being a child, so instinctively headed for Foyles to pass some time. It was at that point and with that single decision that the *Law of Attraction* seemed to come into play. For unknown to her the quantum universe of interconnectedness was about to make a big hit that would impact on her life forever.

Serendipity smiled as she chanced to enter the shop right by the promotional book stand. Normally she would abhor such commercial vulgarity and head for the more intellectual shelves but today was different. Today she found herself, quite out of character, sifting through the brash titles on offer. Under the third pile she unearthed a *Trojan horse* in the form of a large French paperback entitled *L'Affaire Jehanne d'Arc*. The book had somehow inexplicably become entangled in the mêlée of popularly promoted titles. She thought momentarily about the probability of it all but was immediately captivated by the bright red lettering that made the edition standout and the portrait of a kneeling Jehanne d'Arc. It drew her subconscious attention like a magnet.

Oh my God - she thought, she looks just like me! The face, the pose, the attitude, they all collided with her subconscious which then connected head on in a single revelatory moment with her conscious mind. The connection had been made. All hesitation and inhibition was suddenly lost as she realised that the book was destined for her and that her subconscious mind had drawn it towards her in connection with this extraordinary journey. Opening the book with her delicate and now shaking hands she flicked briefly through the pages. Echoes of her school girl French illuminated the dark recesses of her mind as she started to hesitantly comprehend the foreign text. It was readable, concise in factual content and the information seemed invaluable to her emerging sense of identity. She also felt sure that Yann and Lily could help her with the more difficult passages should she get bogged down in the detail. Decision made, she took the book to the cash point and paid the assistant. It was now hers to keep and study at leisure; the vagaries of fate could no longer snatch it from her grasp. She also realised that fortune in that very moment had smiled on her.

Feeling satisfied with her precious find she headed for the *des Vins café wine bar* and ordered a pot of Earl Grey. Soon she was lost like Alice in an abstract world of medieval chivalry and violent bloodshed. She began to read the text and make sense of the key concepts. A quick glance at the back cover caused her to splutter on her tea; according to the two investigators Jehanne had not been burnt at the stake as told in the conventional history books!

The authors presented a case of classical heresy in declaring that the beloved French icon and saint had escaped her fate on May 30, 1429. They challenged conventional dogma with a presentation of evidence gathered from many original suppressed documents. It felt like a *Da Vinci code* moment and Roselinde revelled in the conspiracy of it all.

She felt like a blind woman that could suddenly see, as she lurched and waded through sections of difficult prose. She began to grasp the strange yet blurred facts. Certain keywords leapt off of the page at her and started to form concrete images in her mind. The details seemed to resonate with her soul and within minutes she found herself unexplainably emotional. The most amazing discovery beckoned, it was the picture of an old carved wooden door with two faces, it was tucked in the corner of a page, adjacent to a coloured picture of the illuminated chimney breast at Chateau Jaulny.

It was a face she recognised, she looked again in disbelief but there was no mistaking it. The mouth was so distinctive; it was Yann Baillieu the very person she was going to meet! She quickly glanced at her mobile phone and was surprised to see that the time read 13:33hrs. It was time to head for the platform and board the waiting Eurostar that would effortlessly speed her under the channel and onwards to Lille in just one hour and twenty minutes.

Exactly on time at 14:04hrs the train pulled out of St Pancras Station and started to pick up speed through the suburbs of London and then the Kentish countryside.

As she sat back in her comfortable seat Roselinde flipped open her mobile and texted Yann that she had forgiven him for messing up the ticket arrangements. At the end she added the cryptic sentence; I know who you were! :-)

Abandoning thoughts of reading further Roselinde was content to gaze out of the window and let her mind wonder. The bright light stung her eyes so she pulled down the sunglasses that perched neatly on her blonde hair. After several minutes she found herself drifting in and out of reality. The journey continued and soon the Eurostar entered the dark womb like *tunnel sous la manche*. The hypnotic effect of the lights passing rapidly by the window only added to the deep altered state she was entering.

She suddenly saw Robert des Armoises sitting on a horse. He was dressed in blackened armour and wore a long black hooded robe. The solid black mass of his persona was broken only by the very distinctive radiating white cross that covered his left breast. It was a symbol of enlightenment, a beacon of hope in a dark world of ignorance, magic and superstition. It was an emblem that she recognised and intuitively knew from the past. He smiled at her, she felt herself smile back but only for a brief moment, then she raised her banner high and spurred her horse towards the fray. The image abruptly shattered and her altered state collapsed as the sound of a voice boomed out.

"Tickets please!" The official said. She felt her body being nudged by sonic waves and immediately awoke. Reaching into her ethnic jute shoulder bag she withdrew the printed ticket and handed it to the inspector. "Thank you, Madam. My colleague will check your passport."

Without hesitation Roselinde rummaged again and produced her claret coloured UK passport, the immigration officer checked the photo ID thoroughly.

"Thank you, Ms Saxmund, have a pleasant journey." He said as he moved down the carriage to the next group of people. Ten minutes later the train emerged from the dark tunnel and the cloudy grey defused light of France hit her eyes. She replaced her documents and adjusted her sunglasses to protect her sensitive eyes from the glare. Roselinde Saxmund was now on French soil and just 30 minutes away from meeting Yann at Gare de Lille Europe.

The Eurostar glided silently into the station exactly on time. The canopy extended high above the train and gave a cavernous feel to the station platforms 43 and 45. Roselinde alighted from the train. She looked up towards the overhead concourse and saw Yann waving in an elegant yet informal way.

Roselinde gripped the extending handle of her suitcase and pulled it along behind her as she made her way to the escalator. Within seconds she was level with Yann who embraced her warmly and kissed her on both cheeks. She felt for an instant exactly like the characters depicted in the large bronze statue at St Pancras.

She was a little nervous and not a tad apprehensive to see her *new* old friend but his warm countenance and strong arms soon dispelled any apprehension she may have had. He was her protector, her rock, her saviour from many lives. The feelings coursed through her veins and filled her soul to bursting point. In his company she knew that she would and could conquer the Franco-phobia that had haunted her all her life. In one single smooth action he took her bag in tow and they headed outside to the Place François Mitterrand. Roselinde was greeted by the sight of a large colourful surreal statue of two giant red tulips with white spots which took her completely surprise and instantly lightened her mood.

"Bienvenue à la belle France mon ami." Yann twirled theatrically and bowed.

The modern stylish space age vista took her breath away. She then took in the quirky L shaped architecture of the Credit Lyonnais building which perched precariously on top of the Gare de Lille

Europe. Together they walked along the Avenue Le Corbusier in front of the modern Euralille shopping centre towards the original railway station, Gare Lille Flandres. Roselinde admired the classical architecture with its stark contrast of the old within the modern space age setting that she had just stepped into.

"The front of the station was once that of the Gare du Nord in Paris! Rather than waste the façade, when they expanded that station at the end of the 19th century they disassembled it and rebuilt it here." Yann was bursting with enthusiasm at seeing his soul clan Saxon princess back on home ground again. It wasn't boasting he just wanted her to catch up with some of the details of his life.

"Fascinating, I feel at home here already. I have always had a phobia about returning to France but have never got to the nub of it. You have changed everything. I feel very safe with you around." It was quite an admission for Roselinde to make for she was normal extremely strong and independent but she felt secure enough in his presence to be totally honest.

He beamed a smile at her as they turned right and strolled along the Rue Faidherbe towards his offices on the main square. Yann pointed out all the points of interest as they walked and shared his world with her. It felt like two soul sisters reunited after a long period of absence; indeed he had experienced several lives in linear time without her physical presence since they last met.

Roselinde admired the classical French late 19th century architecture as she went. Her love of music and opera came to the forefront as they turned into the Rue de Paris and entered the Place du Theatre which sported the Grand Opera house.

"I promise you that we shall go to the opera before you leave. It is one of the finest cultural assets we have in Lille."

It was Roselinde's turn to beam a bright smile. "How did you know I like ballet and opera?" She asked quizzically.

"I know you very well, more than you can ever guess," was his cryptic reply.

Then they entered the main square the Place du General de Gaulle and she was immediately taken by the spectacular Flemish gable of the La Voix du Nord Offices.

"Welcome to my life of the past 30 years." He said reflectively.

Together they entered through the main doors. Yann filled in the guest details in the visitor book and Roselinde signed her name against the entry. They took the stairs to the third floor and immediately saw Lily hard at work on her latest article. She stood up and came over to Roselinde, gave her a big hug and kissed her on both cheeks. "The princess arrives! *Bienvenue à Lille!* We are so excited that you could come and join our quest at such short notice. Yann has talked of nothing else all week."

Yann blushed at the mention of his keenness and busied himself to avoid attention. Friday was traditionally a relaxed day in the working week and mainly consisted of tidying up loose ends from the other days. They all entered Yann's office as he disappeared to get some refreshments whilst Lily made Roselinde comfortable in the guest chair.

"Well, this is our little world." Lily said as she pointed to the simple yet stylishly appointed room. "I've only been here a few weeks, but I have really grown fond of all my colleagues and Yann in particular. It is like we have known each other in many lifetimes. I expect you feel the same way?"

"Yes, I do, strange to say. Even though, we have only just met." Roselinde relaxed visibly in her chair as she now felt very comfortable and amongst friends.

Yann's desk was untidy and arranged in a chaotic way with many piles of different papers and books. Evidence of their medieval memory quest was strewn everywhere which caused Roselinde to laugh and make a joke about house-keeping. Lily joined in with an anecdote about men in general that made Roselinde laugh even more.

"I see that I need have no worries about you two getting on!" Yann said as he re-entered the room carrying a tray of drinks and some Florentine biscuits. "They are gluten free, I remembered."

"I'm impressed. I only mentioned that once last weekend." Roselinde smiled.

Yann placed the tray down on his desk after making a space with his elbow. The girls laughed at the comic procedure and were content not to help but rather to just enjoy the show!

Yann handed around the tea. "It is very non-French Earl Grey just as you like it with lemon and no milk." Finally he relaxed, "Lily has a spare bed for you at her apartment, plus you can share the hotel accommodation with her in Reims if that is OK? We have made all the arrangements."

Lily smiled and sipped her tea which she had acquired a taste for in England, then filled Roselinde in on the itinerary for the Reims visit that would start on Monday.

"That is very kind of you. I am sure that we will get on very well, Lily." Roselinde sipped her tea in a genteel manner as she related details of her journey from Saxmundham to Lille in response to Lily's earlier enquiry.

A convivial hour passed and it was soon time to make our way out of the office and back to the Métro station to pick up the driverless VAL fully automated train for home. Roselinde was disconcerted to find that there were no drivers, so Yann explained that VAL stood for Véhicule Automatique Léger which meant that the system was fully automatic with two unit trains arriving and departing every 1.5 to 4 minutes. Due to clever timing we were just ahead of the main weekend rush and so boarded without a problem. Lily and Roselinde departed on their VAL train towards the Hippodrome whilst I took Ligne 2 to Mons Sarts. The short ride took only 15 minutes and then it was just a short walk to my house at Place Alexandre Dumas.

Lily was making dinner for 20:00hrs sharp so I had plenty of time for a shower and a change of clothes. I checked the post and laid out my evening wear on the bed. It felt like having royalty to stay. Roselinde's presence engendered a behavioural pattern that I had never experienced before; it was automatic and accompanied the irrational urge to bow when meeting her!

I was also determined that Roselinde should have an interesting and pleasant visit. With that thought I phoned the *Carte Blanche* restaurant in Villeneuve d'Ascq to book a table for Sunday night. The restaurant was set in an industrial landscape close by but the atmosphere and food were superb; it would be just perfect because on Monday we would have to be up early to catch the TGV to Champagne-Ardenne and Reims.

On Saturday, Lily and I would show Roselinde the site of the crop circle and then give her a quick tour of Lille. In the evening Vincent was having one of his famous parties so the catering would be taken care of on that occasion; I also instinctively felt that Roselinde should meet Déborah Dubois the beautiful and clever mathematics teacher from Vincent's school as there seemed to be a connection there. It was a subconscious message, my intuition was on overdrive but as of yet I had no idea why?

At 19:30 hrs. I left my house in Place Alexandre Dumas to walk to Lily's apartment. The weather was cloudy and the temperature warm and humid. Everything seemed a lot easier in the summer months especially with the lighter evenings. I remembered to bring a chilled bottle of champagne that I had in the refrigerator as Lily was doing the cooking. I rang her bell precisely on time and was greeted by Roselinde who looked very at home. We kissed on both cheeks and she asked me in. Lily shouted hi from the kitchen and was obviously busy in the final stages of readying the gourmet meal.

As Lily finished her preparations I popped open the champagne and poured out the *Kir Royale* aperitifs into the tall fluted glasses. Entering the lounge I found Roselinde toying with a chess piece from Lily's classic set that sat proudly on her coffee table in front of the settee. It was a present from her father. I then noticed that she held in her delicate fingers a single black knight.

"Do you play?" I asked as I set the drinks down beside the chessboard.

"Of course, I love strategy games; my father taught me when I was a girl, just as Lily's father taught her. We have so much in common." Without thinking Roselinde instinctively placed the black horse back on its correct square.

Roselinde continued to expound her rationale, "I have always loved the knights; especially the way they can jump over obstacles and move in ways that the other pieces can't. It makes them very flexible and able to achieve impossible feats."

I knew that her speech was veiled in allegory. I was aware from her body language that there was far more to her informal observation than she consciously knew.

"Shall we play whilst Lily finishes in the kitchen?" She said as she smiled a feminine feline smile, caressed the stem of her elegant glass and then sipped slowly, allowing the champagne bubbles to tickle her nose. I accepted the challenge and took the two Queens from the board. Holding them up I allowed them to metaphorically eye each other and then placed them behind my back. After shaking them in my cupped hands I held out my closed fists to allow Roselinde to choose her side.

"I'll take the right one."

With that she tapped the back of my left hand. It was a deliberate tactic to wrong foot me and it worked. The electricity of her touch shocked me which added to the effect. I opened my left hand and the white Queen was revealed.

"Looks like I get to move first!" She smiled and took another sip of her champagne whilst smiling over the brim of her glass.

I replaced the pieces back onto the battlefield and slowly turned the board around so that she was in command of the white army. She was exquisitely balletic in her movements which made me lose concentration and I immediately felt incredibly clumsy. Then the battle royal began.

Roselinde opened decisively with a classic King's pawn move. I felt sure she was determined to use her infantry in a full on frontal attack. Responding, I decided to use my two black knights to counter and to cause a little mayhem in the ranks. Over the next 4 moves I moved them into open ground as she prepared her attack.

We eyed each other in turn as the pieces were moved into their initial battle positions and sipped the *Kir Royale*. Roselinde's blonde hair perfectly framed her delicate aristocratic cheekbones allowing her penetrating gaze from those soulful sea grey eyes to lock my thoughts into anything else but the game! There was something incredibly charismatic, almost hypnotic about her glance, it commanded my utmost attention so much so that I found myself losing the tactical plot fast!

My black knights penetrated the white defence and lived up to their name but Roselinde swallowed them whole with her trap of a deceptively weak defence then succeeded in capturing both of them in a devastatingly swift *riposte*. I was suddenly on the back foot and there was no let up. Her army attacked in multiple places with the precision of a surgical knife. I found myself rapidly losing several pieces to her relentless thrusts.

"You are pretty good at this, aren't you?" I said as I scratched my head.

"Of course, I was taught well." Roselinde replied in a matter of fact tone and with a coy angelic smile. "I am as you say, very tricky, no!"

She giggled, flashed her perfectly white teeth and then slowly licked her upper lip with the tip of her tongue. It was a deliberately provocative display of feminine sexuality that confounded my senses. Her eyes sparkled like fire and I found myself sinking under her spell much as a drowning man in quick sand.

I counted with a few brutal but useless moves which were easily out manoeuvred and then I was tied up in knots expertly.

"Checkmate!" The *coup de grace* was administered with a delicate and painless feminine precision which finally put an end to my misery. She took another sip of champagne from her long tall fluted glass and sat back to relax.

"You appear to have the better of me, *Madame*. I am in total awe at your strategic and tactical skill. I salute you!" With that I raised my glass and contemplated my summary demise on the field of combat.

"Come on Robert don't be too harsh on yourself, you confused me with those black knights of yours for several moves and very effective they were too!" Roselinde picked up the black horse, ran her index finger along its mane and then kissed it gently.

I was totally shocked. Her sensual display with the chess piece was obvious enough but she had called me Robert! Why had she done that? Words failed to leave my lips; how did she know?

I sat in stunned silence as she lovingly placed each piece back on to the board. Just as the pieces were reset Lily came into the room carrying the starters.

"Time to eat; up to the table children," she said playfully, "I can see by the look on Yann's face that you have well and truly kicked his butt. He just won't accept that women are the superior race!" Her infectious giggle triggered a polite response from Roselinde who agreed in a demure sort of way.

"Well it's a good job we are all on the same side. I concede! With two dragon princesses in one room I have no chance!" With that I laughed and joined in the fun.

"*Exactement,* we always know what you are thinking and are therefore always one step ahead!" Lily grinned and poured the wine.

I laughed and joined in the fun. The ice had certainly been well and truly broken and the rest of the evening went like clockwork.

Chapter 20

Reims

The weekend proved memorable for several reasons. Revisiting the crop circle at Forest-sur-Marque seemed all the more relevant with Roselinde present for she had been interested in them since their inception in modern times around 1976. As a witness to their development and with years of experience at detecting human made ones it was gratifying to know that she considered this to be the genuine article whatever that meant; with such an esoteric phenomenon?

She conducted a small ceremony of thanksgiving to the circle makers which had echoes of fairy pagan roots totally lost to modern minds. She was an old and very wise soul. Her exquisite elfin beauty belied her age as she seemed the very incarnation of the corn goddess Ceres made mortal.

I was completely enchanted in her presence. Roselinde's charisma seemed to flow and envelope me in a golden light. Lily observed all of this dispassionately for she had taken centre stage in our quest, at least for the moment. Together however they were like sisters, part indeed of the historical sisterhood of dragon princesses and so were amicable partners.

Lille had no need to sell its charms for the blessed city of the north sold itself into Roselinde's heart with ease. Its grand 19th century architecture triumphed over more primitive distant memories. The highlight of course was the evening soiree at Vincent's house in La Madeleine. He lived not far from Lily so it was my turn to walk to her suburb. I introduced Roselinde to Déborah Dubois or DD as we knew her and they hit it off immediately which surprised me as they were polar opposites in terms of academic preferences. Roselinde was extremely literary in her interests and Déborah an analytical mathematician but again they had a certain mysterious chemistry. It was as if they were a double take from the same progenitor, identical to look at, so much so that one could easily be substituted for the other. Yes, they could easily substitute for each other as they looked like identical changelings from a distance.

Both were very similar feisty characters and they appeared more as beautiful enigmatic cosmic twins than strangers. There was obviously some unknown link in the past between them but as of yet I had no idea as to what that could possibly be. They looked like twin sisters with the exception that Déborah was slightly stronger built than Roselinde who appeared the more elven of the two. Both were warriors, independent of mind, muscular, slim yet powerful and with a razor sharp wit. They did not suffer fools gladly! I sat back and quietly observed in detail the interaction that I was witnessing, whilst my subconscious made mental notes on the comparison between these two stunning *femmes fatales*. Both must have been leaders of men in past lives, of that I had no doubt!

By the end of the evening I felt pretty sure that Déborah must also possess the dragon genetic code as she seemed to exponentially radiate energy when in the presence of Lily and Roselinde. I could only liken them to Uranium fuel rods in a nuclear reactor, the closer their proximity the more the neutrons get excited and cause the rods to heat up! My subconscious was also trying desperately to tell me something perhaps DD was the one; my soul twin? I had heard that they did exist but that you would only meet them when you had progressed to a certain level spiritually in life.

Later whilst randomly searching the internet on this point I was to discover a book written by *Nicholas de Vere* entitled *The Dragon Legacy* in which he estimated that some 10% of the European population carries to this day the *dragon gene* and he further confirmed my observation as to the exponential increase in psychic energy when dragon princesses come together! It was as though I had discovered a whole new "lost world" that I never knew existed and more incredibly I was part of it, past, present and I now assumed the future.

The interaction experiment proved a total success as dragons always get on, not only physically and on a conscious level but also and more importantly at a subconscious level too. There was a definite historical connection between the two of them as though they had shared a common past. It wasn't just me that felt this for their physical similarity caused several comments from the other party goers who thought that they must surely be twins or at the very least closely related. After the party had drawn to a close I walked Roselinde and Lily home. Then I departed to wander under the star lit night back to Mons-en-Barouel and Place Alexandre Dumas all the time my mind was drawn to DD. She had only been at Vincent's school for one term perhaps I needed the jolt of Roselinde to fit the puzzle together. Certainly my spiritual progress had rocketed off of the scale since visiting Metz, experiencing the flashbacks and seeing the door. Come to think of it they both looked a lot like the lady on the door!

Sunday morning was declared a morning of rest as I had a surprise for Roselinde and Lily that I had yet to tell them about. I had managed to book three seats for that evening's performance of Bellini's *La Sonnambula* at the opera house. So I had cancelled the dinner date at the *Carte Blanche* restaurant near my house and rebooked an early evening meal at the *Le Pot Beaujolais* opposite to the Grand Opera House in the Place du Theatre. It was one of my favourite restaurants in the city so I knew that we would have a first class evening of *gastronomie et culture – c'est superb!*

The whole day was a monumental success. Roselinde was reduced to tears of pleasure at the performance of *Amina*, the titular Sleepwalker, who performed all aspects of the famous high *tessitura* with the exquisite trills and florid technique required. It was definitely a musical feast for the ears and food for the soul. The joy was accentuated further as I had kept the girls in suspense, not telling them of my surprise until the last moment when we sat enjoying our starter of oysters in the restaurant! That night I was rewarded with several hugs and kisses as we said good night at the VAC station. We then parted and took our respective automatic double carriage metro trains home.

I slept extremely well as I had packed earlier that Sunday morning knowing that I would be late to bed. I didn't know whether the girls had done the same but I knew they would be ready for anything at a moment's notice so I didn't have any real fears.

We rendezvoused at Gare Lille Europe twenty minutes prior to boarding the TGV for Champagne-Ardenne. Roselinde seemed to be in awe at the effortless way we moved around without resorting to the car. I explained that it was all part of living *a la mode* in a modern progressive French city. In England people seemed to strive to live in the countryside where as in France the opposite was true. The city contained all the art and culture that one could wish for so urban living was *d'rigueur*.

The same had been true of medieval life. The cities of France had been the great theatres of the Jehanne d'Arc story. The English may have won a couple of field battles but the French had won the sieges and eventually the war, although it did last a hundred years it has to be said.

England's William Shakespeare had dined out very nicely on the stories generated by the likes of Henry V, Henry VI and Falstaff but it was George Bernard Shaw who much later would write Saint Joan the definitive play about our precious little maid - La Pucelle. The truth that we were now uncovering was very far from the simple legendary mythos that he and hundreds of others had penned in the 600 intervening years. I reflected such notions silently in thought to myself. Yet, I'm a journalist and people like a good story so I mustn't complain too loudly, plus I was enjoying the conspiracy angle which we were uncovering. This gave me a wry smile.

I had already booked the TGV tickets for Saumur in the Loire valley, and Rouen which would be the big one. I had the feeling that the pace of our investigation was accelerating exponentially and that we would soon be swept away as the story took on a life of its own.

Now we were off to the coronation of the Dauphin, following in the footsteps of the miraculous bloodless march from the Loire to the gates of Reims in 1429. It was an astounding feat, for Jehanne had invoked the power of the Lord of Hosts and the English had surrendered to a man without an iota of resistance. She had even penned a letter to the Duke of Burgundy inviting him to attend the coronation service, now that was definitely not the actions of a peasant girl! I voiced my thoughts to the girls as we sped through the flat landscape of Picardy towards Champagne-Ardenne and our date with destiny. The girls discussed the amazing level of feminist power that had been demonstrated by a very modern Jehanne d'Arc and even more so by her powerful mentor Yolande of Aragon. For she was the true power behind the Armagnac throne of the Dauphin who would soon be Charles VII; the true anointed king of France, once the ancient ceremony instituted by Clovis I had been performed. It was the sacred moment of public proclamation that signified the zenith Armagnac achievement and Jehanne d'Arc had been there in person to see it happen; a frail young girl in armour with her sacred white Jhesus Marie banner surrounded by the aristocratic nobility of France. It was a pure miracle; a single iconic moment in history that would echo down throughout the centuries.

With such a high powered and interesting discussion the time went rapidly by. So much so that we almost forgot to alight onto the platform of the ultra-modern purpose built TGV station at Champagne-Ardennne. We carried on the conversation in the midst of the fields of France as we waited for the connecting

TER train that would take us the short seven minute journey into the heart of Reims.

Roselinde was becoming quite excited, "I love Champagne!" She exclaimed enthusiastically, "I can almost taste it from here."

Lily laughed and commented, "Diamonds may be a girls' best friend but Champagne always knows how to show a girl a good time!"

"Hush you two, listen to yourselves this is a dignified historical journey into France's noble past and all you can think of is having a good time!" I put on my best annoyed school masters voice which had no effect what-so-ever! Both girls were transported back to their days of youth and stuck their tongues out back at me; they then looked at each other and giggled in unison. Where upon I burst out laughing, "One thing the French know how to do is – party!" I said then broke into a very retro disco move to show how trendy I was not!

Lily gave me a playful slap on the shoulder, Yann Baillieu, you are the limit!" I was spared further playful comments as the train arrived and we boarded. Within minutes we had arrived at Reims main station in the centre of the city. I was then that I noticed Roselinde's look of horror. In an instant the playful mood had dispelled and a palpable quiet descended.

Despite my frivolity I had the presence of mind to observe that the stark change had occurred at the point Roselinde had physically set foot on the ground as she alighted from the train. Her face had changed in an instant, from one of jollity to one of abject horror and pain. The colour had drained from her cheeks which were now bone white with a greenish tinge.

"Are you alright, Roselinde?" I enquired as I stood square in front of her and grasped her shoulders with both hands in an effort to snap her back into the real world. I was conscious from my own journey that memories could be triggered at any instant and that one needed a reality check. Physical touch had the ability to pull the experience back from the abyss of the time shadows to the present.

"Yes, er yes, I'm f-f-fine, you probably think I'm a real bore?" She said in a weakened voice as the reality of present day space time clicked back into place.

"Don't worry we have both been there before, we know exactly how you feel, although we can't possibly know what you have experienced."

Lily placed her arm around Roselinde to lend comfort and support. She then noticed some strange reddish blue marks that had appeared around her slender neck; they looked mysteriously like pressure bruises?

"It was awful, I felt a constriction around my throat and suddenly had trouble swallowing and breathing. My whole body started to go into shock. Your actions saved me from further discomfort."

"Yes, you seemed to snap out of it once I touched you and applied pressure to your shoulders." I continued to hold her delicate hand in reassurance as I escorted her to a nearby seat.

The minutes ticked by like hours, Lily somehow provided a drink and Roselinde gradually began to regain her natural colour. The marks were still visible but gradually fading. I took a moment to photograph them on my mobile phone as I was anxious to preserve some tangible evidence of what had transpired for later analysis. Roselinde began to regain her composure and I decided that the best course of action was to get her to the hotel as soon as possible so that she could rest.

Lily took Roselinde's bag in tow and headed to the park in front of the station. Taking the right hand path she led us towards the Rue General Ducot.

"Not much further now, the Hôtel Le Bristol is just down here on the right according to my iPhone. Roselinde was too weak to comment and Lily was struggling to drag two bags whilst consulting her map. I supported Roselinde with my arm around her waist and she reciprocated with her arm around my neck. The whole scene must have look totally bizarre in the warm afternoon sunshine. Not surprisingly passers-by tried to avoid eye contact as we progressed towards the hotel.

After what seemed hours but was in truth only minutes we had reached the pavement cafe that fronted the hotel. I sat Roselinde down and asked Lily to order her a cognac whilst I went into the decadent chandeliered foyer to check in at the main desk. The hotel staff were most accommodating once I had explained the situation and had filled in the registration forms that made us officially guests. I collected two sets of keys without further problem. The young lady on the reception desk arranged for our bags to be taken to our rooms which meant that I could return to the cafe to sit with Roselinde and Lily. The cognac had revived our patient's spirits and Lily had ordered some organic Earl Grey tea for her as well which had arrived.

"I know you don't take sugar but I have dissolved a cube in the tea to give you some energy. You still look very pale." Lily added.

Lily and I had both now experienced several episodes of paranormal activity and knew how to cope. This was however all together more sinister and physical. The flash back or whatever had translated into actual physical symptoms which were clearly life threatening. I voiced my observations to Lily and Roselinde who both nodded in silent agreement with my assessment of the situation.

"You are right, Yann. We must be much more on our guard until we get to the bottom of this affair!" Lily spoke in earnest tones as Roselinde sipped her tea. Finally as the colour to her cheeks returned fully she smiled at me so I knew that she was on the mend.

"You don't have to continue with this if you don't want too and if you feel at all uncomfortable we can return to Lille today. I will just change the tickets."

"No, I'm determined to see this through. I have had a phobia about coming to France all my life and I want to get to the bottom of it. I will get to the bottom of it!" Roselinde gave me a steely glance which meant that going back was not an option.

"*Courage mon brave mademoiselle!*" I spoke softly and gave a reassuring smile, "Here is your key. Your room is next to mine and Lily is going to share with you so that she can keep a close eye on you in case anything untoward happens. You need have no fear."

"I trust Lily and yourself with my life. I do feel totally safe in your company." Roselinde smiled up at me and I felt a deep connection going back many lives. A silent inner voice told me that it was not the first time that she had uttered those very words to me.

We sat relaxing in the afternoon sun for another half an hour. Then the girls decided to go up to their room in order to get changed into more comfortable exploring apparel.

"Meet you back here at 16:00hrs!" I said as I started to make some notes on the curious space time anomaly that had just occurred. As I sipped my cognac and coffee, I zoomed in on the picture I had taken on my mobile. The marks had the definite look of contusions caused by rope strangulation yet neither Lily nor myself had witnessed any physical pressure being brought to bear on Roselinde's neck in the minutes leading up to the incident.

After several minutes I made my way to my room which was next to the girls on the 1st floor. I changed into my grey cotton travel and trek jacket and matching cargo pants. I was now ready for the experiment. I was intuitively aware that Reims was Roselinde's journey as I had no feeling of connection at the deep subconscious level. Perhaps for me the events of 1429 hadn't been so memorable in this city if at all. We would soon see?

I sat back down under the white parasols of the pavement cafe that belonged to Hôtel Le Bristol. Within a few minutes the girls reappeared. Lily was dressed in her usual "ready for anything" Lara Croft outfit with her Pentax camera slung around her youthful neck and Roselinde was in a khaki green safari suit. She looked every inch the quintessential English lady explorer crossed with a distinctive World War II theme. As if to accentuate the look she wore a khaki olive British army scrim scarf that gave the whole ensemble a distinctive military feel. She looked intriguing. Her long blonde hair flowed to her shoulders and was held in place by her sunglasses which were perched high on her head where they acted as an efficient Alice band. Around her neck she had an expensive Nikon D 900 SLR camera with a series of interchangeable lenses in cases strapped to her belt. On her back she also had a small hiking pack which seemed to bulge with who knows what? Certainly both girls looked similar in attire and accoutrements. I could see that there was a definite connection between them and that they both meant serious business.

I smiled and stood up as they approached the table. Lily burst into life and was first to speak, "What's the plan, Yann?"

"I'm prepared to let the dice roll on this one, but I thought we would start with the cathedral as it was the focus of attention in 1429." I voiced my thoughts as for me this trip was very much an open ended experiment.

Roselinde slid her sunglasses into place in the same fashion that a medieval knight would drop his visor before combat. "Let's go then!" She said with purpose and determination. It was a simple phrase but delivered with the urgency of a command or order. Her confidence was high, yet I could tell that she was nervous. With that we strode onto the paved surface of Place Drouet D'Erlon.

I let the girls lead the way as I wanted to observe the proceedings so they walked slightly in front of me. As we headed towards the golden winged victory monument in the direction of the cathedral the girls walked with all the presence and concentration of a couple of gunslingers on main-street at high noon. Roselinde even gripped her camera like a carbine and was busy shooting pictures on the move as we progressed. Just then all of a sudden she veered off to the right into a side street. This wasn't part of the plan but I was content to say nothing and see what would happen. I knew that Roselinde was navigating using her intuition as she was engaged in deep conversation with Lily.

They walked for fifty odd metres and then swung left into; I did a double take for the street sign on the wall read - Rue Jehanne d'Arc!!!?

Out of all the streets in Reims how did Roselinde know that this was Rue Jehanne d'Arc? The girls kept walking oblivious to my silent observation. They continued for another 30 metres then Roselinde came to an abrupt halt.

I caught up with them and was concerned to find Roselinde doubled over in obvious pain. "What's happened? You were alright a moment ago. I was having trouble keeping up with this roller coaster of a ride.

"I don't know?" Lily said with a sound of exasperation and a note of desperation. She had one arm around Roselinde and was obviously supporting her dead body weight. Roselinde seemed to be gasping for breath, was turning blue and convulsing into body shock. I removed her sunglasses and was astonished to see her eyes had rolled back into her head with only the whites showing.

I could see that Roselinde was dying. My heart sank as I clutched her lifeless rag doll body to mine. Anaphylactic shock – the words rang in my head as I desperately sought an answer to this monumental crisis. "Quick Lily, check her backpack, see if she has an epipen?" I had drawn the logical conclusion from her symptoms. She wasn't convulsing as an epileptic would yet she was displaying extreme shock symptoms. I checked for swelling to her lips. Lily searched frantically amongst Roselinde's possessions; torch; rope; knife. "Who now-a-days carries a torch, a rope and knife?!" Lily exclaimed.

"Obviously our Lady Roselinde," I said half listening as I contemplated her lifeless body, "Quick faster..."

"No, no epipen - what now?" Lily shouted with forceful emotion. Her intensity shocked me into action. "We must start her heart and get her breathing; CPR."

I undid her blouse buttons and exposed her bare chest, then undid the catches of her brassier. Checking her windpipe for obstructions, I gently tilted her head backwards to open her airway. It was then that I noticed the return of the reddish blue rope mark bruising to her neck. Putting that to the back of my mind I pinched her nose and gave Roselinde three rescue breathes to re-inflate her lungs. Then I placed both of my hands over her heart and rhythmically pumped five times; Lily watched transfixed, "can you hear us Roselinde, don't slip away like this, you're a fighter."

I cupped my mouth to her blue lips and inflated her chest once again. Then I continued with the rhythmic pumping action on the breast bone. On the third count she spluttered into life, convulsed and begun breathing again. Gasping for air like a drowning person surfacing she opened her eyes wide and started coughing freely. I checked her pulse – it was strong.

"Thank God you are alive, Roselinde. I thought we had lost you. Keep breathing, deep and long." She seemed to comprehend my words and deepened her breathing as Lily cradled her head into a more comfortable semi-reclining position. The backpack made an excellent pillow.

"Where am I?" Roselinde stammered, finding it difficult to speak.

"It's OK. You are safe. You've had a nasty turn that's all. We just need to find out why?" It was then that I looked up and saw the possible answer to my question; it immediately sent shivers down my spine.

SQUARE DES VICTIMES DE LA GESTAPO

The forbidding epitaph was mounted in large capital letters on a stark rectangular concrete lintel that surmounted a large iron railing designed to look like prison bars. The iron grille faced onto a tranquil garden in which stood a simple monument. It was composed of two pillars side by side containing what looked like embossed plaques. It was difficult to make out the detail from where I was standing so I resolved to return later to record the details. It was a sign from the universe I knew that, there had to be a connection. My computer like mind quickly put the clues together yet I said nothing so as not to reinforce the trauma or bias the experience.

Several passers-by attracted by the commotion asked if we wanted and ambulance. Roselinde now quite recovered and with the colour returned to her lips and cheeks positively declined and waved them on. She readjusted her clothing and miraculously stood up without assistance; albeit shakily. "That was a novel experience. I've had worse days at the office though!" She said in a jesting tone. "See France and die!" she continued flippantly as she brushed herself down. Leaning against the railings she regained her serious composure.

"This is where it happened." She suddenly said in an emotional quivering voice. Tears started to well up in her eyes and she gazed beyond the railings into the quiet garden. I noticed she clutched the cold iron bars like a prisoner condemned with a look of lost hope in her eyes.

"What happened?" I spoke softly in her ear. I could half guess the answer from my observations but I wanted her to say it without coercion.

"This is where I died, May 30, 1942. I had been tortured relentlessly for several weeks and finally they lost patience and hung me from a rope over there." Roselinde pointed with a quivering finger through the railings to a space now filled with the scented flowers of a memorial garden. "It was a big building, gothic in appearance like a small chateau with a tower. The headquarters of the Geheim Stats Polizei; the dreaded *Gestapo,* I was a Dutch resistance worker, an undercover agent working for the French underground here in Reims."

"What did you see when you had the psychokinetic episode just now?" Lily asked softly.

"It was totally real. I was marched out to a courtyard by two soldiers in black uniforms with white lightning strike collar badges and steel helmets bearing swastikas. I looked down at their shiny jackboots which clattered metallically on the flagstones. I couldn't bring myself to look at the noose and scaffold. I wanted to die bravely without fear and signs of trembling. I didn't want to give them that pleasure. Without ceremony they stood me on a chair and fastened the noose around my neck. I could feel the rough hemp chafe against my bare skin. I found myself praying to Mary mother of Jesus and Saint Catherine. They then kicked the chair away and I just dangled there in fee space, convulsing like a macabre marionette, slowly choking. The last thing I remember was the face of the hideous man who had tortured me smiling and smoking a cigarette. He wore a black leather coat and a fedora hat with a large brim. He had compounded his torture by playing a concert piano in the evening as I lay in my cell weeping. The combination of my love of classical music superimposed on my daily regime of pain, humiliation and relentless questioning was more than my soul could bear. Yet I did not break and betray the names of the underground workers who were helping me hide the Jewish refugees in the Champagne caves nearby. I was glad to die and put an end to my suffering. It was my only escape..." With that her voice faltered as she clutched her bruised throat.

Lily and I just stood in stunned silence. The experience was totally beyond words. I put a reassuring arm around Roselinde's delicate shoulder as she stood trembling and white faced, all muscle tone drained from her body. Lily did the same and the three of us just embraced for some several minutes as we all came to terms with what we had just unexpectedly transpired. Lily was first to break away and began collecting up the spilt belongings from the pavement. I just hugged Roselinde with both arms and repeatedly kissed her soothingly on the forehead as she sobbed into my chest making my shirt wet. I could feel the life returning to her body as she regained her composure and collected her thoughts.

After adjusting our apparel we finally began walking back to the Hôtel le Bristol. On arrival Lily accompanied Roselinde to their room for a rest, both girls looked thoroughly drained. I slipped anonymously into my room next door after ordering a cafe cognac to be sent up to the girls and one for me also. Lying on the bed I went repeatedly over the events that had just transpired and decided to record them onto paper whilst they were fresh in my memory. I first noticed the strange coincidence of the numbers 1429 and 1942 being composed of the same digits only rearranged like an anagram and then Roselinde's identical May 30th date that she quoted, the same as the execution of Jehanne d'Arc, which was yet another bizarre coincidence.

My thoughts were interrupted by a loud knock at the door that pushed me into action. I greeted the porter with my coffee and tipped him. After jotting down my thoughts, feelings and observations I had the presence of mind to return to the scene and photograph the details for the record. Using the HD video facility on my compact 12 megapixel Fuji camera I recorded the garden through the railings. I was able to zoom in on the plaque that bore the names of those executed there by the Gestapo. I knew that this might prove important and it would save us a lot of time for we would have to get the authorities to unlock the gate for access and that would take days.

I sensed that once the wounds had gone cold and begun to heal Roselinde would want to exorcise this ghost in her memory. I was sure that any evidence would help, so behaving like a CSI forensic officer I gathered every possible shred and clue whilst it was still fresh. I found the whole experience extremely disconcerting and uncomfortable. My emotions ranged from anger to sadness, I had trouble remaining objective as the horror of Roselinde's description sank in.

Somehow the events of 1429 being that much further back in linear time seemed strangely more acceptable. It was an irrational thought as I knew that in truth, there was only the *eternal now* in the higher dimensional universe, I felt sure that this was the true abode of our conscious and subconscious minds. A strange thought occurred to me, the men in black uniforms with white insignia had executed *her* here on this spot, yet the men in black uniforms, the black brethren, had saved *her* from execution in 1429!

It was a magical *eureka* moment of revelation into the deeper workings of the universe - we always have to experience the opposites in order to learn and truly understand the lesson. The resurgent memories of several other incidences suddenly reinforced and confirmed my observation. Perhaps I had discovered a universal principle? I made several pages of notes with the prefix - must discuss this with Lily double underlined.

Returning to the hotel for a second time I went to my room on the first floor. Dinner was at 20:00hrs, so I had time to shower and change I guessed that we would dine in after our traumatic experiences and the long unexpectedly eventful day. My assumption proved correct as no sooner had that thought crossed my mind than a text came through from Lily.

All OK! Fully recovered see you in the dining room at eight... Fleur d'Lily X

Well all must be right with the quantum universe if I can pre-empt Lily's thoughts that accurately! I allowed myself a smile, what a journey this was and it is only day one of our expedition to Reims. I felt literally mind blown yet again at the frequency of these quantum coincidences which seemed to be speeding up exponentially. This was yet another topic that I was eager to discuss over dinner with the girls along with my findings.

At five to eight I descended the elaborate stairway into the chandelier lit lobby and made my way to the atmospherically lit hotel restaurant. The plush claret coloured velvet booths each surmounted by an imposing walled arch bearing a large single back lit fleur-de-lys affixed to the wall made for a perfect gothic ambience. In one of the larger alcoves of the restaurant there was a large copy of a famous 15th century painting by Albrecht Dürer two flying angels receiving a blue banner containing three gold fleur-de-lys from God and hovering above a procession of noble women being given the same banner by a saint. They then appear in the Cathedral of Reims presenting the arms on a shield to Clovis ceremonially at the site of the original sacred coronation scene. It was a weighty reminder of the true purpose of the mighty Reims cathedral the hereditary enthroning centre of the Kings of France. For Sainte Remi had baptised Clovis the first King of France at the very spot nearby where there now stands the church of Sainte Remi. I mused in my head that the angelic beings were what we would call ETs today and that history was somehow an orchestrated pageant of intranet galactic proportions. The thought vanished instantly as I considered the irony that our first encounter had been distinctly non-gothic and very close up and personal. The shadow of the Nazis clouded my mind as I sat at our reserved table below the sacred gold fleur d'lys and waited silently for the girls.

Fashionably late, they appeared five minutes later looking none the worse for the trauma that we had experienced earlier that day.

"Bon soirée Yann!" Roselinde said with a charming elegant almost royal smile. She looked stunning in an all-electric blue off the shoulder Chanel cocktail dress that simmered in the candle light with tiny gold flecks. She looked fabulous, long loose luxurious blonde hair cascaded down and framed her elven features. The dress perfectly complimented her willowy sinuous body regally and I couldn't help thinking that she would fit perfectly into the portrait of angels on the wall. She was simply the divine manifest. A very different lady to the one I had seen earlier that day.

"Bonsoir Roselinde," I rose from my seat and taking her right hand kissed it reverently, then I kissed her softly on both cheeks. She blushed being unused to French manners. Lily coughed theatrically. "Bonsoir Yann!" She echoed in a somewhat mocking fashion and curtsied theatrically. I laughed at her comedic performance and likewise kissed her theatrically on the hand and both cheeks. "I get the distinct feel that you are more used to wielding a sword my Fleur d'Lily than engaging in courtly niceties."

"Of course! She riposte with lightning speed and struck a theatrical musketeer's salute minus the sword. "But I am still very beautiful am I not!" With that she tossed her beautiful chestnut hair back over her shoulder and laughed!

Roselinde smiled at our jesting which alleviated the obvious fact that Lily might just be a tad jealous and that we would soon be engage in a much deeper and darker discussion. We settled into our seats. Lily ordered a super champagne aperitif and passed the a la carte menu around. "After the day we've had we deserve a treat, if our paper won't cover with expenses I will!" Her air of self-assurance visibly impressed Roselinde.

"Then I shall stand the wine!" Not to be out done I quickly stepped up to the mark. "Whatever you desire?" I added with a flourish and a smile.

"My word you do live well!" Roselinde exclaimed as she glanced over the top of her half rimmed designer reading glasses whilst perusing the imposing menu.

"Of course we are French you know - Un pour tous et tous pour un!" I replied in jest as I quoted the famous musketeer phrase. "No, actually not really, we are splashing out because you are in town and our honoured guest."

Lily and I deliberately kept the mood upbeat throughout the excellent meal. After several courses with matching wines we started on a light dessert and settled down to listen to Roselinde's account of her experiences. In a series of intense and vivid flashbacks she recalled the last six weeks of her previous life as a resistance worker in Nazi occupied Reims. I felt my grip on the table cloth get tighter and tighter as I listened intently to the barbarous nature of the torture inflicted on her. She talked steadily without pausing and showed no emotion. Lily and I could see that she was releasing all of her blocked memories and thereby healing herself at the same time. Without warning as she neared the end she suddenly grimaced, stammered and burst into tears. The dam of emotion had burst, it was important to let her expunge the horror of the psychic wound in order to complete the process. After that the memory could no longer hurt her.

The details of the execution were horrendously matter of fact. It was obviously a well rehearsed perfunctory process carried out with German efficiency. Allowing the victim to dangle and choke slowly to death was particularly cruel and old fashioned as modern societies had perfected the trapdoor technique to snap the neck and cut any suffering mercifully short. It was all terribly macabre but again very necessary in order to complete the debrief. I empathised as I had been hung in a previous life, as a Druid, by the Romans in the time of Vercingetorix. There was a definite parallel with the Romans and the Nazis perhaps the same malevolent soul group reincarnating. Roselinde's account stirred dark and painful memories in my soul. I felt my throat constrict and found it difficult to swallow. The memory was a fleeting shadow in my subconscious but like a hungry wolf in the pit of my mind it began to howl. It needed release but this was not the time or place. This was Roselinde's moment.

Roselinde remained disciplined and behaved with dignity as a military prisoner in her demeanour. She had suffered in many many lives, always willingly, selflessly and for the greater good. She continued to recount other sundry facts and the graphic nature of her flashback experience. I poured her a large glass of wine and gestured that she should take a sip as I too needed to clear my throat. Both Lily and I could see that she was obviously reliving those terrifying moments in character but her soul was now recounting them in the third person. With that the emotional pain was disconnected thank goodness.

I leaned forward with a tear in my eye and clutched Roselinde's trembling hand. "It's all gone now. You can just float above it and heal in the warm sunlight."

Lily smiled and placed her hand gently on top of ours. Her warmth and love penetrated my skin and as my hand warmed so the heat conducted through to Roselinde. "Many lives, many sacrifices," She said melancholically and with a deep philosophical resonance that belied her tender years.

Roselinde smiled and broke free of our touch. Then she raised her champagne glass and toasted the proceedings. "That was yesterday, this is today, let us enjoy the NOW!" With that she emptied her champagne flute with swift but elegant decorum.

By now it was midnight the waiters were eager to clear away the debris of our exquisite repas. The girls excused themselves from the table. It had been a very long and unexpectedly eventful day. We embraced and kissed on the cheeks then they turned and left me alone as I had been not 4 hours earlier.

Tomorrow would be another day and our journey would continue, of that I had no doubt for Reims wasn't finished with us yet.

Chapter 21

Visite des Caves

he morning dawned and I awoke early. After the drama of the day before I was still thinking things over in my head, somewhat unexpectedly World War 2 had taken over from the anticipated medieval scenario but at least Roselinde was able to tune in to her subconscious memory. I hoped that today would bring a more expected result in line with our quest. It was however up to Roselinde, as simple as that.

I shaved, showered and dressed. I then made my way down to breakfast to await the girls. I hoped that they had at least had a restful night, we would see shortly, I then text Lily a cheery note whilst the waiter took my order, a light continental breakfast with a couple of soft boiled eggs. The eggs arrived and proved perfectly boiled, the sign of a good kitchen as it requires precise timing.

The girls arrived after a lull of 15 minutes during which time I perused the morning paper; they looked sleepy.

"Morning Yann, hope you slept well? We slept a bit but Roselinde had a strange vivid dream. I think it may have some bearing on our investigation today?" Lily poured a glass of orange juice and left to check out the buffet.

"Morning, I had a chance to reflect on yesterday's events, it was quite a baptism of fire!" Roselinde was still ashen faced. "We will have to visit the basilica Saint Remi today it figured large in my dreams last night and I really need to get to the bottom of this immediate past life. I understand the mechanisms involved now and feel confident that I can control the psychosomatic effects. I don't think we are going to have a repeat of yesterday's extremes." She seemed reflective and calm even though her neck bore mute witness to the incident she referred to.

I offered her a seat and placed my hand on hers in reassurance as she sat to the table. She smiled and we exchanged a knowing glance of empathy. It was a look that we had shared before in some other life of that I knew instantly. "OK the ball is in your court we will follow your lead and support you in any way we can."

"Thank you I can't begin to tell you how happy that makes me, I am determined to get to the bottom of this black morass that is blocking my mind." With that she studied the breakfast menu peering periodically over the top of her designer reading glasses. Lily returned and smiled, the colour was returning to her cheeks as she found her appetite. We made pleasant conversation and finished with some strong French coffee. The girls then left the room and I sat making a mental note of our plans in my head. The large brown wooden fleur de lys on the wall all the time reminding me of our medieval mission.

Returning to my room whilst checking my weather app I noticed the day would be somewhat overcast with a possibility of heavy summer showers later so I packed my French army Gore-Tex light weight waterproof in my bag. Handy and practical it was extremely easy to carry and totally weatherproof yet breathable. The threatening weather added a certain dramatic emphasis to the darkness we had encountered yesterday. I shouldered my bag and camera, walked down the stairs, then through reception to the pavement beyond the cafe, at the front of the hotel. The girls arrived at 8:30 on the dot and were eager to get going. Roselinde was determined to follow the clues in her dream and said straight away that we would head for the Basilica Saint Remi at the lower end of the town near the champagne caves.

We had a clear purpose and direction so I let the girls lead as I had done the day previous. The pavement was busy with cafes and hotels going about the early morning breakfast trade. It was the height of the tourist season and Reims was very busy. Place Drouet-d'Erlon was a thriving hive of activity even on a cloudy day passing through we marched steadily onward towards la Fontaine Subé. At the fountain we took the right fork into Rue des Capucins the scenery was more town like and less tourist orientated, traffic thronged the streets as the local populous made their way to work.

Roselinde seemed to know exactly where she was going despite her never having set foot in Reims. Straight as a die she continued until we reached Rue du Ruisselet which crossed our route at right angles immediately in front of the Saint Remi business administrative district. The large imposing buildings were obviously linked to the champagne industry of which Reims is the world centre. We took a left and walked the short distance to Rue Simon.

Roselinde immediately went right and continued her linear journey following her subconscious instincts. We didn't have far to go and soon passed the imposing gated entrance to the Musée Saint Remi. Just beyond that was the western facade of the basilica Saint Remi, its imposing twin rectilinear steeples standing tall either side of the classic quintuplet of porticos surmounted by five beautiful stained glass windows above which an enormous many spoke wheel rose window grandly sat, yet again above that was a trinity clover leaf window just beneath the apex of the roof gable end. The basilica Saint Remi was a master piece of gothic ecclesiastical design, its architectural perfection assailed the senses with a celebration of the masons' art.

Without hesitation and as though in a trance Roselinde entered the basilica Saint Remi via one of the lesser porticos that had an open door; Lily followed as did I. The outside gave way to a vast cavernous space of gothic limestone architecture which seemed to stretch to the sky. The air changed instantly, it was much colder and musty to the senses. The smell of damp and old relics pervaded the air.

Walking up the main aisle as though on a divine mission Roselinde continued, "Jesus holds the key; Jesus holds the key; Jesus holds the key," she kept repeating over and over still in a semi hypnotic trance. We finally reached the mausoleum of Saint Remi at the eastern end of the basilica. The stone frieze of five life sizes bishops from antiquity surrounded the large enclosed reliquary on the right side, kings to the left. It was an affirmation of holiness and the blessing for the bones of the saint within; a lesson for the ordinary people that proclaimed the authority of the church over them. Everything was designed to overpower the senses and impress.

Having completed a circuit I peered through the bars of the sacred monument and came face to face with Saint Remi who had baptised the Frankish king Clovis I on December 24, 496AD. This eventually led to the conversion of all the Frankish people to Nicene Christianity, a seminal event in European history. The reason for this miraculous conversion was the recent victory of Clovis I over the Alamanni at the battle of Tolbiac earlier that year. I thought of the irony of how much blood had been spilt for the great Christian god in the name of peace and progress. Even the Nazis had *'Gott mit uns'* on their belt buckles in World War 2, I baulked at the thought, perhaps this explained my own individual spiritual path as a rejection of established pre-revolutionary religious dogma.

My thoughts were swept aside as Roselinde came back around the tomb still chanting her monotone mantra, "Jesus holds the key." She continued without blinking back the way we came down the main aisle but this time she took a hard left into the transept. She continued onward and only came to a stop in front of the most beautiful life size stone sculptured tableau of medieval figures surrounding the body of Jesus lying on a shroud post crucifixion.

"Jesus holds the key; he shall set my children free." The words came automatically out of Roselinde's pale lips as she stood observing the scene without blinking. She was literally like a blind woman feeling her way by tapping into her pre-programmed subconscious memory. The once familiar pattern of a previous incarnation was playing its haunting message for us to hear. Lily and I stood back one pace on either side not wishing to disturb the process and trance like state. We silently willed her on - come on Roselinde, remember, you can do this! I kept repeating those words over and over in my mind as though joining in with her mantra and sharing my own ethereal energy with her. I guessed Lily was doing the same.

Then she clicked into action like some automaton released from its mechanical bondage. She suddenly ducked under the partitioning rope, then past the small tributes of flowers in pots of various sizes and disappeared behind the large plinth amongst the figures. In the ensuing pause I had time to take in the group of sculptures. Jesus lay supine on a shroud with two medieval renaissance figures at his head and toes. They showed some signs of fire damage as I could see the marble of the front two figures was slightly discoloured with the brownish hue of burnt residue.

A hooded Virgin Mary leant over the body praying and being supported by Saint John. I guessed this as the cross displayed on the plinth was of Knight Templar origin so the Knights of Saint John would not be far behind. A well dressed woman stood to the left of Mary and to the right was an extremely voluptuous Mary Magdalene who was most obviously pregnant with child, her arms up raised in distress with tears running down her cheeks, around her head was the inference of a halo denoting her heavenly status. She again was supported by another well dressed woman. From the life like quality of the statues and style of carving I estimated that the whole ensemble was from the renaissance period around 1530.

I stood momentarily transfixed by the sheer beauty of the workmanship. My mind connected to the Templar mind that had commissioned this masterpiece. The significance of the story of the bloodline of Jesus being transferred through Mary Magdalene down to the descendants of the Merovingian kings suddenly hit me. This was undoubtedly the reason that the remarkable sculptures had found their place of honour in the basilica Saint Remi, the traditional resting place of the holy ampoule containing the anointing oil of the monarchy of France. For had not Mary Magdalene anointed Christ with scented oil and thereby gained the disapproval of the disciples for wasting money. Legend has it that she died in Provence in 63AD giving yet another French connection.

My train of thought was disturbed by the sound of stone grinding on stone. I looked at Lily; she had heard the same unmistakable noise. Roselinde must have found a secret compartment at the back of the plinth! Then a triumphant Roselinde stood up straight amongst the statues like a living carving being raised from the dead and holding aloft a large rusty iron key.

"Jesus holds the key; now he shall set my children free!"

Roselinde smiled a euphoric smile of both revelation and vindication all rolled into one. "This is what I dreamt of. It's all true! The rest of the dream must be too!" With that she ducked back down and we heard the now familiar grinding noise of stone on stone again. Lily and I looked around to see if we were being observed, we were quite alone, so our dramatic discovery had gone unnoticed.

Roselinde crept stealthily back around to the front of the sculpture plinth and ducked back under the rope. She looked like a naughty school girl that had just broken the rules. A huge grin lit up her face. Lily and I looked at the large intricate rusted key that was obviously several hundred years old.

"Wow, I wonder what it unlocks and what it has seen during its history?" Lily was dying to hold the key as if she intuitively knew she could use her psychometric powers to discover its dark secrets.

But there was no time as Roselinde triumphantly declared, "We shall find out very shortly, follow me!"

Using my iPhone I snapped a quick couple of pictures of the key in her outstretched hand and several of the sculptured tableau for reference. They would come in handy later for analysis during our debrief over dinner. Lily did the same but with her much more expensive camera which she had expedited from her rucksack in an instant. Without waiting of us to finish Roselinde was off, she spun on her heels and headed back across the transept into the north wing.

"West to east, south to north; then underground we travel forth!" She repeated the words from her subconscious like a magical spell in a child's fairy tale. We reached the north quarter of the cross shaped basilica that adjoins the cloisters of the abbey Saint Remi. "We have to look downwards now." Roselinde whispered in a hushed voice, "The crypt, we must find the crypt." Lily spotted a sign and we took a small doorway leading to some well-worn stairs. Daylight disappeared and was replaced by a subdued subterranean hue composed of minimal safety lighting and flickering prayer candles burning in large black iron candelabras that illuminated the darkened alcoves and recesses. We had descended to the original level of the sacred basilica. The vaulted ceiling was repressively close compared to the airy cavernous space above. Its forest of thick limestone columns were much closer together and extremely claustrophobic.

"This is the site of the holy ampoule, it is all strangely familiar. I've been here before!" Lily spoke in hushed tones to herself but it was audibly loud enough for us to hear given the perfect acoustics of the darkened crypt. My eyes lit up at this unexpected revelation. I knew she was right as I too felt the same déjà vu feeling; we had hit medieval pay dirt! My heart leapt into my mouth as I realised my initial intuitive feelings at the beginning of the day had come true. Perhaps Lily and I had been involved in the fetching and the sacred procession ceremony of retrieving the holy oil and escorting it to the coronation of the dauphin Charles VII in 1429. It felt right every bone in my body knew the truth of that thought. Lily smiled at me a knowing smile, I knew she felt the same and like me was remembering the same thought synchronistically. The medieval quest was back on track and somehow mysteriously entwined with Roselinde's World War 2 memory.

"What are we looking for?" I said quizzically as I snapped back to the present NOW moment. My, what I thought were whispered comments, boomed back in the echoing darkness of the void.

"Ssh... not so loud! We are looking for the door which fits the key." Roselinde said in a matter of fact way as if stating the obvious for she was totally unaware that Lily and I had slipped out mentally for a moment and were only now rejoining the plot.

"Not a buried treasure chest then?" I quipped in a desperate attempt at humour to lighten the moment and cover up my own appalling lack of grasping the blatantly obvious.

"No, certainly not!" Roselinde's verbal chastisement for my levity cut to the quick. "We are not children playing pirates!" With that she softened her visage and smiled as if to confirm that I had not been totally obtuse. "Treasure comes in many forms, mine is knowledge."

She was right we were hot on the trail and might discover something of import; wise words indeed. By now we had come to the eastern most wall of the crypt underneath the reliquary of Saint Remi who lay in sacred repose just above our heads. A solid wall confronted us. This was obviously a very special place as several small tributes of flowers had been placed at its base. It was also highlighted with its own spot light. I knew it was the resting place of the holy ampoule and the baptism place of Clovis. Roselinde stopped in her tracks and started tapping the flagstones of the floor. They appeared pretty permanent and very solid to me. The sound was completely dead denoting solidity to the touch, chalk or limestone obviously lay under their shiny smooth surface. Lily and I stood in complete silence as Roselinde persisted with her tapping, our collective ears strained for the slightest change in pitch. We instinctively knew what she was doing as it echoed in our minds for this was something we had done in another time and place.

Then we heard a distinct change in pitch that rose from a dull thud to something altogether lighter in tone, almost metallic. Roselinde tried again several times just to make sure. It was definitely a different sound. She dropped to her hands and knees and produced a torch from her knapsack. Shining the beam on the joints surrounding the flagstone she examined the detail. "This is it!" She excitedly exclaimed, "See the joints are not solidly compacted with mortar, the stone is removable. It's been used many times over the centuries and still works for those with eyes to see!"

The penny dropped as Lily and I both understood simultaneously, "Of course a trapdoor!" We exclaimed in unison, it had to be. "But we will never shift it." Lily said with a tone of dismay in her muted voice, "It must be way too heavy and I'm not breaking my nails for anybody!"

"Maybe not?" replied Roselinde stoically, "I have just the thing." she replied with a wink and a smile, then reached into her knapsack to retrieve a small crowbar! Was there no end to this lady's talents; a crowbar! Who on earth carries a crowbar in their luggage? Obviously this lady; came the silent reply in my mind. Roselinde never ceased to amaze me, much as Lily did all the time.

Swiftly she inserted the flattened end into a small worn groove that would escape the notice of the casual observer, especially in the dark. Sure enough the flagstone started to move, it was indeed much thinner than imagined and the reason became apparent as the flagstone lifted. It was a dressing of stone veneer underpinned by a well oiled shiny manufactured iron sheet of armoured steel. Within seconds Roselinde had the slab up with the familiar ease of an operation performed many times. Lily shone her torch into the gaping abyss, it was pitch black except for the remains of a simple iron ladder to one side of the opening that was just big enough for a single human being to slip through; it was in short a medieval manhole. The riveting and flaking wrought iron workmanship covered in rust stood testament to its great age.

"So a medieval bolt hole for the monks of the Abbey to be used in times of duress, very ingenious and very logical." I said as I admired their handy work from long ago.

"Yes and used up until recent times if my memory serves me correct for this is where my dream runs out and I awoke!" Roselinde pondered the darkness of the abyss she was not scared but seemed apprehensive of what she might encounter below. Lily had no such qualms. "There's one sure way to find out where it goes; follow me!" With that she sat immediately on the ledge of the gaping blackness, placed her torch in her clenched teeth and her feet firmly on the rungs of the ladder and deftly disappeared from sight. It was the perfect demonstration of the agility of youth, executed with all the swiftness of the magician's art at making anything disappear.

I smiled at Roselinde, "It's what she does!" I said with an element of pride in my nimble assistant's élan, "*Après vous mademoiselle!*" I extended my hand elegantly in a cavalier flourish as I helped Roselinde find her balance, "I will act as rearguard in this instance, for I am no match for you girls!" I gave a cheeky smile as I accentuated the girls. After repacking her trusty crowbar into her knapsack she attached a thin but strong chord to its harness and lowered it with a smile and then descending into the darkness below shouted, "and I didn't even break a nail!" Roselinde emulated Lily's deft movements with surprising ease as if polished by years of practice, she was an amazing lady.

Bringing up the rear I squeezed into the small gap and dropped down onto the rungs of the ladder and then carefully dropped my bag down to Roselinde in the darkness below. I took a last look around, no one was there, so satisfied I eased the false flagstone back into place above my head much as a loft hatch cover, with a few jiggles it fell into place with a snugly fit. I was pretty sure that no one would be any the wiser above. I made a mental note in my mind that we should go back to check at the end of the day just in case.

The ladder dropped for several meters and then opened into a larger tunnel of roughhewn appearance. I switched my torch on. The ancient pick marks from the excavated walls could clearly be seen and it was obviously built for people of a much smaller stature as it was no more than a little over one and a half metres high. This was starting to give me déjà vu. I had experienced this before but not here for I had experienced no clear flashbacks as of yet which puzzled me. I could hear the girls up ahead talking as they went. Lily was still in the lead. Both were in their element Roselinde seemed empowered in total contrast to the day before.

The tunnel went due east in a straight line. I estimated by pacing that it extended some 300 metres. Unfortunately the gps on my iPhone wasn't working due to lack of signal but I could work it out later from memory.

"We've found the door!" Lily's muffled voice exclaimed from the dimly lit murk ahead. I caught up within a few seconds of the shout. The passage was still very narrow but I could tell that Roselinde was passing the key to Lily in the dark by the shuffling. "It's an iron bound oaken door with a lock. I'm giving it a go."

An audible click and a turning noise could be heard in the oppressive stillness. Surprisingly it opened with ease. The door swung open with a creak into the space beyond. I guessed this as I had not received word to back up. I followed the girls through being relieved to finally stand upright and stretch my back. The girls were busy shining their torches around to investigate the dimensions of the cavernous space and check for obstacles. It was a fair size at least, I estimated that it was a good 3 metres high by 10 long and 5 wide. At the far end gaping black tunnels went off in 3 directions but there were no sign posts to indicate anything.

"Interesting, this does seem somewhat familiar, I must say!" Roselinde half muttered to herself.

"Right take a tunnel each, ten minutes to explore, all meet back here - agreed?" Lily sounded decisive so we all agreed without question.

"I'll go straight on." Roselinde said using her intuition.

"I'll go right then." Lily stated without hesitation.

"Ladies prerogative; guess I'll take the left then!" I finished the sentence without blinking. Looking at my iPhone, I continued, "Synchronise watches, 10:13hrs exactly, on my mark, three, two, one, mark." The girls checked their timepieces and then melted silently into the darkness like apparitions.

My tunnel ran on for some 100 metres overall but doubled back on itself at least three times. Preceding each twist was a cavernous space some 20 metres in length off to the side opposite to the bend. I check for booby trap wires at each entrance before cautiously entering but they contained only discarded champagne racks against the ancient walls interspersed with neat piles of old woollen blankets folded with care. I examined them perfunctorily. They were full of moth holes for the most part and covered in dust and bat droppings so I knew that there was ventilation somewhere. I rapidly scanned with my torch and simultaneously drawing my lighter struck a flame and watched it flicker in confirmation but the draught came from the direction I had come from.

The labels on the blankets showed that they were of French manufacture mainly but there were also large numbers of German blankets. Then a breakthrough occurred I found a smaller than normal one with personalised hand embroidery in the corner, the blanket was obviously that of a child with the name and date clearly displayed next to a large faded yellow Star of David; Joseph Jakob Epstein 7-7-36. It was definitely of World War 2 origin.

We were in the right time frame. I visualised Jewish refugees fleeing Nazi persecution making their tortuous way across Europe trying to avoid the anti-Semitic killing machine that surrounded them, their only hope to make it to Vichy France and beyond; seasonal grape pickers were always in demand, so what better cover story.

In another cave further on I discovered a half burnt pile of documents and ID cards bearing Jewish names. Half mutilated photographs of children and adults lit up under the glare of my torch. Time was pressing so I hurriedly continued on abandoning some of my initial caution. Finally as time was running out I turned a corner and came face to face with a cunningly constructed large door blocking my way. It had several bolts and was spring loaded with an elaborate mechanism. I paused taking it all in to my memory, then hurriedly took several flash photographs on my iPhone to show the girls. My eyes stung at the brightness of the flash as they had become accustomed to the darkness. My time was up so I retraced my steps back along the roughhewn labyrinth to the room with the iron reinforced oak door. I was first. The girls returned in quick succession, each clutching some more pieces of the puzzle.

"Right, who wants to go first?" I said as I greeted their torch lit faces.

'I will," Lily said impulsively, "as I didn't find much just caves and blankets and a ventilation shaft, it's narrow but navigable and I could see a faint glimmer of daylight up ahead.

Roselinde spoke next, "Mine was more fruitful, I found a cave with tables, old lamps, sewing machines, photography equipment, chemicals, sleeping quarters and a small printing press. The placed abounded with old blank ID documents and Nazi rubber stamps. It's worth another look as it must be the nerve centre of this underground complex, definitely World War 2 and very, very familiar."

I repeated the details of my findings and I could see Lily nodding in appreciation as the evidence mounted. I showed the girls the photos of the elaborate door. "It must be the way out." Roselinde surmised, "It's very elaborate, let's try it after we have explored the command centre and the ventilation tunnel, at least the air is breathable and there are bats!" She smiled half expecting a reaction.

"Nice!" Lily said stoically, "They are a protected species now, such irony when you think of the extermination camps for people seventy years ago."

"Interesting, so Lily's ventilation tunnel must be a way out for them." I said.

"It's definitely worth a look?" Lily added nonchalantly.

We followed Roselinde into the dark. Her torch lit the way and we were soon in a very large cave with a breeze coming into it from the opposite end. Bats could be seen clinging in their hundreds to the ceiling and droppings covered the floor. We began searching for artefacts, anything that could tell us the story of what had transpired here some 70 years previous.

"It looks undisturbed," Lily commented from under a desk in one corner. "Ouch! I've bumped my head!"

I giggled in mock sympathy, "Poor old you, good job you are thick skulled!"

"Certainly, it's one of my best attributes!" She laughed and carried on.

Roselinde had come to a grinding halt at the entrance of a small recess off of the main cave, the sleeping quarters as she now called it. "I got this far last time, but I can't go in! I've got a terrible feeling, my mind is blocking the memory and I feel nauseous."

"OK let me take a look, sounds like your subconscious has detected something of import?" I moved to her side ready to defend her against the unknown. My response surprised me, for it intuitively felt natural and was the same as that I felt in my flashback at Patay. It was the overwhelming urge to defend the princess, the name echoed in my head.

Without questioning further, I plunged in, re-engaging with the NOW moment. There was a small bed with an old oil lamp on a battered desk next to it. I then spotted an old brown leather case half pushed under the bed together with a couple of mouldy canvas medical bags in Wehrmacht grey. I reached for it and held it up to the light of our combined torches. It felt important. It was a civilian medical bag with a large printed red cross on it. I opened the now green with corrosion clamp fastening to examine the contents.

Bandages, field dressings, scissors, forceps, and a small brown bottle that reeked of iodine despite its contents being long crystallised; all standard World War 2 Wehrmacht issue.

Then my heart raced for inside there were some old photograph and a nurse's ID card, printed on the white card were the words

- Deutsches Rotes kreuz - Personal Ausweis

The official looking words were emblazoned on the front of the card in large black Gothic letters under a heraldic Nazi Eagle with a white swastika on its chest. I opened the card to examine the photograph and ID details inside and was stopped dead in my tracks as the torch light shone onto the face in the photograph. It was Roselinde! Roselinde in a German nurses uniform! Roselinde, yet it was not Roselinde? It was her, but not her, same face, same bone structure, same eyes, just younger and with much darker hair in a very different but contemporary for the times style! It was definitely her, I knew immediately we had struck gold and held it up to her face as I turned around.

"Oh my God, Look at this, look at this!" Lily immediately squeezed in behind my back to look over my shoulder, her reaction was instant.

"Wow! Same eyes, nose, chin everything, incredible!" She kept glancing backwards and forwards between the photograph and Roselinde's puzzled white face.

"May I see please?" Her shaky hand extended to grasp the ID card.

Roselinde saw the photograph and tears rolled down her cheeks as she connected with her past self in the NOW moment. This was a moment of supreme recognition, healing and of unblocking. No longer would the past haunt her soul and hold her captive, she held the proof in her hands.

"This belongs to you I believe." With dignity and quiet ceremony I handed over the brown case to her. With shaky hands she took it and replaced the Ausweis inside, finally shutting the clasp with a definitive click.

Undoing her knapsack she stowed the precious evidence and then re-shouldered her burden. With wet cheeks she gently smiled, her lip quivering, "Thank you, both of you thank you." Her voice was soft and faltering. "None of this would have happened if we hadn't met at Devizes. Crop circles have a lot to answer for!"

I smiled gently back and my eyes started to water as small tears formed and ran down my cheek. The emotion of the moment was something I could understand having had my own journey of revelation in Metz. I fully appreciated how she felt at this particular moment.

"Come on you two break it up we have work to do!" Lily was firmly focused and in the zone. "Right on to target two, the ventilation shaft, follow me." With a quick about face she spun around and left the small recessed bedroom. Roselinde and I followed. This time Roselinde took the rearguard position as she needed time to reflect on and remember her movements leading up to the discovery. For her the rest of today would be a blur as nothing could surpass the personal life changing experience that she had just experienced in that single moment.

Lily started up the right hand passage from the original room with the iron bound oaken door. It was narrow and rough much as the original passage way from the basilica. It also had a distinctive upward slope that made the going harder. We followed in hot pursuit torches illuminating our footing and the rough tool marks in the hewn limestone chalk. To the left after 50 metres I noticed a vent in the wall and surmised that it must be the conduit causing the draughts in the command centre cave. I continued upward and onward following Lily, she could certainly shift when she wanted to.

"I've found the end!" She shouted from up ahead in the darkness for her body blocked the light. "Yes, there's definitely light at the end of the tunnel!" She quipped and laughed at her own joke. This brought a smile to my face for I wasn't sure how to turn around in this tight space. There had to be an opening, it was only logical, a ventilation shaft and an escape route, two for one. "There is an iron grille, I'm going to pick the lock, wish me luck, otherwise we are stuck!"

Suddenly light shone in my eyes, Lily had exited the shaft and I could indeed see the light at the end of the tunnel! I squeezed through the small opening into green foliage and the overcast sunlight of a typical Reims day. It was grey but still bright as the sun was at its apogee in the summer sky.

Roselinde followed my lead emerging behind me into the same daylight. She blinked and shielded her light sensitive eyes then unslung her knapsack and reached for her sunglasses. "That's better, now I can see where we are?" She enquired in a ladylike tone, her composure had returned.

"Looks like we are in a wood, but I can hear traffic close by. It has to be part of a vineyard as we are surrounded by famous champagne houses. Perhaps it belongs to the champagne house who owns the caves?" Lily was busy scanning the wood with quick frantic movements and shielding her eyes. "There is a beautiful statue over there and some large concrete works built like a wall with steps. It backs onto a mound with trees."

I was just glad to be breathing clean air, unpolluted by damp, dust and bat droppings. I sat taking stock of events then took some photos on my iPhone. "Drink anyone?" I held up my water bottle and offered it around to the girls who gratefully sipped from its contents. I followed and we all then stretched out on the grass in a clearing among the trees. It was nice just to enjoy a rest and appreciate the fortuitous burst of sunshine that pushed momentarily through the clouds.

After twenty or so minutes rest the cloud returned as did a sudden drop in temperature, "Time to get moving again, I guess." My suggestion met with approval so we got up dusted ourselves down and started to explore. It seemed to be a designated green space composed of trees in a park like setting. Lots of paths crossed the grass, following them we soon stumbled upon the strange Greek like statue of a bearded man sat on quarried blocks of regularly dressed stone arranged as a wall with his arms resting on skewed block either side of him. It was a stunning evocative statue to man the builder cleverly set juxtapose amongst a natural woodland setting. "It says - *Le 1er Architecte* on the plaque by Paul Landowski. It's a good example of modern classical art in the Greek style." Roselinde spoke aloud as she read and was genuinely surprised by the find which turned a common semi-urban green space into a work of art.

"We are French, it's what we do!" Lily shouted back with pride as she ran up the concrete steps of the bunker like wall behind the statue. Two minutes later she returned into view. "You'll never guess what? We are right next to a main road! In fact it's a major five way junction like a huge roundabout but with no centre. That's the traffic noise you can hear, amazing, we are in an urban landscape yet it feels so rural."

Roselinde and I climbed the zig zagged concrete steps to the top and looked around. We could see neat organised vineyards to the South east, a woodland with an impressive Gothic inspired villa, but apart from that we were completely surrounded by buildings and roads. It was all an illusion! "Incredible, I could have sworn we were in the countryside!" I added, "Just shows you how disorientating it is when you are scurrying around in tunnels. Time to head back it's gone 2 o'clock now."

With that we descended the steps and found ourselves once more in what we now knew was a small park. Back we went into the green foliage and amongst the trees to the opening to the tunnel. We re-entered and Lily carefully locked the iron grille that prevented public access to the champagne caves below.

Daylight was replaced instantly with darkness as we stumbled on the rough passage floor. Soon we returned to the tunnel nexus, paused and then continued onward towards the elaborate door and the final piece of the puzzle. Within 20 minutes we had reached the mechanism. Roselinde took over. She seemed to understand what she was looking at. Sequentially she removed the bolts and slid the door, it was stiff with age but with help it started moving. The spring mechanism acted as a counter to the mass of the door making it easier to move than it should have been. Once open Roselinde slipped through the gap. Lily and I passed the knapsacks and my bag through and we followed.

We suddenly found ourselves in electrically lit dry modern tunnels and surrounded by champagne. The racked bottles lined the tunnel and the space between. Our mysterious door was in fact a rack filled with full champagne bottles hence its weight. We moved it back into position and Roselinde soon found the hidden catch that reset the bolts. We stood for a few minutes to admire the ingenuity and skill that had been put into the secret door; it was totally invisible to the uninitiated, "Vive le résistance! If I had cracked under torture it would not still be here untouched! I took the secret to my grave." It was a remarkable statement that only we who knew could fully appreciate.

Shouldering our baggage we set off to find our way out. As a working cellar, signposts abounded as did memorabilia. Following the sound of voices we soon stumbled across an organised tour and with care discreetly tacked ourselves onto the end of the group. We merged seamlessly with the crowd and I even started to enjoy the tour guide's talk. Soon we found ourselves sampling free champagne at the end of the *short version* of the tour! "How absolutely splendid, I feel I am celebrating my liberation from the past." Roselinde said as she smiled elegantly and raised her glass.

After the tasting we made our way up a magnificent spiral staircase to ground level. On the way out I glanced at the simple white washed wall which in large black painted letters read - TAITTINGER - VISITE DES CAVES.

To our surprise and delight a mounted black knight adorned the main gate. How appropriate I thought to myself and smiled.

Chapter 22

Dauphin

By now it was 4 o'clock in the afternoon so we decided to head back to the Basilica Saint Remi in order to make sure the trapdoor was securely in place. Roselinde talked as she walked with pace and determination. Lily and I listened sympathetically as we knew the whole episode had been deeply personal and certainly a reality check. We were not sure what she would make of the whole experience as it depended entirely on her belief system and paradigm base. Would she go public with the discovery of the secret tunnels or not that was entirely up to her.

'"I would rather we just let it be. I'm not sure what to make of all this, as far as I am concerned I would rather it stayed sealed forever; too many painful memories." Her voice was barely audible, her face blanched and she was totally lost in thought.

As we reached the entry door of the Basilica I turned to her and gazed into her soul through her sea grey eyes. I could see many lives and such pain. I held her gently and spoke with a softness that I was unaccustomed to. "We respect your feelings and you can be reassured that we will never write a word of this unless you give us permission; we promise."

I shot a sideways glance at Lily for confirmation. She simply nodded her approval and stared bashfully at the ground. The moment passed and we swiftly moved on through the now familiar gothic spaces. Down the stone steps to the crypt and through the labyrinthine forest of limestone columns to the East wall where the enigmatic trap door waited. Lily looked around to check that we were alone and then shone her torch at the floor. It was very difficult to tell which flagstone had been the cover as there was no evidence of any disturbance what so ever. The flagstones were perfectly polished and contained no dust to give away forensic clues as to our previous nefarious activities.

Satisfied Roselinde turned to leave, her mind lost in a multitude of questions. Her silent contemplation was palpable, for her regularly ordered English life had been turned upside down and inside out. It was a lot to digest. Lily followed and after a brief pause for thought so did I.

Then just as I galvanised myself into motion the familiar flashing lights and tunnel vision returned unannounced and with a forceful vengeance. Without protest I surrendered to their fairy like ethereal beauty. Observing I remained calm and centred for I had become accustomed to these cerebral forces in my head. I rationalised briefly that it must have been the sudden release of the collective focus that had allowed me to return to the medieval period and the memories held captive in the stones and my mind. Time and place had now conspired to trigger a vivid flashback of vibrant intensity. The intense energy imprint in the limestone walls was of such highly charged emotion that it now dragged my subconscious back to a past that I had experienced in another physical body.

I was a willing servant of the energy for I had been waiting for this very moment. The lighting changed, torches flickered in wall mounted iron braziers and the smell became much more agricultural. I felt heavier and confined in my movements. Looking down I could see that I was wearing blackened armour and an azure blue surcoat with saltire argent upon which was emblazoned a red winged beast. From my viewpoint I could only see the tail and lower half of the strange heraldic creature but I knew exactly what it was! It was the red dragon that I had seen so overtly displayed at Landremont, the very same icon that we had discovered at Chateau Jaulny. I was Robert des Armoises, sieur d'Tichemont, Chevalier noir de Metz. I stood fully caparisoned engaged in a solemn and sacred occasion of great importance. I felt an immediate sense of pride and stiffened my sinews accordingly. In my right hand I reverently held the black oak staff of a furled banner to protect it from the dust and dirt of the crypt. It felt extremely precious and of great import. It gave me a buzz of electricity that surged through my body and I knew that I had sworn allegiance to its Lord that I would die defending it for it was much most than just a tattered piece of cloth. The space was full of knights and priests engaged in a ceremony. Lesser knights and men-at-arms stood in hushed silence monitoring events.

At the centre I could see four exquisitely attired knights of great wealth kneeling to receive a golden dove from the ecclesiastical monks present. I recognised their coats of arms which proclaimed that they were the Marshal Jean de Brosse, Lord of Boussac, and of Ste Sévère, Gilles de Laval, Baron of Rais, Jean de Graville, the High Master of Crossbowmen and Louis de Culant, Baron of Châteauneuf-sur-Cher, Admiral of France.

In their midst barefoot was the Abbot of Saint Remi Jean Canard, his hands firmly clasped in prayer. The abbot and an extremely solemn man placed the dove in the now outstretched hands of the bishop. His presence told me that this could be but one occasion; the coronation of the Dauphin July 17, 1429.

The four hostages of the sacred ampoule had come to escort the divine oil given by God to Saint Remi to anoint Clovis all those years ago. God had appeared as a dove and handed the oil to the saint, this was the significance of the golden dove. I knew that inside would be a crystal vial containing the holy oil. The entourage would be joined and assembled in its full glory for the procession to the Cathedral of Notre Dame.

Directly following the Sacred Ampoule procession I could see the Royal Sword entourage. The Royal Sword blade was engraved with fleur-de-lys in a column from the hilt to its point. The naked blade with its point uppermost was carried and held aloft and would be for the entire ceremony by the Constable. At the coronation of Charles VII, the honour of carrying the Royal Sword should have gone to Arthur de Richemont, Constable of France. But the honour has been given to Trémoille's nephew, Lord Charles d'Albret. I recognised his distinctive quartered red and blue surcoat the fleur-de-lys modern proudly emblazoned on their azure blue field. Richemont had been the Dauphin's favoured advisor but had been driven away in disgrace from the court because of the political intrigues of the Duke de la Trémoille who had taken Richemont's place.

The traditional Royal Sword came from the 13th century. I knew it was called in French "of Charlemagne" surnamed "Joyous". This sword along with the other French coronation regalia was stored normally in the Abbey of Saint-Denis, near Paris. It had been fetched just days before.

The peers came next, six laymen and six churchmen that recalled the original coronation of King Clovis when these men made themselves subject to the newly crowned King by holding the crown above the monarch's head during the coronation.

Had France not been in the midst of a civil war, the six lay peers would have been: The Duke of Burgundy, The Duke of Normandy, The Duke of Guyenne, The Count of Flanders, The Count of Toulouse, The Count of Champagne.

Because they were all enemies of Charles VII, substitutes had to be named. I recognised them as: Jean de Valois, Duke of Alençon, Charles de Bourbon, Count of Clermont, Louis de Bourbon, Count of Vendôme, Guy de Montfort, Count of Laval, Georges de La Trémoïlle, the Grand Chamberlain, Raoul de Gaucourt, Captain of Orleans.

Then leading them the duke of Alençon who would dubbed the Dauphin on the morning of the coronation for he would have to be created a knight before the ceremony.

Everyone was dressed in their finest regalia and harness of war; surcoats, armour, and banners newly cleaned by teams of squires and pages. Such battles they had fought against all odds and now the miracle was unfolding as foretold by a little peasant girl - La Pucelle - the maid. My eyes started to mist over as the full force of emotion of the moment hit me and a giant wave of realisation swept over me. I swallowed hard savouring every second of this special time, for France was about to regain its King and restore its dignity as a leading power.

The four knights on bended knee stood and turned to leave the crypt via the familiar staircase. The Abbot bearing the golden dove and the monks followed. I found myself in the retinue of Raoul de Gaucourt, Captain of Orleans. I'm clinging to a banner, it can be only one thing, the banner of our Liege Lord Charles Duc d'Orleans, the very banner that was flown at Agincourt 14 years previous when I was 12 years of age and but a page to my Lord of Orleans. My heart races as I have to wait until I am outside the basilica to unfurl it. Sadness then wafts over me as I think of Charles my Duke languishing in English captivity for even though he is in a gilded cage he is still cut off from his beloved city and France. We represent him today Raoul de Gaucourt, my humble self Robert des Armoises and our brave men at arms. We are Orleans! We are France!

As we enter the spaciousness of the gothic basilica above I am amazed at how many people there are. The men at arms in their various multi-coloured household liveries struggle to keep order. Our horses wait at the entrance, silently we mount in a flurry of activity, each hostage with his own retinue in attendance; many lesser knights attend these great lords and lay peers.

Mounted, the procession pauses momentarily. Raoul leans around, his distinctive white ermine surcoat with two red barbel fish back to back fluttering in the breeze and shouts, "Unfurl the banner Robert! Let Orleans be seen on this great day."

I obey and out flutters the gorgeous azure butterfly from its chrysalis emblazoned with three golden fleur-de-lys modern and a label of three points argent, the personal arms of Charles Duc d'Orleans bloodstained, tattered and unbowed. Today it proclaims his presence for all to see. Roger smiles at me and I smile back my visor raised on my sallet, we both have tears in our eyes.

"You have the honour Robert, for you were the youngest among us at Agincourt."

My mind leaps back instantly to that terrible day. I instinctively grip the banner tighter and thrust it high into the sky! Modestly and with a sense of occasion I refrain from my urge to cry Orleans at the top of my voice but as if in accord with a psychic connection the crowd do it for me. "Orleans, Orleans!" They shout with one voice in recognition; for we were the turning point in regaining our country from the English Goddons and the Burgundians.

With dignity, panoply and a certain amount of medieval organised chaos the procession made its way to the Cathedral. The houses are very different, half timbered and huddled together, the sun shines and the people line the street, my horse rears its head champing at the bit as if preparing for a charge but not today I tell it with a gentle pat of my mailed gauntleted hand to keep calm, this is not Patay. Soothing words take their affect and she calms down. We are one, horse and rider, a mystic union from time immemorial, tempered by trials and tribulation. For Guinevere and I have been together these past five years including one year hard campaigning with La pucelle, today we reap the reward for our devotion and loyalty.

All too soon the procession halts at the entrance of the mighty Cathedral. Inside like an expectant groom the Dauphin awaits his coronation on bended knee. No one could have predicted this moment just six months earlier, except for one demure frail girl whose faith and love for the Dauphin set a country ablaze and miracles followed.

On the steps stood Jehanne with her Jhesus Marie banner fluttering in the breeze, utterly stainless trimmed with gold and painted with God and his angels for all to see. To her immediate right centre stage stood the Archbishop ready to receive the sacred ampoule from the Abbot of Saint Remi and his for dutiful knights. The knights ascend the steps and stand at four corners to protect the Abbot and his holy charge. The Abbot raises the golden Dove for all to see and places it in the hands of the Archbishop. An almighty cheer erupts from the joyful crowd in approbation. The Archbishop raises the dove skyward a second time and the crowd repeat their adulation many are overcome with emotion and fall to their knees.

I ascend the steps, banner in hand, Orleans first in order of seniority as of the Boubons and leader of the Armagnac faction whose victory this is. As I did so with slow reverent steps the crowd cheer with shouts of Orleans, Orleans! I come face to face with La pucelle her eyes bore into my soul with pure love, then she smiles and I find myself looking at Roselinde, she has the exact same face. I knew then with certainty that she had been La Pucelle, she smiles "Are you OK? You've been awfully quiet back there."

"Yes awfully quiet." I respond echoing her English accent, "basically I have been physically present but elsewhere in time and space, it's a bit complex but Lily understands." I smiled a faint smile at Lily and she smiled back then coyly dipped her chin in a typically engaging fashion that is so characteristic of her demure femininity.

"Tell you later when we have more time over dinner, but today is your day!" I became upbeat as I realised that I knew her secret.

Lily nudged me, "Let's go in we are not here to stand and gossip!"

I blinked in reply still dazed from the flashback, "Yes of course, no rush, it'll keep."

We entered through the open entrance to the might west facade after pausing to take in the magnificence of the medieval stone carving. It was as if the basilica Saint Remi was merely a prelude to the might and utter splendour of La Cathedral Notre Dame de Reims. Its giant Rose window dominated the vista as did the imposing both towers either side.

The sounds of tourists thronging the nave filled my ears as I entered. They spoke in hushed tones and footsteps could be heard echoing as their feet struck the smooth polished flagstones. I breathed in the air it had that distinct old smell and taste. The limestone felt cool to the touch as I ran my hand along a huge column. I was in no hurry and content just to watch Roselinde discover her own truth. I wanted that to be without suggestion or bias. I acted with the thoroughness of a scientist engaged in a ground breaking experiment. The result must be genuine.

Roselinde felt comfortable her expression had changed and she became much lighter in her mood, almost celebratory, her voice more regal and assured. We walked the length of the nave. I then sat on a seat in the front row of the congregation and silently watch Roselinde and Lily proceed towards the altar illuminated in the distance in front of the Chagall stained glass windows that now replaced the bomb damage from World War 2. I took a quick video on my iPhone just to record this moment and the atmosphere for the record. Then it happened, Roselinde dropped to one knee. I immediately leapt out of my chair and strode swiftly to her side. Lily stood transfix with one hand gently on Roselinde's shoulder in support. Roselinde was gently sobbing, she wept silently and without the painful emotion I had come to expect. I put my hand softly on her other shoulder without speaking.

"This is the place," she spoke quietly, "it was here that I was overcome with emotion all those years ago."

"World War 2?" Lily asked in a hushed tone.

"No, much further back 600 years. I knelt before the Dauphin and wept tears of joy, for we had achieved the miracle promised by Saint Catherine, Saint Margaret and the angels. He wore the crown, my beautiful wayward Dauphin. He was trembling in sheer disbelief that the moment of his coronation had finally come to pass against all odds and as foretold by myself, his half-sister. The congregation watched in stunned silence. It was a moment like no other in history, so powerful and so poignant. The destiny of France was changed in that instant."

A rapture descended on her face as she looked up her tears stained eyes raised to the heavens and her hands clasped in prayer.

"It was a miracle." She cried softly, "a miracle."

Lily and I paused for breath, swallowed and gently rubbed her back as she froze in silent memory.

"Well now we know the truth of it." Lily broke the silence with a whisper, her eyes watering with emotion.

"Yes, the miracle has come to pass exactly as I have seen in my mind's eye." I added. I paused as the import of Roselinde's statement hit me like a ton of bricks. "Half-sister! Did you say, Half-sister?" my voice jumped an octave and several decibels in loudness.

"Yes, I was the Dauphin's half-sister." Roselinde answered matter of factly. "Well Jehanne d'Arc was - that is I mean." She started to splutter as her logical mind kicked back in

"Sacré bleu! Eh, ben quelle putain de surprise!" Lily gasped as the connotations of the statement hit her. "That's one for the history books!"

"Yes, perhaps it is something that we have yet to remember?" I added quickly. Roselinde looked confused and mystified at our rapid conversation in French. For me that was somewhat of a relief as Lily was adopting more soldier like language due to her experiences! That made me smile as I attempted to put Roselinde in the picture with a quick explanation. "It has been conjectured as theory that Jehanne was not the simple peasant girl as made out by legend and the history books but that she was the illegitimate 12th daughter of Ysabeau of Bavaria and the Duc d'Orleans. She was a substitute born in the year 1407; interestingly your revelation just now appears to support that theory."

"Ah I see. It seems I have put the cat amongst the pigeons as we say in England!" Roselinde gave a wry smile, "It is quite genuine I definitely felt connected to the Dauphin in that instant." She blushed.

I looked at Lily and finished her thought; it was everything we had worked for in that life. We had been supporting actors on the stage of life and had helped events unfold in a minor but important capacity.

The chivalry and people of France had been the true heroes of the drama. They had suffered and fought hard to free the land from the English "Goddons" and the Burgundian yoke. They had freed themselves inspired by one small girl and a banner. A child divinely inspired by Saint Catherine and Saint Margaret, she had led them to victory against all odds, it had indeed been a true miracle.

As Lily held Roselinde, I went over and lit 3 small candles. In my mind I knew this was a seminal moment in the quest that had begun just a couple of months previous when we visited Metz, for the Porte Allemand had been the trigger that fired the first shot in this amazing adventure and it wasn't over yet.

After several minutes Roselinde stood up and took a deep breath, "can we go now? I don't think I can take much more of this." She looked pale and in need of rest so we turned silently around and made our way through the myriad of tourists to the exit.

Immediately the sunlight stung our eyes as we left one of the open doors of the main west facade and Roselinde pulled her sunglasses over her damp sea grey eyes. I noticed that they glistened with tears just before the visor slammed shut and cut them off from human view.

We walked over to the statue of Jehanne d'Arc that stands on a large plinth just to the left of the main steps of the west facade. Roselinde couldn't bear to look directly at it but chose instead to sit with her back against the plinth.

"Are all your trips like this?" She said with an air of casual nonchalance and a wry smile, "I'm not sure what to make of it all? I believe in the now. I shall have to think long and hard about what has happened in this city. I hope you can forgive me if I seem less than enthusiastic. Lily and I understood the paradigm shift that must be occurring in her mind and tried to raise a smile.

"We know how you feel, been there, done that and got the t shirt!" Lily broke the uncomfortable silence with a youthful response. I was lost for words and was happy just to admire the workmanship of the equestrian bronze of our heroine with her sword raised high. After several minutes lost in contemplation Lily slapped me on the back," Come on Yann Baillieu let's go I'm hungry!"

With that she shouldered her camera and helped Roselinde to her feet. "Good idea, I could do with a nice shower and a change of clothes.". Roselinde agreed as she dusted herself down and shouldered her rucksack. With that we marched together along the Rue Libergier, turned right into the Rue des Capucins then on to the golden angel and place Drouet Erlon. Within 20 minutes we were in sight of Le Hotel Bristol. Stopping at the pavement cafe attached to the hotel I broke the silence, "Anyone for goûte? I'm for a cognac café, it's been one of those days!"

"No thanks Yann, us girls have to make ourselves beautiful in time for dinner, catch you later. Dinner at eight, don't be late!" Lily tossed her hair back with an incorrigible smile that denoted the confidence of youth and her own sexuality.

Roselinde tried to smile and followed Lily into the reception and I lost sight of them amongst the colourful umbrellas and tables. I sat in silence and ordered my drink. When it arrived the caffeine and alcohol stimulus hit the spot and I began to unwind. I mused over events and drifted into silent contemplation. The tourist crowds hummed and thronged the street a few metres away blissful unaware of the events that had transpired and the potential impact on history that would occur should we publish our results. A million stories, a mass of human conscious memory machines each one a book, the thought ran through my mind like a wayward child kicking a ball down a silent street; what an amazing planet this truly is. I smiled at the thought and sipped my café cognac savouring its warmth and comfort.

Twenty or so minutes passed when I noticed Roselinde walk by and sit at a table in the corner with her back to me. I found that strange as surely she knew that I was still sat in the same place that she had left me in. Impulsively I shouted out, "I'm still here!" I raised my arm to wave but got no reply. I tried again but this time a little louder. Other people in the cafe began to look and raise their eyebrows but not Roselinde. Puzzled and perplexed by the negative reaction I decided to wander over and tap her gently on the shoulder, perhaps she was lost in thought after the day's events?

As I did so she turned around with a start! I recoiled instinctively as it was not Roselinde but instead Déborah Dubois! "I do apologise!" I said in somewhat of a fluster, "Please excuse me but aren't you DD, the mathematics teacher from Lille?"

Déborah looked quite amazed and then burst into laughter," Oh my God it's you Yann, what a coincidence! I only saw you a couple of days ago at Vincent's party. I had no idea that you would be in Reims, what a pleasant surprise."

"I am certainly surprised too, you look just like Roselinde from the back, same hair style and colour. I do apologise please come and join me. Let me buy you a drink. I'll put it on my tab as I am staying here together with Lily and Roselinde; you met her at the party." I adjusted her chair as she slipped out from her table and made her way to where I was sitting.

"You are very kind Yann. I am still totally amazed at the coincidence but I guess that is how the universe works!" She sounded genuinely in awe. "I'm staying here too!"

DD ordered a glass of Pinot grigio and we carried on our conversation. It transpired that she had been following our articles in the paper as they had struck a chord with her. Finally her curiosity peaked and she decided on the spur of the moment to take a random trip to Reims to break the monotony of the school holidays. Her mother had kindly offered to look after her two girls and take them to the seaside at Saint Valery sur Somme for a few days. It was one of their favourite holiday spots but DD felt that she needed a break from it all. She was after all a busy single mum.

I listened effortlessly as there seemed something so natural and familiar about her manner and conversation. It was as if she were filling in the missing bits in a conversation that we had had forever. As she talked I became more aware of my own emotional feelings of warmth and connection between us, for we had always met in crowds and never on our own.

Time stood still, in fact the whole universe appeared to stop momentarily as I listened. An hour went past in a flash and I only became aware of the time as the shadows grew longer on the pavement. "Hey, it's a quarter past seven and I haven't showered and changed yet!" I stood to leave abruptly then remembering my manners I add courteously, "Say would you like to join us for dinner? I will ask the girls I am sure they won't mind. In fact they will probably be glad to see you!"

"Are you sure? I don't want to barge in uninvited." DD said politely then relaxed and sipped her aperitif.

"I'll text you. What is your number?" Without hesitation she gave me her mobile number and I pumped it into my iPhone. Quickly I pressed the call button on the screen and after a short pause her phone rang. "There you go my number will be stored in you recent calls. Catch you later I see that you are already dressed for dinner."

"*À plus tard!*" She stood and we kissed on both cheeks, her Chanel Number 5 perfume electrified my senses. I hesitated but then tore myself away from the random encounter that had been completely unexpected. Déborah sat back down and resumed her people watching.

I hurried upstairs to my room, text Lily about DD and the amazing coincidences and jumped into the shower. Twenty minutes later I was dressed and ready to roll. I checked my iPhone, Lily's reply was affirmative so we would join forces at eight for dinner and the debriefing. I immediately copied the text to DD. Events appeared to be speeding up and I was beginning to fit the pieces together in my head. We just needed the evidence.

On the stroke of eight I entered the dining room DD was already sat at an alcove table waiting. We made light conversation and I briefly outlined what had happened since we arrived in Reims so she would be able to follow the twists and turns of the conversation without getting too lost. DD appeared fascinated by the whole thing, the history, the physics and the emotion. Her mathematical mind began to click and she made several comments about coexisting multidimensional state spaces and how that might figure in our flashbacks experiences. Our present reality was probably only one facet of such a complex geometrical construct. She concluded that somehow we were able to navigate between realities due to the ability of our subconscious to connect with our other conscious selves and feed through to our present contemporary conscious mind. It strangely all seemed to make sense and I realised that there was more to our chance meeting than met the eye.

Just then the girls entered both looked tired but triumphant. Lily wasted no time and ordered four Kir royale aperitifs and we perused the menu. The waiter returned with our drinks and we set down to business. Roselinde was still visibly shaken. "I really don't know what to make of all this it conflicts totally with my basic core belief system." She said quiet firmly. "I believe in the NOW and what we do in this life. I don't want to dwell on what may have been in the past."

Lily and I were shocked by Roselinde's blunt statement but we realised that each person must find their own truth so we respected her honesty and integrity at being upfront with us. DD listened intently. Dinner arrived and I found that without consciously thinking DD and I had ordered the exact same main course; salmon. Roselinde steered the conversation away from anything heavy and chatted politely about Reims in general and asked DD what she had done since arriving. As at Vincent's party they seemed to have a natural empathy for each other.

Having had sufficient of the main course we ordered light desserts, a lemon sorbet in my case and then the cheese arrived.

Just a taste of Abondance and a glass of red wine was sufficient for my waist line. Roselinde then cleared a space and placed the Ausweis card on the table.

"I have decided that I need time to digest what has happened here. The pain is too great in this place, so I have decided to return to England and visit the crop circles in Wiltshire in order to restore my energies. They are in full flow at the moment and I need an energy boost. Then I shall return to Aldeburgh to write up my journal and analyse all that has transpired. I hope you don't mind but I really need to rest and heal?"

Silence descended as we all took in exactly what Roselinde had said. It was quite a shock for Lily and I as we felt enthusiastic and hot on the trail. After a long pause I broke the silence. "You must do what you must do and follow your heart. I respect that."

"Me too," Lily added quietly as she held up her wine glass to the candle light in order to observe its beautiful dark blood red colour.

"We look forward to hearing of your deliberations in due course. Meantime we will continue to get to the bottom of things this side of the channel."

I went to continue but Roselinde gently placed her hand on top of mine in reassurance and to halt my flow. "This is not the end Yann. I feel that there is much more to come before you find the truth. We shall meet again I am sure of it. Meanwhile just to inspire you onward I discovered this." She spoke with all the deliberation and candour of a poker player holding four aces as she pushed the Ausweis towards me.

"Open it!" She said without looking up. I opened up the simple white card and was immediately transfixed by the photograph exactly as I had been initially, it was Roselinde for sure. "Now read the name." Roselinde added a smile.

I hurriedly read the German print.
Name: von Bogen
Vorname: Johanna
DRK Dienstgrad: Helferin
Geburtstag- und Ort: 8.4.20 München

Then the penny dropped. "Oh my, no it can't be! Von Bogen is d'Arc in French and Johanna is Jehanne! Johanna von Bogen in German is Jehanne d'Arc in French."

Lily snatched the Ausweis from me. "It is you know! It is written here totally for real in black and white." Her jaw dropped as the realisation of the intricate workings of the universe hit home. DD took the card and looked for herself as Lily and I sat there dumbfounded and frozen like statues in time. "It is an identical likeness, so exact. Totally amazing I have never seen such a thing in my life!"

"And look at the birthplace - München in Bavaria. The Bavarian connection! I looked up the Von Bogens' on the Internet whilst Lily was in the shower and it said that they were a noble Bavarian family, she was of aristocratic birth."

"Oh my God it's all there in black and white." DD added as she handed the Ausweis card back to Roselinde.

"Now on that bombshell I think we should all drink lots of champagne." Roselinde summoned the waiter and ordered two bottles of Reim's finest. "My treat as you have looked after me quite Royally!" Roselinde giggled and started to visibly relax. The healing had begun.

Chapter 23

Luxembourg

he party mood prevailed eased by the flow of champagne and tempered with good humour. A sense of perspective returned as Roselinde kicked back and memories of hatred, death and destruction were mercifully forgotten. DD caught up rapidly as the stories and anecdotes flowed freely. It was a baptism of fire for her but the normally insane ramblings of a few psychic questers seemed to make increasing sense to her analytical mind and she was able to make several acute observations that shed light on the overall mental process that was occurring. Our discussions in the hotel bar went long into the night as we were all too aware that there would be *a parting of the ways* come dawn. Finally we hit bed around three o'clock much the worse for wear. Our alarms set for a masochistic six o'clock start as we all felt that we needed to get going in the morning. Before turning in I text Jean my boss at *La Voix du Nord* and suggested that instead of returning to Lille we push on with our research as we were hot on the trail.

Lily had suggested this as she wanted to visit Luxembourg to see if we could pick up any clues as to our next move. I was only too happy to go with the cosmic flow and be guided by her dragon princess instincts. I was sure that Jean wouldn't mind us not being in the office as August was traditionally a quiet month and we could submit our articles electronically thanks to modern technology.

The good news was that Déborah had decided to come along for the ride. She had no commitments for the week and could therefore spare the time to join the quest. I noticed that she had become much more engaged in the story as we talked freely about all that had happened since that fateful day in Metz. In fact even the very mention of the word *Metz* seemed to have drawn a subtle reaction from her. She could certainly drink and was excellent company. It almost felt that she was somehow part of the unfolding events. We would see by doing the experiment. Perhaps it was all meant to be?

The alarm went horribly quickly and I crawled out of my bed and into the shower. The sun had already been up a good two hours so that eased my pain a little. The initial cold water woke me up as it hit my face, it was a good couple of minutes before the hot came through and it reached civilised temperatures. Ablutions finished I felt at least back in the land of the living if somewhat jaded after our titanic session.

I text Lily and DD - *Bonjour les enfants!* I hope you slept well ;) lol are we ready for another glorious day. Breakfast at seven, taxi at seven thirty!!! Xxx

I needn't have worried for being more efficient than me they were already up, packed and waiting in the dining room.

"What kept you?" Lily giggled as she sipped her hot chocolate from an enormous French coffee cup. The aroma was to die for. She held it two handed and that allowed the warmth to penetrate her body through her hands. Then placing it down on the table she dunked her croissant into its luxuriously warm contents and took a dainty bite.

Roselinde was amazed at how we ate our croissants as she struggled to apply her apricot comfiture and butter in a lady like fashion. DD explained that you had to break a croissant rather than cut it with a knife as you would with toast. A quick practical demonstration made the point.

Leaving them to it I walked over to the buffet and poured myself a large steaming bowl of French coffee. Its aroma assailed my nostrils with delight and my mood instantly improved no end. Taking two fresh croissants on a white porcelain plate I returned to the table and attempted to explain to Roselinde the origin of this French delicacy.

"It's all due to the Battle of Vienna in 1683 which put the Hapsburg dynasty on the throne. Having defeated the Ottoman Turks, the pastry chef produced a crescent shaped croissant so that the royal court could eat the crescents of the defeated enemy! In French it is known as Viennoiserie, and it is believed to have been introduced into France by Marie Antoinette who of course was an Austrian dragon princess."

"Your encyclopaedic knowledge never ceases to amaze me Yann! Lily spoke with a genuine note of affection in her voice.

"It's totally politically incorrect now of course but we are French!" DD added with a smile and a glint in her eye. They were different times."

I dipped my croissant in my coffee and took a bite. It melted in my mouth like hot butter. It was the only proper way to enjoy a croissant.

"Well I never knew that!" Roselinde said positively and attempted to emulate the technique. "Yes I see what you mean. It does work rather well."

Lily and DD smiled, *"Sante!"* They said in unison as they simultaneously raised their croissants.

Breakfast over we settled our accounts and headed out into the street. The pristine white umbrellas and tables guided our way. Turning right we made the short walk to the Boulevard Foch. The taxi was already waiting. The azure sky, green trees and cafés completed the perfect scene.

I greeted the taxi driver. *"Champagne-Ardenne TGV s'il vous plait et rapidement."*

"Certainement Monsieur." The taxi driver was obviously well aware that time was of the essence as he was no doubt familiar with the TGV timetable. Effortlessly he navigated the early morning traffic free roads and swiftly made the short journey to Bezannes and the TGV station. We barely had time to take a last look of the Vesle river as we crossed by road bridge into Courlancy. As we passed the Hippodrome Roselinde enquired

as to its purpose. Lily obliged with a description of the unique horse and trap racing that is so characteristic of northern France.

"Ah yes I remember you mentioning it briefly in Lille." She said enthusiastically. DD delighted in explaining the betting system that accompanied its popularity and helped to finance the sport.

Barely 15 minutes later we were at la Gare Champagne-Ardenne TGV. I paid the driver, tipped him and thanked him for being so efficient. We purchased three tickets to Gare Lorraine TGV. Roselinde already had her return to Gare Lille Europe so waited quietly as we organised ourselves. The air became rapidly charged with emotion as we realised the hour of parting was approaching.

"You will have to see us off." I said rather awkwardly as we stood on the southbound platform. "Our train is at eight sixteen."

"Yes I know." Roselinde interjected. "Mine is at eight twenty eight, you needn't worry Lily explained everything last night and it is my decision to return to England." A tear appeared in Roselinde's eye as she spoke. Emotion was getting the better of her despite her English stiff upper lip.

"France is your home." I said softly. "It is stained with your blood."

She became very tearful and wept, "I know." Those two words of recognition were enough for me as it signified that Roselinde had accepted her soul memory and removed the mental blocks; the reconciliation was underway and she would now heal given time.

"Be brave as you have always been." I said finally and found myself saluting. As I spoke the southbound TGV came coasting in silent as a silver wraith, the hum of the electric motors barely perceptible. We embraced and kissed on both cheeks and then again once more. Lily and DD followed suite. I boarded the train without looking back in order to disguise my pre-emptive feeling of loss. I hated long goodbyes for that very reason. Finding a window seat I looked for Roselinde through the glass. She seemed so small and frail as she stood on the platform. What a remarkable woman, I thought, so noble and proud but my contemplation was shattered by the sudden noise and bustle of Lily and DD as they stowed their luggage and sat down. The train started to move off without a sound true to its spectral qualities. I turned and looked once again out of the window but Roselinde had already disappeared.

To fill the energy vacuum of her missing presence Lily chirped up, "How long does it take to Lorraine TGV, Yann?"

"Forty one minutes according to the timetable." I answered precisely and logically like an automaton, my left brain had kicked in to retrieve the situation and relieve the emotion of parting.

"That's quicker than I imagined." DD added, "It's hardly enough time to get comfortable." As she spoke her leg momentarily brushed against mine and I felt a jolt of electricity. There was something strangely familiar about her vibratory energy, personality and voice. Just her presence seemed mysteriously to inflame my soul with passion. It was a totally novel experience for me, the palms of my hands became suddenly moist and my heart suddenly began to race in response to my feelings. This for me was an entirely new sensation that I had not previously experienced in this present life. I was puzzled.

Lily sat opposite and had already plugged into her iPod. She smiled as my glance caught her. We had chemistry but more as a father-daughter and an equal. I loved Lily plain and simple, we had grown very close and there was without doubt a soul bond between us, intangible and unbreakable. I knew that I would sacrifice my life for her should it be necessary, she was beautiful, strong and intelligent but DD had all that and more. With DD I sensed raw passion and a fire within my soul. The smouldering embers of which were beginning inexplicably to flicker into flame. The more I thought about it the more her energy resonated with my soul and the more I felt alive. I knew then that this was much more than a random encounter, this was destiny, fate, kismet call it what you will but it was damn powerful whatever it was?

I abstractly looked out of the window to engage my conscious mind but the feeling of attraction towards DD just accelerated exponentially. My mouth became dry and my heart rate increased yet again. I knew from past experience that my subconscious was screaming in my ear for it knew the truth, but my conscious mind was deaf to its protestations. DD sat closer and I could feel her body warmth penetrating my being. She was reading *Elle* magazine and an article about French women and sexuality; it was tantamount to pouring petrol on a fire! Her cheek protruded from her blonde hair, her skin soft and without flaw. I observed every molecule of her being, there was something so wonderful about her, she shone, she was radiant and for me she was beauty personified. Her profile seemed perfect.

Then DD turned her head and smiled, our eyes met and our souls embraced. I was lost, totally lost in her beauty. The world stopped and time froze, nothing seemed to matter, only our unspoken love. The words came naturally and just entered my consciousness from nowhere. It was the signature recognition of a soul twin. I was lost for words and smiled back. She just carried on reading her magazine.

Without realising we had passed Gare Meuse TGV and were on the final approach to Lorraine TGV. Time had contracted like a piece of elastic. The train was audibly slowing down and I could feel the change in inertia from the deceleration.   Silently the platform came into view and the train stopped. We then exited.

We headed for the Avis car rental desk and using my credit card I signed for a black Renault Megane diesel. I knew that we would be travelling a fair few kilometres and this gave us range and flexibility in our movements. We had cut loose and who knows where we would end up. Three days had become the standard procedure now, so three days it was. We were literally living three days at a time. The chase was on and Lily was leading the charge.

Having taken delivery of the documents for the car we walked to the rental parking lot. Lily adjusted the seat and took control for this was her shooting match. The station resembled an oblong box placed in the middle of nowhere; it was geometric, simple and effective.

I decided to take the back and let DD sit in the passenger seat so that she could chat to Lily. I wanted time to think about my feelings and the messages that they were giving me. It was nine thirty when we set off. Lily drove with purpose and used her natural inbuilt compass for she was going home.

"I've booked us in at the hotel Le Royal, seemed appropriate and we are on a vacation of sorts. I managed to find a very good internet deal, half price!" Lily said with a giggle. "I want to get to the bottom of who I was and the Bibliotheque national de Luxembourg should have the answers, it is right next to the cathedral. I don't expect to recognise much though as the Haute Ville part of the city has been rebuilt so many times and dates mainly from the early 17th century, but we shall see. It has been called the Gibraltar of the North due to its fortress like qualities, independence and the fact that it is all built on a giant rock formation overlooking a bend in the river Alzette."

Lily talked rapidly as she drove out eastward along D918 towards Louvigny, at the roundabout we headed north up the D913 towards Verny and Fleury. The route nationale road was nice and straight which gave it a Roman like quality thanks to Napoleon's love of straight lines. Just before Metz, Lily took the N431 ring road east to circumnavigate the city; the city where our adventure had begun. The landscape seemed familiar and friendly, for me it had a home like quality that touched my soul. At Maizieres les Metz Lily turned north up the E25 to Thionville and from there to Dudelange in Luxembourg.

"Welcome to Lëtzebeurg, the castle of light!" Lily's sudden exclamation and use of Luxembourgeois language woke me with a start for I had been silently dozing due to the late night session.

"Wow, you can see its fortress like qualities from the way it sits above the landscape, are we going in over one of the viaducts Lily?" DD asked as she became aware of the proximity of our goal.

"I'm going to skirt left around the city and enter through the route d'Arlon as that takes us straight to the hotel." Lily had certainly done her homework and seemed extremely confident. I was glad of the rest and looked on with pride as my able companion led the way.

"Just over there is a place called Le village les Dragons!" Lily said pointing towards the southern part of the city below the rock corniches. "I would say that that is a bit of a clue wouldn't you?"

I laughed, "Sure is you couldn't make it more obvious to those that know! It is a shame that it is all so built up, it would have been so much better had some more of the original medieval architecture survived but I suppose re-development is the name of the game in such a small country."

As we came into the city it all seemed so modern and clean. The wooded green areas outlined the course of the river as it wound around the fortress burg. A few minutes later Lily pulled up outside a very large hotel that resembled an office block but with greater architectural style; the T shaped relief use of concrete between windows was clean and pristine. We parked the car and went to check in. Lily took charge and soon had our keys, as with Reims we had adjoining rooms and DD like Roselinde before would share with Lily.

The rooms were extremely spacious and plush as one would expect from a 5 star hotel in an extremely wealthy city with a strong economy. Luxembourg sits at the heart of Western Europe and is near to the European parliament at Strasbourg, its power confirmed by ancient roots and our own medieval era. It was no coincidence that Robert des Armoises had found himself working for the Grand Dowager Duchess of Luxembourg, Elisabeth Görlitz, Dragon Queen par excellence. I hoped Lily would find out more about her former mother in the Bibliothèque. Nationale de Luxembourg

I had barely unpacked when my iPhone buzzed, it was a text from Lily it simply read - ready! XXX

We met in the corridor and made our way to the reception. "I've taken the liberty of ordering coffee, hope you don't mind."

"Of course not what's the plan chief?" I said respectfully, emulating the tone of a voice heard in a TV cop show.

Lily giggled at my joke and laid out a sketch map that she had drawn. This impressed DD and I as it showed much forethought and planning. We recognised the big X that marked the position of the hotel. "I shall head straight to the library as it is open until six thirty tonight. I intend to spend most of the day rooting around old manuscripts and history books, so I thought that it would be more interesting if you and DD play tourists. How does that sound?"

"Perfect," I said after some thought and a short pause looking at the map, "Provided of course that DD is happy?" I looked up at her and saw that she was beaming a smile. Her beautiful face shone and gave me the answer I needed.

"Why not?" she confirmed verbally and sipped her coffee coyly. "I am on holiday after all!"

"OK that's settled. I will mark the possible places of interest on this map and you can search out a nice restaurant for dinner tonight." Lily had the bit between her teeth and her meticulous agenda had all the hallmarks of a well-planned military operation. She had obviously thought about this for a good number of weeks; it wasn't just a last minute whim.

Coffee over, Lily stood, shouldered her rucksack and placed her trusty camera around her neck. I stood and kissed her on both cheeks and once again, then gave her a big hug. "Go get 'em tiger!" I smiled and Lily grinned.

"And you Yann Baillieu behave yourself!" She sounded just like a mother packing her wayward son off to school. She could obviously sense the power of the chemistry between DD and myself, which must have stood out like a sore thumb to a dragon princess. As she turned she winked at me and then disappeared.

I sat down again and DD moved her chair nearer to me. She studied the map intently in a military fashion I leant forward to get a better view as she pointed out several possible areas of interest. Her Chanel perfume caught my senses and again that profile of her soft cheek and distinctive nose protruding from her blonde hair triggered my subconscious. I could feel my mind screaming again in my ear but the message still alluded me. I just felt an overwhelming soul connection and buzz of electricity between us. Perhaps we would discover the connection as the day wore on? I hoped so with every fibre of my being, I hoped so.

DD was dressed in a very bright printed blouse of cobalt pink and purple, sky blue jeans and opened toed mules. She carried her handbag awkwardly and freely admitted that she didn't like handbags, preferring to carry change and keys in her jean pockets normally. She looked fabulous, her long blonde hair fell down around her square strong shoulders, her athletic figure tapered at the waist and flowed effortlessly into powerful legs packed into her tight jeans. She marched like a soldier and kept pace with me easily.

We headed south down the Boulevard Royal and passed the famous Nana sculpture "La Grande Temperance" by French artist Niki de Saint Phalle. The huge primeval blue woman stood on the plinth like a prehistoric fertility goddess yet dressed in a garish red and yellow striped circus costume with a weightlifter's dumbbell in red and sporting two golden balls. On her shoulders either side of her disproportionally small faceless blue head were asymmetric wings, the one on her left shoulder like a giant B, her left leg cocked sideways to give her a jaunty look. DD and I stood transfixed for a number of minutes and discussed the many connotations of the sculpture. As with all good art it provoked thought. I was reminded of the phrase "Art disturbs, science reassures" a famous quote by Georges Braque, the blue goddess certainly fulfilled that criteria! I took several photos on my iPhone of the statue and DD, she was a very different goddess, beautiful, strong and athletic; a warrior goddess.

As we walked we took little notice of the bland office blocks and shopping areas that made up the city vista, for we were so lost in each other's company. Soon we reached the city wall and the view of Pont Adolphe the famous viaduct bridge that enters the south west corner of the fortress on the rock. Turning left we strolled along Boulevard Franklin D Roosevelt that parallels the old Spanish fortified wall to Place de la Constitution. We descended the balustrade lined steps to the well-kept garden space below the road level that provides spectacular views over the Val de Alzette. A giant flag pole sat centre stage with seven smaller flag poles arranged in a neat line along the edge of the rectangular space above a triangular ravelin of the fortress.

We sat conversing on a bench and admired the panoramic vista before us. A sense of history gripped us and we found more common ground as we talked. It was as if we were cosmic twins separated at birth and now reunited, each a mirror image of the other. I was reminded of a play by the famous English playwright William Shakespeare, Twelfth Night, I think it is called? I would be Sebastian and DD my Viola except we would not be brother and sister, the feeling of passion and soul connection was far too strong for that. After what seemed like a few minutes but was in actual fact an hour we continued our walk along the city wall. The Cathedral Notre Dame came into view on our left as we continued, but I was not drawn to it. Instead we passed by the collège des Jésuites and then cut across to the Chemin de la Corniche via a quaint narrow old cobbled street that reeked of age. Coming out into the sunlight again on the eastern side of the city we found ourselves amongst the delightful period streets of the corniche. Leafy trees lined the inclined streets dotted with old fashioned lamps and all around we were over shadowed by the massive

Vauban parapets of the fortifications towering above us. The view over the confluence of the Alzette and Pétrusse rivers was beautiful and we could see the Grund area in the distance. We stood for sometime in silence admiring the view. Then without warning DD kissed me on my right cheek. It was like an electric shock but so much more so; a long forgotten sensation that kick started my subconscious memory with an almighty jolt.

"I'm sorry. I don't know what came over me! It just seemed the right thing to do. What must you think of me?" She spoke in hushed tones with her sparkling blue eyes fixed on mine. In that moment my heart melted and I just held her close. We needed no communication. The gentle touch of that first kiss had said it all.

After several seconds that seemed like an eternal moment I began to listen again as DD told me more of her life story and the sad loss of her sister through illness just a few short years ago. Her story touched my soul so deeply that I just wanted to sweep her up in my angel wings and enfold her with love such was her tangible pain.

We continued our walk in the old part of the city but nothing seemed real, I just floated along barely touching the ground beneath me. It was a feeling like no other that I had ever experienced in my present life. Time *the sneak thief of all things* told me that Lily would be waiting for us as it was now gone six o'clock. Obligingly we hurried up the inclined narrow roads and back through the crenulated gate into the Haute Village as it is called. Back to the world of governments, administration and shopping; an emotional desert for the soul. But the connection had been made and now I had DD by my side. I felt invincible.

Nowhere is very far in the city of Luxembourg. Like naughty children late home from school we hurried through the busy streets into Place Clairefonteine. There was just time to look at the Grand Palace and the beautiful statue of the Grand Duchess Charlotte who reigned from 1919 to 1964. Depicted in bronze she stands as a young woman with her hand out stretched to the people. Inscribed beneath is the simple phrase "Mir hun lech gaër." - we love you - in the native Luxembourgeois; immortalised she stands surrounded by official government buildings and Notre Dame Cathedral.

Whilst DD admired the statue I texted Lily to say that we were in the neighbourhood and could meet her in front of the Cathedral quite easily. Within a minute she sent a text back saying that was great and that she would see us in five. So DD and I took a short cut through the churchyard to the great west door. Within a couple of minutes Lily appeared clutching lots of photocopies and handwritten notes.

"I've found loads of information! I knew I would." As she spoke a gust of wind came and she dropped several pieces of paper. We rushed to help her recover them. The one that I picked up had a large heraldic diagram of a shield with 12 blue and yellow sun rays and a centred small shield vertically divided half white and half red. The title read Armoiries des Armoises, Lords of Differdange. I knew then that Lily had been really busy as she had found out information about me as well as herself.

"Looks like a successful day! Well done my dragon princess." I said encouragingly. "I look forward to hearing all about it back at the hotel."

"Yes exactly, but first it's time to hit the spa!" Lily shot a glance at DD who nodded her approval.

"Excellent, *on y va!*" Lily exclaimed as she turned on her heels and set off in the direction of Pont Adolphe and Boulevard Royal.

Within 15 minutes we had covered the length of the Boulevard Royal and turned the corner into view of the hotel. As we entered the reception Lily spoke up, "I have some difficult information to discuss over dinner, but first us ladies must hit the spa in order to make ourselves devastatingly attractive! See you at eight in the restaurant; the table is booked so no worries." With that she bid DD to follow her and smiled a quizzical smile. I was perplexed at Lily's sudden sombre mood but it did explain her non-triumphalist stance as she met us outside the Bibliothèque. I would have to freshen up and wait for the appointed hour. Still thinking deeply about the events of the day I entered the lift and headed for the shower in my room.

As I showered my euphoria at having spent the day with DD subsided and I found myself puzzling more and more over Lily's comments. Finally dressed and ready for dinner I descended in the lift and headed for the hotel restaurant *La Pomme Cannelle*. The hotel information in my room had described it thus:

"With a passion for fresh ingredients and true European gastronomy, *La Pomme Cannelle*, has earned its reputation not only as Le Royal Hotels & Resorts - Luxembourg's gourmet restaurant, but the city centre's address for excellence in innovative French cuisine. The restaurant serves a delicate blend of classic French dishes enhanced with choice ingredients from around the world. The restaurant's warm colours of cinnamon and bamboo in bright decor are reminiscent of colonial times during the spice trade."

It certainly sounded exceptional so my mood lightened somewhat in anticipation.

"Ah Monsieur Baillieu your table awaits you, please follow me." The Maitre d' had somehow recognised me and escorted me to my seat with courtesy and efficiency. I was immediately struck by the black Iris centre piece and black serviettes that set our table apart from the others in the restaurant. Lily's idea of a prank was my first thought but then again she had been in a dark mood just before we parted; perhaps not?

As I perused the menu with approval at the excellent choice on offer the girls entered the restaurant and the Maitre d' escorted them to our table in the same way that he had me just a few short minutes before. Lily and DD both sat down. They looked radiant, whatever magic had been performed in the spa had worked extremely well and now both glowed with vitality and health. I ordered Kir Royale aperitifs which arrived promptly as we chose from the menu.

Finally Lily looked up and said, "I suppose you are wondering why the black Iris and serviettes? We are here to celebrate my death!"

My jaw dropped and I suddenly went cold. "But you look so young, beautiful and full of life Lily!" it was as much as I could do to utter those words in denial without tears. DD just looked stunned and sat there in silent shock. Lily just laughed much to our amazement and started to relate to us her discovery.

"I was once Marie-Yvette Elisabeth Görlitz, daughter of the Grand Duchess Elisabeth Görlitz of Luxembourg. My father was Antoine, Duke of Brabant, killed at Agincourt 1415. They were married in 1409 in Brussels. He had helped my mother secure the throne and helped to defend her from three uprisings by the nobility of Luxembourg. My maternal grandfather was John of Görlitz Duke of Lusatia and Görlitz, Elector Brandenburg, Third son of Charles IV Holy Roman Emperor, my maternal grandmother was Richardis of Mecklenburg-Schewerin and daughter to Albert King of Sweden. I was born on the fourth of June, 1412 not several hundred metres from this very spot, the second and last surviving child of Elisabeth my beautiful Royal dragon princess mother. My older brother William had been born on the second of June, 1410 but alas he survived only five weeks before he died.

My mother remarried in 1418, he was a terrible man, John III also known as the Pitiless. He was poisoned in 1425 and my mother free of his evil influence then ruled alone. My mother never talked about his death and I never asked but she poured all her love, wisdom and knowledge into me, her only daughter."

Our drinks arrived and we sat there spellbound as Lily unfolded her findings. She grew more tearful but resolute as she continued. "I died in 1429! I found details of my death recorded in an old leather bound tome entitled Codex Draconis, Maison du Luxembourg. The entry under our family history simply read; Marie Yvette Elisabeth Görlitz 1412-1429 - Draco

Princeps fuit in proelio interfectus - Dragon Princess was killed in battle - her heraldic symbol, an Iris noir on a field gules. I have made a sketch here." She took out a piece of paper meticulously drawn in black ink, hand coloured red and placed it on the table.

I studied it closely and passed it to DD. "How beautiful!" She said.

"But I saw you at the wedding in the L'église Sainte Ségolène, Metz! I married Jehanne d'Arc and your father was there, he gave her away." I frantically searched my memory for the truth, " and you, you had a brother and sister! You can't have died?"

"Well that is a big mystery I guess we are going to have to find out the hard way? May be the Codex is wrong? Anyway, I'm here, I'm flesh and blood and very much alive so... Sante!"

Her smile returned and we all raised our glasses. "Un pour tous et tous pour un!" DD raised her voice with the customary musketeers' toast as she too was familiar with the works of Dumas.

"Hey that's my line you stole that!" I joshed and slapped DD on the back in a friendly way that seemed perfectly natural between us. "Where did that come from? It just seemed the right thing to say.

Perhaps I'm in this too!" DD quipped.

"I think you are Madam, there is more to you than meets the eye." Lily chinked DD's glass. "But first let's eat, I'm starving!" The waiter brought the starter and after that the main course.

The cuisine was superb and the hotel certainly lived up to its reputation; in fact the chefs surpassed themselves.

After the main course Lily produced another piece of paper with a direct translation copied from the Codex Draconis. "This concerns you Yann or should I say Robert. Read the details closely it gives us a clue as to where to search next!"

I studied the archaic middle French and then read my poor modern translation to DD and Lily. I knew that Lily had probably worked it out already but I wanted to check that I had it right.

"Le vingtième jour du mois de mai 1436, la Pucelle Jehan ne qui avait été en France, vint à la Grange-aux-Hormes, près de Saint-Privey. Elle y fut amenée pour parler à quelques seigneurs de Metz. Elle se fai sait appeler Claude. Le même jour, ses deux frères arrivèrent auprès d'elle. [...] Aussitôt qu'ils la virent, ils la reconnurent, et elle les re connut aussi. [...] Elle fut re connue par plusieurs détails pour la Pucelle Jehanne de France qui amena Charles à Reims. [...] Jehanne revint à Arlon, et là fut fait le mariage de Messire Robert des Her moises, chevalier, et de Jehanne la Pucelle."

Ces lignes sont extraites de la Codex Draconis Maison du Luxembourg-Thibaut ou Chronique de Metz. Ainsi donc, Jehanne réapparaît cinq ans après son procès.

"The twentieth day of May 1436, the Maid Jehan who was not in France, came to the Grange-aux-Hormes, near St. Privey. She was brought to speak to some lords of Metz. She is known to call Claude. The same day, her two brothers came to her. [...] As soon as they saw her, they recognized her, and she knew also them.

[...] She was re known more details to Joan the Maid of France who brought Charles to Reims. [...] Joan returned to Arlon, and there was made the marriage of Sir Robert of Her moises, knight, and Joan the Maid. "

"Interesting it is actually like going back in time, Arlon that is not far from here, it in Belgium I believe?" DD was quick off the mark, "It seems a familiar name, I've never been there but somehow I feel that I know it?"

Lily and I glanced at each other and she gave me that look! "Well we shall soon find out as we are going there in the morning. It's the first Sunday in the month but who's counting? We are all on holiday, so to speak; so no peace for the wicked."

She laughed at the last remark and took a sip of her wine. DD and I remained thoughtful and studied the exact wording more closely. "It's all here in black and white, very precise dating too." I added.

Lily then had a couple of final aces to play. "Oh and I've been playing with your images from the door and rotated them, take a look!" With that she handed me a photographic copy she had had made and one to DD.

As I rotated the picture to the left I was astounded at the dragon that leapt out, for Robert des Armoises' hooded hat transformed into a dragon devouring his head! The stunned look on my face was enough to tell Lily that I had spotted the cryptic message and she giggled at my discomfort, "*Mon Dieu!* It is a message I have left myself about the Dragons."

"Madam des Armoises has the same, her flower hat transforms if she rotates the image to the right. It's not quite a clear though." Lily shot a glance directly at DD. "Now sit sideways and hold up the picture so we can see it!"

DD did as Lily requested. The resemblance was striking! Lily whipped out her camera and clicked away merrily.

"Your profile is an exact match!" I exclaimed barely able to contain my joy and surprise.

DD looked embarrassed as she disliked having photos taken. Her shyness caused her to turn away so Lily stopped clicking immediately.

"We shall soon see if I'm right?" Lily said triumphantly but I suspected that she knew the answer already.

The dessert came and went and we finally settled down to liqueurs, cognac and coffee. As we settled down Lily began to speak quite grandly but in hushed tones, "And now for the bombshell, which is not for public consumption and must remain a secret for fear of ridicule but I am of the opinion that it is all true. See what you think? It concerns the origins of the dragon genes and dragon line of inheritance. In a nutshell the human race is the product of Extra-terrestrial genetic engineering and manipulation. Three races were created around 200 000 to 100 000 years ago. The first was part reptilian and part hominid but not successful. The second was an improved reptilian-human hybrid species that were overseers of the third pure human species. The project was to create gold mining slaves to extract the valuable metal for their ET overlords who would periodically return to collect their tribute. They ruled by using mystery and ritual to control the masses. As the ET dragon lords moved on only the hybridised humans with dragon genes and the pure humans were left. Those with dragon genes and the associated psychic abilities became the guiding aristocracy of the old world. They were the leaders and organisers of the human race. As their genes became diluted so the system broke down. The medieval period was the last hurrah of the dragon princesses and dragon knights so says the Codex Draconis of the House of Lëtzebuerg."

DD and I sat there in complete stunned silence. "Is that for real?" I said finally to break the awkward silence and sniffed the warm aroma of my cognac in order to ground my mind.

"That is quite some statement Lily and if it had come from anyone else I'm not sure I would be able to believe it." DD added with a deep intake of breath.

"Oh yes I believe it!" I added quickly, "if you had seen what I have seen then you would believe it. It does explain our ability of being able to navigate time streams and harvest data and it may even explain my extra blood supply and associated plumbing to my brain; amazing! Well done Lily."

I sat back in my chair and studied the Jehanne and Robert des Armoises translation again. "It says they were married in Arlon, not Metz? How can that be? I have come to trust my flashbacks implicitly."

Lily thought for a moment and then spoke. "I think, and this is only a rough hypothesis, that you viewed an alternative time stream, a reality that only exists if I survive my death in 1429. If I die in battle as it says then the present time stream as recorded in the Codex Draconis exists? Does that make sense?"

I sat and thought over Lily's profound words and found myself doodling complex annotated timelines in the form of geometric diagrams on my serviette. "Yes, yes I think you might be right. If we view our reality as just one cell in a multidimensional geometric construct then all realities can co-exist. It would make sense of the comment Jesus made in John 14:2 – In my Father's house are many mansions: if it were not so, I would have told you; I go to prepare a place for you."

"Wow, you amaze me Yann Baillieu, how do you manage to remember all that?" Lily exclaimed.

"Simple, I've puzzled over that phrase since I was a child and now at last it kind of makes sense!" I said with quiet satisfaction.

"Yes, it makes perfect sense to me!" DD added, "As a mathematician at university we routinely played with multidimensional constructs and of course the famed hypercube. They could easily contain more than one 3D space capable of sustaining a complete reality. Imagine a 200D shape, that would blow the mind of the average human being or even and infinityD shape, an entire multiverse where all realities that are possible co-exist at any one given moment!" DD positively enthused as she spoke with the conviction of a personal revelation. In that moment she was more adorable than I had ever seen her and I found myself falling deeper and deeper in love with her.

Chapter 24

Arlon

Sunday morning dawned and we assembled for an early breakfast in the dining room of the hotel Le Royal. Everyone had slept well after the busy day before so we were all in good spirits. At nine we met in the hotel reception and headed out front to where our black Renault Megane had been valet parked for our convenience.

Lily took control again and we soon sped out along the Route d'Arlon, the very same road that we had travelled in on the previous morning. This time instead of heading south at the interchange we continued on towards Strassen and beyond. In quick succession the villages of Mamer, Capellen and Steinfort came and went. The journey progressed rapidly and we soon found ourselves over the border into Belgium and approaching the outskirts of Arlon.

The town appeared prosperous and bustling. The houses neat and well kept. The streets clean.

"Hey it looks like they are having some sort of a market," Lily shouted from behind the wheel so that I could hear in the back seat.

"Yes, it seems to be some sort of *Braderie* similar to our own annual one in Lille but on a much smaller scale." DD enthusiastically joined in the conversation as she observed the many roads lined with trestle tables and brightly coloured awnings.

The concentric ring roads built around the old part of the town were clearly sign posted with parking instructions so we had no problem finding our way in as close to the old castle mount as possible. As it was still early the traffic was not busy and we finally found a good parking place in the Rue du Marquisat. I had studied Arlon on the Internet before going to sleep the night before so I knew my way around and I was therefore able to deduce Lily's plan of attack from the terrain and historic landmarks of the town. Sure enough Lily indicated whilst checking her camera that she was determined to explore the old castle mount which lies at the centre of the original medieval town and is now the site of the impressive L'Eglise and convent of Saint Donat, built in the 17th century by the Capucin monks. I like Lily knew that it was built on the exact site of the old medieval castle, church and summer residence of Elisabeth Görlitz, Dowager Duchess of Luxembourg. I didn't need to consult any information I could just feel it deep in my soul memory.

As I stood by the car waiting for the girls to get their belongings together I was able to appreciate the beautiful large rectangular tower that loomed above me on La Knipchen hill, it was surmounted with a stone balustrade and a tall ornamental spire. The cross at its summit reminded me of the holy purpose of this sacred site and gave me hope that I would have a time slip experience. To the right just across the road was an impressive fortified gate with the date 1634 in large iron numbers, the 16 being separated from the 34 by a statue of Saint Donat. After some discussion we chose to go left and explore further.

The links with Luxembourg are quite plain to see in this part of Belgium for even the province is called Luxembourg and the town of Arlon proudly uses the Luxembourg coat of arms as its municipal badge. Such a cultural heritage makes a non-sense of the cartographer's artificial lines drawn on a map purely for administrative convenience. The people themselves definitely know who they are and this could be heard quite clearly reflected in the distinctive Flemish accents that surround me in the early morning sunlight.

Whatever happened I was determined to make it to the top of the tower and access the commanding view of the surrounding landscape. I was sure that this might trigger a déjà vu experience. Being the summer tourist season I hoped that it would be open despite the busy Sunday market. The market had come as an extra bonus and somewhat of a pleasant surprise. I thought it might prove interesting to look at after our investigations, should we have time? I loved the *Braderie* in Lille and always enjoyed a good rummage through the junk and the more up market *bric a brac* stalls that attracted tourists from far and wide. I very quickly ascertained from the signage that Arlon's market was only held on the first Sunday of every month which for us was lucky as today just happened to be the first Sunday of August.

Blending in with the tourist crowds we made our way through the stalls and tables to some wide stone steps that led up to the church on the mount. In the distance the tall spire of the other larger church of Saint Martin of Dessu could clearly be seen in the distance rising above the western skyline of the town not too far in the distance.

However, the wide stone staircase beckoned us with open arms so we ceased admiring the view and turned towards them. To the left a small stone statue of Saint Donat dressed as a knight stood proudly on the end post of the balustrade, to his right on the other end post stood Jesus holding a large cross in his left hand ; both were permanent reminders of the nature and purpose of the patrons that had built such a magnificent edifice. I was reminded of my own memories of being a knight of Metz in the service of my Lady the Dowager Duchess of Luxembourg.

DD examined the figures and took a picture of the knight. She moved close to me and reaching out squeezed my hand gently. "He looks a lot like you, if you had a beard that is!" Then to compound my amazement she mysteriously leant forward and whispered in my ear. "You are *my* black knight." she then kissed my cheek softly and gave me a gentle loving smile that transcended the boundaries of time and space.

Again the shockwave was overwhelming it seemed to strike a chord deep within my soul that resonated throughout my whole being shaking me to my core. But how did she know? I hadn't told her that Robert des Armoises was known as Le Chevalier Noir de Metz and also had a beard! Perhaps she was picking up the information from me intuitively or perhaps she just somehow *knew*? I looked around to see if Lily was watching, perhaps she could intuit something to solve this new mystery, but all I could hear was the constant clicking of her camera as she snapped away looking for good shots.

"That's one for the family album!" Lily exclaimed with a giggle. I suddenly realised that her lens was pointed straight at us. I immediately went red and became self-conscious having been discovered by my companion in arms. DD by contrast was extremely at ease with the situation and kissed me again.

"Shall, shall we get on? It looks a lot of steps." I said with a slight stammer and in desperation to move on from the embarrassing moment. DD just held out her hand for me to hold. It was a watershed moment in time, without thinking I found myself taking her hand in mine; it felt familiar, warm and reassuring.

"*Après vous!*" Lily said as she broke the silence and so we ascended the stone steps as a king and queen, hand in hand with Lily following. As we reached the top the world went silent and I magically stepped through a rose tinted portal into another dimension of space time.

The change in smell was the first thing to overwhelm my senses and indicated that I was in a different time zone. It was sunny and much quieter, devoid of mechanical sounds, filled with nothing except bird song and the quiet bustle of medieval life. The language seemed archaic yet somehow familiar and I found that I could understand it perfectly. I took a moment to examine my clothes and I could see that I was dressed in blackened armour with a large black cloak. I could feel the weight of a heavy *hand and a half* "bastard" sword dragging on my left hip. It seemed natural though and something that I was well used to. I entered the church with a sense of commanded urgency.

To my shock it was empty apart for a priest and a couple of bystanders, one I recognised as the Dowager Duchess' cook and the other the Captain of the Guard of the House of Luxembourg. I recognised the coat of arms clearly displayed on his black nailed jack. He held a particularly handsome German sallet in his left hand. I strode the length of the aisle and stood at ease in front of the altar. Quietly I knelt at the altar rail, prayed briefly, stood and crossed myself. I then nodded to the cook, who curtsied politely and bowed her head and then to the Captain who came to attention and smiled warmly, for we were good friends and knew each other well. The priest smiled but said not a word for it was as though I had arrived on time for an expected appointment. After a considerable pause a bell struck once and the east door opened. In walked a woman dressed simply in a white lace chemise and a long flowing gown. Her head was veiled. She looked iridescent framed as she was in the bright light of the doorway. To her right stood the Constable of Luxembourg, resplendent in his shining white armour and to her left the Dowager Duchess, her face stern and resolute yet beautiful.

She looked older than when I had seen her last. I guessed that several years must have passed since *the mission*. I observed her face closely; she had the air of stoic fortitude that comes from loneliness about her. My heart wept for her condition. She was exquisitely elegant, noble and commanded all her subjects with a firm hand that had caused a series of rebellions early in her reign. I knew that she was my liege Lady and I served her with all my heart for she was a great lady and one didn't cross her lightly. The feeling of loyalty was overwhelming and sharpened my attention profoundly.

The woman in white walked slowly and steadily towards me. I could hear the distinctive clip of metal on stone. I knew instantly that it was the sound of armoured sabatons striking the flagstones of the church for it was the sound that I had made as I walked up the aisle not several minutes before; she must be wearing armour under her white samite gown. My curiosity piqued as she drew near. Like a metronomic automaton she approached with slow regular steps. Finally she reached the altar, bowed her head and crossed herself. She then turned to look at me, nodded her head again and then looked back towards the priest.

The Duchess stood one pace behind the woman in white with the Constable directly behind me in the centre of the aisle. The priest uttered a few Latin phrases and then the woman in white slowly lifted her veil.

My heart leapt into my mouth immediately for it was DD! In an instant I knew the truth of all things. DD was Jehanne des Armoises! I fought hard to suppress my conscious mind from disconnecting from the time stream as I desperately wanted to witness the crucial events that were about to take place. Surrendering to my subconscious I floated back into the flow and viewed Jehanne in all her strength and glory. Her hair was darker than DD's and deliciously rich chestnut in colour but her distinctive facial profile remained the same; a constant in time exactly as lovingly carved into the door in the Musée Cour d'Or, Metz.

We stood together at the altar. I focused on the stain glass window as the priest performed the service of matrimony. Periodically I glanced at Jehanne and smiled. Thoughts ran through my head as to the events that had led me to this point in time and space.

Elisabeth had taken Jehanne in after she had fled from Köln in fear of her life as the Catholic Church tightened its noose. She had been declared a witch and summarily excommunicated due to her high profile and association with the young Count Ulrich of Württemberg and his unwise dispute in ecclesiastical politics within the diocese of Trèves. He had spirited her away from Metz soon after she first appeared in early 1436 believing that she was in fact Jehanne d'Arc returned from the grave. He even purchased for her a gleaming cuirass which she wore with her armour but he did not know her secret.

It was a secret like no other, a secret that only I and a few others knew, that she was the real peasant daughter of Jacques d'Arc of Domrémy and his wife Isabelle Romée, that she had struck her mother and had been persuaded to seek absolution from the Pope. After which she dressed in men's clothing and enlisted in his army under the male identity of Claude.

Thus it was that Yolande of Anjou was able to substitute her changeling a dragon princess who would become the La Pucelle of fame. After five years the real Jehanne d'Arc had returned from Italy. She had been recognised by her brothers and her mother who embraced her again as their own.

Now she resided under the protection of my mistress Elisabeth Görlitz, Grand Dowager Duchess of the House of Luxembourg who had generously taken her in. I believed in truth that this was because she was missing her only daughter Marie or Yvette as we had come to know her, who had fallen in battle during our rescue attempt to save the royal Jehanne d'Arc, the half German dragon princess changeling; for she had been trained specifically for the task from birth to stir up the peasant classes against the English and fulfil the prophecy that a maid should lead the Dauphin to his crown. Now the Dauphin sat on his throne and the House of Bourbon was restored to its rightful place. What of that Jehanne d'Arc; I know not what?

I had been married to Marguerite de Baudricourt the sister of Roger de Baudricourt one of the original knight companions of La Purcelle in 1429 but Marguerite had died in child birth leaving me recently widowed with two young children. So it was hurriedly agreed that I should marry Jehanne formerly known as Claude in order to prevent her from being burnt at the stake as a witch. We had met on several occasions recently at my summer residence in Marville not far from Arlon and near my chateau of Tichemont, but always she was in the company of Elisabeth and we were never alone.

It had come therefore as quite a shock when it was proposed that I marry this feisty beauty who swaggered like a man, had adopted a man's name, worn men's clothing and fought for the Pope. She had even killed two men whilst in his service! That much I knew for certain at this point but not much more, no doubt I would find out the whole truth in due course as our life together unfolded.

Yet I could feel a soul chemistry that linked us as we stood side by side at the holy altar about to become man and wife. We exchanged vows and with the joining of hands the ceremony was complete. At that very moment I found myself falling through the rose tinted portal back to the present. The transition was instant and gentle as the present day scene was not so far removed from the past. I stood in front of the altar of Saint Donat's church holding DD's hand gently. I could still feel her warmth as she squeezed my fingers tightly and I suddenly caught the subtle fragrance of her Chanel Number 5 which told me that the transition was complete. The light from the stained glass windows was noticeably brighter as the windows were larger now but even so it still had the same bluish hue as in medieval times.

I looked at DD and gazed into the same sparkling blue eyes that I had seen in my time slip, she seemed a veritable angel as she stood there in her jeans. The moment seemed endless and I felt myself magnetically drawn to her lips. We kissed. A deep long lasting kiss of passion and of an intensity that I had never experienced before. A kiss like no other, it was the kiss of two soul twins spiritually reunited in sacred union.

As I finally pulled gently away she kissed me again deeply and even more passionately. I knew then that the feeling was mutual. We had found each other after a separation of some 600 years.

"OK you two lovebirds break it up!" Lily's voice entered my head with a jarring discord, "do you want to let me in on the secret or do I have to wait until later?"

I seized the moment and blurted out intuitively that which I knew to be true, "I know who DD is!" I spoke excitedly barely pausing for breath and still holding her hand. "I have just been back there and seen it all. DD you are, were Jehanne des Armoises the truly beloved wife of Robert des Armoises, Sieur d'Tichemont, Chevalier Noir de Metz.

DD's face looked amazed but as the information sank in she finally gave voice to her feelings. "That would account for the powerful chemistry and the electricity between us. I felt attracted to you the moment I first saw you in Reims. It was instant. I've never felt like this before, never ever. Well not in this present life."

"Say DD, how old are you, if you don't mind me asking?" Lily stood there quizzically putting all the pieces of the puzzle together.

"I'm 42." DD replied without hesitation or embarrassment. "I have just had my birthday a couple of weeks ago it was the twentieth of July. Why is that significant?"

Lily racked her brains in deep thought for a good few minutes and paced up and down. "Yes, that's it! I've got it, Jehanne des Armoises was 42 when she died in 1453! She was therefore born in 1411. That means you have met in this life casually before but the sparks of passion were not rekindled until the exact same age that you were suddenly parted in the medieval life!"

"Of course that would make sense!" I added as I thought it through in terms of quantum physics. "Time is an illusion there is only the continuation of consciousness; the eternal NOW! Time merely separates events to stop them colliding in order that we may have meaningful experiences. Yes, case solved; well-done Lily, an excellent observation and conclusion."

DD stood there taking it all in as we rapidly delivered our astonishing conclusions. I could see her mathematical mind going through all the permutations of our deliberation.

"That's what has been bugging me about your profile, it's the same as the door!" Hurriedly I held up the photo of the door that I kept on my iPhone. Zooming in on Jehanne's profile I put it to the side of DD's right cheek.

"Amazing, it is a perfect match!" Lily agreed.

"Let me see!" DD said excitedly.

I showed her the photo of the door and then to make it easier I took a photo on my iPhone of her right face profile. The hair, the cheek, the nose, the smile were all identical. I flipped the pictures back and forth to show DD and Lily in turn. "If we make a composite of DD's photo and the door you will see what I mean. I will do that when we get back to the hotel, I can use my laptop." Finally I gave DD the phone so she could look more closely herself.

"Yes, well I never, completely the same, even the hair covering my ears, completely identical, totally amazing." DD smiled as she could see the visual proof of our discovery. "Such love we had, I never thought that I would find love in this life but there we are gazing at each other throughout eternity our portraits immortalised carved in wood in another."

"Absolutely my love, welcome home!" I embraced DD fully and buried my face in her hair to hide the tears of joy that welled up in my eyes as I felt the full force of our discovery. My life had been an emotional wilderness up until that point and now I knew why? I had waited for my only true love, my twin soul flame and now she stood before me, radiant, mirroring my spirit perfectly. DD felt the exact same way, as she too realised that we were identical in every way except of course physiology! It was pure alchemy; spiritual chemistry of the highest and most beautiful order.

"I feel I should catch the bouquet!" Lily said with genuine feeling. "Quite a discovery and it is only ten past eleven on a Sunday morning in Arlon."

"Yes but we have all the time in the world now that we know the truth." I added as we gathered ourselves and began to think logically again. "The rest will keep until later and I'll tell you it in full over dinner."

We climbed the tower and looked out over the landscape before us. The panoramic vista rotated a full 360 degrees as we walked around the tower walk way. At one point Lily suddenly stopped and then started to converse with the air. DD and I stood silently gazing at the view and hardly noticed this strange occurrence at first but gradually the sound of Lily's voice began to penetrate our hearing and we looked around. Sure enough Lily was standing there at the South West corner of the tower engaged in polite conversation but we both recognised that it was not French she spoke but fluent German. DD started forward to interrupt the moment but I restrained her gently and found myself cuddling her back. I held her lovingly with my two arms around her waist. She felt warm and wonderful, very feminine and very beautiful yet she had a muscular strength about her that said - warrior.

After ten minutes or so Lily said goodbye in very formal language which I found out of character and turned to walk towards us.

"Such a nice man, army I think? He had an air of aristocracy about him." Lily seemed to think he was real and spoke as though we could all see him.

"But you were talking to the air!" DD said as her curiosity got the better of her.

"We saw nothing!" I added to back up DD.

"Well he was there and I spoke German to him. Somehow I just knew what to say even though my German is a bit rusty. I'll draw you a picture of him later he had a very distinctive hat on, carried binoculars and said that his horse was nearby. Right, come on time is pressing and I still haven't seen my mother yet!" Lily was obviously referring to Elisabeth Görlitz, as I knew she was still in search of her answers and her own fate. We followed her as she swiftly descended the tower stairs. For an hour we walked the ramparts of the citadel but to no avail. Lily was disappointed so I tried to console her, "Maybe we will have more luck back in Luxembourg city. There is still a day to go."

We descended the wide stone steps that led from Saint Donat's church to the street level below and became once more immersed in the busy commerciality of the *bric a brac* market that thronged the streets of Arlon on that Sunday morning.

As we walked I spied a jewellery stall displaying its wares. I was taken by the silver pendants as I had noticed that DD favoured silver jewellery over gold. Glancing quickly I noticed a large distinctive *Cross of Lorraine,* devoid of ornamentation it stood as a symbol of freedom and faith. Without hesitation I asked the lady vendor if DD could try it on. She was happy to oblige and quickly found a suitable heavy silver chain from which to suspend it. I placed it around her neck and fastened the clasp at the back; absolutely perfect, it matched her warrior strength and shone beautifully in the afternoon sun.

"It was meant for you; a symbol of our timeless love from the past," I said softly which made DD blush instantly.

Lily snapped a picture of DD and then a couple of the two of us in the same pose as the door. "Now I feel really like a tourist!" She said and laughed.

DD and I laughed too. "We don't mind at all, we are in love. It is an amazing feeling." DD added with a glint in her sparkling blue eyes.

I turned to settle up with the lady and handed over €40 in notes, she acknowledged the payment and gave me a €1 coin as change. Fully satisfied that we had cemented the occasion of our discovery with a tangible keepsake we continued our walk.

As we continued our walk I found myself drawn to a militaria stall that contained many artefacts from World War I and II. I guess I was still subliminally thinking of the unexpected discoveries we had made in Reims just a couple of days before. Rummaging I noticed a collection of World War I postcards and photographs that contained scenes of Arlon. In many were pictures of victorious German troops taken at the time as snap shots of the belligerent events of August 1914. I pointed them out to Lily who always had a keen eye for photographs and architecture.

"Hey this one is of Saint Donat!" DD exclaimed as she joined in the hunt with interest. "You said your invisible friend on the tower balcony spoke German. I wonder if it is to do with this." No sooner had DD finished speaking than Lily recognised the distinctive hat which I now recognised as a Uhlan's helmet based on the traditional Polish czapka.

"That's it. That is it, look it is him, same height, same face, same uniform; he is even wearing the binoculars I saw him with!"

DD took the picture from Lily to have a look. The photo was of a confident young German Lieutenant dressed in a cavalry uniform, on his head he wore the distinctive mortar board topped head gear of a lancer.

"I wonder if it has anything's written on the back? Old photographs often do have an inscription." DD flipped the snap over. "Does the word Richthofen mean anything to you? It just says - Manfred von Richthofen, 1914 - in faint blue ink."

DD handed the photograph back to Lily who marvelled at the quantum coincidence. This was nothing to what was to come next because as I looked down I found that I was holding an old original copy of *The Red Battle Flyer* by Captain Manfred, Freiherr von Richthofen, it was open at page 40 and my eyes caught the word Arlon. Scarcely believing my own senses I read on to see if it was real or just wishful thinking triggered by Lily and DD's conversation. Sure enough at the bottom of page 40 it read:

"At Arlon I climbed the steeple in accordance with the tactical principles which we had been taught in peace time. Of course, I saw nothing, for the wicked enemy was still far away.

At that time we were very harmless. For instance, I had my men outside the town and had ridden alone on bicycle right through the town to the church tower and ascended it."

I stood there in dumbstruck amazement and just handed the little brown book to Lily.

She laughed out loud and read the exact same words, "Well I never he did say very politely would I excuse his bicycle and assured me that he was indeed a proper cavalryman with a real horse!"

After a pause to take it all in I finally found my tongue, "You may not have found your medieval mother today but you've definitely just met the Red Baron."

Chapter 25

Sierck les Bains

After showering back at the hotel I met the girls for dinner at eight. This was our last night in Luxembourg so I wanted to make it memorable.

We told each other tales of what we had witnessed in Arlon. A large part of that consisted of my description of the low key wedding ceremony that had taken place between Jehanne and Robert des Armoises. Lily and DD listened intently and tried to visualise all of the details. I listened with extreme interest to Lily's account of her brush with the Red Baron.

As she talked I got the distinct feeling that she was tuning into yet another one of her past lives set around World War I. The number 1896 kept surfacing in my mind and I intuitively felt that this was the year she was born, also that she had been German or Luxembourgish in that life which accounted for her fluent use of the language when talking to the red battle flyer.

Despite the excitement of this encounter Lily remained sad as she was bitterly disappointed not to have had an encounter with her medieval mother Elisabeth Görlitz. The feeling that I had to be proactive and do something about this state of affairs built exponentially in me as we continued through our excellent meal. Finally as I mellowed, relaxed and sank into my café cognac the seeds of a plan began to germinate in my fertile mind.

"Right, time for action!" I suddenly declared much to the astonishment of DD and Lily. "It's our last night in Luxembourg and I can't go to bed without resolving this issue. You need to see your medieval mother, you have to see your medieval mother and you shall see your medieval mother! I think we should do an experiment, who's up for it?"

I looked earnestly into Lily's sad eyes and saw the beginnings of a sparkle. It was a faint glimmer of hope that needed fanning into a blazing fire of controlled psychic energy. DD positively glowed with enthusiasm for the challenge and was up for anything having heard of our remarkable experiences.

Knowing she had been Jehanne des Armoises now fired her up. She began feeling her latent power, the latent power of a dragon princess waking up for Jehanne had been no ordinary peasant girl. Her psychic gift of prophecy and adventurous nature testified to the inherent genetic ability of looking beyond the normal material world. All she needed was a jump start to remove the mental blocks that had imprisoned her mind since birth in this life. Today had provided that jump start and now she was beginning to feel her own power rising like a phoenix in her corporal body. It was her birth rite and she was champing at the bit for action.

"I'm in!" She finally said as her passions rose to such a height that they could no longer be contained by her logical thought.

"Me too!" Added Lily as the electricity of the moment became infectious. It was the dragon energy resonating between the three of us that was causing the effect. Just as harmonic tuning forks resonated in empathy with each other when one is struck and begins to vibrate.

"OK, un pour tous et tous pour un!" I placed my right hand palm down in the middle of the dining table, in quick succession DD placed her right hand on mine and Lily hers on top of DD's. Then I placed my left on top of Lily's and they followed suite. As we engaged in this strange spontaneous ritual I could feel the energy multiplying and increasing exponentially with each touch. I could tell from the girls' expressions of satisfaction that they were feeling the exact same phenomenon.

"Together we are strong, we can make this happen. Now do you believe?" I said in triumph as I could feel my own power rising up from the base of my spine and flowing out of the top of my head connecting directly to my higher self and beyond.

"Let's go! Follow me." With that dramatic statement of intent I broke the hand fast and stood up. The girls followed my lead and we left the dining room to exit the hotel.

Although not dressed for the night air, as I was acting on impulse, I didn't feel cold for my blood was up, my psyche on fire and I radiated pure energy.

We exited the hotel by the main reception door and turned left then left again, very quickly we found ourselves out on the familiar streets we had come to know. It was rapidly approaching midnight and I felt that the time was somehow significant as the bewitching hour would soon be upon us and the whole rock upon which Luxembourg city is built would act as one giant generator to provide the power for what I was about to attempt.

With unity of purpose we strode through the Uewerstad and continued along the whole length of the Grand Rue. Despite the late hour tourists could still be seen wandering the street under the bright waxing Moon and clear sky. I was navigating using my inner compass, a medieval memory of once familiar territory now long forgotten by my conscious mind.

As I walked I began to believe. DD and Lily followed in a tight arrow head formation with enthusiasm and speed. As we reached the end of the *Grand Rue* I turned right into *Rue du Fossé* and followed the curved street around into *Place de Clairefontaine.* Finally we halted in front of the bronze statue of *Grand Duchess Charlotte* as a bell somewhere tolled the stroke of midnight. The large multi-level circular dais with its five tiers reinforced the energy point status of the scared position chosen for the statue. To our left the cathedral fed energy into this metallic artistic antenna as a giant generator feeds a radio beacon. The bronze statue stood beckoning us to come closer with the Duchess' out stretched right hand extending a welcome. Subliminally I knew that she was reaching out from beyond the grave to connect with her beloved people. I hoped with all my heart that she would now be able to make good that promise as Lily was in desperate need to see her beloved medieval mother once more.

"MIR HUN LECH GAËR"

Slowly I read the epitaph inscription to Lily as DD already knew what it said and that made my task easier as I could concentrate all my energy on Lily.

"WE LOVE YOU"

I repeated the words in Luxembourgish several times as we gazed upon the face of the statue. Lily changed position and moved silently to the centre of our arrow head formation. Her eyes transfixed on the beautiful kind face of the bronze statue, she never wavered. It was as if she was remembering and reconnecting with the past as I had hoped.

Silently as misty wraiths DD and I moved forward so that we paralleled the exact circumference of the dais perfectly and we joined hands with Lily.

"MIR HUN LECH GAËR - MIR HUN LECH GAËR - MIR HUN LECH GAËR"

DD took up the mantra that I had begun chanting. Softly and with love we felt the vibratory shape of each sound syllable as it emanated from our vocal chords. It was the vibration of a lost language of magic preserved now only as an archaic language barely spoken. The octave difference of DD's feminine voice provided the harmonic required to elevate the sound to beyond the dimensional curtain of our 3D physical existence. It seemed to be working.

Then slowly as if following an unspoken command we advanced onto the first ring of the dais. Gently we guided Lily towards the statue and the out stretched arm of Grand Duchess Charlotte. At first she resisted our invitation but as we continued chanting the mantra her body softened and she started to enter the magical flow of the time stream beyond the 3D curtain of illusion.

"MIR HUN LECH GAËR"

Her voice joined our chorus in perfect harmony and I could feel the exponential jolt of the increased vibration resonate throughout my body. As our psychic frequency ascended to meld with the higher dimensions I could see the power of the moment take hold of Lily's body.

We advanced another step without noticing our physical movement. Our minds joining in a zeitgeist gestalt of power and trinity that focused through Lily with laser precision.

"MIR HUN LECH GAËR"

We advanced again.

"MIR HUN LECH GAËR"

Then again we now reached the fourth ring. I knew that Lily would have to make the final step herself if and when she was ready. My heart pounded rhythmically in time with the mantra, the pulses communicating through my fingers with Lily and transmitting the energy of my intent into her.

Finally Lily floated away from my grasp and ascended the final step of the dais with a gentle weightless glide. DD and I let go simultaneously as one lets go of a small boat to cast it adrift on the waters.

Softly we maintained our invocation. Then the most amazing event took place, a curtain of white light descended from the sky to envelop the statue, it grew in width to encompass first Lily and then DD and I.

The diameter of the ethereal beam seemed to mimic precisely the matching diameters of the respective rings of the dais. A silence descended.

The statue took form in spirit and manifested the body of Elisabeth Görlitz, the morphing of the face and the body coinciding with the fall of silence. Then fully formed the spirit became animated.

A spectral spirit hand lowered from the out stretched right arm of the statue and Lily instinctively lifted up her left hand to join with it.

"My beloved daughter, we love you too." The voice entered my head without effort. It was the voice of Elisabeth Görlitz, I recognised it immediately by its distinctive dulcet tones and intonation.

"You must follow your destiny my child. You were born to do this, heed not the consequences for we are eternal in spirit. I am always with you as you are with me. Do you not recognise yourself in this statue? You my darling precious daughter were once mortally Grand Duchess Charlotte of the House of Luxembourg.

Your love for your people and this place anchors you here. It is your constant."

Lily raised her face towards her mother's spirit, "What must I do? I am you and you are me. I feel the truth of your words. We have been mother daughter, daughter mother many times since coming to this world."

"Merge with me my child and you will see everything that you desire."

The silence intensified as the beam now grew brighter. The sense that this was a timeless place beyond our physical dimension became even more apparent; a construct of thought without substance.

Lily stood gazing at her mother and gently nodded in agreement, as she did so her eyes flickered and closed. She then began downloading all the information she longed for from the Akashic record of her medieval mother's soul. Eons of time yet no time at all seemed to pass in this higher dimensional world. I watched in silent enchantment scarcely believing what I was witnessing. It was a miracle; a miracle that I had initiated and it had come from deep within my subconscious.

I glanced towards DD, she had the look of an angel and was transfixed in a pose of adoration that I had seen many times often illuminated in medieval manuscripts.

Gradually the light dimmed in intensity, it flickered erratically, then for a brief moment flared up and was gone.

As though waking from a dream I was suddenly conscious of the cold night air caressing my cheek. The clear sky above me sparkled with countless billions of stars and galaxies in its jet black heavenly vault. The Moon ever counting the passage of Earthly time had moved several degrees through the sky and was now low on the horizon.

Somewhere a dog barked and the transition was complete.

"I think that answers your question." I said without emotion, my mind quiet and lost in contemplation as my voice returned automatically.

The vibrations of the sound seemed to awaken DD and Lily from their psychic slumber. They moved, blinked and then sat down.

I joined them. Together we sat in a row on the dais steps with Lily in the middle exactly as we had stood.

"I can never thank you enough, Yann. I feel that tonight I have come of age. I know who I am and I can navigate this reality once more with confidence, the potential confidence that I have always had within me but never harnessed fully. I no longer fear what we may discover in the coming few weeks. We will complete the mission." Lily spoke solemnly with her head bowed as she absorbed all the details of her experience.

DD placed a friendly arm around her to keep her warm and silently say; you are not alone. After several minutes of deep thought Lily fired into motion, "Right, I am the navigator. I know where we must go and what we must do in order to complete our quest for the truth about La Pucelle. I can guide you up until the point that I physically die in 1431 but after that you must walk the last steps on your own, exactly as I have just done."

Her voice was resolute, strong and armoured with a new super confidence that fully justified her surname – Chevalier; for she had all the mettle of a knight of old.

Dragon princesses are incredible I thought in total respect. DD stood and extended her hand to Lily to help her up. Then she did the same for me. We momentarily embraced and she kissed me passionately on the lips. "I love you with all my heart and all my soul, Yann Baillieu." The force of the statement rocked me and I felt a warm glow permeate my body as the truth of DD's words hit home.

"And I you, my thrice beloved Jehanne." We embraced again and then I turned towards Lily. "I will follow you anywhere my Fleur d'Lily, to the gates of hell and back and that is a knight's promised."

I knelt on one knee and bowed my head. DD did the same and repeated my words. It was true recognition of the royal blood that flowed through Lily's veins, for she had come of age and so had her powers.

Silently she stood before the statue of her former physical self and instinctively stretched out her right hand. It was a double take. "Arise, my black knight of Metz. We are all equal in spirit; arise also my warrior sister of light for you too are of the sisterhood of the Black Iris. It is no accident that you have joined us at this moment in time. We are united across, through and around time, sometimes we are masculine and sometimes we are feminine but always together." Lily sounded uncharacteristically grand and I suddenly realised that she was feeling her royal power and that she spoke as her former Grand Duchess self.

"You are a very old and very wise soul, Lily." I acknowledged as I stood up to my full height, shoulders square and ready for battle.

"Mir hun lech gaër." DD added and smiled.

The walk back to the hotel was relaxed and we all fell into our beds completely exhausted after the joint mental exertion that we had exercised. The experiment had been a success and now Lily had a head's up road map of the way forward to solve the mystery. DD was totally amazed by the vivid experience and now rapidly adjusting to life in the psychic fast lane. Her old paradigms were being well and truly dismantled whole sale and she was loving every minute of it!

Breakfast was early and we had checked out by 9 am. It was another warm August day with just a hint of cloud and the forecast was good for the week.

"What's the plan?" I asked Lily as we climbed into the Megane.

"We are off to Sierck les Bains home of the Dukes' of Lorraine. It's an amazing chateau ruin overlooking the Moselle. My mother said we should go there to gather our companions in arms for the breakout attempt. I'm hoping that we may catch a glimpse of who they were. Mother left that choice up to Robert des Armoises, so it is down to you Yann to conjure up the magic again and fill in the gaps in our knowledge."

With that she fell silent as the short journey progressed. Just before the suburb of Strassen we turned left off of the *Route d'Arlon* and onto the south section of the ring road, the same road that we had used on our way into Luxembourg city just a couple of days previous. DD had changed positions to ride in the back with me, she nestled her head onto my shoulder in order be close and to gather some shut eye as we drove. Lily was quite chatty and commented that she felt more like a chauffeur as she had no passenger in the front seat! I laughed and made a comment about wearing out the young ones first as us oldens needed looking after.

We had soon reached Dudelange but this time Lily headed east on the A13 *Route de la Sarre* to Schengen on the Moselle, the journey went quickly as it is a major highway and we soon found ourselves at our destination.

In no time at all we headed past Montdorf les Bains and beyond into the double road tunnel on the final approach to Schengen. As we emerged from the artificially illuminated darkness we were treated to a panoramic view of the Moselle valley. The sight never ceased to give me goose bumps throughout my life yet I had never known why? Now with full conscious knowledge it was even more of a thrill as the river for me led to my home. I gently nudged DD awake and kissed her on the forehead.

"We are almost home! It leads all the way up river to Metz where we used to live." I held her hand tightly and gave it a squeeze.

She smiled and kissed my cheek. "It's as if there is no time my sweet black knight." She added thoughtfully.

"It will be a tight squeeze time wise but I want to take DD there on the way back to Gare Lorraine TGV." Lily added loudly from the driving seat over the noise of the diesel engine.

"If we miss our train; who cares? We've cut loose now with nothing to lose and everything to gain. I vote we push on!" I felt suddenly energised and was eager to communicate my sense of urgency to Lily and DD. The quest was taking on a life of its own.

"I'm in!" DD said excitedly. "We can sort out clothes and other stuff along the way."

"I'd hoped you would say that DD. It is the only limiting factor as Yann and I are familiar with chasing stories and following up leads." I could see Lily smile in the driving mirror as the matter was settled. We would stick with the trail until the end or until it ran cold.

At the interchange overlooking the river we took the first exit. It looped sinuously under the autoroute and then joined the local single lane road. Driving into Schengen Lily took the road bridge over to the opposite east bank so that we would be on the correct side for the chateau as we entered Sierck les Bains. We then turned right onto the *Route de Treves* and headed south along the river upstream. Very quickly we hit the outskirts of the town and turned right down the short Rue de l'Europe to the riverside. The fortress could be seen rising above the houses at the opposite end of the town. Slowly we made our way along the riverside to the Quai des Ducs de Lorraine and into the car park below the chateau. The massive towers and curtain wall completely dominated the skyline and immediately impressed upon us the functionality of this place as a pressure point to exercise power over the medieval river trade.

"My mother said that even though old Duke Charles II of Lorraine was engaged in his own political intrigues with Burgundy and Luxembourg, he was now aged, infirmed and very near death. She felt that the tide was turning in our favour. His son-in-law René of Anjou was sympathetic to our Armagnac cause and freeing La Pucelle. He had fought at her side in the campaign for Orleans and was a son of Yolande of Aragon who was a fellow dragon princess of the sisterhood and the mastermind of project virgin the d'Arc Conspiracy. Yolande had therefore given leave to Robert and Yvette to gather their companions here on that fateful January night in 1431. Who they are and how many she had no idea? That is the question we must answer here." Lily talked as a general outlying her plans to company commanders before a battle so that each was clear on their mission in order to ensure its overall success.

I thought for a moment and my subconscious volunteered an answer. "Ritter Freiherr Johannes Jakob von Eltz is one of them!" I felt sure that Robert's young German comrade in arms was bound to be one of the companions as he had been at Orleans. "But who is the third knight? Knowing our use of the power of three I sense that there is another. Each will also bring three men to assist. The answer is lurking in my subconscious mind I just need a visual nudge to extricate the information!"

Just before entering the narrow steep cobbled streets that climbed from the riverside we paused several times to look at the magnificent river view of the majestic Moselle. On the opposite west bank we could see orderly Vineyards with their neat rows of grapes set amongst the trees and I could immediately imagine the delightful bouquet of their flowery white wines on my palette. The short walk to the entrance was steep and wound through medieval streets now lined with typical French town houses in various states of repair. Finally turning a corner we found the modest entrance to the chateau and paid to go in. All around us were the echoes of long past medieval splendour and raw military power now turned to mere shadows of their former wealth and glory. As I climbed on I became more tuned in to my medieval memories, Lily was right it was up to me to remember and all I needed to do was recreate the feelings of being back there in that specific time and place. This was the nudge that I needed in order to access the universal data stream.

DD and Lily were enjoying the climb and savouring the same atmosphere. Both were in tune with chateaux and the medieval way of life it represented so both found it interesting and I could over hear them chatting away and comparing details. At the end of the long cobbled slope we approached the main tower gate. This was the business end of the chateau thick substantial stone masonry confronted us with its impressive strength. As I entered the tower the characteristic rose coloured archway formed so I knew that I was about to start time travelling.

It was night time and the Moon was shining brightly. I immediately noticed the sudden drop in temperature and I could see the white glisten of snow on the battlements. Two guards in cloaks with hoods and carrying halberds stood either side of the tower gate. They were saying that Duke Charles was not long for this world and they were worried about what would happen when he passed on.

I found myself conversing with them in medieval Alsace dialect which sounded part French part German. We joked about the weather and drinking wine to keep warm. I preferred cognac which they thought was very extravagant. They obviously knew me and I had the feeling that this was a regular occurrence as I had been in town for about a week.

I was waiting for something to happen and this was a way to pass the time. It was a natural extension of my job as Captain of the Sainte Barbe gate in Metz just up the river. I too had my loyal troops who I treated with love and respect, much as a father would treat his children. I had always found that I could command more loyalty and get the job done more efficiently if I got them on my side. Due to this approach I had the best squad of guards in all of Metz.

My blackened armour and attire was all part of the theatrical show as it discouraged braggarts and swaggerers from causing trouble. For them I was the black knight, a raven angel of death. A handy rumour that I did not take pains to deny as it served my purpose admirably. To my *les enfants terribles* I was kind, just and equal handed.

The guards respected me and knew that I was a soldier that shared the hardships of his men and that I never asked them to do anything that I was not prepared to do myself. I asked them if they had seen any strangers today. I was waiting for two knights and their men at arms. Ritter Freiherr Johannes Jakob von Eltz he would be recognisable by a silver and red shield bearing a golden lion rampant and Ritter Matthias Habicht von Schweiz, a Swiss mercenary knight who I had made friends with at the siege of Orleans a couple of years ago. They would recognise him by a distinctive red shield with a Northern Goshawk standing on a small green hill. This was a depiction of his family name Habicht which means goshawk in the Germanic tongue.

We had become good friends and I had sent a message to Chateau Chillon on Lac Léman where he resided in the service of the Count of Savoy when not actively engaged in a military enterprise. Like me he was a poor knight that had to work for a living. My other comrade Johannes however was from and extremely wealthy family but he had been sent out to gain experience and serve the Armagnac cause which is where we had met just two years pervious. Now I had been tasked by my liege Lord Elisabeth Görlitz, Dowager Duchess of Luxembourg to attempt a rescue mission. It was going to be dangerous, daring and audacious. So much so that the English Goddons would not know much about it until it was too late! I therefore needed men that I could trust and who would fight for a greater cause than money or women.

The target was La Pucelle herself who had been captured by the Burgundians at Compiègne, sold for 10 000 livres and was now imprisoned by the English. I had no idea of exactly where at the moment but once our party was assembled I was to lead them to Saumur on the Loire and receive further instructions from none other than Yolande of Aragon, Grand Duchess of the House of Anjou. It was on this account that I had been granted access to the fortress at Sierck les Bains as the Duke of Lorraine in waiting was of the House of Anjou. In my purse I carried a signed and sealed letter of marque and reprisal from Yolande herself. Elisabeth had given this to me personally along with the safe keeping of her only daughter Marie-Yvette who would assist me in the venture by using her psychic powers. Now I waited.

It was well past midnight, an owl hooted and the Moon shone high in the sky overhead. I pulled my black fur lined woollen cloak tighter around my body as I stood near the brazier giving out its glowing life preserving warmth. My face stung with the cold but roasted when too close to the fire. We shared a little bread and cheese to keep the wolves of hunger at bay. This had become a nightly ritual as by day I made myself scarce for no one was to have the slightest inkling of our mission. English and Burgundian spies were everywhere. *Trust no one* had become my motto. As far as Metz was concerned I was on business with our ally Luxembourg. This had become accepted and a routine part of my job as Sieur d' Tichemont.

I suddenly detected a noise and immediately drew my bastard sword and came *en garde*. My two companions at arms levelled their halberds and shouted out a challenge.

"Who goes there? Surrender up the password of the watch or suffer the consequences."

"Hawk moon!" Came the reply in a female pitched tone that I recognised instantly. It was Yvette's distinctive voice, steady, calm and in total command. I knew that she was safe and not under a captive's duress. We had agreed a false password that would indicate that such a scenario was afoot and thus allow us to act accordingly in order to save her.

"The Goshawk flies free and the lion prowls the night!" This voice had a distinctive German accent to it and I knew immediately that it was my old comrade Johannes. He had made it up river with our mutual companion Matthias Habicht a Swiss mercenary. As they neared the firelight I could see that each had bought three trusted men at arms as instructed. Lily led the way with the hood of her black fur lined cloak pulled up over her head and carrying a small candle lit lantern. She had cleverly masked the light from our eyes until the very last minute in order to not attract unwanted attention.

"Fraternal greetings Johannes and Matthias, you made it! Wonderful to see you both, a little delayed but here now and safe." I was genuinely pleased to see them as I had not done so since the Dauphin's coronation when we had gone our separate ways.

"I received your letter in early December and came with all speed." Matthias spoke in warm tones. He was an extremely strong stocky man of good courage and excellent wit. "Travelling down the Rhine is always swift and I reached Koblenz within the week. Business is quiet this time of year as the campaigning season is over so I am free until the Count summons me." He paused to heat his hands by the fire.

"Good to see you my old friend, welcome!" I embraced him warmly and could feel that he was fully armed and ready for action at a moment's notice.

"Apologies for the delay Robert but we had to wait for a fair wind to make it up steam, the Mosel is in winter flood and the current strong. Schloß Eltz sends its greetings and again I am hoping for a little action to cure the winter boredom. One tires of eating and drinking too much. It is not good for the health and one becomes fat and lazy." Johannes spoke with a clipped Germanic tone and was as ever to the point. He would provide the logical thoughtful approach to any problem we would face. Matthias was more down to earth, good in a tricky situation as he could talk his way out of anything. We had a deep soul connection of some sort but as yet I had not thought further on the matter.

After a suitable pause to make acquaintances with the men at arms I addressed the troops.

"Welcome one and all, we are about to embark on a dangerous mission with little reward. I will outline the plans as much as I know and after that if any wish to leave they may do so for this may not be to the liking of all.

We will take on supplies at my home city of Metz and then we will make for Saumur on the Loire to learn further instructions as to our exact target. In order to avoid difficult questions we will disguise ourselves as Knight Hospitaliers of the Holy order of Saint John. This will be accepted without question by the English Goddons when we enter their territory as we surely will. That is when it becomes dangerous. If we stick together we will have a much greater chance of success.

Our guide will be Marie-Yvette Elisabeth Görlitz only daughter of my Liege Lord Elisabeth Görlitz, Dowager Duchess of

Luxembourg. Every man here will swear a sacred oath on whatever they hold to be holy to protect and defender her to the death whatever the peril."

After the last part there were one or two murmurs but these were soon quelled by Yvette who spoke up bravely. Yvette pulled back her hood so that all could see her youthful face in the glow of the firelight she paused dramatically then spoke with eloquence and passion. Her beauty commanded respect as did her station in life.

"I may have the body of a woman but I have the heart and soul of a princess of the House and lineage of Luxembourg. I have abilities that can see beyond the normal world and I shall guide you faithfully and true, so help me God and the Holy Trinity. We go to free a prisoner who at this very moment is being tortured and cruelly abused by the English having been betrayed by the Burgundians and their avarice. It is a Holy crusade that we embark on and our souls shall win eternal redemption for our pains and suffering should they occur. Who is with me?"

A pause ensued which although only lasting seconds seemed like hours. Then one of Johannes' men Ruprecht of Müden by name stepped forward and said, "Aye sweet lady I will follow you!" The prevailing silence broke and so everyone with one voice acclaimed Yvette as their leader in this sacred mission.

I smiled and was much relieved at this turn of events for I wanted the unanimous trust of all. Yvette had stolen the show, her intelligence, beauty and oratory had welded the men into a single unit. Smiling yet still serious she addressed us all again, "Thank you, my army may be small but what we lack in number we make up for in quality. I commend you all." With this everyone cheered. "You will take your orders from Robert des Armoises who is my chosen field commander and then your own knightly Lords. Now we must away to the boat and set sail before dawn for Metz."

With that she replaced her fur lined black hood and stepped back into the shadows. Leading with the lamp Yvette set off back down the sloped cobbled street in shadow of the curtain walls. As I went to move off last in line the rose coloured archway appeared and I suddenly found myself in broad daylight and another +30 degrees Celsius of heat.

"Where are you going Yann? We've only just got here!" DD's concerned voice brought me crashing back to the here and now with a wallop.

"Sorry I wasn't quite with you my maths angel." I abruptly did an about turn and resumed my position at the Tour de l'Artillerie gate. "How long have I been gone, Lily?" I asked to ease my confusion.

"Only about a minute." She replied looking at DD.

"Ah I get it!" DD said with a smile as she suddenly understood what had happened. "You can tell us all about it after we finish our tour. I think we should get our money's worth." With that she winked and laughed.

"Absolutely!" Lily added and stepped off through the Tour de l'Artillerie gate and continued up the inclined slope to the chateau. The layout was that of a large semi-circle with the flat side facing the river. Even though the towers had been shortened somewhat they still gave an impression of the power and majesty of the fortress in its hay day. Continuing up the inclined slope we turned left under a small arch immediately in front of the arsenal magasin des vivres et des armes and entered into the large flat courtyard area of the chateau. The views over river were spectacular and gave us a clear sight both ways as it was situated at the apex of the bend in the river. It was well chosen and a perfect strategic site.

After walking around the vestiges of the grand buildings that once existed we stretched out onto the grass in the sun. The day had proved highly successful so far and Lily outlined her plan to have some lunch in the restaurant by the quay side and then we would continue on to Metz by way of Thionville.

It was now around one o'clock so we descended the slope and entered the town once more. The walk to the car was considerably easier as it was downhill all the way. Turning into Place Jean-de-Morbach we entered the restaurant *La Vieille Porte* – The Old Gate. Lily enquired as to the availability of a table for three and this proved no problem as it was a quiet Monday.

The decor was modern and fresh, stylish black modern upholstered chairs surrounded the crisp white linen table clothes. Grey serviettes complimented the grey and yellow abstract paintings that graced the walls of the restaurant and modern tracked spotlights shone their beams down from the ceiling to highlight the sparkling glasses and silverware.

Everything met with our approval. We chose *Le menu du jour* and chatted over a glass of house red as we waited for the entree. Water was provided separately and much appreciated as we had built up quite a thirst walking in the hot morning sunshine. It was now time to relax so I related my experience to the girls in the form of a story acting out the parts.

The meal was delightful and extremely good value at €14.50 a head. I opted for the obligatory cafe cognac after the assortment of cheeses; the perfect way to end the meal.

Lily settled the bill and DD and I gave her €40 to cover the tip and our meals. "Time to go *mes enfants terribles!*" Lily obviously liked that part of the story. She was excited to hear the details of her speech and the response of the men at arms. The boost to her confidence was visible and she felt a little safer in the new knowledge that they would protect and defend her to the death.

Leaving the restaurant after complimenting the chef on an excellent meal we sauntered to the car. After a last look downstream at the vineyard slopes and then the chateau we started our journey to Metz by following the riverside road to Königsmacker and beyond that to Thionville.

In the back I put my arm around DD and whispered in her ear, "We are taking you home my love."

Chapter 26

Sainte Barbe Gate

 t was 3 o'clock by the time we arrived in Metz. Lily drove straight off of the *AutoRoute de Lorraine-Bourgogne* into the old part of the city via the *Pont Elbé bridge.*

"This is the Rue Sainte Barbe." No sooner had Lily informed us than we were across the next longer bridge the *Pont de Thionville.* I had always been fascinated by the way Metz had been founded on the Moselle where it contains a number of mid-stream islands of varying sizes, some large, some small all interconnected by a series of bridges that join the north bank of the river to the south and the old city.

We approached a large roundabout at Les Iles and took the second exit into Boulevard du Pontiffroy. Lily was looking for the old Sainte Barbe gate which had been home to Robert and Jehanne des Armoises from 1436 to 1453 when she passed away due to an illness. The only time she went away was for more adventures during their third year of marriage when her fighting spirit got the better of her for the best part of a year. After many adventures in the Vendée area of France she became Captain of the Guard for the notorious Gilles de Rais but left quickly when she discovered his child murdering occult ways, after that she went to Paris to see the Dauphin Charles VII now king. When asked about *"their secret"* she was unable to answer correctly that she was his half-sister and so she was exposed as not being the royal protégé of Yolande d'Aragón and the saviour of Orleans. Humiliated and made to confess in public she finally made her way back to the loving arms of Robert in Metz and then finally settled down in 1440. That was when the door was carved as Robert was so elated to have her back. He loved her so much yet he wished never to stifle her beautiful adventurous free spirit. They then lived many a happy year over the Sainte Barbe gate and from that time she called herself Jehanne de Lys, the Lady Armoises of Tichemont and even had the arms of Jehanne d'Arc displayed over the gate where they lived, as she was indeed the peasant girl daughter of Jacques d'Arc and Isabelle Romée.

As we drove I knew that we would tune into those happy and tragic memories as soon as we set foot in that place. It was therefore with mixed apprehension that I entered the old city of Metz once again. DD was blissfully unaware of what I already knew and that was as it should be for I wanted her to discover the information for herself first hand and to enjoy the journey to revelation that would undoubtedly take place. The quest had become all-consuming and was exponentially gathering pace. I was prepared to trust Lily 100% as she was the navigator, her psychic intuition sharp as a razor. She had planned this to the last detail.

"The museum closes at five, so we need to go straight there once we have parked. I want DD to see the door first-hand, "Lily sounded excited and this infectious enthusiasm communicated perfectly to DD as she resonated in total harmony with all the information.

Within minutes we drove over the *Pont des Grilles* and into the *Sainte Barbe* quarter of the old city proper. Lily turned immediately left into Rue des Remparts then at the next junction she turned right then took the next left into *Rue du General Fournier* adjacent to a distinctive red surfaced football pitch. As we entered the city wall area DD commented on the unusual amount of greenery and space. I explained that it had been part of the geographical history of Metz to keep this part clear due to the needs of defence and river flooding. Several old maps show this and I offered to show them to her on my computer later.

The road was lined with commuter cars parked to the right. Lily finally located a vacant spot and parked the car neatly nose first into an available gap.

"This is the *Pont Sainte Barbe!* We are actually parked on the bridge of the barbican gate house. Look there is the railway line going north crossing over on its own bridge just in front of us." She then leapt enthusiastically out of the car to check her bearings. "It's exactly as I saw in my dreams, not bad driving using my inbuilt psych-nav even if I say so myself."

"Absolutely perfect, most impressive Lily you are a marvel. I thought you had been here before. This is so exciting I'm getting goose bumps already!" DD said as she embraced her with a big hug.

"It doesn't look much now but you have to imagine how it was 600 years ago. It was a major defensive work covering the north east sector of the city and ran along the west bank of the *River Seille* from its confluence with the *Moselle* to the south side of the city. *Porte Allemande* is just up there on the right and beyond that the *Mazelle gate* near the modern railways station." Lily added rapidly as she pointed out the geography. She had certainly done her homework or rather her headwork I thought to myself; very impressive indeed!

"*Porte Allemande* is where our adventure started, Église Sainte Ségolène is just over there back the way we came and Place Jehanne d'Arc is right opposite it. Beyond that and to the right is *Musée La Cour d'Or - Metz Métropole* our destination." Lily continued brimming with enthusiasm.

"What a brilliant place to park! I thought we were going to have to walk a long way to reach our goal. You are a total gem, I could kiss you Lily!" I was euphoric and so overwhelmingly happy to be back in Metz with at last full conscious knowledge of my life as Robert des Armoises, Sieur de Tichemont.

"If there is any kissing to be done, I will be doing it Yann Baillieu!" DD suddenly grabbed me from behind and then started to tickle me under my arms. I immediately wriggled and was amazed at how she knew my one and only weak spot?

"Look at you my brave Sir Knight; reduced to a quivering wreck by a mere woman!" Lily found the whole episode hilarious and reached for her camera to capture my momentary but pleasurable discomfort.

"Not fair, there's two of you and only one of me!" My protestations fell on deaf ears and just made the girls laugh harder. As DD's face came closer to mine I smiled and then kissed her long and passionately on the lips. That did the trick, she immediately lost concentration, let go of her under arm grip and embraced me fully. "Welcome home my love." I said softly with tender emotion and then kissed her again long and hard.

Click went Lily's camera surreptitiously, "Another one for the family album when you two are grey and old; what fun!" She declared triumphantly.

The moment of *l'amour fou* over, we recovered ourselves and set about gathering our equipment from the car. The distant hum of traffic hardly disturbed the tranquil atmosphere of the bridge and the birdsong in the park like green space that was now the Sainte Barbe gate. Time was pressing so we set off at pace back towards the city and past a red football pitch. We would return later to explore the city ramparts and the old city wall in full as they had no human entrance closing time. Now we focused objectively and exclusively on getting to the museum and 'our' door.

We marched purposely along the curved *Rue Marchant* to Église Sainte Ségolène and then crossed over the road into *Place Jehanne d'Arc*. The distinctive bronze fountain still squirted its narrow jets of water into the ornamental shallow dish shaped bowl that formed its centre piece. The sound of the trickling overflow as it cascaded into the hexagonal stone pool beneath came as lilting music to my ears in DD's presence. Yet, I had no time to stop and stare. On we marched relentlessly into *Rue des Trinitaires* past a *trompe-l'oeil* fresco of three men hauling a large seascape painting up the side of a building. Coming to the next junction we turned immediately right into *Rue du Haut Poirier* at the end of which stood the museum entrance.

It was now nearly four o'clock, plenty of time to visit the door. My pulse was racing, I found myself holding DD's hand tightly, the same way that a nervous school child holds the hand of a designated partner when queuing on a school outing. Lily purchased the tickets which came to €13,80 and we entered. She appeared just as excited as us to be back. She would be the witness to the supreme moment that DD, myself and the door would finally be reunited again as one entity in material reality. It would be such a special moment in history when timelines collide past and present all one.

Rushing headlong through the many exhibits of the museum we headed directly for the medieval section heedless of the other exhibits. Then our personal climatic *moment suprême* arrived as we reverently approached *La Porte*. The sacred memorial to our love, carved in perpetuity so that the world and a future 'us' would see its poignantly beautiful message, an eternal message of our love calling from beyond the grave.

In silence it lay at an angle in its resting place, waiting for the day that we would return. Tears welled up in DD's eyes as she felt the pure emotion of that supreme moment and knew truly that she was loved and had loved. It was a sublime moment in time, a moment like no other; the reunion of lost twin souls that had been cast adrift in the tempestuous seas of time and space to wander as rudderless ships with no purpose or direction but now somehow as if by a miracle the true compass of their love had brought them safe home again.

Our faces mirrored the detailed wooden carving perfectly. Lily arranged us in the exact same position and began happily snapping away with her camera for all she was worth.

"Closer, closer, lower, lower, look at each other, that's it perfect. Amazing, I can hardly believe what I'm seeing through my lens you are still the same. My you two have aged well. You don't look a day over 600!"

Her laughter made the camera shake and blurred one of the photographs. "I'll take that again. I must stop laughing at my own jokes when working!" She muttered under her breath.

Finally after reviewing the shots and video footage Lily was satisfied that she had captured the definitive images for posterity. "This is going to make such a great story for the paper! A tale l'amour like no other, the readers will love it! It is a shame we can't buy the door and take it back to Lille."

In a spontaneous moment of verbal reflection I said quietly, "That would be lovely Lily but this is truly where it belongs as it not far from where we once lived and it was created."

"Besides it is nice that the public can see it for it is a universal story of love that belongs to everyone." DD added magnanimously as she smiled at me with her sparkling blue eyes.

"And where would we put it? We are not even married or

live in the same house even." I added thinking as ever of the practicalities.

"That may change!" DD was quick to reply and winked and smiled lovingly at me.

I blushed like a young girl.

"Madame des Armoises is as quick and forceful as ever I see!" Lily joined in using her incisive wit to underscore the truth of the matter and aid my discomfort yet again. "Some things never change, past, present and future they are all the same, there is only the eternal NOW and you two are married, it's just that it happened in 1436! You are the same people inside. We shall have to re-write future laws to include a spiritual as well as a physical union."

Time and events were blurring into one. Perhaps this is what they meant by the post 2012 effect? We are learning to deal with our multidimensional existence in a totally new reality. Perhaps it is the reality that has always been but we just didn't recognise it? As all these heavy thoughts permeated my head DD just smiled as she gazed into my eyes and then kissed me. It was a long lingering passionate kiss that was worthy of Auguste Rodin's famous sculpture and sealed our rediscovery of the door perfectly.

Click went the camera, "Ah perfect! It's made me go all shivery." Lily whispered, "This is going to look so good in black and white; very artistic! I might even win a prize with that one?"

Finally we stood for several long minutes hand in hand staring at the door and the carvings of ourselves as we once were; ourselves looking at ourselves from the perspective of another time and place the same yet different. For me personally the quest was over. This was the pinnacle; anything else would now be the icing on the cake.

An hour passed before we made our way reluctantly out of the museum and back onto the street. Tourists walked to and fro without an inkling of the miraculous moment that had just taken place. Perhaps I would write a book one day to tell our story. Yes I would! The idea came rushing into my head and in that second I resolved to carry it through once I had retired from *La Voix du Nord.* It would be a story of love interwoven with the medieval history of France. It would be a story like no other ever written. I would call it *La Porte - The Door.*

My thoughts were suddenly interrupted by an enthusiastic Lily exclaiming, "Let's take DD to see the *Graoully* in *Rue Taison* it is only just up here on the right."

"Yes why not, it is after all part and parcel of Robert des Armoises for sure. We can tell her about the legend and the dragon connection with Metz." I added in agreement. This prompted a sudden look of interest from DD which spurred us on to make a positive decision.

Walking back the way we had come to *Rue des Trinitaires* we turned right instead of left and continued to a small Y junction. Taking the right hand fork we continued into *Rue Taison.* At the next junction Lily pointed out that the *Cathedral of Saint Etienne de Metz* was just down the road to our right.

Then we saw the *Graoully,* the two winged, two legged green dragon suspended over Rue Taison. DD looked up and stiffened as her subconscious was delivered another jolt from the past.

"I know this so well. It has been in my dreams since I was a little girl." She said in a hushed voice. "I'm sure it also has an allegorical meaning?"

"You are quite right on both accounts." I added quickly seizing the opportunity to explain for we were all involved in the intrigues of the dragon princesses and their political machinations.

"We still are!" Lily said then laughed, "Once a dragon princess, always a dragon princess." With that she looked at DD and winked knowingly. She then proceeded to relate the tale of the vanquishing of the dragon by Saint Etienne and the allegorical meaning of the triumph of Christianity over Paganism that it alluded to in the minds of the simple country folk.

"Yes the *Graoully* or *Vouivre* is a member of the dragon family, and is considered to be one of the most beautiful species of winged serpents.

According to old legends and traditions, this mythical reptile lived in swamps, lakes, abandoned chateaux and monasteries of Franche-Comté - Doubs and Jura; Burgundy - Yonne, Nievre, Côte-d'Or and Saône-et-Loire; Lorraine - Meuse and other such regions of France, Belgium, Switzerland; oh and not forgetting the Aosta Valley in Italy.

It is described as a dragon; part woman, part bird and part snake. The *Vouivre* wears a jewel in the middle of her forehead. This jewel is what allows her to see, and she can only be killed if it is stolen, although it is removed for bathing.

It is said, in an old story from Franche -Comté that a greedy and fearless man, living in the village of Mouthe, wanted the carbuncle jewel for his own. He took the advice of an evil sorcerer who told him to slaughter a bull and steal the carbuncle from the *Vouivre* while she was busy drinking its blood. He did this successfully, but once he had the gem, he refused to share its riches with the sorcerer or the people of the village and it turned into horse dung in his hands! It was said he smelled of dung for the rest of his days, and the *Vouivre*, whose power was diminished without her magical stone, went into hiding.

Yes my little children, the *Vouivre* wears but one eye in the middle of her forehead, and that is a carbuncle; when she stops to drink at a fountain, she lays it aside; that is the time to possess yourself of the jewel, and she is blind ever after. The Christians demonised the *Vouivre* even further by turning her into the scary dragon you see above us!

Oh and the *Vouivre* flies through the air like red-hot iron, whatever than means?

Of course this story was for the peasants. We know better, the Vouivre was in reality a dragon princess and the jewel her third eye – the pineal gland which allows her to have psychic powers with which to see into multiple dimensions and other realities beyond this physical world. DNA is the key. You are either born a dragon princess or not. It cannot be attained. It is a birth right, our birth right!"

DD found the story eerily fascinating for she was now tuning into her own past memories which were surfacing by the minute and becoming ever clearer as she felt her own dragon DNA abilities and focused on the artefacts to be found in the surrounding Metz cityscape.

After Lily finished telling the story we continued on into *Rue de Ladoucette* it was now gone six o'clock and we talked of our plans for the night.

"I think DD and I will spend the night in the *Tour des Esprits*, variously also called the Tower of Spirits, the Tower of Witches, the Tower of Sorcerers or the Tower of the Mind and see what occurs?" I used a theatrically spooky voice to make it sound more interesting and macabre. I was totally fascinated by the complex etymology of the name and stressed its many meanings as they were exactly in tune with our quest and own discoveries.

We can have dinner first and then wander around the *Sainte Barbe* ramparts when it is dark. It is a shame we can't light a small fire, that would be nice but I don't think the authorities would take too kindly to that in a public park!" Lily and DD laughed as it seemed so absurd now that we lived in a world of authority with rules over such trivial matters.

Lily spoke next, "That's fine, I shall sleep in the car then, one night won't hurt and we all have to be at *Gare Lorraine TGV* by eight in the morning otherwise we will be charged for another whole day on the car. We can then head to *Saumur* and a nice hotel to get cleaned up in; modern life does have some compensation."

"I can use my phone to book the hotel and check the TGV times." DD added wishing to join and be more actively involved in our quest, "Even if the restaurant has no Wi-Fi connection I can use my download allowance to find the information." She smiled and her eyes flashed a deep azure blue. It was a glimpse of the determined Jehanne des Armoises of old. She was now definitely part of our team adventure and rediscovering that sense of excitement that had been all but washed away by bland modern life.

It sounded a good plan so we headed onward and into the appropriately named Rue Serpenoise where we found a large impressive department store which looked as though it would probably sell travel blankets. I was sure we would need them come nightfall and especially in the damp cold early morning.

Whilst browsing at the department store we chanced upon a 1/6th scale collectors doll dressed as a *Vouivre!* The quantum coincidence was all too much so I weakened and purchased it on behalf of DD and myself and then we gave it to Lily for it reminded us of her and it would make a nice souvenir of our Metz adventures for her to keep. Dressed in a stunning red Gothic dress with long dark chestnut hair and a black net petticoat the doll looked every centimetre a dragon princess; the most distinctive feature being a jewel on her forehead representing her third eye. The likeness was so spooky after what Lily had just been discussing that I could hardly believe my eyes. Strangely it somehow balanced the gruesome brutal image of the green dragon *Vouivre* hanging in *Rue Taison* just up the road. Finally after a lot of rummaging we found some tartan fleece travel rugs in the sports department that were light yet waterproof on one side, perfect for the night manoeuvres that we had planned.

It was now time to eat so we walked back along Rue de Ladoucette and back into the street of the green dragon, Rue Taison. The *Graoully* still hung menacingly overhead like the *sword of Damocles* it could only be judged by the outcome of its actions good or bad with and not by purely preconceived judgemental dogma. On the one hand it was said to be a symbol associated with Satan, plague and pestilence and then on the other it was associated with strength and protection in battle, it alluded to the power of the dragon princesses and their ability to see into other dimensions and into the future. The *Graoully's* actions in life would determine whether it was good or evil? Handsome is as handsome does as with dragons, people and all things. Perhaps this was why Robert des Armoises had adopted it for his enigmatic heraldic emblem? It had certainly served him well as a badge of mark and was sown onto the clothing of all those who served as men at arms under his orders. Either way it did add a certain mystique to his small command at the *Sainte Barbe gate.*

My *Vouivre* was bound to make an appearance tonight in my time slip, I felt sure of that. We would wander the ramparts through the Devil's gate into Devil's alley and make our way to the *Tour des Esprits* after dark and see what transpired? I would tell the girls more of my insights over dinner which would set the scene and command the night to conjure forth its dark secrets.

Turning left at the end of *Rue Taison* we leisurely walked down to the riverside in order to find a pleasant restaurant in which to pass the evening. Lily knew of several that came highly recommended, it was just a question of price and availability. We could easily stay until dark as the meal was something to be savoured and enjoyed not rushed and hurried as in other cultures.

Entering the Rue des Piques Lily pointed out *Thierry Saveurs et Cuisine* the atmosphere looked in keeping with our noble enterprise, as was the interesting gourmet section of the menu described as – *a Bistrot chic fusion food and wines, perfect for a delightful evening.* Reading through we decided to go for the *Ardoise du Marche* which looked excellent value at €26,50. Lily ordered for the three of us after we had decided and DD carefully chose the wines to suit, we then settled down for an interesting evening of discussion and conjecture as to what events would follow in the darkness.

It was now a little past ten when we left the restaurant in a very relaxed mood and started to stroll along the river side. I had wanted to catch the last of the summer twilight so that we could gather our bearings. It was a beautiful clear sky and the waxing rising Moon provided plenty of light for our journey. We were not on the Moselle proper but rather the lesser branch used for navigation that led from the small harbour along the north side of the old city and rejoined the main river at Saint Julien les Metz. These were the old medieval quays that Metz had based its independence and wealth on in the *Moyen age*. The first was the tree lined Quai Felix Maréchal that then led to the Quai du Rimport this had less trees and joined with the Pont des Grilles that we had entered the old city by that very afternoon. Beyond was the Sainte Barbe quarter of the city, I mused that the best thing about geography was that it hardly ever changes when measured in the ephemera of human lifetimes; most convenient.

The rampart walls and towers started immediately beyond Pont des Grilles. They were much reduced in height but as with the geography they were still where they had been 600 years ago. The atmosphere changed immediately which was something we all felt. Lily declared again that she would stay with us until around 2am but after that we were on our own as she was tired from driving and our Luxembourg foray. I was happy with that as was DD. We needed some time together so that we could connect with our own timelines and see what we could discover?

With Lily I hoped that we would tune into the gathering of the company so that I could identify the names of the men at arms under my command. That was the one piece of information missing from the puzzle that I desired before we proceeded to Saumur and thence to Rouen. Who were my three chosen men? Men who I had asked to risk life and limb in a calculated gamble to save the heroine of France - *La Pucelle.*

The Graoully, the Habicht and the Lion all three houses would be represented and recognised by their own distinctive heraldic devices and badges of mark. They would be worn as distinctive insignia on the armour and leather nailed jacks of the men, my friends, all comrades in arms. Also each would wear over the top a disguise of a black hooded robe with the white radiant cross of the *Chevaliers noir de Metz.* Thus we would pass easily as *Knight Hospitaliers* of the Order of St John and so avoid the suspicion of the Burgundians and English *Les Goddons* whilst on our mission.

As we walked and talked in the warm night air darkness settled with black inky fingers and the street lights twinkled ever more brightly dancing as mystical reflections on the gently rippling surface of the ever flowing river. The cloaked city now took on a magical quality that seemed timelessly enchanting and enticing. Modernity with its infernal machinery receded and we began to travel back in time. Like silent shadows Lily, DD and I began our haunting of the ramparts. In a ritualised ceremony we would visit each tower one by one and talk softly to the stones, the same stones that had witnessed our passing all those many years before. Just physically touching the stones would secure our connection with that past.

As we proceeded I could feel myself reconnecting with my own past self. How often I had walked these same walls as part of my watch. Countless times I had toured the curtain walls to ensure my men were at their posts, awake and alert. Now I was performing this duty once more and like a Necromancer of old summoning dark spirits I began to feel their phantom presence.

"Oh my God look at those orbs of light." DD cried out in genuine amazement.

"Ssh... stand silent and see what happens, radiate positive thoughts, don't scare them. I will try to get some shots on camera." Lily focused her lens and snapped away but far from being shy the orbs came closer and closer.

"I can see them *mon Dieu*, they are my men. I recognise them. They wear my badge. Can you see their faces?" I could scarcely believe my own eyes as I whispered hardly daring to breathe. I desperately sought confirmation from DD that I wasn't hallucinating from the Absinthe aperitif and too much cognac consumed after the meal.

"Yes, I can see them clearly too." DD answered back. "Each of them has an individual face, head and shoulders within the orb. They seem to recognise me too." As silent as soap bubbles on a summer's breeze the orbs moved towards DD. As I stood there transfixed they then came towards me and gathered around in two's and three's. One even took his cap off in salute as he recognised me. I then suddenly realised why the locals had named this corner bastion of the ramparts the *Porte au Diable de Metz* - The Devil's Gate! Perhaps these trapped souls would not be so charitable to those they didn't recognise for they in their own minds were still performing their faithful duty beyond the grave. Gathering my thoughts and emotions, I saluted my men and told them quietly to stand down, I thanked them for their service and assured them that all was well and with that bade them go to the light. At first nothing happened as they were reluctant to leave my side but eventually they did. In turn each of the orbs brightened, flickered and then went out leaving us totally alone in the darkness again.

A sense of peace descended on the place. "I suppose it is the concentration of their soul energy that we can see? Like the much illustrated halo often illustrated in medieval manuscripts and paintings."

The girls mulled over my insight whilst Lily reviewed her film. "Well remarkably whatever they were they have shown up on the camera. Zooming in you can even see individual faces quite clearly!" Lily passed her camera to us and we saw the evidence for ourselves. Young and old they were there as plain as a pike staff. It was yet another piece of a very big multidimensional puzzle that we were now routinely navigating with ease and increasing excitement.

Then we turned the corner into the *Allée de la Tour au Diable de Metz* and headed along the *Seille* to the *Pont Sainte Barbe*. The show continued unabated as more orbs came to visit us. Lily was ecstatic and continued shooting away with her camera. Her concentration was so intense that she did so uncharacteristically in complete silence.

On the way DD and I paused by a fortified small bridge with three pillars that I did not remember from our time. It was now only a short walk to where we used to live and I wanted to compose myself for the big moment as the Sainte Barbe gate was next on our phantasmagorical tour macabre.

Holding hands tightly DD and I started towards our home as it was some six centuries ago. The trees beckoned us onward. The silence was broken only by a freight train passing slowly by on the railway track leading northward. The noise of the steel on steel reminded me of swords being deflected off of heavily armoured knights. It was that same grating texture of metallic sound. I could feel the metal grinding my teeth as the noise penetrated my being.

When we reached the actual position of the gate I suddenly realised that Lily was no longer with us. I called her name but there was no reply. DD began to get concerned as did I after several minutes for there was no sign of her. I switched my torch on and started scanning the undergrowth, the earthen mounds and the trees. Wooden sculptures in the park cast eerie shadows that played tricks on my mind.

"I bet she is time tripping?" I whispered just loud enough so that DD could hear me clearly in the inky darkness.

"She's over here!" DD shouted back.

I walked towards her voice and came to a clump of trees. Shining my torch beam frantically to and fro I suddenly saw DD kneeling over Lily. "Any damage?" I asked immediately. "Airway, breathing, pulse?" My voice was steady as it went into a well-rehearsed man down drill.

"She seems alright. Her pulse is slow and her breathing shallow but detectable. I'm frightened to shake her in case she is startled and becomes shocked." DD said with deep concern and feeling. She now knew the symptoms of our time tripping and not to disturb the experiencer.

"Good girl DD, we will just monitor her. Put a blanket over her and grab one yourself. We may be a while?" I pulled the tartan fleece travel blankets out of their large carrier bag that had been supplied by the department store and passed two of them to DD. She gently placed one over Lily, fleece side to skin and tucked the waterproof side under her as best she could. Then she placed hers on the ground next to Lily. We huddled together to share warmth and I spread my blanket over the two of us.

"Perfect all warm and water tight now all we have to do is wait a while." I kissed DD on the cheek in reassurance and lay back holding her close so we could observe the myriad of stars and galaxies that floated across the night sky above us. An hour passed and still Lily appeared to be sleeping like the dead. To pass the time DD and I caught up on our life stories. I wanted to know everything about her as she did of me. Everything seemed the same; we were twin souls and without a doubt made for each other.

Another 40 minutes went by and then all of a sudden Lily began to wake up. Her breathing increased suddenly then her eyes flickered and opened.

"How long?" she said without pausing for another breath.

"About an hour twenty." I said sitting up and leaning over DD.

"That's not too bad, thanks for the blanket. I don't feel cold at all." Lily then laid back in order to relax and stretch; I caught the moonlight reflecting in her eyes. For an instant she had an otherworldly look about her. I couldn't help but wonder what she had seen? I knew however that I would have to wait a little longer whilst she gathered her thoughts.

"Don't mention it. It's our pleasure." DD said as she twisted over to face Lily. "I tucked the blanket under you to gain the maximum benefit of the insulation as best I could." Lily smiled. Then after several long minutes she was ready to speak so we all sat up together.

"It was amazing, lots of vivid detail of our meeting in Metz. I think I was meant to come here to this precise spot in order to connect with my medieval self. Perfect, I'm glad it is much warmer here it was so cold back there! I'm getting better at this time tripping it doesn't faze me anymore and strange to say I am actually enjoying it."

Lily had obviously been back to January 1431 with snow on the ground as I had seen in *Sierck les Bains*. "What time is it?" She asked.

"Five to two." I answered as my iPhone lit up. "Perfect timing you said you would stay with us until two. It is just as though you set the alarm in your head to go off and wake you up in time."

"Yes something like that. Right I'm off then. It's time for you two to take to the *scène de l'histoire*. The car is just along here if I'm not mistaken and I've got to drive in the morning. Take my rope you may need it?" Lily reached deep into her rucksack that she had carefully placed on the grass beside her previously and after ferreting about for a minute or two she extracted a neat coil of climbing rope which she gave to me. "Always useful I carry it everywhere, old habits die hard!" She said with a bemused giggle.

"Thanks I've got a feeling we might need it." I said gratefully and set about re-coiling it so that I could sling it around my body and over one shoulder. DD looked amazed as though Lily had performed the most wonderful piece of magic ever. Lily and I both interrupted simultaneously before DD could ask. "It's what we do!"

"I call it Lily's rope trick." I added theatrically with a flourish. DD laughed and exclaimed, "Well that's a new one on me."

Smiling Lily checked for the car keys and then bade us goodnight, "Sleep well *mes enfants terribles* and don't let the *Vouivre* bite!" Please at her parting shot Lily disappeared off into the darkness towards the car carrying her blanket and rucksack like the good soldier she truly was.

"See you bright and early I know where to find you; have fun!" Her last few disembodied words floated through the trees on the still night air and she was gone.

Quietly we rolled up the two remaining blankets and then continued our nocturnal journeying along the *Seille* towards the mysterious *Tour des Esprits* and the unknown frontier of our minds.

Chapter 27

Tour des Esprits

It was only a short walk from the *Sainte Barbe gate* to the *Tour des Esprits* in 3D space but it was a giant leap in time. I could feel the memories closing in on me as we silently walked slowly along the old city walls that had weathered the centuries. In the moonlight I could see that the path suddenly forked, we intuitively took the left smaller branch towards the river. Then as gnarled as an old broken tooth we saw the tower in the misty gloom. Circular and strong it stood but with a giant triangular shard broken away from the side facing the river Seille. Pausing at the base of the gash I shone my torch into the structure and saw that it reflected off of a number of arched ceiling pillars that still performed their task stoically in maintaining the flat roof structure above. The Witches hat timber and tile roof proper had long since gone and now only the bare bones of the defensive work survived.

The height of access via the missing shard proved impossible to negotiate it was far too high and too smooth to climb effectively. Scanning again with my torch I noticed an iron grille gate half way up that obviously led to the battlements on the city wall side of the tower. DD and I looked around in order to locate another point of entry or at least a way of climbing up onto the battlements that rose above us some eight metres high from ground level. The torch beam illuminated a flying arch that had been carefully built to link the broken town wall immediately to the right of the tower with a further section some 20 metres distant. This allowed passers-by to continue their walk and to directly access the football pitch and sport facilities we had seen earlier. On the left hand side of the tower the river walk continued to run parallel to the city walls and the river bank but it was narrowed and did not have that spacious park like feel of the *Sainte Barbe gate* area.

I surveyed the brick structure with DD and noticed that whoever had dismantled the wall had left convenient foot and hand holds in the form of exposed bricks protruding from the flat smooth surface. Perfect, I knew instantly that I could easily climb the eight metres to the battlement and then I could secure the rope to the iron gate like grille and drop the loose end to DD below. Just like old times I thought to myself and smiled as I un-slung and uncoiled the rope. I outlined my plan to DD who was totally amazed.

"This is one event I hadn't dreamed of a week ago!" She exclaimed with a note of shock in her voice.

"Treat it as an experiment. It will be just like old times; bring back all those happy memories!" I said half in jest yet in all seriousness.

"OK I will give it a go and see what happens?" DD replied with renewed confidence. I had obviously struck a familiar chord with her subconscious, she watched me with incredulity as I began my careful ascent. As a precaution I attached the rope with a bowline around my waist and then threw the remaining coil over the arch. DD instinctively knew what to do and ran to take up the slack. Should I fall at least I had some insurance. Thank goodness for a piece of rope I thought, Lily was right it is an essential piece of kit.

Not a soul stirred in the early hours as it was now well past two. I knew therefore that we would not be detected. Once safe inside the tower we would be out of sight and out of mind to the casual observer and the authorities.

I began the climb. The first part was extremely easy but as I progressed higher the bricks protruded less and it became a little more challenging but I had faced much worse in both this life and others. Finally I made it onto the battlements and a minor sense of triumph coursed through my body. DD let go of her end of the rope and I gathered it in safely so that it was completely free of the arch. My subconscious acted with all the expertise of a seasoned sailor of tall ships as my body went through the somehow familiar drill of coiling the rope.

I untied the bowline from my waist and secured it to the strong iron grille that covered the bottom half of the doorway into the tower from the battlements. I then dropped the rest of the newly coiled rope down to DD waiting below in the darkness. She fastened the rope around the blankets and I hauled them up onto the battlements with ease. I then threw the loose end back down and in the darkness I could hear her clothes rustling as she tied it around her waist and then tugged three times to indicate that she was ready to make the climb. Taking up the slack I re-secured the rope to the iron grille with a clove hitch.

Satisfied with all our preparations I whispered below that she should begin her climb. Again it was fairly easy and DD made rapid progress over the first half then came the trickier bit. The rope gave her confidence and she continued the climb without loss of pace. Within half a minute I could see her blonde hair and face appearing at my feet and I helped her onto the battlements with a firm grasp.

"Just like old times!" I said with a smile.

"I guessed that you would say that! But now you come to mention it, it does seem strangely familiar." I helped her to untie the rope and adjusted the knots on the iron grille so that the rope was now doubled and dangled into the tower chamber. Twice I checked the knot for strength and made sure that the iron grille would take our weight. The one thing I didn't want to do was lower us into a trap from which we would not be able to escape.

Satisfied with all preparations I climbed over the iron grille and started to abseil down the wall using the friction of my jacket to control my rate of descent. The drop was negligible and only some five metres to the floor. The wooden joists had long since rotted and only the foundation that I stood on was left. It would be a cold hard bed but it would have to do.

DD threw the blankets down to me then dropped down in the same manner that I had used. "I didn't know you abseiled?" I said in astonishment at her professionalism.

"I didn't either! I just watched you and somehow I just knew how to do it?" She replied with humour and honestly.

"A hard bed my love but one I would not trade so long as you are by my side." The words just came out of my mouth without thinking as I spread the first blanket onto the cold damp floor.

"I'm back now forever and I will never leave you again Robert." DD's voice was unmistakeable as she whispered in my ear. I barely had time to stop my conscious mind from puzzling over the Robert reference but that I began to fall headlong into a well of dreams. I felt DD's body next to me as I passed silently from this world into another long ago.

I found myself in a bedroom of sorts with a roaring log fire and a four poster bed. Two large black giant Barbet water dogs sprawled on the stone floor in front of the blaze absorbing its radiant warmth in sublime bliss. They stretched and dozed again, the cares of the day gone from their canine minds. I looked down and saw that I was dressed in tight black hoses and a doublet over my linen shirt which felt different to the soft modern cotton that was now receding in my memory. Over my doublet I wore a fur trimmed long dressing gown that kept the night chills away when I was not in front of the fire. I felt sad and lonely. I had known brief happiness and thought briefly of my two young sons that were now rapidly growing. They were close by being looked after by a wet nurse so I knew that they were safe and well. I missed my beautiful Jehanne now Madam des Armoises, she that previously had fought like a warrior under the name of *Claude* and led men as though born to it.

Now, I was sad because the one I loved was far away, God knows where and I was sad that she had chosen to depart of her own accord in order to follow her adventurous heart. The passion for adventure still burned brightly in her bosom and so I had let her fly free for I desired no tame caged bird. She was a wild and passionate spirit that flew on the wings of eagles. She needed to soar and feel the wind in her face and the sun on her back. She was beautiful, so beautiful.

We had married by a chance meeting at the request of my liege lord the Dowager Grand Duchess of Luxembourg, Elisabeth Görlitz. It was a strange affair but her beauty, of body, mind and spirit had won my heart and so I had agreed, but the hawk must fly free in order to live so reluctantly I had let her go. For a year I had waited patiently with not a word. In my heart the last flickering coals burnt low as barely glowing embers but as of now they were not yet extinguished and cold.

Day after day I had discharged my duty faithfully as *Captain of the Sainte Barbe Gate*. The burghers of Metz slept soundly in their beds at night because my men watched over them. Oh how I missed my Jehanne, she who fought like a man yet made passionate love like a woman without equal. Yet every day I was reminded of her presence as her chattels and effects surrounded me. Every day I waited and yearned for her return.

Just at that very moment there came a sudden knocking at the door. The dogs became instantly alert, stood up and started barking. I hushed them and then left my chair. Midway to the door it burst open without warning and in strode Jehanne travel stained and weary. I stood speechless hardly daring to believe the evidence of my own eyes, my hand already on the hilt of my trusty bastard sword ready to draw. Without warning she flew at me and embraced me in a long passionate kiss. My heart raced and I knew from her physical touch that I was definitely not dreaming. I relaxed the grip on my sword and kissed her back savagely as my animal passion got the better of me.

We paused and looked into each other's eyes searching for the soul spark behind the physical forms that we wore like clothes. Her sparkling blue eyes pierced my heart once again as we connected at the deepest level. Jehanne went to open her mouth to explain and I placed one finger on her lips in a gesture of silence. Words were unnecessary. She was back in one piece and whole needing nothing more than food and rest to heal and become the angel I knew and loved. I kissed her again this time tenderly, soft and long. She reached for my gown and loosened it from my shoulders. It fell silently to the floor and I reciprocated with her cloak and tunic. Silently and deliberately she kissed me and started to untie the chords of my hoses from their supporting belt

The feel of the sheer woollen material being pulled free from my skin was electric and instantly burnt into my memory. We stood together separated only by our thin linen shirts. Holding each other and feeling the fire's radiant heat warming our flesh beneath the ephemeral garments. Slowly I untied the chord at the neck of Jehanne's chemise and she mine. Stretching the fine linen I revealed her bare shoulders to the warmth of my kiss. Then without warning the loosened shirts fell to the floor and we embraced fully, warm naked skin caressing warm naked skin. I kissed her breasts and she beckoned me towards the bed which waited cold and silent. I pulled back the blankets and bed linen and together as one we plunged into the cold.

The shock woke me with explosive force and I felt the exact same cold from the stone and mortar foundation I was lying on. My body ached with stiffness and pain. It was dawn and the first rays of light had penetrated the trees surrounding the tower. They were now illuminating the columned arches with a pink hue. I looked towards DD who lay cradled in my arms which suddenly felt dead from loss of circulation. She was sleeping like an angel and her quiet breathing felt as light as gossamer on my cheek. I kissed her gently knowing that she was safely back in my arms forever.

She stirred and murmured my name; Robert. It was definitely Robert! I guessed that she was experiencing a time slip of her own. We would have to make comparison notes later on. I kissed her again gently on her forehead as I resisted the temptation to pull my arms away and restore the much needed blood circulation to my limbs. Her eyes opened and she smiled. I knew then that she had seen and felt what I had. "I love you so much." The words just formed in my mouth without effort.

"I will love you forever." She replied without reservation.

"And I love you both!" Lily's voice cut the atmosphere like a hot knife through butter as it came from out of nowhere. Now let's get going we've got a train to catch!"

I popped my head over the top of the gash and saw a dishevelled young lady who had obviously had a rough night.

"Morning, lovely day!" I said cheerily trying to jolly the proceedings along. "Won't be a minute old girl." I added affectionately.

"Less of the old girl, I'm 23." Lily said indignantly, "Its 5am time to get moving."

I ducked down threw the rolled up blankets out of the tower and then got DD up to the breach by using my cupped hands as a stirrup. She obliged by placing her foot automatically in the recess and I boosted her upward with a heave ho!

"Over you go." I said without allowing her a pause for thought. With help she scaled the wall without difficulty and then eased her way safely down to Lily who nobly offered her shoulders as a step.

"It's not far, you shouldn't need a rope." DD shouted back at me.

To her surprise I appeared on the battlements as I had scaled the wall back up to the iron grille by using the rope and then climbed over it as quick as a flash. I then hurriedly untied the two knots.

"I didn't know this was a race." Lily shouted.

"It's not but you did say to get a move on. Grab the rope and hang on." With that I threw one end of the now freed rope down to the base of the arch. The girls took up the slack. Using the other end I abseiled down the raw edge of the city wall and smoothly touched down on the soft ground. Taking the rope from Lily and DD I flicked it several times and pulled the loose end from around the iron grille so that it dropped to the ground by me.

"There you go neatly done; thanks for the assistance, I couldn't have done it without you." Smiling I coiled the rope and handed it back to Lily who stowed it back in her rucksack.

"Shame I had to use two hands to hold the rope that would have made a good picture." She said in a complementary way.

"Of course but it might get me arrested by the Gendarmerie, best to have no evidence." I said thinking out aloud.

With that we made our way along the river to our faithful black Renault Megane parked on the *Pont Sainte Barbe*. Having stowed all of our gear Lily started the engine and we were soon on our way to *Gare Lorraine TGV*.

Chapter 28

Saumur

Despite the disrupted night we all felt exhilarated at the progress we had made in uncovering the mission to save *La Pucelle*. Lily chatted freely as she drove and told us of her experiences the night before. She had witnessed the fateful meeting of the companions in Metz on that cold January day in 1431. They had discussed the plan in rough detail and had made arrangements to travel by horse to Saumur on the Loire. There they would have an audience with the Grand Duchess Yolande of Aragon who would give further precise details and silver in order to finance the mission. Robert carried a letter of marque from the Grand Duchess Elisabeth of Luxembourg but it was phrased in code so that should it fall into enemy hands the plot would not be discovered. It stated that they were a religious order on a pilgrimage on behalf of the Duchess' late husband John the Pitiless, of Bavaria. This would conveniently explain the mixture of Swiss and German accents in the party and it was a common enough practice to support such pilgrimages in order to ensure that the sponsor would go to heaven. John had been murdered so needed as much help as his widow could muster to ease his and her passage to the afterlife.

Then Lily mentioned the crucial piece of information that I had been seeking the names of the three men that Robert had chosen from among his Metz militia. They were Tomas, Thibauld and Enfant Guilliame a young fresh faced lad of no more than thirteen summers. All bore the insignia of the red *Vouivre* surmounted on a black and white shield of Metz which were the arms of Robert des Armoises and the Sainte Barbe gate guard. Each of the *chosen men* had a particular skill that would be of use on the mission. Tomas was a wiry fellow with a neat light colour beard and a clean cut appearance. He was extremely intelligent, dexterous at picking locks and adept at the black arts of alchemical magic. Thibauld his comrade was a tall giant of a man, extremely strong and would provide muscle should the occasion arise. Enfant Guilliame was good at gathering information and mixing unnoticed in crowds. He would be useful undercover in Rouen to ascertain the strength of the enemy and mix unobtrusively with the brutal *Goddon* soldiery in the taverns when necessary.

Robert des Armoises himself held the key to the escape plan for only he knew precisely the location of the secret passages in an out of the dungeon fortress of Rouen. He had stated this at the meeting in order to inspire confidence in his companions. It all went back to 1415 in the months leading up to *Azincourt* when as a page to the *Duc d'Orleans* he roamed the mighty chateau in Rouen like any adventurous boy would. There he discovered the secret ways in and out of the keep. All chateaux had them for various cryptic reasons but the main one was for escape should the enemy penetrate the final defences.

Lily's contribution as Marie Yvette was of a psychic nature as she was able to see events in the future which would be most useful on the road to Saumur and in Rouen. The information was received with interest and a certain amount of awe by the party, although only events would tell if her predictions were accurate.

By the time Lily had told us her story we were at *Gare Lorraine TGV* and had to say goodbye to our car. Shouldering our luggage we headed into the station to purchase our tickets to Saumur. The first train available was the 7:25 to *Aeroport Charles de Gaulle* on the outskirts of *Paris*. From there after an hour's wait we would be able to catch the 10:01 to *Saint Pierre des Corps* near *Tours*. That would get us in at a fraction before twelve just in time to catch the local TER train to Saumur at 12:01. Travelling along the Loire we would arrive at 12:31 precisely, the journey would be like clockwork and in total comfort which would be in stark contrast to the journey undertaken by our medieval selves!

"I've booked two rooms at the *Hôtel de Londres* in the centre of *Saumur*." Lily announced as we waited on the platform, "It's not far from the chateau which will make our trip easier and more efficient; no car hire necessary."

"I'll look for some coffee my mouth feels so dry." I said and then disappeared off quickly to find some. Several minutes later I returned without success. "No luck only machines we will have to wait until we get to the *Aeroport* they will have proper facilities there and we can have a civilised breakfast with decent coffee and fresh croissants. It will be worth the wait."

"I have some bottled water if anyone is thirsty!" DD added. Quickly reaching into her luggage, she took out a bottle of Evian and passed it around. Lily and I took a long sip and were most grateful as it assuaged our parched throats.

"Well at least we know where we are going and how we are going to get there unlike in 1431. Thank goodness for the information age." I was most upbeat. Living with modern technology was just so cool. The girls smiled and as I spoke the TGV, like a shiny silver serpent, glided silently into the station precisely on time.

The journey to Paris was quick and we arrived at *Charles de Gaulle* just before nine. The terminus felt dark and confined as the trains ran in below street level. With little under an hour to wait for our next train we set off in search of fresh coffee and croissants. Taking the escalator from the platform we emerged at ground level into the myriad of grey fluorescent lit corridors that ran hither and thither. Blue illuminated signage greeted us cheerily with an endless stream of updated information that twinkled and flashed amongst the ultra-modern urban architecture. Above us swept the elegant curves of the wide arching canopy over the main concourse. It was a miracle of engineering, pleasing on the eye and perfectly suited to the functionality of the space. Light flowed in through hectares of glass and lit the massive floor space below with ease. All around an elegant forest of girders and columns supported the vast sinuous curves of the roof. Eventually we found a patisserie and purchased our *petit dejeuner*. As we sat in the ultra-modern decor it seemed to whisk us as far from the medieval period as we could possibly be; this was definitely more space age than *moyen age*. We therefore contented ourselves with people watching and enjoying the much needed refreshment.

Descending to the subterranean platforms once more we boarded our TGV train for the hour journey to Saint Pierre des Corps. Smoothly the silver serpent snaked its way around the Paris suburbs and then into the open fields beyond where it was able to get up to its maximum speed. In the distance the wide open spaces of the *Centre* flashed past. As they did I thought of *Orleans* and our adventures there. I knew it was somewhere just south of the mainline that we were on and I was equally aware that we were now heading into strange territory as the west of France had long been wild, sparsely populated and steeped in the occult. Now DD held my arm and slept quietly with her head on my shoulder. She was the final piece in my own personal puzzle and I was overjoyed that she would be able to witness the final climax of our quest.

My reflective thoughts were disturbed by the sound of our train hitting the myriad of points that denoted we were arriving at our destination of *Saint Pierre des Corps*. Lines, carriages and freight were neatly waiting everywhere as we entered the busy station for this was a major junction on the Bordeaux route. From here we would take the local train along the Loire valley to Saumur, beyond which lay the city of *Nantes* and the wild-west coast of France. I looked at my iPhone, it was a little before twelve and we only had five minutes tops to find our connection. This we did with surprising ease thanks to the clear signage and we were soon sat in our seats ready to enjoy the views of the ever expanding river as it continued westward.

The journey took just over thirty minutes. It appeared slow by comparison to the TGV but that was just the illusion created by its *grand vitesse* which seemed to condense the very fabric of time and space in an Einsteinian way.

The station of *Saumur* was by complete contrast to the previous was extremely understated; a small box of a building greeted us which belied the fact that this was a busy line and the city an ancient centre of historical power. It was however pleasingly undergoing rejuvenation and there was evidence of new building. After pausing to look around we stepped out into *Avenue David d'Angers* and grabbed a taxi.

We were all tired after the adventures of the night and so we sat in silence. My attention kept being drawn hypnotically towards the impressive *Chateau de Saumur* that dominated the skyline on the south bank of the river. Its solidity emphasised by the thin narrow spire of *l'église Saint Pierre* which pointed heavenward like a thin black needle protruding from the flat city skyline.

"No doubt who is in charge here, look at that fortress, it's simply magnificent." I passed the comment just loud enough so that the girls could both hear me clearly. DD leaned over to get a look out of the passenger window on my side. The aroma of her Chanel No5 perfume instantly transported me to another world and I forgot all about history, knights and chateaux for a brief moment.

At the first junction east the taxi turned right onto the central many arched *Pont des Cadets de Saumur* that spans the northern branch of the Loire to the *Ile de Offard* in the middle of the river. The driver informed us that it was the *Route de Rouen* which jerked me back to our mission. Just the very mention of that place was enough to grab my subconscious by the scruff of the neck and make it jump through hoops. The climax of our quest was clearly building and I could feel the adrenaline starting to pump around my body. Goosebumps ran down my arm as I tightened my grip on the door panel hand rest. My knuckles went white and drained of blood before I realised what was happening and eased my grip.

The road then continued straight as an arrow over the *Pont Cessart* towards the centre of the old city. I knew from the Internet that the hotel would be just ahead of us midway along the *Rue d'Orleans* just beyond the *Rue Franklin Roosevelt* that we were now travelling along.

The taxi driver pulled up outside the *Hôtel de Londres*. Without ceremony we disembarked and took our luggage from him. Lily exchanged pleasantries and paid the man. The hotel was clean, neat and brightly decorated in red and grey, its close proximity to the chateau made it the perfect staging post for our purposes. On the notice board was a poster advertising the *Cadre Noir*. The very name struck a chord with me as I read the detail regardless of the checking in procedure which Lily was engaged in. DD wandered over to me and together we discussed the poster that was more of a coincidence than it should have been. The picture of a soldier dressed in black sat on a rampant horse with the chateau in the background was extremely enticing. Even more remarkable was the fact that out of the whole of August the only day that the stables and ménage would be open to the public was the following day! That was just too much of a quantum coincidence it was a sign. I talked hurriedly with DD and she agreed that it would be a good idea to go and see them in the morning.

Without further ado I called Lily over and pointed out the poster with a smile. She was immediately intrigued and suggested that we should definitely go and take a look the following morning.

"You read my mind!" I said with a big grin for I knew that Lily would be way ahead of the game when it came to deciphering the cosmic clues to our quest. "We hereby declare the rest of the day a public holiday in celebration of this magnificent coincidence." I royally announce which was only common sense as we had not had much sleep the night before. The girls gave a mock hurrah and we headed for our rooms. The first thing was a shower and rest so we decided to meet at five for an aperitif. That would allow us time to recover and research the mysteriously named *Cadre Noir* on the Internet.

Whilst in the long hot shower I cast my mind back and re-examined every second of our experience in the *Tour des Esprits*. She was definitely Jehanne des Armoises without a shadow of a doubt. Her behaviour and character just cried out the fact that she was. As with everything it was so obvious once you knew the truth. I couldn't believe that I hadn't spotted it before but then again my eyes hadn't been opened. This was the beauty of a quest for knowledge as only by looking, really looking do we discover the blindingly obvious all around us. That thought echoed and reverberated in my mind as a profound statement about the nature of the universe and the fact that we have to use our conscious mind in tandem with our subconscious to puzzle out the myriad of cosmic clues that surround us. Only then will we truly understand their relevance as signposts to our many physical lives.

Just then a knock came at the door. I opened it and was surprised to see DD in a towelling dressing gown, her beautiful blonde hair still damp and tussled from the shower. "Lily's is asleep so I snuck out to see you!"

Somewhat flustered by this unexpected encounter I invited her in. She smelt divine. As we talked we moved closer together like two magnets of opposite poles relentlessly attracting each other to join forces and be one. The tension was too much and I found myself embracing her and kissing her neck just below her left ear. She melted in my arms and then kissed me passionately full on the lips. This was our time we had waited 600 years in linear time for this moment. Silently she slipped off her robe and we slid beneath the covers. I set the alarm on my iPhone for four o'clock and we were suddenly lost in a roller coaster of sensual ecstasy.

In what seemed an instant the alarm buzzed in my ear. We awoke enfolded in each other's arms. The bed was warm and comfortable unlike our few hours in the Tour des Espirits. Awakening DD gave me a kiss and then gracefully dressed very, very slowly. As she did so the soft late afternoon sunlight from the window accentuated her perfect curves and stunning breasts. "I had best be getting back to our room and wake Lily up. I don't think she will mind my little foray?"

"Dragon princesses see all and know all, she will be well aware of what has transpired even if asleep – *bon chance!*" I smiled lovingly and blew DD a final kiss. "Until we meet again my only true love; À bientôt." With that DD quietly slipped out on my room leaving me to get dressed.

At five I went down to the reception and booked a table for dinner that night. I figured that it would be easier for all of us to eat in the hotel. The menu looked good and we would not have far to go in order to fall into bed.

Within several minutes the girls appeared. "I see *La Porte* has been working its magic!" Lily said without batting an eyelid and to break my awkward silence. She then burst into a knowing grin and gave me a big hug. "I'm sooooo happy for you both it is just like a magical fairy-tale but all true,"

"Ah yes exactly." I said thoughtfully looking bashfully at the floor. "It - *La Porte des Armoises* - is a declaration of love unlike no other. Who else on this tiny blue planet has such a testament to their undying love? It is totally unique and the miracle is that we have found each other again."

"And I feel exactly the same." DD added with deep emotional sincerity as she supported my *de facto* statement. "The magic works both ways it is not just Yann's wishful thinking. The door is but a pale reflection of the intensity of emotion that we felt, still feel for each other." As she spoke she took my hand in hers and electricity filled every corner of my being.

Lily thought for a moment. "It is so wonderful to witness this first hand. It would make a great story of love beyond the grave in its own right. I really feel blessed to be part of it all." DD hugged Lily as did I.

"And you my dragon princess can be the bridesmaid! But only if you want to?" I said without thinking.

"That sounds very much like a proposal to me." DD said in affirmation, "I think we should celebrate!"

"I shall be honoured the *Bar d'Orleans* is just back down the road towards the river that looks an appropriate place; *on y va! Allons-y mes enfants terribles!*" Lily said with a big smile.

It was just a short walk along the road to the bar. The atmosphere was relaxed and we chose a secluded corner table. The waiter soon came over and we ordered *Kir royale* aperitifs and began to chat about our immediate plans, but as we talked my attention was drawn to a tall fair haired young man dressed in black that sat alone quietly at the bar. The object of my focus was not the man but a shiny silver object on his left hand that caught the light. It was too big to be a ring and extended the whole length of his little finger. No matter how much I focused on the conversation my subconscious kept tugging me back to the shining silver glint that fascinated me.

Eventually my curiosity got the better so I walked over to the bar to order some more drinks and take a sneaky peek. As I neared I could see it was articulated in several places and on closer casual inspection that it was a miniature piece of armour; an elaborate and unusual finger ornament of some distinction. The medieval coincidence was too much so I just had to say something, "Nice armour; a very interesting piece; where did you get it from, if you don't mind me asking?"

"*Oceania Legends*; I bought it in *Cornwall*, England." he replied without looking up and then continued. "I've been waiting for you. My name is Jay."

His reply took the wind out of my sails as it was totally unexpected. "I'm sorry. I didn't quite catch that?" I said hesitantly, "Did you say you have been waiting for me?"

"Yes, I've been expecting you. My dreams have been sending me all sorts of messages this past few weeks, in the end I just had to listen to what they were saying and so here I am. It seems the universe is on my case and won't let it drop, most disturbing. I could do with a good night's sleep."

As he spoke he stood up and turned towards me, his deep blue eyes spoke volumes. It was as if he had decided to drop his visor and let me glimpse the powerful being that lay beneath his physical form. I recognised instantly the same energy that I had observed in Roselinde, Lily and DD; it was dragon power. Yet Jay was clearly male? This puzzled me but I was now more open to the ways of the universe so it didn't faze me.

"I can feel their sacred dragon energies from here." He said glancing at Lily and DD. "It radiates like a beacon. The one with the darker hair is decidedly *Royal* in countenance. She has a light violet to purple auric field, really quite stunning." His observations were too near the mark to dismiss as pure coincidence.

"I think you had better join us. I'll introduce you to my companions." I collected the tray of drinks from the barman and we walked over to our table in the corner. I formally introduced Jay to Lily and DD and he drew up a chair to sit down with us. He was a fascinating young man, very deep and intense..... He talked freely as though he had known us forever and in his own words told us all about his life.

454

"Living in the chateau alongside all the 'ghosts' gave me, or switched on, what I now understand to be trans-temporal perception. I only seem to be able to reliably access time-periods in which I am currently present. It is less to do with memory and more to do with experience. I know the two are almost in separable. However when I perceive something is plays out as if it were my present not my past.

I saw a lot of my past including my death and the hands of the Gobelin tapestry weavers, equivalent to the modern media I suppose!" He said with a wry smile.

His mother was a famous artist and he had been brought up at *Chateau Haute Rivière, Sainte-Gemmes-d'Andigné* near *Angers*.

His story touched me as it was a perfect example of how we develop our own innate abilities when not brain washed by education. For being left to his own devices with only the ghosts and spirits to play with he had developed his psychic abilities to an advanced degree. His mother had then sent him away to a Catholic boarding school in England when he was twelve and he had finished his formal education there. Since then he had developed a talent for computers and now had his own successful IT business.

He then continued and gave us a gruesome example of the practices that had gone on in his chateau back in earlier times.

"Have you seen the tapestries at Chateau d'Angers? They were woven by the Gobelin who assassinated the original Lord of Chateau de La Haute Rivière; my house in France.

They are called the Apocalypse Tapestries, morbid name! Although why a celebrated band of Dutch weavers took to assassinating French Lords is beyond me? Michele's blood stain, which had soaked into the slate step, was still there. We had it chemically erased and it came back within a month. When we eventually had the step removed, which was no simple task as each step was about half a ton in weight of stone, we found the bodies of two infants and a cat buried together with some stones in a grave filled with red-brown dirt. This was most odd as the native dirt is orange-yellow in colour. It also hid a sealed off chapel that we didn't even know we had under the stairs. The local Mairie came to the conclusion that it was ritualistic in nature and buried the find under a ton of paperwork, probably because the area was having an expensive face-lift and ritualised killing of children might scare away tourists!"

A chill went down my spine as I thought of our encounter with Gilles de Rais and *Les enfants perdus* in *Orleans*. Perhaps then this was why of all the bars in Saumur we happened on the bar d'Orleans. The connection was there a quantum sign post that we had subconsciously followed to the next link in the chain.

As proof of his abilities he told Lily all about herself for she was the strongest dragon princess in our group and her royal past fascinated him. He talked effortlessly without pause or hesitation and I started to see the past life connection that he shared with us. It was something to do with Saumur and Yolande of Aragon but as of yet I could penetrate the mystery no further. We would have to journey together awhile for me to find out as unfortunately my psychic abilities were not so well developed as his. The girls of course had female dragon DNA which made them adepts. DD was catching up fast as she accelerated the activation of her abilities with every step of the quest.

By universal non-coincidence Jay was staying in the same hotel as us so I invited him to dine. I was sure that it would not be a problem as he must have already booked in for the meal so it was just a matter of changing tables.

The girls found him charming, intelligent and charismatic. He fitted in extremely well. I kept looking at the finger armour which tugged at my subconscious continually. It was a perfect example of people wearing their memories for others to see; a subconscious desire that we all manifest whether we know it or not.

The time flew past and as the clock approached eight we made our way a few doors along to our hotel. I was still reeling from the coincidences that were stacking up with increasing frequency and magnitude. Dinner was extremely pleasant and we took it in turns to fill Jay in on our adventures to date. Lily dealt with *Metz* and *Reims*, I took the grizzly story of *Orleans* and DD finished off with our latest visit to *Luxembourg* and *Metz*. It was a pleasure to listen to her talk. She was so beautiful, animated and strong. As she spoke I discovered several points that I had missed as I had naturally perceived events purely from my point view. She had experienced far more than I had ever imagined in the *Tour des Esprits* which confirmed my time slip experience in both detail and accuracy.

As we came to the end of the meal the atmosphere mellowed and the girls said good night for they were extremely tired and wished to get some unbroken sleep. Even though I too shared their fatigue I decided to stay up with Jay until the midnight hour in order to listen to his tales of *Le Côte Sauvage, the Vendée* and *Catherine de La Rochelle;* also to fill him in on tomorrow's plans. He knew the *Chateau de Saumur* well and would be an invaluable guide, but his real passion was for *Chateau de Angers* near where he had grown up. He told me more of its strange and occult history that included the *Tapestries of the Apocalypse.* He had investigated the many secret passages that riddled the fortress which further confirmed my suspicions that somehow this complete stranger had been a part of our mission in 1431.

My curiosity satiated and my head stuffed full of tales of medieval France and the lawless wild-west coast we parted company around one. I slept very well and it was soon time to rise. At eight thirty I made my way down to the dining room and waited for the girls and Jay whilst enjoying a steaming bowl of fresh coffee. They duly arrived fifteen minutes later looking clean and refreshed. Over breakfast we agreed to tackle the chateau head on and leave around ten.

The walk although not far was steep. We traversed the *Rue Dacier* to the *l'église Saint-Pierre* and found ourselves in a quaint district of bars and cafes with a few timber framed buildings. A board with a portrait of Cardinal Richelieu hung near an inspiring red carved timber town house which was now a cafe and we noted that it would be a good place to have lunch later. Continuing on we passed the *Maison des Compagnons du Devoir* an impressive pristine limestone and slate medieval building with a courtyard. Looking back we could see the magnificent old city hall in the distance. Turning left we continued up the *Rue des Remparts* towards the main entrance of the chateau. To gain access we crossed over a narrow masonry bridge midway between two projecting angular ravelins that led to an arched opening in the curtain wall and beyond into a courtyard. Lily paused to take some pictures.

Then as I set foot into the chateau from the bridge the now familiar rose arch appeared and I step through it across time several hundred years into the past. The shift was silent and instant. I was now well aware of the process so immediately became alert and started to record the information that my senses were giving me.

The courtyard was suddenly alive with hustle and bustle, grooms scurried to and fro. I could smell wood smoke and dung all around me. I looked back and saw that they were rushing to tend the horses of our party. Mine was a particularly fine black mare with a white blaze on her forehead. We also had several pack animals in tow. I counted them, thirteen of us and twenty horses. We made quite an impressive sight each of us dressed in long black habits with hoods, on each of our chests was a large white Germanic cross.

Johannes, Matthias and Yvette wore a black cloak each with a small similar white cross covering the left breast above the heart. This was to difference the knights from the men. Marie-Yvette Görlitz had already dismounted and was being careful not to expose her face to view. I knew it was her by the slender willowy build. Johannes and Matthias were busy giving instructions to their men. They would tend the horses and keep guard over all of our effects. Having made due arrangements they joined me and we headed into the chateau proper. As we approached the impressive barbican entrance the guards became alert and crossed their halberds to prevent entry. Not wishing to antagonise them I sent word that we were expected and produced my letter of marque from the pouch worn on my belt.

After several minutes the Chamberlain arrived dressed in his sumptuous fur trimmed finery and with the gold chain of his office around his neck. The rich red and gold colouring of his clothes contrasted totally with ours to good theatrical effect. He greeted me courteously and said that the Grand Duchess had been aware of our imminent arrival for several weeks. He examined my letter in detail to confirm our identity and when fully satisfied that we were who we appeared to be bid us enter the main building.

He led us to a disrobing room and we removed our travel stained cloaks, swords and daggers. He was even more surprised to see us take off our black habits to reveal our court dress underneath and that one of our party was a woman dressed as a man! Each of us wore our heraldic colours with an embroidered coat of arms on the left breast over our heart.

Johannes resplendent in red and gold with the half rampant lion of Eltz, Matthias in red and green with his Habicht coat of arms of a hawk natural on a green mound, Marie-Yvette with the arms of Luxembourg, silver and blue stripes with a rampant red lion surmounted with a crown and myself dressed in black. Looking at my left breast I could see the characteristic black and White arms of Metz surmounted with a splash of red that I knew to be the *Vouivre*.

Realising that Marie-Yvette was of royal birth the Chamberlain immediate changed his demeanour and his language became much more courtly and respectful. This made me laugh as it seemed a fine trick for us to masquerade as humble knights.

"Appearances can be deceptive my dear chap, sometimes that which seems plain can hold a golden treasure inside, just as the humble egg dull with camouflage contains a golden yoke!". I spoke eloquently and with a great flourish.

"Are you saying I am an egg Robert!" Lily sounded indignant.

"Not really, it is just that our disguise reminded me of an old Lotharingian riddle - A box without a hinge or lid inside golden treasure is hid; what am I?" I was conscious that all the others had stopped to listen alerted as they were by Lily's tone of voice.

"So you are saying I'm an egg!" Lily continued her mock interrogation. Then she burst out laughing, "I'm only joking. I wanted to see how big a hole you could dig and then throw yourself in, shovel and all."

The tension broke and everyone laughed including me. "You had me there. I really thought you were annoyed, very funny."

"Yes, my mother told me that riddle when I was little too." Lily graciously put me at my ease. "Now I must see my mother's cousin." The Chamberlain jumped to attention immediately and asked us to follow him into the grand hall.

The chateau was labyrinthine and designed to confuse would be attackers. Eventually we came to a large set of impressive oak doors and the Chamberlain disappeared within leaving us to stand outside. After several minutes the doors opened and we were invited to enter. At the far end on a raise dais sat Yolande of Aragon, Grand Duchess of Anjou, Countess of Maine, Countess of Provence and Forcalquier, Countess of Piedmont and titular Queen Consort of Naples, surrounded by her gentle women. She radiated power; dressed in a red bodice trimmed with ermine and an exquisite blue dress of rich velvet. On her head she wore a gold coif richly entwined with a string of pearls and trailing a protective veil. In her left hand she held a gold sceptre to denote her status as a Queen.

Walking slowly in a chevron formation we approached and knelt before her. Lily was first to rise when given leave. "Greeting from my mother Elisabeth Görlitz, Grand Duchess of the House of Luxembourg and greetings from her only daughter who stands before you great lady." Lily's youth and aristocratic bearing spoke volumes as she spoke with measured respect and royal formality.

One by one she introduced us and we took a step forward, bowed and gave thanks to her royal highness. To each of us in turn Yolande smiled and waved her hand.

"Thank you my child. We are pleased to see you and you are most welcome to enjoy what time you have with us freely. My love and protection is absolute. Now to the matter in hand, Robert des Armoises, Sieur d'Tichemont, Chevalier noir de Metz step forward."

I took a pace forward and bowed once more with a flourish. "My gracious lady, your royal highness I am at your command." as I looked up Yolande extended her right hand which bore her personal seal. Touching her fingers lightly with my right hand I kissed the ring and then stood to attention.

"It grieves me Robert that I may be sending you, your men and my cousin's only daughter to certain death at the hands of the English but I am at my wits end. We must save my protégé known to the populous as *La Pucelle* the Jehanne d'Arc of Orleans fame, for she is of royal blood. Unfortunately as you may or may not know in a headstrong fit of pique she foolishly exceeded her original remit and raised her own army. She thus exposed herself and was captured at Compiegne and so became a prisoner of the Burgundians who have now sold her to the English; a dreadful business indeed. She is however still a royal daughter of France and a dragon princess. I will therefore not rest until she is safe!" Yolande banged the arm of her throne forcefully to make the point.

"They will do for her, mark my words. She will be tortured and executed viciously as an example to all those who dare to oppose the English and the Church, for whilst she is alive she remains a thorn in their side. They abhor the power of women and are desperate to smash the Armagnac cause by any and every means possible. Even more they know that she is a daughter to my cousin Ysabeau, Queen mother of France and mother to the King.

At this very moment they have her incarcerated in Rouen and it is only a matter of time before they eliminate her. Captain La Hire on my orders has been dispatched with an army to attempt a rescue by frontal assault but I fear he will fail for the

English are too strong in defence. It therefore occurred to me to dispatch a second party to attempt a rescue by the backdoor so to speak. Hopefully whilst the Goddons are being entertained in the open a covert operation will succeed through stealth and cunning. You are my chosen man for that task Robert, are you up to it?"

I swallowed hard and thought for a moment weighing up the lives of my companions with the destiny of France and the sacrifices that everyone had made since the siege of Orleans two years previously.

"How can I refuse my gracious Lady? We have all bled for France and what she might become in the future. I was at Orleans with *La Pucelle* as was Johannes. I withdrew the arrow that had struck her and then helped her to heal. I can but show the same courage. Of course I will accept the mission it will be an honour and I will not rest until the lady in question is free to breathe the good clean air of France again."

"Excellent I knew I could rely on you Robert. You will need some help and of course some monies to prosecute this action? Charlotte of Angers another of my protégés and a dragon princess in her own right will accompany you. She is highly adept at the black arts and she will report back to me using her powers."

As she spoke she clapped her hands and a beautiful young blonde woman entered the room. Her hair flowed like a river of gold framing her fine cheek bones and contrasted perfectly with the sky blue dress of the finest silk that she wore. Slowly she drew near; gliding effortlessly across the great hall her face suddenly became clearer to my sight. I took a deep breath in astonishment for I realised that I was looking at the incarnation of Jay as he was 600 years ago.

Yolande smiled. As she did so she extended her hand again. I kissed her ring again and as I did so she whispered in my ear. "God's speed Robert, fare you and your companions well. Charles the Duc d'Orleans always spoke well of you, in fact he still does in his letters. He told me that he could never find you in Rouen before Azincourt! You were always hiding and up to mischief, that is how I knew you were the man for the task. His father was also the father of Jehanne d'Arc! You will therefore render your captive duke a great service by freeing his wayward royal stepsister. You must swear on my ring never to divulge this to anyone."

"Sweet lady I so swear on my life and my knightly honour never to reveal what you have imparted to me in good faith; I now know for what I fight which will comfort me in my time of trial. Thank you."

As I turned to leave the rose arch appeared and I found myself assailed by the noise, heat and bustle of a room packed full of tourists. The transition was complete and instant. As I adjusted I noticed that I was looking at a portrait of Yolande on the wall in the same great hall.

"It doesn't do her justice. She was much more beautiful than that." I said out loud.

Jay just looked at me, smiled and said, "Of course she was!"

Chapter 29

La Gabarre

The climax to our quest was taking shape and a sense of urgency busied us along. As we left the mighty fortress of Saumur high on its plinth of rock over shadowing the town of the same name and the mighty river Loire, Jay's presence amongst us suddenly assumed a new stature and importance. I hurriedly filled in Lily and DD on my discovery and Jay seemed to naturally accept the role that he had now assumed. It made perfect sense to him and he wore the feminine part well. For many lives he explained that he had sought patronage and that he always worked best when under direction and given a purpose. My description of his association with Yolande and the task she had allotted to him fitted perfectly his core *raison d'etre*. It seemed that our meeting was far from random and that the universe was speeding up the frequency of coincidence as we neared the conclusion of our odyssey.

Retracing our steps we descended the slope of the *Rue des Remparts* to the restaurant Le Richelieu that we had spied earlier. It was an impressive old timber framed building set in the *place St Pierre* with a distinctive Cardinal Richelieu sign of a red cardinal's hat that hung high above the square. It was time to plan and digest the enormity of the task that we were being asked to perform. The boundaries of time were merging and I felt an enormous burden of pressure building on my shoulders. It amused me that it was all so tangible and real. Talking helped as I began to share myself imposed yet obligatory task with Lily, DD and Jay. One question remained; how did we get to Rouen back then?

By water seemed the natural option for Yolande would be able to supply a vessel fit for purpose and with that we would be able to slip into the enemy port relatively undetected. Breton crews regularly conducted commerce along the coast between Bordeaux and Normandy. Our disguise and cover story of travelling from the Holy land having been on pilgrimage would fit well with the profile of the many travellers that commuted these parts. We decided to walk the quays for inspiration and to see if our intuition was correct. Lily felt sure that she would be able to use her dragon senses to check the validity of our supposition. Our plans made we paid the bill for our light lunch and left. It was now late afternoon as we emerged onto the water front. It all seemed so familiar. Minus the modern trappings of mechanical traffic we were swiftly back in medieval times. We decided to walk westward along the *Quai Mayaud* towards the *Quai Lucien Gautier* in the direction of the *Pont Cessart.*

As we walked I noticed a small landing stage made of stone that gently sloped down towards the water's edge. I was immediately drawn to the water and fascinated by the way that the slope merged land and water together. We continued walking and reached the *Pont Cessart* with its many stone arches that elegantly span the Loire at this point. We stood near a small roundabout with a rich display of summer flowers that marked the town end of the bridge. Then just along the river bank I spied a couple of tall wooden masts rising into the sky. The name *Gabarre* leapt into my mind and I knew in an instant that I was on the right track.

"Hey look I think we have just found our next clue!" I called excitedly to the others. Carefully avoiding the traffic we made our way to the other side of the bridge to get a better look. The river level was low which was normal for this time of the year and the sand bars could clearly be seen above the meandering flow of the river current.

We then continued on along the quay side and came to a gap in the bank. I followed the gentle slope of the slip way down to where the two flat bottomed craft were moored. A seasoned river worker busied himself tidying the various ropes that rigged the bigger of the two craft. The large square sail reminded me of a Viking ship. It was an elegant age old solution to the problem of getting along on the water. The only variation in technology was the pronounced horizontal windlass that was mounted on the cabin aft of the mast. This clearly assisted the raising and lowering of the mainsail and enabled two able bodied people to easily adjust the sail as required. A large steering oar mounted on a long pole completed the rig. As I sat observing the tranquil scene in silence all sorts of memories flooded my head.

I was so absorbed by my thoughts that I failed to notice that Lily and DD had engaged the man in conversation whilst Jay was busy looking at the second smaller craft.

"Pierre says he will give us a ride as the wind is good at the moment." Lily called out to me in a loud voice that meant hurry up you'll miss the fun. DD was already aboard and chatting away with her new found friend Pierre. Jay and I started towards the boat. "This is a bonus." He said cheerily. "I wonder what we shall find out, hey ho, here we go."

"Some answers I hope? I have a hundred unanswered questions in my head." I replied. "This is the universe at work, seek and ye shall find."

Jay stepped onto the deck of the large craft which was a good fifteen metres long and took a position up near the small rudimentary shed like cabin aft of the main mast. On the roof of this was fixed the A frames supporting the windlass. Pierre asked him if he could help to hoist the sail. Looking aft I noticed that the smaller craft had no cabin. My memory distinctly remembered the boat we sailed on as having a cabin. DD busied herself untying the mooring rope that held our craft to the smaller one and the quayside. Lily held the bow line tight and awaited the orders of Pierre - to cast off.

Still observing the scene I stepped onto the deck from the slip way, as I did so the familiar rose arch appeared and I was transported instantly back to a busy medieval river scene bustling with craft and life some 600 years ago.

Totally un-phased I found myself checking cargo which was being loaded carefully from the quayside under my supervision. I noticed that my attention was being drawn constantly to several studded iron bound strong boxes which had extremely secure hinges and large padlocks. My eyes never left them. They were obviously of the utmost importance to my mission yet I knew that they were not of monetary value per se. The money was being handled by Charlotte the dragon princess protégé of Yolande of Aragon. I could see her busy with the task of securing that valuable part of the cargo. I knew that she had a tight hold on the purse strings of our expedition and I was not in the least concerned with that aspect of our mission. My cargo was of far more strategic importance. In fact it was absolutely essential and also deadly dangerous; the last two words flowed through my mind and lingered there hovering.

As I contemplated my charges I noticed that Johannes and Matthias were busy stowing their kit and directing their men accordingly. My men were nowhere to be seen but I trusted them implicitly and knew that they were usefully employed somewhere in the town. I had sent them to purchase some more crossbow quarrels as I was not happy with the quantity that we had for our weapons. One could never have enough ammunition and I knew that we would have plenty of opportunity to use our long range weaponry before too long. It was always better to neutralise the enemy at a distance rather than coming to close quarters and cutting blows. We were small in number and I didn't want us losing any more men than necessary. Yolande's words echoed in my head as she felt that our mission was suicidal but there is more than one way of skinning a cat and so I had used my alchemical knowledge to even things up a bit.

The boxes kept drawing my attention. What did they contain? What had I thought of that was so important? I knew that they were the ace up my sleeve in this deadly enterprise. Just then Marie-Yvette came to me and dropped her black cowl. She was the image of Lily and of course I knew in my own mind that she was Lily beyond doubt in my present future reality time stream.

Yet I could never get over the shock of seeing her as she was and it was an effort not to call her Lily in front of the others. I decided to attempt an experiment in order to resolve my curiosity.

"Ah Marie-Yvette how goes it fair lady?"

"I am well sir knight, better to call me Yvette from now on it is less conspicuous and I think it better to blend in whilst we are undercover. I see you have your several boxes of tricks safely stowed. We shall be in need of those before long."

Her reference confirmed my feelings of excitement and unease with regard to the iron bound boxes.

"Yes, all are safely aboard, shall we check that our precious cargo has not been broken in transit?" I knew this would be an opportunity for my future self to observe the contents of the chests. With that I hitched up a large ring of keys from my waist belt and moved towards the iron bound strong boxes stacked within the confined of the rudimentary shelter on the deck of the boat. Yvette followed and knelt beside me as I selected the correct key for the first box.

"Does the name Lily mean anything to you?" I deliberately selected that moment to casually slip in my question as I hoped to catch her ever watchful conscious mind off guard and thus allow her subconscious to answer the question directly without interference.

Yvette looked at me with a quizzical piercing stare. "How do you know that name?" her reaction told me all that I wanted to know for it had struck an obvious nerve.

"It just came to me. Does the name mean anything to you?"

Yvette thought for a moment and then replied, "Yes of course that is one of the names that the dream people call me." She looked at me as though this was common knowledge and continued nonchalantly. "Ever since I was a small girl I have had visions of other worlds. I dream constantly even when I am awake yet my mind is always alert. I remember all of my dreams. You are in my dreams too you always have been, even before I knew you in this life."

A tingle ran down my spine as I realised that consciousness was timeless and operated both ways into the material future as well as the past. This was quite a discovery but I kept my emotions under check and responded with an even tone, "It is good to know that we are always together. I will always protect you."

"Yes Robert you are always there in some capacity and I always recognise you. You always protect me."

I returned my attention to selecting the correct key and inserted it into the padlock. With a loud audible click it turned easily as the well oiled mechanism worked flawlessly. With a creak I lifted the hasp and raised the heavy lid. A red velvet cloth greeted my eyes which I duly removed carefully to reveal a dozen or so hand blown glass wine bottles, deep azure blue in colour. They were neatly stacked top to toe on each other six abreast. I checked that the wax sealed stoppers were still intact and read the labels carefully. The Latin inscription told me all that I needed to know – *Conium maculatum - Hemlock, Hyoscyamus niger - Henbane, Atropa belladonna - Belladonna, Digitalis purpurea*

– common foxglove and extract of Amantia muscaria - Fly agaric mushroom. I handled each bottle with all due respect and every care aware that I had enough narcotics to wipe out a small town. I knew that each box contained the same deadly cargo or a more potent variation. So this was my secret weapon, very smart, don't get mad get even. I knew that I had decided to even the odds in our favour somewhat and I smiled at my decision to use alchemy.

In my head I knew that the hidden power of plants would be a useful ally in my mission to free La Pucelle. We would not kill the *Goddons* but merely neutralise them just long enough to steal their prize prisoner from right under their very noses! I planned that they would be blissfully unaware of our covert action until it was way too late. Then they would awake with an almighty hangover and a lot of explaining to do. Cauchon would have their heads not me! I smiled to myself at the thought of this as I replaced the precious deadly bottles one by one, much as a loving father puts his children to bed, tucking them in carefully.

"So that is what you have been up to Robert! Very clever I was wondering how we were going to pull this off now I know for certain. I had thought you were bringing wine to the party but this is much more interesting."

As I clicked the padlock shut with a swift turn of the key. I heard a commotion outside. Rushing on deck I spied Tomas, Thibauld and Enfant Guillaume hurriedly jumping onto the boat as it cast off. "That's good timing boys!" I shouted, "I thought I had lost you to those serving women we met in the tavern last night."

The boys laughed at my levity and swept back their cloaks to reveal four dozen new crossbow quarrels. "These do you Sir Robert!" Tomas quipped as he laid them on deck. "Exactly as you ordered with the recesses behind the head to take the liquid potion as you said, anyone copping one of these won't know what hit them even if it is only a scratch!" Tomas grinned as he wrapped them carefully back up in batches of six.

"Good work boys, we will need every advantage we can muster, remember sneaky is best!" I patted him on the back and took my place on deck next to Yvette to watch the town of Saumur slip away from view. "Oh when you have a minute boys check the crossbows. We might be in need of them before long."

"Now what have I done with those ferrets?" I said out aloud to myself as if to make a mental note. I had lots of plans for my ferrets very useful they are too at rooting out things, ideal for rabbit burrows, secret passages and the like. I had brought a half dozen aboard in baskets of twos. I now went to find them. After several minutes I located the baskets which were at the rear of the vessel. I had started to handle them back in Saumur just after I had purchased them in order to get them used to my scent. They seemed pretty friendly and just like horses they responded to a confident person's energy. Also they couldn't really escape from the confines of the boat so one at a time I stroked, played with them and fed them tit bits of raw meat. I had also a small harness made for each so that I could attach a length of line. I was certain that they would earn their keep come our nocturnal activities in the Chateau Rouen.

My solitude was disturbed by an annoying buzzing sound and the rose archway appeared just as I was starting to relax. The now appeared and I found myself sat on the deck with my back to the mast. The river view was identical to my time slip so I effortlessly slid back into the present. I discovered that the noise was the outboard motor which was pushing the *Gabarre* back up stream towards Saumur. We had obviously travelled several kilometres and an hour had elapsed since I boarded.

I didn't think anyone had noticed me slip off mentally so I just seamlessly inserted myself back into the proceedings. DD was still chatting to Pierre whilst Jay and Lily we swapping stories of their experiences of travelling by water in France. All was well.

Returning to the quayside from whence we had departed I thanked Pierre for his kindness and settled up with a €50 Euro note. Lily, DD and Jay also thanked him and shook hands. As I left the vessel for the solidity of terra firma Lily whispered, "How are the ferrets?"

"They are fine." I whispered back and smiled. This was getting spooky. Her powers were obviously increasing exponentially with time and now she was tuning in to what I was seeing and experiencing mentally. "Not much point in telling you what I discovered I suppose as you probably already know but I will have to fill DD and Jay in on the details over dinner."

"Absolutely, I know all your secrets Yann Baillieu but they don't. Don't worry I won't spoil it. Also we will have to have an early night as we need to be in Rouen by the morning. If we can get to St. Pierre des Corps by 6:15 am there is a direct TGV at 6:19 that will take us straight there. It gets to Rouen Rive Droite at 9:50 precisely. That means we can have the whole day to get set up.

I took the liberty of booking us in to the *Hôtel de Bourgtheroulde* in the middle of the old town just off of the *Rue Jehanne d'Arc;* what else! It looks contemporary to our medieval time period so it should set us up well for our final series of time slips. Part of me doesn't want it to end but we need to solve the puzzle once and for all." Lily stood thoughtfully quiet after her outburst of information and especially the last comment. Jay and DD were still talking to Pierre and saying their goodbyes so our discussion went unnoticed.

Waving a final farewell to Pierre we headed up to the roundabout and the *Place de la Bilange* opposite the bridge, then straight through to the *Rue Franklin Roosevelt*, joining the *Rue d'Orleans* and our hotel. It was fast approaching eight so we decided to go straight to dinner without bothering to freshen up. The concierge recommended *Restaurant le Gambetta* which was just a short walk of 300 metres west of the hotel so we made tracks for there.

The ambience was perfect intimate and romantic just what we need after a busy day. The food was exceptional and we were not surprised to notice that it had recently been awarded a Michelin star. I told DD and Jay of my discoveries and insights into the nature of our secret weapons which went down well whilst eating the main course! "I'm not surprised you did confide in me once that you had wanted to be a pharmacist before you ended up as a journalist." DD added as she finished her last mouthful of her smoked eel and cod.

Jay was positively enthusiastic about the revelation of our narcotic secret weapon and added a whole lot more detail to the conversation which obviously came from his deep memory as he could not recall studying it. He seemed to know all about the effects of ancient poisons which gave me confidence that I was definitely correct in my observation and description. Charlotte of Anger obviously been an adept at poisons and potions and had studied under none other than Yolande of Aragon herself but Jay's knowledge seemed also to go back to ancient Greece and he enjoyed relating the tale of the death of Socrates from hemlock poisoning. It was so clear and precise it was almost as though he had witnessed it first-hand.

After coffee and a *deadly night cap*, as I joked, we made our way to the *Hôtel des Londres*. Lily had ordered a taxi for 5 am so we all agreed to set our alarms for 4:30. It only remained for us to settle the accommodation bill before turning in for what would in all certainty be yet another very short night.

Chapter 30

Rouen

he taxi arrived at five. All four of us stood bleary eyed in the reception waiting by the main door of the *Hôtel de Londres*.

"Taxi for Mademoiselle Chevalier and party!" The short rotund man was far too cheerful for the unearthly hour that we now found ourselves catapulted into.

"Over here, Monsieur!" Lily sounded equally cheerful which spoke volumes for her youth and the rampant enthusiasm that she had for our adventure. "Lovely day!" She continued unabated without pausing for breath and mimicking my sardonic Tour des Esprits comment. That may me grin momentarily despite my thumping hangover.

I stood there silently with a gut wrenching tightness in my stomach much as the gladiator in me had stood in the tunnel of the Coliseum in ancient Rome. There I had waited sweating silently for the bright light to blind me as the doors opened to reveal the arena of death and the noise of the crowd baying for blood. My senses were now poised ready to strike once again.

I was reliving the exact same feelings of that fateful journey into the jaws of death that I had taken in April 1431.

Being hypersensitive Jay was silent too as he could feel the tension that I radiated. DD put her arm around me and her head on my shoulder. Her mere touch provided me with a tangible comfort which reassured me that I was not alone.

Lily shot me a painful sideways glance and I realised in an instant that she too was putting a brave face on it by masking her true feelings with an artificial cheerfulness.

"Ave, Imperator, morituri te salutant." The words just slipped out under my breath – Hail Emperor, we who are about to die salute you. The others in our team needed no translation.

Then we quietly helped the taxi driver load our bags into the cab and all squeezed into the large red Peugeot 807 people mover. The sun was just up and shining on the river as we said goodbye to the *Pont Cessart*. We crossed over to the central midstream island and then over the *Pont des Cadets de Saumur*. At the roundabout we turned right onto the E60 *Route de Tours* and I allowed myself one last glance up at the imposing chateau. With the *Loire* on our right and the railway line on our left we made our way swiftly up river towards our destiny. The roads were quiet and there was very little traffic this early in the morning.

We passed *Villbernier*, several small villages with no name and then rolled ghost like into *Chouze-sur-Loire*. All the while the bright orange summer sun rose steadily into the sky turning the mighty Loire into a river of shining fire. It was all too beautiful for words.

In no time at all we were over half way and speeding through *St. Michel-sur-Loire, Langeais* and *Cinqt Mars-la-Pile*. Nearing Tours we continued through *St Etienne-de-Chigny* and skirted *Luynes* and *Fondettes* all the time hugging the ever flowing river.

Reaching the city we were met with the modern functional urban architecture of the *Pont Napoleon* which contrasted starkly with the much older many arched *Pont Wilson* that we came to next. Another two bridges came and went. Then a spaghetti junction of main roads before finally we turned off to the right down the *Boulevard Jean Jaures* and finally to *Avenue Fabienne Landy* which took us to the station entrance. The whole journey had taken no more than 40 minutes door to door which left us plenty of time to buy our tickets for the 6:19 TGV to Rouen.

Lily thanked the taxi driver with courtesy for being so prompt and gave him a generous tip. His mood lightened considerably and he wished us well on the next leg of our journey.

DD and I went to purchase the tickets whilst Lily and Jay hunted down some coffee and croissants. Within 15 minutes we had both and made our way to the platform to await the arrival of the silver serpent. The sense of adventure was back upon us as the coffee revived our flagging early morning spirits. Right on time the sleek beast slid silently into the station and greeted us with its shining presence.

The train was reasonably busy but we were able to find four seats together after some searching. Stowing our luggage we all sat back to relax and let the train take the strain. The journey was direct and would take three and a half hours so there would be plenty of time to catch up on sleep. In my head I contrasted this with our epic journey of 1431.

Having found our way to the mouth of the *Loire* via *Angers* and *Nantes* we took ship at *Saint Nazaire*. The neutral Breton crew were wary of us at first but soon became more enthusiastic when they could see that we would pay them in gold. The April weather was passable and the journey around the northern tip of Brittany was interesting to say the least! So much so that the captain decided to put into *Brest* to ride out a particularly nasty three day storm that was passing through. As the seas calmed and with a fair westerly we continued our journey hugging the coast putting onto *Cherbourg* to off load some cargo and then sailing on to the north of Guernsey.

The Breton cog from *Bordeaux* was carrying wine bound for Normandie. This was a normal occurrence and very low profile as it was a regular trading route. In port we kept ourselves to ourselves hidden in the hold. Our cover story of being German knights returning to our homeland via the Rhine and Mosel en route from the Holy land after a pilgrimage seemed credible. The story worked well as we were deemed politically neutral by all we met and thus no threat. In port our men dressed as crew and wandered the wharves in disguise to find out the latest gossip; anything that would help our cause without arousing suspicion.

I was acutely aware that there was more than one way of completing this mission just as Roselinde had mentioned in our game of chess back in Lille in what seemed another lifetime and place. The knight can attempt impossible manoeuvres and jump over obstacles which other pieces cannot do.

Her words now guided my strategy. As Robert des Armoises I would use a two pronged approach there by not showing all of my cards on the table for when we reached *Rouen* a small party of German knights would pose no threat to the ever vigilant English *Goddons* and we could easily explain our presence as we had been doing. Whilst our men including our two ladies dressed as men would continue in disguise as common seamen and busy themselves in delivering the prize cargo of Bordeaux claret to the chateau. Once inside they could mingle with the kitchen staff and prepare the ground for our stealth night attack when the time and opportunity presented itself.

Confidence was the key, blending in and remaining anonymous until the appointed hour when we would unfetter the prisoner and spirit her away in the blink of an eye. The wind was fair and the captain had no reservations after some gentle persuading about releasing his crew so that our men could take their place. I sped them happily on their way with a pocketful of coins and tales of the *Dunkerque pirates* that would slit their throats as soon as look at them as we journeyed north after Rouen. The money would suffice their needs until God willing the ship returned. The captain likewise was bought with gold and the promise of more on the successful completion of our journey. We would have one passenger extra no questions asked and sail for Zeeland and the Flemish islands at the mouth of the Rhine. From there we would take a barge to Burg Eltz on the Mosel the home of Johannes. Thus we would keep to our story of returning from the Holy land but with one extra very special passenger that we would deliver to the Grand Duchess of Luxembourg.

My mind made up we set sail for *Le Havre* and the *Crique de Rouen* at the mouth of the Seine

"Yann, oh Yann, we are nearly there, time to wake up!" Lily's gentle voice and a nudge returned me smoothly to our current reality although I wasn't too sure now which reality was real anymore as they were all equally as vivid. DD yawned, stretched and poked me in the eye which stung. I knew instantly that my pain sensors were telling me in no uncertain terms that this was the present physical reality.

"Oh sorry, I nodded off!" She said apologetically.

"You and me both my love, we are just so the same." I kissed her gently on the cheek and brushed her shoulder length blonde hair away from her sparkling blue eyes.

Jay was busy on his laptop and so completely oblivious to our exchange of banter.

"Did I miss something? We here yet?" He said in a laconic voice after removing one ear piece.

"We sure are." Lily replied as she started to retrieve her bag from the storage compartment.

"I'd better save my blog." He swiftly pressed send and then shut down all his programmes and the mobile Internet connection he had been using. He then started to focus on our joint physical reality which required some effort as he was always elsewhere in his head. I knew how he felt.

"I've decided to blog this adventure as it looks to be outstanding! It's live as of a couple of seconds ago." He smiled and I realised that he was just reliving the same pattern as when he was Charlotte of Anger in keeping a record of the *Rouen Rescue*. I duly noted my thoughts and was pleased with the alliteration as it had a nice ring to it. I would use that in my story when I came to write it up for the paper.

Silently the silver serpent applied its brakes and we slowed our forward motion. Effortlessly it came out of the tunnel and in to the shadowy sun light. Finally coming to a standstill the intercom announced that we were now at *Gare de Rouen Rive Droite*. I looked out of the window at the overhead car park that sat like a huge grey asphalt crêpe on top of the old art noveau decorated platforms. Gathering my belongings I caught up with the others as they detrained and the fresh salt laden air immediately blew away the cobwebs lingering in my head. I could instantly tell that I was near the Norman coast as the air tasted different and the temperature was noticeably cooler.

Climbing the stairs we entered the lofty booking hall which was full of character from a bygone age. It was now well over one hundred years old and built before World War 1 tore Europe apart. People sat at the cafe tables of the *Rue de Station* restaurant beneath two large frieze wall paintings depicting a bustling city and riverscape dominated by the architecture of the *Cathédrale Notre-Dame de Rouen* and the *l'église de Saint Ouen*. Whilst the others looked around and availed themselves of the convenience I took the time to text Roselinde in England with an update on my iPhone:

Bonjour Roselinde!
We are in Rouen and about to rescue you!!! We have just arrived from
Saumur a few minutes ago. You are welcome to join us for the finale?
Un pour tous! Robert Xxx

I pressed the send button and the text flew off into the ether. It was only then that I realised I had signed it Robert not Yann! This demonstrated to me just how blurred the boundaries had become between then and now. I gave myself the luxury of a wry smile before the others rejoined me.

"I've just text Roselinde. I'm not sure she will want to be in on our little adventure it might be a bit much for her after the Reims episode?"

Jay looked quizzical so Lily briefly filled him in on the World War 2 details from just a few days previous. As she talked I thought silently that it seemed a lot longer back. It was amazing how time appeared like a piece of elastic when we were discovering so much in such a short space of time.

Leaving the art noveau booking hall we went out into the bright morning sunlight of the forecourt. Looking back at the building I noticed the time on the tall decorative clock that adjoined the right side of the building, it read ten past ten.

"Time to get going, On y va! Allons-y mes enfants terribles!" I said with gusto as I clapped my hands theatrically; for the game was at last afoot,

We headed south across the *Place Bernard Tissot* and over the subterranean *Rue de la Rochefoucauld*. We then entered the *Rue Jehanne d'Arc* which was straight ahead and I knew that our hotel was only a short walk along its length. Avoiding the busy traffic we crossed over the *Boulevard de l'Yser* via the many pedestrian crossings that seem to haphazardly litter the road junction like so many horizontal ladders.

Calm returned as we started to stroll more casually and take in the scenery. "To our left is the *Rue du Donjon*. You can see the tower a paltry reminder of the once great chateau that we shall visit in our quest. Even so it is worth looking at and we shall of course return as and when to confront its secrets but on our own terms." I sounded just like a commercial tour guide as I pointed out the tall black witch's hat slate roof of the donjon that dominated the immediate skyline.

I felt strangely in control as if *Rouen* belonged to me. I didn't belong to *Rouen*. I was its master. The feeling gave me renewed confidence. I wasn't afraid anymore, the vibes were good and that reassured me that we had been successful in our expedition of 1431.

"Who's afraid of the Goddon wolf, the Goddon wolf, the Goddon wolf." Strangely I found myself singing the children's nursery rhyme, well a politically incorrect variation of it which drew smiles from DD and Jay. Lily just replied nonchalantly "Not I." under her breath.

Further on we passed *Square Verdrel* with its leafy green trees, pond and waterfall. Beyond it lay the *Musée des Beaux-Arts de Rouen* with its impressive grand facade. We walked another couple of blocks and crossed over the *Rue Guillaume Le Conquerant*. "Not far now!" I confided to the troops. At the next junction I turned right into *Rue Rollon* and then after two short blocks left into *Place de Pucelle d'Orleans*. On the corner we were suddenly confronted head on with the infamous *Place de Vieux Marche*.

The hackles on my neck stood on end. I didn't need a guide book to tell me where I was and what I was looking at. The old timber framed buildings still looked the same only their colours had changed and now a modern looking church with its strange weird hat like roof stood in atonement for the sins of Cauchon and his evil Catholic inquisitors. I spat on the floor in disgust! I could feel the hatred so long repressed rising to the surface of my mind like so much bile vomiting forth.

My whole body started to warm up as the hormones pumped adrenaline into my circulatory system. All this caught me totally off guard and I had to use my conscious mind to regain control of my rampant emotions.

My blood was boiling and my passions ready to explode as I resisted the urge to shout several expletives out loud. DD and Jay stood there in shocked silence, totally amazed at the sudden transformation that had come over me. The look of horror on their faces said it all. Lily stood silent with an icy vacant stare like a cobra waiting to strike. She had obviously had a similar reaction but it had manifested itself in a different way. I could see the uncharacteristic cold dragon hatred in her eyes and I knew exactly what she was thinking.

It was up to DD to break the spell and snap us back to the here and now for she had not been with us on that fateful quest in 1431 and so was emotionally unattached to the horrors we had seen. As such she was the only one able to think logically.

She kissed me on the on the cheek and her electric touch snapped me back to the now just as a needle pricks a soap bubble.

"God that was intense!" I said as I leant forward with my hands on my knees in order to gather my breath.

DD shook Lily with a gentle but firm clasp of her shoulders and likewise she came to. Jay was also profoundly affected, "This is and bad, bad place." He murmured as he stared through Lilly into the ether beyond. He was beginning to divine his involvement in the whole *Rouen affair* it being also his only mission with us as far as we knew. For him it was not the culmination of several previous adventures as with us, for he had followed his own timeline without back then. No doubt we would discover the truth of the matter in due course as there was certainly much more to Jay than met the eye.

"Right let's move on. This place is decidedly unhealthy. I think it's this way!" DD picked up her bag and started walking towards the *Hôtel de Bourgtheroulde* which was just along the road.

Moments later we entered through an ornate renaissance carved archway surrounded by two supporting rampant lions and an achievement of *Three Lion's heads Or, divided by a chevron Argent on a field Azure above which rested a golden helm with coronet.* It was the grandest entrance to a hotel that I had ever seen and dated to between 1486 - 1531. On the ground a red carpet beckoned us in. Stepping through the archway we entered a world of bygone enchantment. The courtyard was an intimate human space with ornately carved heraldry in beautiful buff coloured stone. To our immediate left in the corner stood a quirky first floor reddish brown timber framed room supported quaintly on two wooden pillars of the same colour. Our mood immediately began to soften for we had found our sanctuary.

Without further ado we headed for our rooms after booking in. Three nights seemed a reasonable length of time in order to see the mission through. The hotel was a fascinating blend of the old merged with the ultra-chic modern. The large bar area built as an extension onto the back was breath taking with a suspended glass floor mid-section running the length of the cavernous space and affording vertigo inducing views of the swimming pool below which was just so cool!

To one side there was a swish bar in white running the whole length of the wall which contrasted perfectly with the black cubic style leather chairs and sofas that lined the central glass floor walk way and the alcoves underneath the balcony on the side opposite. The walls decorated all in red gave it a warm welcoming feeling that enveloped the body in a cocoon of luxury unknown by our previous time travelling selves.

At one end there was a grand double staircase the ascended to the vault like roof and balcony. A modern abstract statue of a walking man adorned the mezzanine landing as it attempted to walk up the left stairs in frozen perpetual motion. Above the sunlight cleverly shone bright yet diffused through the overarching glass tiled roof and gave the whole space a Roman villa feel. Like so many well designed spaces that play with the mind it was a complete surprise. Being nothing like one imagined from the classic late medieval exterior of the building outside. It was in short a veritable Tardis! Yes that's it! It was a set straight out of the long running English science fiction series Dr Who. I smiled to myself as only I being a fan of that show understood the cosmic joke that the universe had played. We were indeed time travellers and we had landed in the middle of Rouen in this fantastic ship that had taken the form of a hotel instead of a blue Police Public phone box. It was perfect!

"Oh my, it feels just like a Tardis!" Jay exclaimed. I knew then instantly that he too must also be a fan.

"Of course and we are the Time Travellers." I said with a cryptic sideways glance and a smile.

I didn't waste time trying to explain my impressions and inferences to the ladies so I tucked them away in my mind for a later time and place when I could entertain the team with a story over a late night drink or two.

Ascending the staircase we headed for our rooms which were tucked away in the roof space of the old building. The wooden beams and angled ceiling of my room gave me a cosy feeling which again made me feel very comfortable. The pale biscuit coloured tiled bathroom had a medieval feel to it which was further enhanced by the massive roof beams that were of castle like proportion. Three turret windows completed the old yet new illusion. Again it was the perfect fusion of the ancient with the modern. As I cleaned my teeth and freshened up I admired the sense of history that the space communicated.

Just then my iPhone buzzed which indicated an incoming text.

See you in five we are raring to go!!! Lily XXX

I read the message and returned my phone into its protective black leather case that shielded it from harm. That's quick I thought to myself Lily's got her fight back. I changed into my grey travel trek cotton jacket, grabbed my battered grey fedora and headed for the bar area. Within a couple of minutes Lily, DD and Jay arrived suitably attired and ready to go.

"Let's kick some ass!" Lily said in a very unladylike voice that showed her resolve in no uncertain terms. Turning on her heels she strode towards the main door and the bright sunlight beyond. Her backpack brimming with who knows what and her camera shouldered like a carbine.

"I think she means business!" DD quipped and smiled.

"I think the lady does!" Jay replied with a stunned bemused look.

"Watch out Rouen Lily's back in town! I'm starting to enjoy this - after you." I said in a mock American accent as I touched the brim of my hat and gestured the way forward with a slight theatrical bow.

Jay led the way following in Lily's wake, then DD and myself bringing up the rear. I guessed, well I knew that Lily would head for the quayside as it was the logical starting place for our *Rouen Rescue*. We had worked together now for several weeks and I had tuned into her mind with infallible accuracy.

Once through the small arched gate that ejected us back into the *Place de la Pucelle* we turned right into the *Rue Saint Eloi* and headed south towards the river. Immediately we found ourselves in front of L'église Saint Eloi. The magnificent flying buttresses towered above us but what caught my eye were the many dragon gargoyles jutting from the roof with necks extended and wings folded. That's a bit of a coincidence I thought to myself?

I pointed this out to the team. "Home from home eh? It feels like we are on the right track?"

Lily laughed, "We sure are. What better sign that we are in the right place!"

"And right next door to our hotel, how fascinating. It's against all probability!" DD joined in the conversation as she marvelled at the many dragons that seemed to be everywhere we looked.

"It says Temple of Saint Eloi on the sign that's very non-Catholic! Curiouser and curiouser - Alice said..." Jay added a spooky voice to his quote. "It's going to be fun running around in the dark. I like!" He was definitely getting into Gothic mode as the architecture simulated his memory.

We continued walking towards the *Quai du Havre* between the modern apartment blocks and offices that rose all around us as we neared the river. Breaking out into open space we crossed the busy main road using the painted ladder pedestrian crossings that afforded scant protection against the four lanes of traffic. Having negotiated that successfully we then crossed over the minor tree lined road that skirted the banks of the river. Finally we emerged unscathed onto the *Promenade de la France Libre* and could view the mighty *Seine* in all its glory. The sight of its waters flowing unvexed to the sea gave me goose bumps as I immersed myself in the eternal moment of time and place that I had arrived at.

Thoughts of 1431 dominated my head as I scanned the opposite bank for the river was our escaped route out of here, a silver ribbon lifeline that would spirit us and our prisoner away from under the very noses of the English Goddons. I sensed the deliciousness of that audacious thought and smiled to myself.

In the distance I could see tall yellow cranes demonstrating that *Rouen* was still a commercial port importance. How different they were to the archaic enclosed wooden cranes that we had used to unload our wine barrels from Bordeaux all those years ago. I could still see the large hamster wheel that contained several sweating stevedores as they operated the treadmill to raise the hog's heads from the hold of our Breton cog.

My silence was disturbed by DD's voice that penetrated my thoughts like the mewing of the seagulls above calling me to pay attention to the now.

"Look at this! It's one of those old wooden ships you described to me." She was gesticulating wildly and pointing to the far side of the bridge in front of us. Lily and Jay were already running to see what she had discovered. Without further loss of precious time I jogged to join them under the *Pont Guillaume Le Conquérant* road bridge.

I could see immediately the unmistakable silhouette of a fat wooden cog with its distinctive single mast and barrel like crow's nest. It was definitely tangible and not a mirage as it sat silently fastened to the Quai. In the distance the yellow cranes and the distinctive Y topped columns of the new *Le Pont Gustave-Flaubert* vertical lifting road bridge reminded me that I was very much in the present. I had read of this remarkable bridge when it was built in 2008. In order to solve the problem of admitting the famous tall ships armada and the larger cargo ships to Rouen port it was necessary to construct a road bridge that could lift the two carriage ways high into the air. But it was not that which caught full attention as I rushed into the sunlight from beneath the *Pont Guillaume Le Conquérant.*

I could hardly believe my eyes for there was the wooden ship of my dreams still tied neatly alongside the *Quai de Boisguilbert.* It was indeed a full sized working reproduction medieval cog of the exact same dimensions that I remembered! I marvelled at the coincidence and had to pinch myself to confirm my senses.

"It's definitely real. We are not dreaming!" Jay's voice came floating back on the breeze as he arrived at the gangplank leading up and onto the main deck amidships.

"Look at the flags and shield on the aft castle!" Lily shouted as she joined him. I looked again and got yet more goose bumps for there flying proudly from the stern deck were two large white over red banners bearing German crosses of the opposite contrasting colour.

"Hey, Yann look at the main mast flag!" Lily shouted as she disappeared up the gangplank without ceremony or pause for reflection.

DD came over to my side and gave me a big hug. "It is exactly like the cross on that black hoodie you showed me. The one Lily bought. It is the Phi proportioned cross of enlightenment. What's the probability of that?" With her last comment she tugged at my t shirt beneath my open grey cotton jacket and gave me a big kiss

.

Jay and Lily had disappeared and were nowhere to be seen. DD and I strolled arm in arm the final few metres in order to view the colourful information board that was on display more closely. Together we read the fascinating Gothic German script:

"Ubena von Bremen"

Hanse Koggewerft e.V. Bremerhaven.

Underneath the proud heading were placed several large photographs of the many voyages it had been on. The distinctive red and White striped sail with its black key emblem reminded me of its Viking heritage. The only difference being that it was carvel built by nailing the planks directly to the ribs of the ship as opposed to the lighter clinker construction of Viking vessels which nailed the planks to each other and then lashed them to the ribs and keel. The cog was literally a tub compared to the sleek wave horse that was the feared *Drakkar* of Viking fame. I mused over the dragon name connection of that type of vessel as I read the details. Another innovative feature was the barrel like crow's nest at the top of the 21 metre mast just below the large triple tailed red flag bearing a quintessentially white Germanic cross.

On further translation I grasped that the *Ubena* was only in *Rouen* for two weeks as part of a tour of coastal ports. Remarkably it was due to leave in three days' time which coincided with our expected departure exactly and return northward to Germany! For me this was the ultimate perfect cosmic coincidence!

"Have you seen the shields hanging from the aft castle?" DD said as she pointed upwards drawing my attention away from the information board.

"Oh my goodness you're right, will you look at that it is the Flemish rampant lion!" I exclaimed as I recognised its distinctive form amongst the highly decorative heraldic shields that denoted the ports that it had visited whilst on its travels. It was the same rampant lion form as used on the Luxembourg coat of arms and so familiar to my memory. For me that was the final sign connecting all points of the eternal now perfectly into one gigantic web of universal quantum coincidence.

DD took my hand and led me up the wooden gangplank to join the others. As I ascended I stepped across time and through the now familiar rose coloured archway that beckoned me onward.

Chapter 31

Les Furets

The moment I set foot onto the ship I was transported in an instant back into the hustle and bustle of the medieval port of Rouen. We had been in the port a few days and it was the last week of May 1431. I was pleased that our plans were coming to fruition slowly but surely. Looking down at myself I saw that I was dressed as a sailor in very poor ill-fitting garments. Feeling my face I tugged at an unfamiliar beard that was a foreign entity in my modern 21st century life. It felt however natural and I soon became accustomed to it. Curiously I could only see out of my right eye and on further examination I found that I was wearing a leather eye patch. My hair was long lank and greasy. The most distinctive thing about my person was that I smelt awful, a sort of body odour mixed with essence of ferret! It was a perfect disguise. I posed absolutely no threat whatsoever to the *Goddon* soldiery that patrolled the wharves with their vicious halberds and a total contemptuous disrespect for the Normand citizenry around them. To all and sundry I was anonymous.

I chuckled to myself and thought if only they knew what a surprise we had planned for them? Content with my observation

I retrieved a couple of my ferrets from their basket and then sat on the deck cross legged to fuss with them. They were now use to me and with my free hand I fed them small pieces of freshly cut up meat. There were now my favourite familiars. Amusingly I called them Warwick and Bedford after the two most prominent *Goddons* in Rouen. That made me laugh and as such it reduced my enemies to controllable puppets in my hands. Yet my ferrets like my real opponents were capable of a vicious bite should I be incautious and inattentive. The thoughts of all that I had heard and seen reiterated in my head as I compared my experiences with the intelligence gathered by my other more human ferrets.

The English were losing patience with la Pucelle. They kept her locked up in the chateau donjon of which I was intimately familiar with, where she was cruelly chained day and night to a block of wood. A few days earlier I had witnessed them bring her to the old Market place and show her the stake in an effort to break her spirit and sign a document of abjuration. They were like cats toying with a captive mouse, she looked half starved, beaten and wore shackles; a small defenceless girl guarded and bullied by so many brutal thugs. It was a pathetic inhumane display that was as far from the code of chivalry as it was possible to be. It turned my stomach with revulsion. I would have intervened then but that would have been certain suicide, better to wait my time for the appointed hour when I would hold all the aces in my hand. Then I would strike as a coiled serpent and bury my fangs in their fat over fed necks.

In truth Couchon, a so called bishop of the holy church and chief English lackey wanted Jehanne dead and out of his hair. Ever the political puppet master it was easier for him to deal with a corpse, for corpses can't answer back! That was one thing La Pucelle was certainly good at, answering back. His own ego was now clouding his judgement as he had shown in an open display of anger in the square for he was becoming heedless of making her a martyr for the French Armagnac cause. That would be the fatal chink in his armour and I would exploit it fully when the time came.

La Hire and Dunois were at Louviers just 5 leagues from the city gates in a renewed attempt to free 'our Pucelle d'Orleans' at this very moment. The English soldiery had refused to march out against them whilst the witch still lived but were arrayed in preparation. This was yet another reason why Cauchon wanted rid of her. With the Goddon soldiery in the field the chateau was minimally guarded from within which for us was the single most important factor.

Étienne de Vignolles called La Hire and Jean de Dunois known as the "bâtard d'Orléans" a first cousin to the king were two of Jehanne's most loyal adherents which spoke volumes for the fickle nature of the other aristocrats that only a year before had hailed her the saviour of France. To them she had become an embarrassment and an obstacle in their gaining favour with the Pope. Even the Dauphin in public if not in private had washed his hands of his now troublesome stepsister.

Due to their close proximity I decided therefore to dispatch two of my most trusted human ferrets, Tomas and Thibauld. They would entreat these gallant knights to renew their efforts as a distraction towards the end of the month when I sensed that the English would make their fatal mistake.

Ultimately we moved on the word of Yvette for she was our psychic navigator. For days now she and Charlotte had been attempting to contact La Pucelle telepathically as only dragon princesses can do and they had had some success. The dim flickering spirit that was Jehanne could still be reached although she was a shadow of her former self. At least they hadn't yet taken her maidenhead which they surely would do just before they burned her, for a virgin cannot be executed. My stomach turned once again in revulsion at the twisted logic of the church and state. Any excuse to defile and degrade the victim was allowable under the law and pandered to the base carnal instincts of the masses. They must break the power of the virgin to avoid their wrath from beyond the grave or so they believed. I would show them what wrath meant when the time was right if I had to but most probably my alchemy would speak for me and like magic we would spirit her away. In that way we would play far more with their fears and suspicions. We would in short sow fear and doubt into their souls. The armies of France would do the rest.

Returning to the now the captain was ashore haggling with the Vintners guild over the price of our red Bordeaux wine or *claret* as the Goddons called it. Once the price was agreed and the guild had taken its pound of flesh from the transaction we would be allowed to deliver the barrels to the chateau. No doubt the guild would charge the English three times the price that they gave us but it mattered not as I had already covered the cost of the voyage handsomely with the captain. Such is the wicked world of business but that didn't trouble me so long as we gained access to the *Chapel Royale* of the chateau, for that was where the secret tunnel emerged. I had made this fortuitous discovery as a boy of 12 in the disastrous year of 1415. It would be the final piece of the puzzle and I would hold a full house in my game with the English Goddons. After that it would be in God's hands.

Stroking the ferrets I carried on watching the quayside. I found myself singing quietly the old French nursery rhyme Il court Le Furet:

Il court le furet

Refrain:
Il court, il court, le furet
Le furet du bois, mesdames
Il court, il court, le furet
Le furet du bois joli

Il est passé par ici
Le furet du bois, mesdames
Il est passé par ici
Le furet du bois joli

Refrain

Il repassera par là
Le furet du bois, mesdames
Devinez s'il est ici
le furet du bois joli

Refrain

Le furet est bien caché
Le furet du bois, mesdames

Pourras-tu le retrouver?
Le furet du bois joli.

The ferret runs
Chorus
The ferret, it runs, it runs,
The ferret of the woods, my ladies.
It runs, it runs, the ferret,
The ferret of the pretty woods.

It passed by here
The ferret of the woods, my ladies.
It passed by here,
The ferret of the pretty woods.

Chorus
The ferret, it runs, it runs,
The ferret of the woods, my ladies.
It runs, it runs, the ferret,
The ferret of the pretty woods.

It'll pass by there again,
The ferret of the woods, my ladies.
Guess if it's here,
The ferret of the pretty woods.

Chorus
The ferret, it runs, it runs,
The ferret of the woods, my ladies.
It runs, it runs, the ferret,
The ferret of the pretty woods.

504

The ferret is well hidden,
The ferret of the woods, my ladies.
Will you be able to find it?
The ferret of the pretty woods.

After several minutes of singing and fussing which Warwick and Bedford I placed them lovingly back in their wicker basket. As I fiddled with the catch making sure it was secure I felt a gentle shaking.

'Yann, Oh Yann are you going to sit there all day singing? We've got things to do. Lily and Jay want to see the *Gros Horloge*. I wouldn't mind seeing it either as I understand it is a miracle of renaissance technology.' I awoke to see DD standing over me with the sun behind her, her strong legs bracing the deck and her golden hair flowing in the gentle breeze.

'Why not my beautiful pirate princess of the high seas? I've seen what I wanted to see.' With that I slapped her thigh in a playful gesture of affection and she extended her hand to pull me to my feet. I ached considerably which indicated that I had been sat in the same position for quite some time. Still brushing myself down, she turned my head and kissed me fully on the lips. Her electricity and passion immediately ignited my soul with a lightning bolt discharge causing me to leap fully into the present.

"That should keep you focussed on the NOW! You can tell me what you saw later on. Meantime let's follow Lily and Jay." DD said with a wicked smile.

I looked around for the ferrets but alas there were none, due no doubt to health and safety! They make fine rat catchers I thought to myself as I followed DD back down the gang plank. Absentmindedly I found myself whistling the nursery rhyme tune as it still kept going around in my head.

"Ah you have been playing with your ferrets again. You are in incorrigible Yann Baillieu!" Lily said laughing as she recognised the tune and started to sing the words that she remembered from her childhood as Yvette.

She then explained to Jay and DD the traditional game played with the song. "You slip a ring on a string and tie both loose ends together after measuring a length that will form a circle around the outside of the players, use about half a metre of string per player as a rough guide. A child or adult is placed in the centre and the others maintain the circle around him or her. They hold the string with both hands behind their backs. The ring runs from hand to hand. As soon as the child or adult at the centre guesses correctly who has the ring, he or she says so and they switch their roles. The song was sung as the game was played. The game was very popular in the court of Louis XIV and with the aristocracy.

As Lily talked I had a sudden flash of inspiration, it really sums up the Rouen rescue. I now knew exactly why Robert des Armoises had had two ferrets carved onto the wooden door over his portrait! Of course that was it! Up to then I had been wondering why I had had visions of ferrets since Saumur, Robert regarded himself and his human compatriots as the living - *Furets de Rouen*.

I hurriedly explained to Jay and the girls but by the look on their faces I knew that I would have to elaborate over dinner. Lily understood immediately I could tell that from the look she gave me as she turned to take the lead with Jay so I was content that it wasn't just my fanciful imagination.

I took DD's hand and we wandered along the quay behind them for the now was just as important as the then. As we walked towards the *Pont Jehanne d'Arc* I tried to imagine the busy wharves now quiet and tree lined as they would have been covered in stores and cargo not that long ago. A light blue Metro tram rumbled over the bridge in front of us as we. We headed northward to the *Theatre de Arts* and paused for several minutes to admire the large bronze statue of Pierre Corneille the 17th century playwright an illustrious son of Rouen. Another Metro tram emerged as if by magic from the ground in front of us. As it snaked its way out of the tunnel that marked the beginning of 1.7 kilometres of subterranean track under the centre of Rouen I couldn't help comparing the old and the new Rouen separated only by time in my head.

As ever Lily noticed my interest and quoted from her memorised research notes, that it was constructed in 1994 to link the two suburbs of the *Rive gauche* with the centre. As ever she totally impressed me with the thoroughness of her research and the depth of her knowledge. She was a formidable ally and I was definitely glad she was on my side! If only La Hire and Dunois could have taken the Metro tram our mission would probably have been unnecessary!

On our left were the remains of an ancient tower now with a curious modern octagonal collar fixed two thirds of the way up to stop falling masonry from causing damage this curious mixture of ancient and modern stood to reinforce the point. It was almost a piece of art looking as it did like some ancient radio telescope pointing heavenward. I used the tram and the tower to illustrate my La Hire and Dunois point which amused Lily, DD and Jay.

Just two more block and we reached the *Rue de Gros Horloge,* turning right we headed towards the cathedral. It was obvious to see why this was a tourist mecca as it's half-timbered crowded walkways made it look so quaint. It connected in a direct line the old Market place and the *Cathédrale Notre Dame de Rouen* seat of the Archbishop. As the buildings began to swallow me up I squeezed DD's hand tighter for I could feel the spiritual presence of the buildings that had witness our adventure first-hand 600 years previous.

It was amazing to think that they still stood as silent sentinels to the atrocities that went on in that barbaric age, atrocities we had witnessed first-hand. Suddenly the fantastic giant clock loomed over us with its associated tall bell tower, the single hand relentlessly telling out the time since 1529. Before that a simple clock had been present on the site since the 13th century, the business of the day being regulated by the striking of bells on the hour, half hour and quarter. Like Pavlov's dog the citizens of Rouen would regulate their daily lives within the city's confines. The clock is a masterpiece of renaissance technology and ingenuity, its automatons indicate the day of the week in tableau and the phases of the Moon are shown by a rotating sphere set into the top of the clock face.

Lily and Jay explored the intricate bias relief carved stones, Lily taking many photographs. As she did DD and I talked about the illusory nature of time, all the while I could hear the constant clicking of Lily's camera reverberating from the ornate reflective surface of the *Gros Horloge* archways. Finally satiated Lily indicated that we should move on towards the Cathedral.

On moving through the archway I could immediately see the imposing cast iron steeple that for a time 1876-1880 was the tallest structure in the world at 151 metres. As a giant colossal steampunk icon it protruded above the two original lesser stone towers of the west facade. The very same facade made famous by Claude Monet's studies of light falling on the impossibly ornate stone work. He had spent the year 1892-93 continually painting the same scene at different times of the day and produced over 30 paintings. In 1894 he finally re-worked them in the studio and then placed the best 20 with his Paris dealer's where they were well received

Strangely I felt no urge to enter the cathedral as I had done in Reims and Orleans, maybe it was to do with my aversion to the evil perpetrated by Cauchon in order to secure his personal ambitions? Maybe it was to do with its turbulent history and the continuous natural destruction caused by many lightning strikes in its 700 year history? For me it was a sure sign that the powers above were displeased at man's inhumanity to man. Whatever the reason for my phobia I still had to admire the tremendous workmanship and skill displayed by the countless generations of stone masons.

"You can tell the English were in control of Normandy there is a distinct lack of good restaurants in this part of the town!" Lily said absentmindedly as I continued gazing at the west facade using Monet's eye for colour and texture.

"Funny you should say that I'm getting a little peckish" DD responded as she stretched out her arms high into the air in an effort to shake off the fatigue of the early morning start.

"That works for me too, good idea." Jay joined in agreeing with the girls. "You may not like it but I think we will have to go back to the old Market place to find somewhere to eat."

"We must be brave the past has no hold on us only if we let it, we have to face our fears." Lily commented laconically.

"Yes you are right, perhaps I need to put it all into perspective? This place has a habit of getting hold of you." I added as I pondered our next move. "OK, OK, I agree, so long as no-one orders steak!"

The audience groaned at my gallows humour but then relented with smiles all round and so we made our way once more westward along the Rue du Gros-Horloge and then turned northward into Rue Jeanne d'Arc heading towards the Tour Jeanne d'Arc near the Gare de Rouen Rive Droite. Passing the tower on the right we continued momentarily and hunger getting the better of us we decided to get a bite to eat in the Subway next to the Café le Metropole opposite. Chairs and tables abounded so we ate our subs voraciously outside the former establishment then moved next door to the Café from where we could take our leisure over coffee as we eyed up the tower across the busy junction. The black witch's hat of the tower peaked at us over the tops of the more modern buildings as the blue articulated Metro buses plied their trade to and from the station. Finally as the ominous dark clouds above us rolled in the tension built up to breaking point and as I settle the bill with the waiter Lily, DD and Jay suddenly stormed the tower.

Chapter 32

Rue du Donjon

The others went straight in but I couldn't the past life memories were being amplified by our proximity to the actual matter fabric of the tower which was exactly the same as in 1431. I stood contemplating the gaping black void of the open doorway surrounded by red stained stonework. It was as if the very limestone had taken on the hue of dried human blood to mark the countless victims that had been tried, tortured and sentenced to death in this bloody place. Summoning up my courage I made myself inch forward foot by foot, my eyes observing every detail of the pock marked stone now some 800 years old. For the tower was part of the chateau built by Philip II of France upon his capture of Rouen from the Norman English 1204.

The tower was built of extremely thick walls with three main floors all connected by a spiral staircase. The vaulted ceilings were of the same construction technique as the *Tour des Esprit* in Metz and were extremely familiar to me as I had once dwelt in the Sante Barbe gate house.

I ascended the claustrophobic winding steps that were lit only by the dim daylight from the archers slits towards the voices of Lily,

Jay and DD chatting above. The ambient illumination improved as I entered the middle room due to modern electric lights. The damp limestone with its distinctive musty smell assailed my nostrils and conjured up multiple images of old churches and castles in my mind. The circular room closed in on me with a feel that was alien to the modern world with its obsessive rectilinear cubic architecture. We continued up to the main room above which had more windows and a number of subtle bright electric lights set like twinkling jewels in the wooden boarded roof.

Centre stage was a large glass cased model of the chateau in its original pristine lime washed form as constructed by Philippe Auguste. To one side in a recess hung a wrought iron pulley wheel suspended over a well shaft, its black menacing structure echoing the many instruments of torture that had been employed in the room below. Jehanne d'Arc indeed had herself been threatened with those self-same implements of pain as part of her incarceration in the chateau between December 1430 and May 1431. In response to their threats she said loudly that she would subsequently deny any confession torn from her by such foul means. Her same defiant spirit rose now in me making my blood start to boil and was further fuelled as I felt the trapped energy of the thousands of victims that had suffered in this place in such an agonising way.

"Don't get mad, get even." The well-known phrase echoed in my head as my rational mind took control to limit my blood pressure to safe levels. It made good sense for irrational emotions led to poor decision making and failure, something a good commander could not afford. I felt my nerves settle and the tension was replaced with the ice calm of cold steel waiting to strike. I knew then that I was feeling the exact same emotions as I had felt back in 1431 whilst I readied myself to attempt the most audacious exercise in military history; the freeing of La Pucelle from under the very noses of the English Goddons!

With Lily, Jay and DD I studied the excellent 3D model of the chateau and simultaneously overlaid it with my memory of the structure from my lifetime some 200 years after its initial construction. It was more elaborate then but essentially the basic ground plan was the same.

La Pucelle was being held in the tower immediately to the west of the donjon or *Grosse Tour* as it is also known. I remembered the distinctive hexagonal room structure which made it unique among the other six towers. I also remembered then that I had mapped it accurately in a rôleplaying game that I had written back in 1982. Even though the setting was a Dark-age fantasy the details were all deadly accurate. I now realised that I had written the game at the exact same age that I was when I and my comrades in arms had attempted the rescue!

Robert des Armoises was 28 years of age in 1431 having been born in 1403. I had been 28 years of age in the spring of 1982 when I wrote the game complete with detailed maps and illustrations. I cursed my luck that I had given all my gaming material to some young boys of a good friend of mine in a clear out of my garage just 12 years previous. The valuable documents had lain undisturbed for 20 years before my tidy up. If only I had kept them another 12! They would have provided excellent evidence for what I was now discovering about my previous medieval self. Some photographs however did exist of a *Moyen age* costume that I had made for a fancy dress party at that time. I made a mental note to track the photos down together with the costume which was still in a chest in the attic of my house. Perhaps it would give me a glimpse of what I looked like as Robert des Armoises?

How had I known about the hexagonal room structure unless I had been there? The game even had as its main feature the freeing of a shackled princess who was being held prisoner on the first floor of a tower in a heavily fortified chateau! Incredibly now all these memories re-emerged as I gazed at the pristine white model with its brick red conical roofed towers. I wanted to tell Lily, Jay and DD immediately but I decided to let it wait until later as I didn't want to disturb them for they too may be having their own revelations.

I smiled contentedly to myself, moved to where DD was standing and placed my arms around her waist. Gently I kissed her ear without the others noticing and observed the goose bumps that formed on her bronzed arms as she responded to my caress. I felt safe and secure as I held her tight for she was my rock in this sea of medieval madness. Death by burning, torture and violence, it had all been part of daily life back then. Thank God it was only a memory now. Whatever happened then could no longer hurt us.

Even the weather started to change as we left the Grosse tour, the grey clouds observed at the café started to grow ominously darker as more storm clouds rolled relentlessly in from the west in ever increasing number. Perhaps we were in for one of those infamous thunderstorms that seemed to have plagued the cathedral of Rouen with monotonous regularity throughout the centuries?

"Looks like the universe knows what we are up to!" I said jokingly out loud. Lily frowned as she was feeling in no mood for a light hearted comment at that precise moment. The tower had obviously affected her more than I thought. By contrast Jay seemed unaffected although so I thought until he made his own curious comment.

"Did anyone notice the World War 2 Germans strutting around the tower? They were typically serious and no fun to talk to!" He smiled upon finishing but I knew that he wasn't joking.

"I think I saw them out of the corner of my eye?" DD spoke up. "I know that that the tower was used as a German bunker in World War 2 so I thought I was just generally tuning into that. I think I'm becoming psychic? It is either that or hanging around with you lot is rubbing off on me!" She laughed and that seemed to break the ice as Lily patted her on the back. "Well done Madam des Armoises I think you have indeed been hanging out with us too long. Just you wait to your full Dragon gene potential kicks in. Then you really will have to hang on to your mental hat!" With that we all laughed and the atmosphere lifted.

I was secretly pleased that DD was with us as we needed someone not directly involved in the events of 1431 just in case we went over the edge with our emotions and experiences. I was well aware that we could literally walk over a cliff so to speak whilst reliving another time and place as reality had a tendency to become awfully confusing.

We re-entered the *Rue du Donjon* and turned right heading back to the *Rue Jehanne d'Arc* which had become our main thoroughfare. Turning left we walked a short distance and stood outside number

102, in the exact same spot that the *Tour La Pucelle* had once stood. A large dark slate coloured plaque with imposing gold lettering proclaimed this as the 'very place' Jehanne d'Arc was imprisoned complete with the correct dates from December 25, 1430 to May 30, 1431. It was so matter of fact in its preciseness and completely devoid of emotion. To the right a bas relief in stone of the chateau as it was in its entirety at the height of its power stood above the door archway. The detail was remarkable and I recognised it immediately as an accurate representation of what I remembered. I pointed out the names of the towers to the others who were amazed at my accurate recall.

I also knew that the tower had still stood in a dilapidated state until the beginning of the 19th century when it was finally demolished in 1809. Even I was amazed at my recall of information that I had no conscious recollection of learning. Obviously my subconscious had been paying attention throughout my present life and noted places that were very important to me.

The energies however were too confusing to be read for the fabric of the present building obscured the psychic history of the tour. So we moved southward and came across an intriguingly elaborate stone statue known as *Le flambeau de l'escalier*. It reminded me of my silver candelabra at home for it had the exact same design of centre piece; a silver flame emerging from an ornate urn shaped. Again I toyed with the idea that possibly my subconscious had wandered here throughout the centuries and had caused my conscious mind to purchase the 18th century candle stick from an antique shop when I had chanced upon it? I was beginning to realise just how intricate my mind was at collecting artefacts. Everything I had acquired or made throughout my life told a story like a secret code. Now I had reached the point when I could finally break that cipher and see it all for what it truly was.

Ascending the steps we entered the charmingly neat garden of the *Musée de la Céramique* which appeared to the right in near middle distance. My eye was immediately caught by a familiar looking old stone building with three arches and a high ornate timbered gable end supporting a black slate roof. The others were looking at an ornate ceramic statue in white which sat centre stage in the neat garden. It appeared to be a male torso on a pedestal. The 'arms' became organic fan like structures which merged with the hair and beard of a distinctly Greek God like character; a deity of agricultural plenty. It certainly made me think which made it good art.

Continuing we entered the *Rue Faucon* and turned right descending a flight of stone steps into the *Square Verdrel*. It was so refreshing to get into a green space with a small lake set amidst a number of beautiful trees in full leaf. We immediately relaxed and simply enjoyed each other's company without conscious thought for history and memories. However I was secretly hoping that my subconscious was still making its own notes and that it might lead me to the correct places after dark when the world became a very different place.

"I'm getting peckish again that sub wasn't big enough!" Lily exclaimed suddenly, "anyone for a bite to eat?"

"I guess that means the Old Market place? Well it's about time we faced the *devil in the detail.*" Jay's laconic voice struck a resonant chord in me for we clearly needed to grasp the nettle of the problem. I therefore found myself agreeing with Lily's unspoken prompt to action and it was after all her ball game.

"We can contemplate the site of execution afterwards!" I added cheerfully in an effort to exorcise my own personal demons with humour.

"Yes, I feel a strange connection with that place but as yet I am not sure what it is all about but not good, definitely not good?" Jay sounded a little forlorn in the timbre of his voice. I duly took note although I'm not sure if anyone else did. "Let's eat drink and be merry, hey!" He continued.

"For tomorrow we die?" Lily added quietly under her breathe with an air of gloom and resignation having obviously picked up some psychic morsel of information from Jay's mind. Jay shot her a sideways glance that spoke volumes.

So without further ado we headed back down the *Rue Jehanne d'Arc* and across a couple of blocks to the *place du Vieux Marché*. Despite getting the psychic chills we chose the *Bistrot de Hallettes* for a late lunch early dinner and sat a table in the open air looking directly towards the Église and *Le buché de Jehanne d'Arc*.

Whilst we chatted freely comparing our experiences of the day so far my computer like memory was busy searching for the answer as to the location of the secret passage into the chateau. Suddenly I looked up into the sky and saw a hawk making its way northward with difficulty as it had to negotiate the increasingly strong westerly wind which gave its flight an uncharacteristic fluttering zig zag pattern.

"The path of the hawk shall set us free! That's it! It's been staring me in the face. I knew the answer all along, just needed to unblock my subconscious." In my excitement I involuntarily knocked the table and spilt a glass of red wine onto the pristine white table cloth. For me it was a metaphor for spilt blood and the price that must be paid for freedom. Much as Jesus had redeemed the world with his blood shed on the cross but who's blood?

"Did anybody notice what is wrong with the chateau?" I posed the question without pausing as I mopped up the excess wine with my serviette. Lily, Jay and DD all looked at me as though I had gone completely mad but before they could open their mouths in reply I was busy rearranging the plates and glasses into a map of the chateau and its immediate environs. A large round serving plate served as the central courtyard around which I arranged various wine glasses as the towers, as I did so I named them all, one after the other together with the internal apartments, buildings and sundry details. Sugar cubes, cutlery in fact anything that fitted the bill was pressed into service to give as much detail as I could to my own model of the chateau.

"That's it, that's it, look the chateau is built the wrong way around! The barbican gate faces inward towards the city and river not outward. It is designed to suppress not defend the population. Most city fortifications face externally so as to protect the inhabitants. Now imagine the wine stain as the small lake in *Square Verdrel*, what connects the chateau to it?"

Lily became excited and started to rise to the challenge. I think the detail of my memory had quite stunned everyone up until that point. Then just as she was about to give me her answer DD chimed in, "*Rue Faucon* - the path of the Hawk!"

"I was just going to say that!" Lily said with sisterly good humour as their minds synchronised.

"Yes that's right! The small artificial lake in *Square Verdrel* is where the tunnel exited allowing the chateau nobles to escape the chateau via the *Chapelle Royale ou Saint-Romain*. The chapelle was originally situated next to the *Tour du coin de la Chapelle,* which was the right hand tower as you entered the fortress. As a young boy aged twelve I spent the three whole months prior to the *Battle of Agincourt* exploring the chateau when not performing my duties as a page to my Lord the *Duc d'Orleans*. I've finally remembered!"

"Well all we have to do now is wait until the bewitching hour and put your knowledge to the test." As Lily spoke her face began to shine for the end was in sight and she knew in her heart I was right!

We continued our meal much to the amazement of the waitress who was at a loss to understand what all our excitement was about. Finally we settled our bill. Lily said she would like to explore the Old Market place with Jay so as to give DD and I some space to be alone. We decided before they departed to eat at the *Restaurant La Couronne* that evening if at all possible. Lily said she would text me the details as they would stop off there first to inquire as to any vacancies before visiting the Église.

It was only 4 o'clock so DD and I decided not to rush as we had plenty of time to kill so to speak. I ordered another cognac café and DD a crème de menthe liqueur. We chatted so easily with synchronous thoughts about all the events taking place that we just knew we were soul twins, each sharing the others memories and secrets as we had done through many lives. We both felt exactly the same about the Catholic Church and its bloody history but we decided never the less that we should visit the Église *Jehanne d'Arc* and visit the old Market place as good tourists should. My heart was now in the fight for I knew positively that I was correct in my memory and the way forward was clear. In the simple modern church DD and I held hands and lit candles for all those lost souls that had suffered torment, torture and death in this place throughout the centuries.

The time went extremely quickly and it was soon nearing 8 o'clock. Lily texted me at a quarter to the hour in order to tell me that they had been unsuccessful in booking a table in *La Couronne* for this evening but had secured one for the following night. She then asked us to meet them at *Les Maraichers* next door as they still had space to squeeze us in. This we duly did.

The meal was light, refreshing and tasty so we stayed chatting until 11:30pm over many delicious courses and had excellent conversation. In some ways this was to be our 'last supper'. Jay held the floor for the main part of the conversation as he had had a distinctly profound if somewhat negative experience when visiting the actual site where Jehanne was allegedly executed. He went to great lengths to describe his emotions, feelings and sensations at that spot. It all sounded extremely ominous but he was determined to carry on and see the mission through come what may until the bitter end.

Finally we paid and left a generous tip, then complimented the chef and staff on their outstanding hospitality and excellent cuisine. We were now ready for anything, fully charged up and ready to assault the *Tour La Pucelle!*

So together we marched purposefully back up the *Rue Jehanne d'Arc* towards the *Square Verdrel* and our appointment with destiny; un pour tous, tous pour un!

It was nearing midnight and the city lay dormant. The warm summer air tinged with salt brushed my face as I led the others into the verdant covered space of the square adjacent to the *Musée des Beaux Arts de Rouen.* Neat paths took us quickly to the *Le cascade,* a small waterfall over some large boulders that are a major feature of the central lake. The rocks nestled in amongst the dense lush foliage and were broken in their dark form every now and then by the glimpse of a silent white swan resting for the night.

As stealthily as church mice we sat down on the grass by the path directly in front of the tumbling waters of the cascade. Lily produced our blankets magically from her rucksack the self-same ones that we had purchased and used in Metz. Relaxing to the music of the waterfall we lay back to look at the stars and silently wondered on how many other planets a similar story was being acted out?

"Well here we go!" Lily said in an authoritative voice, "Good luck, see you on the other side." With that she started to glaze over, close her eyes and was dead to the present world. Jay followed suite and was soon breathing shallowly in synchronisation with

Lily. Gently I covered them with the spare blanket then turned to say farewell to my medieval Jehanne.

"OK my love, you are in charge now, guard us well we may be sometime. Whatever happens we will try to see the mission through to the bitter end. If the Gendarmerie turn up you will have to make some excuses about us! I'm sure you will think of something creative?"

With that we kissed long and hard. The feeling of electricity infused every cell of my body as I started to lock in on the time and place that meant so much to us all. Having DD with me was a real bonus as she was another direct link back into the medieval world that we had known so well. I lay back on the blanket and then she laid on top of me, her sparkling blue eyes glittering in the Moonlight and her long blonde hair falling sensuously over my face was the last thing my senses registered in the present here and now.

No sooner had I lost consciousness than I saw the coloured lights of the archway and I flowed effortlessly through the time slip portal between worlds. I found myself at the wooded entrance of a cave set amongst the same rocks that had formed the cascade in my 21st century reality. The water flowed more vigorously and acted as a fine curtain obscuring the opening to the secret passage way that went directly into the chateau Philippe Auguste the formidable fortress of Rouen. Only I knew it was there for it was not visible to the casual observer.

I looked around, Matthias and his men were with me as were my trusted comrades Tomas, Thibauld and Enfant Guillaume.

We wore black cloaks with hoods over our tunics and armour. Each bore a white radiant Germanic style cross of enlightenment on their chest which flashed clearly in the flickering torch light when their cloak parted. Each had a black band painted across their face covering their eyes which mimicked the markings of the ferrets we kept in small baskets on our back. Each of my men carried two along with the tools of their trade, some rope and the deadly crossbows with venom tipped quarrels.

I nodded to Matthias who drew his short sword to indicate that he was ready.

"Cock, lock and load!"

I gave the simple command and each man placed his foot into the stirrup of his cross bow and pulled the string back with the hook on his belt to the lock position. Then each took a quarrel from his quiver and placed it carefully in the furrow of the stock making sure that the leather flights were the correct way up.'

"Make safe."

My second command sounded in the wooded silence of the night and was followed immediately by another click from each man as the security catch was fastened. The one thing I didn't want was an accident as we manoeuvred in the confined space of the passage way.

I knew that Johannes and his men together with our Captain were guarding the ship and making ready to sail on the early morning tide. The wind was fair and La Hire with Dunois the

Bastard of Orleans had set the diversion in motion the previous day.

The Goddons would be few and relaxed as the main action was taking place on the east side of the city some 5 kilometres away. I knew also from Yvette and Charlotte inside the chateau that Cauchon and the Nobles were planning to hurriedly dispose of La Pucelle in the morning as their own men would not march on Dunois and La Hire until the 'little witch' was dead.

It was now or never if we were to do this. I crossed myself and said a prayer to our Lord. My followers all 7 of them listened with heads bowed and followed my lead.

"On y va les enfants terribles!"

I signified for them to follow me and with that we plunged through the curtain of water into the small hidden cave entrance beyond the waterfall. The rush torches spluttered and sizzled as the cold water hit them but remained alight. My hood and cloak took the water which rolled in beads off of its oily surface so I remained dry underneath. Inside the natural limestone cave a small narrow passage led off northward from the back directly towards the chateau on the hill. We had to stoop to walk and after 20 metres or so we encountered our first obstacle; a locked iron gate. This was a task for Tomas so I called him to the front of the file. He squeezed past me and I caught a flash of his white teeth as he smiled in the dark.

"No problem." He said confidently. Then reaching into his leather belt pouch he withdrew a set of skeleton keys and started to pick the lock. It was well oiled but very basic, just enough to deter the odd curious peasant from venturing further. Within a couple of minutes there was a final click clunk and he swung the heavy iron door open triumphantly.

"Done!" He said in a voice loud enough for the others to hear behind me. With that I released the first two ferrets that we were carrying from the basket on his back and sent them into the tunnel ahead of us. They scampered off happily in to the inky darkness on the prowl. They were my early warning system for the ferrets would soon hurry back if threatened by humans interaction thus we would be ready for any unfortunate surprises. In an ambush any warning and time gained was crucial to surviving.

We continued on our way beneath what would be in future times be called the *Rue Faucon,* now above us it was barely a track through woodland which followed a stream downhill to the Seine. The passage way descended steeply as we approached the foundations of the curtain wall of the chateau. After another 100 metres or so it levelled out and we encountered a second more formidable obstacle, a heavy oaken door reinforced and bound with iron bands and nails. A masonry arch surrounded it. This was the entrance to the fortress and marked that we were mid-way under the mighty walls above. We repeated the procedure. This time it took Tomas several minutes to crack the lock, as he struggled with his black art. I hoped silently that the girls had managed to remove the draw bolts and bar on the other side; otherwise our rescue attempt would end right here, right now.

Yvette and Charlotte had gained employment in the chateau kitchens by using their feminine charms some two weeks previous shortly after we had arrived with our wine delivery. Now at the appointed time they had two functions, to release the catches on the door in front of us and to spike the supper for the guards with our herbal cocktail of deadly alchemical substances. They would then carry the doctored celebratory ale and porter feast to the soldiers in the *Tour La Pucelle* under the pretence of a bonus meal for a job well done for within a few hours they would be permanently rid of their troublesome charge. The girls should in fact be there right now if all was proceeding to plan.

The lock clicked then after a pause that seemed and eternity clunked signifying success and Tomas attempted to turn the large iron ring that lifted the dead latch. It was stuck! My heart skipped several beats as he struggled with the problem. Growing impatient I squeezed beside him and together we tried to free it.

Success!

It finally sprung free with another loud metallic clunk and we shouldered the door open. The heavy door moved a fraction then gained momentum and swung open. The girls had achieved their first task. With that the human ferrets were now in the hen house! We burst through the door to the vertically winding stone stairs beyond. The ferrets I had released previously were nowhere to be seen, perhaps they were feasting of some dead water rats they had caught and killed? So I released another two and up the stairs they climbed with some encouragement. We waited for several minutes listening intently for activity but heard nothing. Silently we ascended to the *Chapelle Royale* above. At last we emerged under the main altar and climbed out into the cavernous echoing darkness. The only light to be seen was a flickering red lantern containing the *eternal flame* that signifies that the Lord Jesus' presence is in this holy place.

Dowsing our torches we moved stealthily in the gloom towards the main door that led to the internal courtyard. I navigated by my memory of 16 years previous and each of the others held the hem of the cloak of the man in front. Matthias was immediately behind me. He would guard the Chapelle with his men to secure our exit. At the door he wished me luck and we embraced.

"Bon chance!" Were his last and only words under muffled breath. I and my trusted chosen men were now on our own. Enfant Guillaume I left with him for the next stage might be brutal, bloody and far too dangerous. He was the same age that I had been at Agincourt but I had no desire that he should risk his life in the frontline.

"Orleans we do this for you!" I said in a muffled voice to encourage my men as I thought of my Lord the *Duc d'Orleans* on that fateful day when he risked all in the hazard and was finally taken hostage. Now he resided *Un prisonnier royal en Angleterre* the island fortress.

With that we slipped into the shadows of the curtain wall and headed towards the *Grosse Tour* to the north side of the chateau. It was a dark night and I was pleased that there was very little activity exactly as I had anticipated. La Hire and Dunois' diversion had obviously worked most effectively. Now only the odd guard patrolled the walls, the rest were probably snoozing in their watch towers by their warm braziers. I quietly thanked my men on a job well done in getting the message to them.

I decided to risk everything and cut straight across the courtyard to avoid the main barbican gate. Moving stealthily we covered the ground rapidly without hazard. Reaching the tower I opened the door trying to make as little noise as possible. I released the last two ferrets and waited for a possible commotion, my crossbow ready with the safety catch off.

"What in God's name?" came a drunken sounding voice from the floor above. I knew then that we must strike hard and fast! Bursting fully into the tower on the count of three we ascended the stone steps at a run. I estimated from the furore that there were a number of guards still capable of action although dulled by our potions that had obviously had some effect judging from the incoherent language being used. This was not the result that I had hoped for but never mind we had to press on otherwise all was lost.

Reaching the mezzanine floor where La Pucelle was being held I took a sharp left into the small guard room that was external to the main cell. I was horrified to see the floor and walls covered in warm dripping blood and a guard slumped in the corner, throat cut, with the lifeless body of Charlotte on top of him as limp as a rag doll. The crimson stream was still pumping from his open wound so I knew without a doubt that this had only just transpired. The other guard was on top of Yvette attempting to force himself upon her, his hose pulled down around his knees. I took careful aim and fired my cross bow bolt fully into his bare exposed flesh. He gave a piercing yell and then started to writhe on the floor as the venom took effect and finished the job that the hallucinogenic sedatives had started. Luckily he had consumed a considerable quantity of the doctored ale so my added dose of Belladonna was enough to dispatch him to hell rapidly.

As Tomas and Thibauld rummaged for the keys and watched the door I heaved his twitching fat carcass off of Yvette. She was barely conscious and in a severe state of undress. I did my best to hide her modesty and checked that she was breathing. No permanent harm was my assessment so I moved to check Charlotte - no pulse! My heart sank, no breath her dagger plunged deep into her assailant's throat. She had severe bruising to her neck and had been strangled, her trachea clearly crushed in the fray.

Spinning around I grabbed the keys from Tomas and spanned my crossbow. Then carefully selecting another poisonous quarrel I placed it on the stock. "Cocked and locked; ready to fire. No quarter!" my blood was up and I was in no mood to take prisoners after seeing what they had done to our girls. Beyond the cell door we would dispatch anything that moved with one exception; our Maid of Orleans.

The ferrets had completed their task and were now busy sniffing the spilt blood which they licked intermittently. I moved out of the room and unlocked the cell door. I remembered the unique hexagonal layout of the room so knew all the possible ambush points. However nothing prepared me for what I saw. The beaten, bruised and tortured La Pucelle shackled to her rough wooden bed by her hands and feet. Luckily the guards with dulled reactions were in no fit state to put up strong resistance. As they rose from their hiding places and drew their weapons, I fired into one of them and Thibauld the other. Their reinforced steel nailed jacks took the sting out of our venom tipped quarrels but the point blank force of the bolt to the abdomen at such a close range was enough to incapacitate them. A similar armour piercing bolt tipped with bees wax would have gone straight through any armour and severed the spine. So we drew our swords and finished them off rapidly without ceremony.

La Pucelle raised a weak smile yet looked confused at this unexpected turn of events and our friendly faces. I comforted her whilst Thibauld unshackled her hands and feet. Dazed, bruised and bleeding from the constant chaffing she tried to stand up.

"They have dressed me up in men's clothes so they can have an excuse to execute me." The words came softly from her dry parched lips.

"I know we have timed this very carefully. Dunois and La Hire are keeping the Goddons occupied. They haven't forgotten their little firebrand and have made every effort to rescue you with their men. Yolande of Aragon has sent us. It is I Robert, the one who removed the arrow from your breast at Orleans." I comforted her as best I could with soothing words and accurate information. "We will soon have you out of this hell hole and you will breathe the good clean air of a free France again!"

"Ah my faithful Robert des Armoises. I remember St Catherine and St Margaret were with me that day! I see you still wear the radiant white cross. I remember it so well." She managed then to raise a smile despite her obvious pain.

With that I escorted her to the door and then re-entered the guard room to check on Yvette whilst Tomas and Thibauld kept watch.

Yvette was badly shaken but standing. She looked mournfully at Charlotte's defiled body and wept.

"Les salauds putain essayé de nous violer!" She said kicking the dead body of her tormentor. "I told Charlotte not to resist but the guard recognised her! He was a Flemish Gobelin mercenary that had been employed at the *Chateau Angers* where he had seen Charlotte. He guessed that she was in the employ of the *Duchess of Anjou* so he started to strangle and then rape her. She would not be defiled so waited like a coiled serpent until the last moment possible when she saw your two ferrets and then plunged the dagger into the Goddon as he finished crushing her tender young swan like neck. I was more fortunate for my guard was so out of it as to be incapable thank God!"

I put my arm around her and she rested her head on my shoulder. "We must go my sweet Lady before the general alarm is raised. We are still in mortal peril." I tried to maintain a respectful composure despite the urgency of our situation but time was of the essence.

"Yes I know but Charlotte can do her Mistress one last service and that is to draw suspicion away from the House of Anjou. I will place my personal signet ring on her finger. It bears my personal arms of the Black Iris together with the Lion of Luxembourg. That way they will think that Charlotte is me and will not connect her to the House of Anjou. Instead they will suspect they have been betrayed by their ally Burgundy my cousin and they will lay the blame squarely there."

I was amazed at how clear headed Yvette appeared under duress and her lightning quick thinking may just save a whole barrel full of trouble for the Armagnac cause, Yolande and the Dauphin. With silent reverence Yvette placed her solid gold ring on Charlotte's slender lifeless finger. I crossed myself and Yvette did the same. Then she conducted a short prayer in Latin. Jehanne joined us and added her own few words to speed Charlotte's soul onward towards the light.

"Right Ladies shall we depart? Time is pressing and we still have to get out of this Goddon place in one piece!"

As I spoke Tomas and Thibauld scooped up my two favourite ferrets and together with the ladies followed me back down the winding vertical stairs to the courtyard below.

Chapter 33

Fin du Début

We exited the tower and started our perilous journey across the open courtyard. Yvette was dazed but able to function physically. She supported Jehanne by holding her under one arm. Battered and bruised they were so far unharmed. I thanked the angels as I moved stealthily towards the Chapelle Royale. Then an arrow zinged past my right ear and another struck the left pauldron of the black body armour that protected my shoulder area, luckily it glanced off at an angle leaving just a gash in my black woollen cloak.

"Merde, il est déchiré! Je vais faire ce salaud payer pour cela!"

Quietly I thanked God that I had bothered to put my upper body armour on earlier despite the inconvenience of the increased weight. Its superior steel and cunning construction did not however restrict my freedom of movement. It was of Nuremberg origin, a composite plate construction, the very latest gothic style to come out of Germany and an investment worth the purchase! We started to run, all caution thrown to the wind. Like nimble fleeting raven coloured storm clouds we flew over the dusty terrain of the chateau. Another arrow thudded into the ground in front of me, and another, and another.

"Zig zag! Don't run in a straight line!" I shouted out the desperate instructions although Yvette had pre-emptied my thoughts and didn't need any further encouragement. Heroically she continued to help and guide Jehanne with her every step of the way.

"Easy for you to say I'm carrying a dead weight!" Yvette shouted back in my direction. It was a taunt too far and Jehanne immediately stiffened. Regaining her fighting spirit she cast off her fellow sister warrior's support and started to run under her own power.

Then I stopped, span around and scanned the battlements for the archer that was attempting to thwart our escape with terminal intent. I literally had seconds to get my shot in before he found his mark as I was now a stationary target and I knew full well the deadly accuracy of the English longbow in the hands of a trained from youth professional archer. At Agincourt I had witnessed a French knight foolishly raising his clenched fist and shaking it at the Goddon archers in anger and frustration. Before he could lower it 19 out of 20 arrows fired at him had pierced it, armour, leather, flesh and bone! As if my sniping antagonist had read my mind another arrow struck my vambrace and glanced off at an obtuse angle of deflection causing me to nearly drop my favourite German jäger crossbow, but it was enough I had him. The Moonlight momentarily glinted off of his helmet which was sufficient for me to draw an accurate bead and aim just below it. I knew from hunting experience to target the space that was his chest area for it presented me with the largest mark, deer or man it made no difference the principle was the same. Holding my breath I gently squeezed the trigger bar of my weapon and the full force of the tensioned steel drove home the wax tipped quarrel with deadly armour piercing effect. A soft thwack told me I had found my target. It was followed by a muffled thud as the body of my Goddon tormentor fell onto the ground immediately below the parapet to my left.

"Mangez mon arbre vous la graisse de porc anglais!" I yelled as I exhaled violently.

There was no time to admire my own prowess as an alarm bell immediately sounded. It's piercing chime cleaving the frozen silence with the clarion call to arms. We now had literally seconds to make good our escape. Another arrow landed in the ground not a metre from my foot and buried itself to half the length of its shaft. I ran. Everything became a blur as I sped gasping for breath towards the chapelle doorway. Yvette and Jehanne had made it thus far and were frantically knocking to gain admission as arrows began to pepper the iron bound oaken form of the main door. Suddenly the door swung inwards and its solidity was replaced by an inky black void into which they plunged and vanished. My delaying tactic had worked and given them vital seconds with which to gain admission to the sanctuary beyond.

Now it was my turn to run the gauntlet of raining steel. I gulped and summoned up the last drop of my adrenaline fuelled rush. As I approached the opening I saw two of Matthias' men step out of the doorway and loosen their bolts in the direction of the main gate. The quarrels clattered off of the masonry, their covering fire bought me the precious seconds I needed to tumble headlong through the portal to safety.

Seeing his men safely in Matthias slammed the door shut to the sound of more arrows striking the oak mass.

"I take it they know we are here?" He spoke softly with a clipped Swiss accent. His rhetorical statement required no reply but I gave one as I regained my composure and gathered my thoughts.

"Of course, time to go!"

The girls were already halfway along the nave as we secured the door. Methodically we made our way to the altar making sure that we left no clues as to our covert exit route. Only the nobles would know of the tunnel for it was their secret and not for common usage. That would buy us time I thought with satisfaction. The common soldiers were expendable and expected to die bravely for their overlords. It was the feudal code of loyalty that was not only expected but demanded by the aristocratic parasites that would always save their own skin at the expense of others. It was the privilege of rank I reasoned although I couldn't stop the emotion of utter contempt from rising in my throat as I walked deliberately towards our salvation. It had taken a small frail girl on a mission to lead the armies of France by example from the front. Something we had forgotten about after Agincourt. Now even more frail and bleeding she was worth a thousand so called English Goddon nobles and we the cadre noir had snatched her from under their very noses. Fortified with that thought my sense of humour returned and I attended to the task in hand with renewed vigour and increased levity.

I made sure that every man was accounted for and that I should be the last one to leave the chapelle. As a final defiant gesture I placed one of my black gauntlets onto the altar beneath the crucifix. It was my calling card and would give the common soldiery a puzzle to contemplate in their ignorance. I then crossed myself and said a short prayer before departing.

With that completed I climbed inside the stone altar, making sure that the cloth dropped neatly into place and then slid the false panel shut with a smooth swishing sound. Down the winding narrow stone step I hurried and back to the chamber with the oaken door far below. Tomas and Thibauld greeted me with a grin and a deliberately nonchalant, what kept you?

"It's a long story, I'll tell you later, time to go!" As I stepped through subterranean archway the familiar rose coloured glow appeared and I found myself lying on a blanket looking at the stars. I felt somewhat disorientated and cut off in mid flow but otherwise was none the worse for wear. The last sound I heard from my medieval world was the distinctive clunk click as Tomas deafly secured the lock once more behind us.

The change in my breathing pattern alerted DD. Her beautiful sparkling eyes now replaced the stars in the heavenly vault above. She smiled and kissed me gently on the lips.

"You are back then?" She murmured, "How was it?"

"It went as well as could be expected," I said, "No lasting physical damage. I think I got away with it? How are the others?"

Putting her finger to her lips to indicate that I should be silent, she added, "Judging for their comatose state I guess that they are still there. Jay in particular is deathly still."

"Is he breathing?" I quickly replied. I became concerned due to what I had witnessed and moved around Lily to check his pulse. It was barely there and he was as cold as ice to the touch. "He's under very deep, deeper than anything we have experienced before. I hope he is all right?" I tried to smile but couldn't hide the anxiety in my voice. "I hope he makes it? We must complete the experiment but if he dies like his other self we will have a hell of a lot of explaining to do to the authorities. I will put an ambulance on speed dial." with that I busied myself punching in the numbers 15 required to ascertain the nearest Service d'Aide Médicale d'Urgence - SAMU unit into my iPhone. The activity steadied my nerves for this was real time and in the event of a fatality it would log the time that I called for help. Just as the answer came I noticed his breathing pattern subtly change and become faintly more audible. Bowing to my intuition I informed the operator that I had dialled the wrong number and apologised. With that I checked his pulse for signs that life was returning to animate his almost lifeless corpse. It was stronger. I checked again and again. It was definitely stronger I could feel the life returning to reanimate his physical form.

Lily by contrast seemed to just be in a deep sleep and her breathing at least was stable and audible. DD left me to it and stood up to shake the stiffness from her body and stretch her legs. She scanned the trees for uninvited guests. Her warrior and worrier instincts were on full alert. We were a team each knowing instinctively what the other needed to do in order to complete the task in hand.

It was gone four o'clock and the first change in the darkness of the night was detectable as it slowly transitioned minute by minute from inky blackness to pale grey. The birds in the trees started to chatter and give voice to the dawn chorus as they stirred from their nocturnal roosts. The early morning dew had settled on the grass and enhanced the new day with a refreshing smell that reaffirmed life itself. Then Lily began to stir and started to come to. "Johannes get the ship underway! We can't wait any longer!" She shouted the words in medieval Luxembourgish dialect but I intuitively understood them with certain clarity. She had obviously made it to the ship and was concerned to catch the tide and make good our escape. A thousand questions went through my head but they would have to wait as I still had Jay to monitor.

Lily stretched, stood up and joined DD in her exercises. "You OK?" I asked with minimum loss concentration and expediency.

"OK," She replied, "Mission accomplished La Purcelle is safe. We are heading north for the Rhine and home once we make it to the channel. It was Johannes' idea as he is prepared to risk the Dunkerque pirates and it will be the last direction the English will think of looking." With that she grinned and continued her warm up exercises.

With that simple statement I knew that we were home and dry. "Well done," I said in quiet reply, "the rest is history as they say."

Lily's grin became a knowing smile which further reassured me. "How's Jay? Do you think he will make it back seeing what happened back there it was pretty brutal?"

"I'm sure he will. His pulse has strengthened and where there is life there is hope." I held his wrist as I spoke and willed him on. Another half an hour passed. The traffic started to move and break the silence. I was still determined that we should not disturb his trip so I ignored the increasing clamour of human activity. At last his breathing pattern changed and grew stronger, an angelic smile developed on his face and colour returned to his cheeks. It was the look of bliss, often written about but rarely witnessed.

Then he spoke, "I'm rising, rising, ascending beyond the mortal physical realm of limitation and pain. I have completed my earthly task. The lamb has been sacrificed." He seemed totally at peace as he muttered and then started to blink.

"I didn't want to come back, but I have work yet to do, yes lots of work still to do in this present life." He spoke confidently and with a new clarity in his voice. "I definitely didn't want to come back but I have places to go and people to see. It is not my time. What a wonderful world this will truly become once we have finished the work we started millions of years ago. The dragon born Illuminati are torn, a divided council is no real council at all. They are not a real threat to anyone. It has been too many years since they sought enlightenment and held knowledge for the future benefit of mankind, now they use the knowledge they have gathered as their power, to wield influence in regimes that are soon to be replaced. They are irrelevant... and they are starting to realize it. These present day Machiavellian performances are nothing more than the death rattle of a weary beast, not long for this world.

We as etheric beings have manifest here as Earthly guides on the path humanity must now walk into our collective future and past; knowledge of where we have been, not through the artefacts that have survived the decay of time but through the experiences of the people that were there, our experiences.

Written through us is an inevitable genetic destiny, we have already succeeded. If we did not have this limiting perspective of time we would understand, we are our own guardian angels, our own higher-selves. We can remember our ancient past and we will remember our future, it is the only way to feel safe in the present. Without that fear of the unknown nobody has any power over us, we can see the lie before it's spoken, we can predict the rain and the drought, the fire and the flood and the famine and the plague. No regime has ever built the foundations to withstand such a storm but we will. So ends the reign of fear.

Welcome to the new plane of human existence!"

It was a profound philosophical statement of being. I knew that he had gone far beyond our mundane psychic experiences and moved to a much higher level. Jay was indeed a light being, blessed and very special. It was the final piece of the jig saw and was more about the future than the past. We had come full circle in our quest for understanding who and what we are.

"Time to eat, I'm starving I could eat a horse!" Lily chimed in with words that struck a chord with us all and brought us firmly back to present reality.

"Back to the hotel then in time for breakfast." DD added as she started to fold up the blanket that we had been lying on. She handed the neatly folded bundle to Lily who stowed it in her rucksack and then folded her own and put that too away with quiet efficiency. I helped Jay to his feet and we watched the swans glide silently on the lake as they too exercised, stretched sleepy muscles and greeted the brand new day.

The walk back down *Avenue Jehanne d'Arc* towards the river was very pleasant. It was as though we had been to an all-night party and were making our way home with assorted hangovers yet in a state of euphoria at having had such a wonderful time. It was in total contrast to the drama and tension that I had experienced in my other world. The emotional dam had burst and now the flood waters had subsided. I felt strangely calm and happy with my lot and the fact that I had found my soul twin along the way. She had been waiting for me all the time without me knowing just waiting for the right moment when we would consciously recognise each other from our portraits on the door. A message we had left for ourselves to find somewhen in time. I now recognised her for the beautiful shining being she truly was. As if to acknowledge my thoughts DD squeezed my hand as we walked and a jolt of emotional electricity flowed from her into my being. I was now no longer a burnt out shadow of my former self, good for nothing, ready for retirement and dotage. I was reborn, fully refreshed, exhilarated at the prospect of what was yet to come. She had transformed me, as Lily and Jay had. They had transformed me too and helped me to reconnect with my higher self. I now knew finally for certain that I was more than the sum of my parts. My spirit was eternal and I had strove through fire and flood in many lives to become the being I am.

"I suggest showers and breakfast in 30 minutes." Breaking the contemplative silence I said the words instinctively out loud as we entered the foyer of the *Hotel Bourgtheroulde*. Everyone agreed with a silent nod of affirmation, for each person was lost in their own world of individual thoughts and words were no longer necessary as we were on autopilot after a long night and needed refuelling. Without ceremony we made our way to our respective rooms. DD squeezed my hand again as we parted as though loathed to cast me adrift and let me go.

"A bientôt mon cher." She said intimately.

"A bientôt my warrior soul twin." I replied lovingly and then we embraced kissing slowly. Time had ceased to have relevance in our lives. We knew that we would always be together so there was no rush.

Over breakfast we each told of our experiences and soon learned that we had indeed all witnessed the same climatic events and each was able to fill in the missing details in the other person's story. All except Jay who just listened quietly and gathered all the relevant facts surrounding his own personal experience up until the point where he had met his untimely demise.

Then he unfolded a most remarkable tale of how he had left his physical body as Charlotte of Angers and had floated above it in the tower and beyond.

"The sense of panic in the English camp was intense. When they suddenly discovered that the star turn of their *théâtre macabre* had vanished. Warwick was beside himself as Cauchon, Bedford and the public masses expected a cathartic burning and an end to all of their self-proclaimed imaginary woes. He then instructed the guards to dress my body in a plain white shift and tie me firmly to a stake that was hurried erected on a tumbrel. They then placed a tall pointed paper hat on my head adorned with the words **heretic**, **blasphemer** and **idolater** in large letters. This was partly to hide my face from the crowds so that they did not recognise me but would assume that I was La Pucelle. Two guards were assigned to travel with me and to animate my body periodically in order to complete the charade. The old Market place was emptied and ring fenced with the remaining armed guards from the chateau. They interlocked their halberds together to prevent the populous getting too close which was highly unusual as normally they encouraged them to get as close as possible in order to witness the tortured expressions and cries of pain of the victims. The faggots of wood had been pre-soaked in oil and extra tallow was added as an accelerant for this would be no long protracted execution, it would be short, sharp and spectacular.

Finally the fire was lit and took hold rapidly, the flames leaping high into the air. The intensity of the inferno could be felt easily at a distance of 30 metres. A guard mimicked my voice and called out for a crucifix to be held up in front of my face. This was prearranged so as to obscure any sharp sighted citizens that may have caught a glimpse of my hair colour and features as the paper hat burnt away. Nothing was left to chance Warwick had used every ounce of his cunning to extricate himself from the embarrassing situation that he had suddenly found himself in.

All the time I floated over the scene watching every detail with quiet satisfaction for my physical body had completed its task and what better way to leave the stage of life than with a theatrical flourish!" Jay couldn't help smiling at that point as he enunciated the words with an actor's eloquence.

"Three times they brought more faggots to re-burn my body to ash for they wanted no trace of forensic evidence for examination as they knew that the ever sceptical Cauchon with his obsessive attention to detail would be most thorough in his investigations. There would be absolutely no means of identification; nothing was left to chance.

Then Cauchon entered the scene in a flurry. He was so annoyed that he had been cheated of his final moment of triumph after so many months of inquisition. The English on the other hand didn't give a damn. They had had enough of his dilly dallying and gave him short shrift. Warwick was more concerned that his troops believed that the witch was dead and would now finally move against La Hire, Dunois and the small French army not 5 kilometres away. Cauchon fumed and continued to protest but to no avail. Everywhere he was met by the same story and a shrug of the shoulders as one and all were totally convinced that they had seen the execution by burning at the stake of Jehanne d'Arc, the Maid of Orleans. It was a *fête accompli*. Warwick was off the hook and like Pilate he could now wash his hands of the whole sorry protracted affair.

As I continued to watch the soldiers cleared the Market place and then marched off back to garrison. About half of their number diverted to reinforce the army in the field. They would carry the tidings to their comrades as to the course of events and convince them that La Pucelle – the little witch, was finally dead.

Then I felt myself ascending into a bright light, the scene vanished and was no more. The rest you know."

With that Jay sat back and sipped his *jus d'orange* with an air of angelic contemplation and a wry smile of peaceful contentment. He was greeted with stunned silence as we all took in the gravity of his remarkable tale and the nonsense it instantly made of all the history books ever written since 1431.

It was the end of the beginning, the culmination of the quest into our collective past; a journey unequalled. We had gone beyond the veil of this earthly matter hologram and seen glimpses of the wheel work of the universe, of other worlds that we had once inhabited on a daily basis. We had our answers but now we had a million more questions?

I was sure that I would spend the rest of my present life in the company of DD, my beloved medieval Jehanne des Armoises. We would marry once again and may even move to Metz from Lille? Who knows? That was for the future, a bright joyous future.

Lily would take over my post at *La Voix du Nord* and what of Jay? Well Jay would always be a special friend for he was indeed special in every way. We would in all probability set up a website to share our experiences with the world so that everyone could read of our remarkable discoveries and adventures. We had even chosen a name for it www.ravenecho.com as ravens are an ancient symbol of reincarnation. In Viking mythology Odin's two ravens are called Huginn (thought) and Muninn (memory) which is very appropriate as they appear to exist beyond death and the physical universe. Likewise our actions in life echo across time as thoughts and memory in the eternal NOW. We are in fact our own past, present and future!

Was it all true? Was it all real? Who knows? For us it is our truth and that is enough.

Love triumphant! And tonight we would dine at *La Couronne* the oldest restaurant in France and not a stone's throw from the place where the world thought the English had burnt Jehanne d'Arc!

With those incredible thoughts filling my head I looked at DD, smiled and said,

"The door says it all my love of many lives, the door says it all."

FIN

www.ravenecho.com © 2014